Tainted Love
THE COMPLETE TRILOGY

R&C CHRISTIANSEN

Copyright © 2020 by R&C Christiansen

All rights reserved.

REGISTRATION NUMBER: 1179871

No part of this book may be reproduced in any form or by any electronic or mechanical means, including information storage and retrieval systems, without written permission from the author, except for the use of brief quotations in a book review.

Copyright registered with THE GOVERNMENT OF CANADA/ CANADIAN INTELLECTUAL PROPERTY OFFICE

❦ Created with Vellum

Dedication

THANK YOU TO MY HUSBAND,
THE R TO MY C, AND THE MAN WHO
HAS CHAMPIONED ME EVERY STEP OF
THE WAY.
YOU ARE THE WHISKEY TO MY VIXEN.
#HFC BABY XOXO

TRIGGER WARNING

PLEASE BE ADVISED THIS BOOK CONTAINS STRONG SUBJECT MATTER IN REFERENCE TO CHILD ABDUCTION. DO NOT CONTINUE IF YOU ARE UNCOMFORTABLE WITH DARK/SEXUAL/ OR STRONG EMOTIONALLY CHARGED CONTENT.
READER DISCRETION ADVISED.
18+

BOOK 1
TAINTED LOVE
The Complete Trilogy

CHAPTER 1
Welcome to Hell
AS TOLD BY KIRSTEN KING (VIXEN)

There are no rules here. Not on the Hill, because everybody who lives here is either rich or related to someone who is. We all know only three things for certain in this place... One, that money is king and women wear the crowns. Two, *nothing* is holy. And three, Friday nights are for partying and fucking. Fine, maybe that's five things but they all go hand in hand in this place.

It's finally Friday and I'm all in on the fucking as soon as I find a party to hit up that my mother won't be attending. The woman is a complete bitch, ruins everything she touches, including my attempt to be a normal twenty-year-old. Well if there is such a thing in this life. The point is, my mother, Helen King, is a walking, fucking plague. She's hot as hell with little effort mind you, but the woman is even madder than the devil.

"Kirsten Evelyn King, where in the hell are my car keys and my condoms?"

Is she fucking serious?

I make my way to the wrought iron railing at the top of the stairs before I answer.

"Same place you left that shit when you got home last night, Mother," I yell down. "On the counter by the empty bottle of Grey."

I roll my eyes as I listen to her stomp around, her heels echoing over the marble flooring and through the entire house as she belts out profanities and smashes what sounds like another priceless vase.

"Why the fuck are there only two condoms here you little slut? I had three and I'm not stopping at the store because you can't keep your trampy legs closed, Kirsten!"

Takes one to know one.

"Don't blame me, Mom. Whiskey only fucks bareback; maybe you should go to the clinic and see if they can't help you find where in that twat of yours the condom ended up!"

I turn to head back to my room. Hearing the march of her heels approaching fast, I duck as the Tiffany explodes against the wall beside me.

I feel the shards hit my hair and my hands as I cover my face and peek my eye open hoping she's not about to launch another one up the stairs.

Shaking the shards off, I turn and glance down at her, now pacified by a mouthful of Jack as she chugs it straight from the bottle.

"Nice aim, Mom, you missed again," I laugh. "Maybe you should get your pitching arm looked at by the doctor while you're in there for your rotting condom issue."

The bottle of Jack comes straight at my head, narrowly missing as I scramble into my room and lock the door.

"Yeah, you better fucking hide, Kirsten. One of these days I'm gonna make you wish you were never born, you little bitch!"

I already do, Mom. I already do.

Like I said, madder than the devil. I grew up here, born and raised straight from the womb of Satan, into money, bad role models, and governed by a woman who not only destroyed my father, but aims to destroy me too.

That's if I don't destroy her first.

It's not yet four and I need to get ready for a festive Friday night down at the Club. It's near the bottom of the Hill about a forty-minute walk through the private gated neighborhood in the suburbs. The Club is a tin-walled party house disguised as a boat storage shack down by Lake Davenport. A few of us pitched in together and got the Marron brothers to build it. It's the only place in this shithole that those of us younger than thirty can go and hang out without being embarrassed by our kin. It's not far from where I met Pax, or Whiskey as I sometimes call him. He's hot AF but broken AF. The guy's been through the darkest shit, things that have given me nightmares, but on the plus side, he can bring me to orgasm with his eyes closed with nothing more than his hand and some dirty talk. He's also one of the only guys I know that hasn't banged my evil mother, so that's a bonus.

I study my freshly-applied cat eye makeup in the mirror and pull my just-dyed Obsidian Black hair back into a high ponytail. Going for the badass bitch look again tonight, I've dressed in my thigh high boots paired with my frayed blue jean shorts and Whiskey's biker jacket. Good to go, I exit my room and tip toe not wanting my heels to draw mother's attention as I listen at the top of the stairs for movement. Assuming the cow got lost in a bottle and likely passed out in the washroom again, I make my way down the stairs, around the shattered vase, and out the door.

As expected, I hear the rumble of Pax's bike up the road, and head toward him as some douche in a top down, stark black Porsche hits a puddle and sprays me as he pulls up and stops outside my house.

Pissed, I turn back toward him, wiping the water from the side of my face and watch him exit his car. The guy looks like some business jock straight out of a formal menswear ad, all dressed to the nines and likely about to lose Mom another shitload of money on some phony investment.

"Hey you!" I shout, walking toward him. "Do your damn eyes not work or something?"

He looks up at me from his phone and stops, near his car just feet from me.

"Excuse me?" he asks, scanning me over.

"You fucking heard me, dickwad, you hit that puddle and messed up my face. You might want to get your eyes checked and watch where the hell you're driving that piece of shit."

The fucker looks baffled and insulted as he takes a few steps toward me and crosses his arms.

"Nice language, kid. Does your daddy know you talk that way?"

I scoff as Pax pulls up; his bike is loud, so I gesture at him to kill the engine as I climb on.

"My daddy," I laugh, "wouldn't you like to know, loser. Why don't you head on inside and ask my mommy instead, but you might have to peel her drunk ass off the washroom floor first, so good luck getting any money out of her, ass wipe."

I slip my helmet on as Pax starts the bike and revs the engine, unable to hear anything the asshole has to say back to me.

Patting Pax on the arm, I motion at him to go, flip my visor down, and give Wallstreet the finger.

There is literally nothing more exhilarating than flying through the Hill doing eighty on the back of Pax's beast. Pax doesn't talk much; he tends to let me handle my own shit the way I see fit. After all, I'm kind of like his Sugar Momma, bought him the Kawasaki a couple years ago and I let him live rent-free at the Club.

The guy's a drifter; a traveling soul he likes to call himself. He takes off for days sometimes, and it bothers me, but so far, he's always come back. We met a few summers ago when I was seventeen. I was walking home from the Club half-cut at like two a.m., because the Marron brothers hid my car keys. I don't know which one either because the jerks are identical twins, Jimmy and Jack. But when they host a Club bash, they either make you crash there or cab, and since I drank until I vomited that night, I decided to take in some air and walk.

I'd barely made it halfway up the Hill before I needed to pee, so I stopped in some bushes in Dellwood Park and hiked up my skirt until I heard Pax clear his throat. He was living in a tent nearby and apparently I interrupted his shuteye with my drunken mumbling.

Even with it being pitch black out and me being drunk as shit, I could see him clear as day; it was an instant attraction I've always referred to as the temptation of sin. The damn guy was walking sex and depravity, with his bad-boy demeanor, low unruly ponytail, steel blue eyes as dark as death, and a five o'clock shadow surrounded smile that'll make a girl wet in a second.

I could tell the guy had a decent body too, even a few tattoos in a bunch of twisted places like his neck. I studied it the entire way as he carried my intoxicated ass the rest of the way up the Hill that night.

After that, shit just sort of happened between us.

He's older than me by eight years, not a huge deal, but he was my first. It seems so long ago when I think about it. Sometimes I miss the way we used to be. But I fucked all of that up in so many ways because of my fear of commitment. Now we see other people and screw when we're bored in between, because Pax is the only guy who seems to understand the way I like it. We have a certain connection when we fuck, an unspoken ritual of sorts. It's a dark link and it's who we are.

I can't complain... our arrangement has its benefits, and besides, when it comes to having my back whether it's to get away from Satan, or I need a ride to the Club, or he thinks he needs to stop me from doing something completely insane, he never lets me down. I consider him to be my best friend.

Pax is my genie… in a bottle of whiskey.

* * *

PULLING INTO THE BACK OF THE CLUB, I hop off the bike and head inside. The place is dead and will be until at least nine when the freaks start to come out. And by freaks, I mean my friends. Nine o'clock is happy hour down here, and until then I spend my time checking the alcohol volume in the bar and mostly shoot the shit with Pax, unless I need to send him on a liquor run.

"So, who was the suit in the driveway when I pulled up?" he mutters in his naturally gruff tone.

"Nobody cool."

"No shit," Pax gripes. "Pass me a rag and tell me what the prick did to make you lay into him."

I toss a rag at him, bothered how the glasses never come clean in the dishwasher, so I always end up hand polishing the damn things.

"The douche hit a puddle and soaked me. It was no big deal, I told him off and I'm pretty sure he'll pay more attention to the road next time."

"I doubt it," he says, stacking the glasses. "Assholes who drive expensive cars are either givers or takers, they don't learn from mistakes."

"Givers or takers?" I ask, confused.

"Yeah, you know, assholes who take what they want, or pussies who bend over and give it to 'em."

"Mmm-hmm, interesting, and which category do you fall under?"

He looks up at me and blows me a kiss.

"Whichever one you want me to."

"Really, Whiskey?" I smile naughtily. "Is your dick bored again, because if it is, I may just be able to fix it."

He smiles back and rubs his stubble in thought, his baby blues dancing with dirty thoughts I can see written all over his sexy face.

"You been using protection lately?" he asks, eyeing me over.

"What the fuck, Pax? I could ask you the same shit."

"No, you can't. I haven't been with anyone besides you since the waitress back in December, and rumor has it you fucked that little weasel Donny the other night."

"Danny," I correct, "and of course we used protection, for your information, I stole that shit off Satan, and it's not like you stuck around to remedy my craving."

His expression says he can tell I'm pissed he would think otherwise, considering he knows he's the only man I'll ever fuck without a condom.

Taking the beer mug from my hand, he lifts my chin and kisses my lips the way only he knows how which ignites a fire in my stomach.

"I had to ask, plus I like it when you're mad, and you know I try not to stick around when you're drunk, Vixen. Now come sit on this dick and I promise I'll give you the orgasm he couldn't."

Still angry, I grab his dick firmly and rub it through his jeans, not surprised he's hard. I'm even more pissed because I know he's right; nobody fucks me the way he does.

"How about I sit on your face instead and you get me off like a real man since you want to act like a bitch and accuse me of shit you know I wouldn't do."

Without warning, the beer mug nails the floor behind him and shatters. Seems I've pushed his buttons.

I step over the glass, ignoring his tantrum and start to pick up the larger shards.

"Leave it the fuck alone, and stand up," he growls, jerking me up from the floor. "Do you see the shit you make me do? I told you... to get. On. My. Dick. So, get on!"

Now we're talking.

He doesn't even give me a minute to argue before he unbuttons my shorts, jerks them down, and lifts me onto the counter. I start to kiss him needfully; his stubble is rough as hell against my face and his tongue whiskey-riddled as I run my fingers down the back of his head and snap the elastic from his hair. No sooner does he get his pants undone and slam his hard cock into me as I brace myself with one hand tangled in his hair and the other gripping the countertop.

"Jesus fuck! Yeah, that's it, just like this," I muster out.

"Don't worry, sweetheart, I know what you like. Spread those legs wider for me."

I spread them further to accommodate his thick body as he continues to fuck me, both of us panting as I arch my back and buck my hips to meet his thrusts.

Taking a fistful of my hair, he yanks my head back as he continues to fuck me harder while he kisses my neck and whispers in my ear.

"I know you want it rougher, Kirsten. You deserve to get properly fucked, so get down and turn around. I want to see your ass. I'm going to fuck this little pussy from behind until you scream."

Fuck me, he always knows what I need!

He pulls out as my heart beats mercilessly and I hop down to give the man his ask.

There is no hesitation with him as he spins me around and shoves himself inside me, stretching me to take in his width. Now he really starts to move, pounding me so hard it hurts, the way I like it. I close my eyes taking in every ounce of his hedonism.

My legs are shaking and seizing as the sheer size of his broad, unyielding body bears down behind me while his fingers work over my clit like it's a fucking guitar solo.

"Shit yes! Hold that rhythm! Fuck, I'm so close!"

I can feel myself on the verge of releasing as I rip his hair knowing, he'll fuck me harder because of it.

He growls and slams into me with brute force; every muscle in my body is twitching and my mind is spinning as I pant out in gibberish while pushing back to meet his every assault.

"Yeah, girl. Fuck this dick," he groans. "Take every fucking inch, I want this pussy broken when I'm done with you."

His words are hot on my neck as I start to climax and dig my nails into his thigh, riding it out as he continues into me relentlessly. As my orgasm begins to subside, he continues tormenting my clit as he holds me steady against the counter not letting me move.

I pant, breathless. "I'm good, you can stop rubbing it now."

"No," he hisses, "you're gonna come again, so breathe through it while I fuck you, because I said broken and I damn well meant it."

Those words rush through my body as I focus on his fingers and I breathe through the pleasure mounting pain of his unbending pace.

It's a sweet torture he can produce for me every time.

"Fuck!" I moan. I'm almost whining as he smacks my ass hard, the sound echoing as I feel my climax start to mount.

"That's it, baby." With each continuous thrust, he speaks a word. "Let. Me. Hear. You. Moan."

Gripping the counter with both hands, I start to convulse, every body part twinging on edge as I gasp for air, embracing the second orgasm as it roars through my throbbing clit.

"Ah! God Whiskey," I exhale through the rippling wave.

"Should I make you do it again? I'm not sure if this pussy has been wrecked thoroughly," he whispers, still slamming into me.

"Fuck! I can't and it's spent, trust me," I plead.

"Alright, then hold still, and clench that pussy for me."

I do it as I work to recover my breathing and my feet throb in the boots from having my toes curled so tightly.

Pax is always a fucking monster when it comes to his turn to get off. He uses my body like he's attempting to destroy it, his hands grind into my hips as he impales me, and I love every fucking second of his pitiless force.

I count ten thrusts in ten seconds and feel him release inside me, listening to him grunt in pleasure in his caveman tone.

"Are you good yet?" I ask, slightly annoyed. "My pussy would like to be dismounted anytime now."

Pax laughs and smacks my ass, pushing himself inside me one last time before he backs off.

"You should know me by now, Vixen," he says planting kisses up my thighs as he pulls my shorts up. "As long as it's you I'm hate-fucking, I'm always good."

I turn and laugh at the stupid grin on his face that always lifts my mood. Fuck, he's pretty. I kiss his cheek and button my shorts before we both go back to polishing the glasses.

There is never a lot spoken between us; he knows my story and I know his, and neither of us questions the other's needs because it is what it is. Sex. It's what gets us through bad days and shitty memories, granted Pax's past is full of moments so dark I've woken up in cold sweats just dreaming about them.

It makes my life with Helen seem like a fairy-tale, and it's how I know Pax can't ever have children. He hates talking about it so I never bring it up much, but I know it's part of the reason he tries so hard to keep a wedge between us emotionally.

"The crowd should be starting to arrive soon and we're low on bourbon, beer, and vodka. I'm gonna take a run to the liquor store on my bike. You want anything?"

I reach into my pocket and hand him my bank card.

"No, I'm good, just hurry because I don't know if Jimmy and Jack are coming tonight to help me with crowd control. I don't want to be here alone in case Danny shows up with his brothers wanting to make a scene over my bad decision to screw him the other night."

"I'll be fast, just lock up behind me," he orders slipping his helmet on. "By the way, I love the new hair colour, but just for the record, black or blonde, nothing will change the fact I'll always see you as my naughty little Vixen."

"Thanks," I grin happy he noticed. "But as *you* already know, Whiskey, I'm solely into you for the hate-fuck therapy. Nothing more and nothing less."

He furrows his brows and growls under his breath.

"I guess we'll just have to see about that," he challenges.

Ignoring his statement, I follow him to the door and lock it once I see him pull away.

Sometimes I worry about him. Not about him on the bike or anything. I trust Pax with my life. The man knows all my deepest secrets and I know they are safe with him. My apprehension stems from knowing who he is, what he is. A broken drifter. I guess I just worry that him being caught up in this place, surrounded by money and trying to commit to living in one place for longer than he ever has, that he may not come back.

CHAPTER 2

The light floods in through the windows of the Club, waking me from a night of insanity and with a pounding headache like clockwork. I rub my eyes and toss the blanket over Pax as I roll off the bed, happy the party went off without a hitch, and thankful that Danny was a no show. I grab the pile of cash scattered across the bar and lock it in the safe before I hit the button on the coffee machine.

As usual, Pax raked in a killing charging his regular rate of five bucks a head for legal partiers and eight for the underachievers. He brought in a nice take by the end of the night.

And as always, he wanted to split it with me, but I told him to save up for the jacket he's been eyeing for months, the one he refuses to let me buy him. He has pride, I get it, but still, his rejection of gifts in general pisses me off.

Besides the Kawasaki, he's never let me buy him anything, and he only accepted the bike A- because I have an issue with drinking and driving, and B- the liquor store is hella far and I can't purchase legally for another year.

"Good morning," Pax says, wandering his way over to the counter.

I glance him over, taking in his shirtless physique and all of its tatted glory.

"It's afternoon actually," I point out.

Pouring him a cup of coffee, I slide it to him and then get one for myself with a side of Advil as I skim through the barrage of text messages from my mother.

"Shit! No! I forgot about the reading of the will! Fuck! Satan's gonna be pissed if I'm late, and the lawyer's going to be there in less than thirty."

"Grab your things and I'll drive you back to the underworld," Pax teases.

"Are you sure you're good to drive? Because I'm pretty sure I'm still drunk from last night."

"That's because you downed an entire mickey of bourbon, so, no, I'm not surprised. But I'm good," he says, slapping my ass. "Now get your things and meet me at the bike."

I nod and take my time sipping my coffee, hoping the painkillers will kick in soon as I gawk at Pax stretching his shirt over his head. The thing is so old and worn down it does nothing to cover most of his body and I can see parts of all his tattoos through the holes. The guy is an avid fan of reptiles and has all sorts of the slimy things inked over his body. I could and *have* literally played Snakes and Ladders up and down his neck, pecks, abs, arms, and his left calf. He's been telling me he wants to get a sea serpent on the other calf, but I keep telling him my mother has no business getting embedded into his body.

"Stop staring and get moving or you are going to be late to meet with the lawyer schmuck," Pax complains, tossing the helmet at me.

"Sorry, I was transfixed by the reptilian exhibit for a moment," I wink. His cocky smile almost makes me want to bend over the counter again, but I change my mind, realizing he's now growling. It's his warning sound, so I've learned.

I buckle the helmet, waiting for Pax to gather his hair into a ponytail before I follow him out to his bike.

The ride home is much faster than I'd hoped. His engine is loud as I hop off, so I gesture at Pax to pull the bike around back by the guest house while I remove my helmet, noticing the same Porsche still parked in front of the house.

I bet Wallstreet not only swindled some cash out of Satan, he probably got a free hand job from her too. It's a good thing Pax knows to wait in the kitchen because he hates anything to do with lawyers, and he prefers to avoid Satan's persistent sexual advances.

I enter the house through the front and catch sight of Natasha dusting the railings.

"Kirsten, I'm so glad you arrive!" she exclaims in her thick-cut Russian accent. "You mother is like crazy banana and break things again!"

Why am I not surprised?

"Shit, that sucks," I shrug, "please go and tell her I'm here, and that I just need a minute to brush my teeth and freshen up. I'm sure it will calm her down."

Natasha nods, looking doubtful as I sprint up the stairs. I don't even know why she still works here after everything she's had to clean up, let alone witness when it comes to Satan's drunken rage fits and my father's recent suicide.

I gaze in the mirror, displeased that I look even shittier than I feel as I wipe the makeup from under my eyes and spit the toothpaste in the sink. This is gonna be a shit day, I can already feel it.

Throwing my hair up loosely on top of my head, I change quickly into a baggy sweater and glide on some pit stick, hoping to disguise the rancid smell of bourbon that's perspiring from my pores.

As I enter the living room, I meet eyes with mother's cold cut glare and then scan over Wallstreet before I take a seat on the opposite side of the room.

"Nice of you to finally join us, Kirsten," Mother bitches, "now we can get the will dealt with. You may start now Mr. Morris."

"Maybe I should introduce myself first," he pauses, turning his attention to me. "I'm your late father's attorney, Gabriel Morris, Gabe for short."

"I already met you yesterday, outside by that piece of shit you so rudely drenched me with, Gabe. So, if you don't mind, just get on with endowing my father's empire to Satan so we can call it a day."

"Kirsten!" Mother slurs. "Can't you be civilized and respectable for once in your life?"

I glare at her and shake my head, laughing.

"You mean like you and the fact Dad hasn't even been in the ground a month yet and you're already fucking Wallstreet here?"

Mother stands unsteadily, ready to toss her glass of wine at me, but Gabe stops her hand mid-air.

"Ladies, please," he pleads. "I know this is a difficult time, but this will go much smoother if you just take a deep breath and calm down."

I roll my eyes.

"And who do you think you are, jerkoff? Just because you slept with Satan does not make you my father. Let the bitch break all the crap she wants; it doesn't matter anyways; she'll just replace it with money she never worked for."

Mother laughs and slams down her drink as Gabe's green eyes narrow, pinning mine. In the moment, I realize he's not bad looking, minus the suit. He has a certain sex appeal about him, a nice build as far as I can tell, and he looks rugged with his unruly dark hair and unshaven face. I kind of get why Mother wanted a piece of him, he can't be a day over thirty.

Gabe clears his throat and opens a folder before addressing Mother.

"Helen, your husband was adamant about leaving you controlling shares of his company, but he left specific instructions that you are not to interfere with how it is run. He's left Mr. Harrison in charge of daily operations. Robert also left to you the main house, the majority of his assets, stocks, bonds, and most of his vehicles. He left orders to split his bank account between the two of you, although Kirsten won't be eligible to access a large portion of the money until she is twenty-four. He has left the boat and motorbike to Kirsten, along with the guesthouse, his library, wine, and record collections, along with a forty-five percent share of the company. Do either of you have any questions?"

"I do," I say raising my hand. "Are there any clauses that say if my father was murdered, and Satan over there is found guilty, that she would have to forfeit her share?"

"Kirsten Evelyn King! How dare you!"

"No, Mother," I say, standing. "How dare *you*! Just because the coroner says he killed himself, it doesn't let you off the hook for being the cunt that forced his hand!"

I can literally see the devil take over her face as her glass nails the table in front of me and shatters at my feet.

I glance over at Pax's watchful presence across the room and wave him away, before I take in the lawyers rattled expression.

"I think maybe I should leave now," Gabe mutters. "Please call me if you need anything, Helen."

"All I need is another drink and a better daughter," she mumbles, "I'll call you just as soon as I am lonely again."

"Slut," I mutter, stepping over the glass. "Here, I'll walk you to the door, Gabe."

Mother yells for Natasha to get her another drink and to clean up the glass as we exit the room.

"I'm sorry she's so embarrassing... you might want to reconsider climbing into bed with her."

"It's fine, I get the whole grieving process... but I think she's lost, you know, she and your father were married for a very long time, maybe you should take it easy on her."

"Is that so?" I snap. "What the fuck would you know about it? She treated my father like shit, for your information. Cheated on him too," I add, opening the door. "Besides I'm pretty sure a man of your stature could do a hell of a lot better than my mother."

He laughs and steps onto the porch.

"Well that's a much nicer tone then the one you took with me yesterday," he says, reaching into his pocket. "Here, call me if you have any questions or need me to come by and take your mother off your hands for a while."

I smirk and take the card.

"I'm going to pretend I didn't hear the last part, Wallstreet, and if you're ever looking for a real party, where the glasses don't get chucked, I think I can help you out, but seriously, Satan is a lost cause and you are wasting your time."

With that, I slam the door in his face and toss his business card onto the entryway table.

The man is insane if he thinks hooking up with Lucifer won't end up backfiring in his hot but arrogant face.

That woman sucks the soul out of everything that lives and breathes, especially men. Just ask my father, after all, she might as well have tied the fucking noose for him and kicked the chair out from underneath his feet.

"How did it go?" Pax asks as I enter the kitchen.

"Okay I guess, although the lawyer is a douchebag. Can you believe it was the same prick from yesterday? The guy's totally banging Lucifer, and he still wants to even after he watched her launch her glass at my head. What a moron!"

"Well," Pax says rubbing his stubble, "The mans a schmuck,

and I suppose even the devil needs to get laid, even if it is by that jackass. You want to bounce?"

"No... actually I have a better idea. Come," I say grabbing his hand.

He follows me out the back door and into the guest house.

"What are we doing in here?" he asks, looking around.

"Moving in."

"What? Why?"

"Because it's mine, and because I say so. Do you have a problem with it?"

"Yeah, I do," he says, nudging me onto the sofa. "I like living at the Club. This place is too sophisticated for my tastes."

"You're kidding right?"

I cringe at him and pull him on top of me.

"But *I'm* not too sophisticated for your tastes, so what's the issue, Pax?"

He kisses my forehead and slips his hand between my legs, instantly arousing me.

"You," he whispers, "will never be too sophisticated for my tastes. But I'd prefer to earn my keep by holding down the Club."

His childishly vacant eyes penetrate mine as his hand continues to massage my pussy, making me moan.

"Fuck, Whiskey, would you stop for a second? Shit! I am trying to have a serious conversation with you!"

Feigning surrender, Pax puts his hands in the air and sits up.

"Fine, I'm listening, but I don't get why you think this is a good idea. Me and you aren't even together, so why do you want me to move in here with you?"

I shrug, knowing my reasons are vain and I don't want to say it's solely for sex.

"I just think it makes more sense this way because you wouldn't have to travel so far between here and the Club to see me. Plus, you are my best friend and it's not like we won't both benefit, so, will you think about it?"

He smiles that wicked grin, the one he does when he's thinking more about sex than my proposition.

"And what about Donny?" he asks, spider-crawling his fingers up the front of my sweater.

"Danny... and what about him? I already told you he was a mistake."

"Only because he couldn't get you off, and if that's the case and you want to live with me, then why can't we commit to each other?"

I slap his hand away and head to the bar at the far wall of the room to grab myself a shot of whiskey.

"I've already explained it to you, Pax. You're a drifter. You leave sometimes and I don't hear from you for days. I'm not going to sit around worrying or waiting for you when sometimes I don't even know if you plan on coming back."

"I always come back. You know me, Vix. When have I ever let you down?"

"When my dad died, Pax, that's when."

I slam my drink to the pained expression in his deep blue eyes. I never meant to sound so blunt but it's out.

"How many times do I have to apologize for not being here, Vixen?"

"I know, and I didn't mean it the way it came out. It would be different if you would at least let me hook up your phone."

"That is not happening. You've already given me the bike, the Club, and your body. I'm not adding a phone bill to the equation. Besides, stealing wi-fi is more my style, now get that ass over here and sit on my dick."

I can't help but smile at his mischievous grin. He always knows how to make me laugh even when I'm trying my damnedest to be pissed off.

"Can't... I need to go shower both you and last night's escapades off of myself. You might want to do the same."

He raises a brow and points to the hall.

"There is a shower in this place, isn't there?"

"Um, that would be a yes."

"Then what's the problem? Let's go test that shit out together."

"Fuck that! I'm not showering with you until you agree to live here... until then, we are showering separately. So, either I can go first, or I can head back to the main house while you do, choice is yours."

"Well why didn't you just lead with that, baby?"

Peeling his shirt off his ridiculously toned body, he tosses it at me and laughs.

"Your turn, Vixen, take the sweater, the boots, and the shorts off, shower with me, and you'll have yourself a roommate."

I smile from ear to ear and don't hesitate, stripping down to nothing before I make him chase me down the hall.

The man is an animal, with the stride of a football player, and he's fast. It's not entirely fair trying to outrun a guy that's practically half man and half beast, and by half beast, I'm referring to his lower extremities.

It takes me less than sixty-four seconds in the glass-encased shower with him to realize why some people are smart and install two shower heads. Pax, the giant man-beast, as fine looking as he is, towers over me. As if that's not bad enough, faultlessly, he's hogging the entire stream of water because of it.

"Hey, Zeus," I mock, smacking his rock-hard ass, "you mind moving a bit to the left?"

Laughing, he turns around to face me as I take in his always ready raging hard-on and roll my eyes.

"If you help me relieve this bad boy, I'll consider sharing the water."

"Or you could move the fuck over and relieve it yourself and not be such a horny prick!"

"I could... but I know that's not really what you want, not what you need," he taunts, slowly stroking his shaft. "So, get on your knees and open that foul mouth of yours."

He knows I love it when he takes control like this; his eyes get all sinister and his words ignite something dirty in my soul. He also knows I never do as I'm told.

I move closer to him, studying his tattoos with my fingers. Running them lightly up the snake's body that begins at his hip and contours over his abs before it crosses over another snake that slithers between his pecks and around his collar bone.

He stops my hand abruptly and jerks me closer before gripping the back of my hair and forcing me to my knees.

I laugh and look up at him, the water beading down his entirely ink sculpted body, his long hair shaping his devious face as he gives me the look. The one that says if I perform well, he'll reward me.

He doesn't need words to command me, his eyes, his touch, and his arcane growl say it all.

I'm purposely slow about taking him into my mouth. I know he likes it when I tease him with my tongue around the knob of his dick.

He groans, tangling his hand in my damp hair, attempting to thrust himself into my mouth just as I catch a glimpse of my mother watching.

"Jesus fuck!" I shout. "What the hell are you doing in here? Get out!"

Pax starts laughing, doesn't even cover his dick as Satan stands there with her arms crossed and I cover my chest.

"No, Kirsten, we need to talk."

"No, you need to get the fuck out! And stop staring at his dick you psycho!"

She smiles cunningly, ignoring my plea.

"I want the library collection your father left you."

"Seriously? Are you insane? We can talk about this later!"

"Well... I'm just giving you a heads up that it's staying in the main house, as is."

"Fine! Keep the fucking books, just get the hell out of here!"

"Hmph. Sure, thing sweetheart. Nice to see you again Pax," she finishes with a wink.

When she turns to leave, I holler out that I'm changing the locks the second I get out of the damn shower and she exits the room.

"Shit, Vixen," Pax laughs, "calm down... why don't we go back to what we were doing?"

I slap his hand off my shoulder and take in his stupid grin.

"You wish, you big dummy! Why the hell didn't you say something to her, or cover your fucking junk at least?"

"She's Satan... I didn't want to end up in her fiery dungeon. Besides, your mom is kind of hot."

I punch him in the ab so hard it sends a surge of pain through my fist as I exit the shower, trying to shake it off.

"Fuck you, Pax!" I yell, slamming the shower door. "You are unbelievable!"

He shrugs and says nothing, just gives me that stupid sad face he does when he knows I'm frustrated with him.

What a jerk. He knows how much I hate the fact people find my mother attractive and that she's literally slept with every guy eighteen and up that lives on the Hill. Married, single, widowed, divorced, blind, even fuckers in wheelchairs... you name him, she's fucked him. She's even fucked two of my underaged boyfriends *while* I was dating them! They claimed it was because I wouldn't put out, but that's beside the point. The worst part is that Dad got wind of it.

If that's not enough to drive a man to kill himself, then I don't know what is. My poor father, I'll never understand why he put up with her for as long as he did. Her and her drinking were always causing problems. Sometimes I wish he would have at least strangled her first instead of leaving her here to mess with my life.

I look up from the laptop as Pax saunters shirtless into the kitchen and takes a seat beside me.

"You still pissed I didn't damn Satan back to hell?"

"You know that's not why I'm mad."

"I wasn't thinking, Vix... I'm sorry, I shouldn't have said it."

"Whatever... it's fine, just leave it alone," I state, searching the web for a locksmith.

"It's not fine. Will you look at me for a second?"

"No... I'm busy."

Without warning he slams the laptop closed, spins his chair around to straddle it, and jerks my chair closer to his.

"I'm fucking sorry, Kirsten, it honestly slipped out."

I can tell by his face he feels guilty, but it still hurts to know he thinks the same thing everybody else does. I've been overlooked my entire life, traded in for my mother repeatedly because of her looks. Pax promised me that would never happen when we met. I don't care if he sleeps with anyone else on the planet. I just can't bear the thought of him laying with her.

He grazes his thumb lightly over my knuckles that are still red from how hard I punched him.

"Do you forgive me?"

"I'm working on it," I mumble, not looking at him.

He lifts my chin and kisses my forehead.

"Okay, well I'm going to head down to the Club to pack up some of my stuff. Want to come with?"

"No thanks, I think I'd better stick around here and see if I can't figure out what that bitch is planning to do with my dad's book collection. Ride safe."

"You know I will."

He slips his shirt over his head and ties back his hair Pax style. It always halts my breath when I watch the way he moves with a sexy charm about him.

I make my way out to the main house as I hear his bike pull away, knowing the second I turn twenty-four I'm getting the hell out of here. I'll be getting on the back of that man's bike and I won't care where in the world he takes me, as long as it's far the fuck away from the Hill.

CHAPTER 3

My father had a strong sense of family, was always determined to mediate the tension between Mom and me. He was good at laying down the law when it came to her booze-fuelled tantrums, he'd often take away her car keys and tell her to walk it off and every few months he'd offer to take her on vacation as an incentive to get her to put down the bottle.

She was never sober longer than a week, but I loved my dad for trying even though I felt she never deserved his loyalty.

He worked hard, built his company from the ground up, and ran it for over thirty years until it became an empire. He was well respected by everyone, except my mother. Thirty-eight days ago, when he took his life, he took a piece of me with him, and the things he left behind don't mean shit to me. What I care about now is making sure that ice cold bitch in the main house never gets her happily ever after. Not with no hotshot lawyer, and not so long as I'm still standing.

"Hey, Natasha," I regard, entering the main house, "did you

take the business card from the entryway table that douche lawyer gave me earlier?"

"No, it should still be wherever you leave it. I like hair by way," she says, pointing at my head. "Dark looks nice on you? No?"

"Thanks... it helps set me apart from Satan. There will be no more confusion when someone comes up behind me. The twat can sport blonde better than me anyway. Speaking of the hell spawn, where is she?"

"Last I saw she was in library, drinking martini, and making big pile of mess in middle of floor. I clean it later when she finishes spat with self, yes?"

I shrug and nod, knowing Natasha wants to avoid being a target during one of Satan's fits. I don't blame her for wanting to stay out of the minefield of exploding valuables.

Creeping the corner, I watch quietly as mother blindly tosses books from the alcove behind her into a pile while slurring some incoherent rant I can't make out.

"Mother... what are you doing?"

She turns toward me, spilling some of her drink down the front of her blouse.

"Damn it!" She hisses. "If you must know, I'm sorting through some of your father's literary abominations... I mean who reads this crap? *One Flew Over the Cuckoo's Nest*? Sounds dreary."

I watch the book land in the pile and shake my head.

"Maybe you should read that one. Fuck, Mom, you're destroying everything Dad loved."

"No, dear, you have it all wrong. It was your father that destroyed everything *I* loved."

"Like what? He gave you everything and you walked on him, disrespected him, screwed him over in every sense of the word, and yet he never quit on you."

She laughs wickedly as if I've just crossed a line.

"I'd say he sure as fuck quit on me the day he killed himself,

Kirsten. You have no idea what you are even talking about. You are just as pathetic as he was."

"I'm pathetic?" I repeat. "Well if that's true, it's not because I'm like Dad. It would be because I was damned to hell and burdened with you as my mother."

I dodge the book that comes barrelling at me but can't avoid the glass as I screech and feel the rigid force of it crack against the side of my head. I hit the floor, dazed for a moment, trying to sort my thoughts as I pick shards of glass from my hair and study my fingers that are covered in blood.

I see Satan's shoes as she stops and looks down at me, and for a second I think she might help me; my heart is pounding in my chest and tears are welling in my eyes from the pain that's setting in.

"Christ, child!" she snorts, "Get yourself cleaned up and stop whining. We are Kings and Kings don't have time to sit around crying... not when there's drinking to do."

She steps over me and hollers for Natasha as I stand holding pressure on my head with my sleeve. I breathe deep, knowing I'll have to fix it myself and unsteadily I find my way back out to the guesthouse.

If I had my wits about me right now, I'd have a good mind to hop on the lawn tractor and drive it straight through the patio fucking doors and into the sitting room. Then I would turn it on and laugh as the blade chewed up her eighteen thousand-dollar Persian rug while I laughed in her satanic face.

Instead, I'm busy picking her bloody martini glass out of my head hoping I don't need stitches because I'll be damned if I'm going to let some doctor shave a section of my hair.

· · ·

"CHRIST! WHAT THE FUCK HAPPENED THIS TIME?"

Pax asks from the washroom doorway. He tosses his duffel onto the washroom floor and helps me down from the countertop.

"I waged war with Satan, that's what happened," I disclose, handing him the lawyer's bloodied business card.

"Shit Vix! Let me see the damage."

I take a seat on the toilet as Whiskey runs his fingers gently through my hair.

"Jesus! This is quite the gash; you might need stitches."

"Nah, it'll heal; these injuries always do. Just get whatever shards I missed out please and pour me a drink."

"How about I get you some Advil instead?"

I roll my eyes as he scoops me up like a baby and carries me into the kitchen, seating me on top of the table.

"Now I can see what I'm doing. So, what's the plan with the lawyer? Are you gonna try to have her share taken away?"

"Nope, I'm going to go for the kidney shot this time."

"You know it will backfire. It always does when you mess with her," he advises.

"Yeah? Well, you're not talking me out of it this time. I'm done being her target practice, Pax. There is no way I'm going to survive another four years here and we both know it."

I swig back the water and down the Advil he hands me as he begins to inspect my head again.

"Well, we could always leave without the money and come back when you turn twenty-four."

"Are you crazy? And leave her here alone to trash the place while she drinks her miserable life away?"

"It's just a thought," he says, kissing my forehead. "There, I think I got all of the pieces out. You are such a good girl… didn't even cry once!"

I laugh satirically.

"I'm a King remember? Kings don't cry."

He sighs, and his eyes meet mine, seemingly dancing with guilt.

"You know," he pauses, tucking my blood matted hair behind my ear, "I think if you cried once in a while you might relieve yourself of some of that pent-up hostility you carry around."

"Why would I want to do that when I have you to hate-fuck it out of me?"

His eyes narrow and I know he's fighting off a smile because he's trying to be serious.

"Come on Kirsten, let's be real... I haven't seen you let out a single tear since the day of Robert's funeral. You need to grieve."

"No, Pax, I don't. His funeral was the last time I will ever shed a tear, I'm just glad you made it back in time to be there. I'm positive I would have shoved Lucifer into the plot with the way she was hammered, staggering, and fake sobbing."

"I remember. I'm the one who undid your anger in the cemetery washroom. It seemed a bit inappropriate to fuck a dead man's daughter on the day of his burial, but I have to admit it was pretty hot."

I can't help but laugh at his twisted humor or the wicked gleam in his eyes.

"My dad loved you, Whiskey. I'm sure he would have expected nothing less from you that day."

"You call him pulling a baseball bat on me love?" he asks doubtfully.

"That was so long ago, and he thought you were committing a home invasion. I mean look at you... long hair, entirely inked with grizzly stubble, and torn clothing like you're a bum. You can't really blame him."

We both start laughing to the point of tears.

"Ha! I finally made you cry!"

"Whatever, dork."

"What did you just call me?"

His face goes completely serious as I contemplate running. He hates it when I call him a dork.

"I meant to say dick."

"I bet you did. Now get on mine, you little badass."

His tone is dark and dirty just like his mind and God knows sex could cure my throbbing head, but the doorbell rings.

"Hold that thought," I tell him.

Shit! It's the douchebag lawyer.

I open the door and unhappily wave him in.

"What brings you back here so soon? Trying to get Lucifer to explain why your pecker is covered in blistering burns perhaps?"

He laughs as if I'm joking as he notices Pax and nods in his direction before he introduces himself.

"Hey, man, my name's Gabe. I'm the family lawyer and a friend of Helen's."

Pax ignores him, saying fuck all as usual, just glares at him from the table with his arms crossed and an unimpressed look on his face.

"Do you want a drink?" I offer. "Feel free to take a seat with my *mute* roommate."

"Sure, please, a glass of water would be great, but I won't stay long. I just came to drop off some paperwork I need you to sign."

"Paperwork?" I question.

"Yeah... I have it right here."

I watch as he rummages through his briefcase, seemingly unnerved by Whiskey's looming presence and the smouldering stare of *hurry the fuck up* on his face.

Personally, I find it hot, but I know it's because Pax hates lawyers, everything about them. He says they're Satan's minions, and right now he happens to be right.

Finding the papers he was searching for, Gabe sets them on the table and takes a swig of water.

I smack Pax on the arm, trying to nudge him to tone it down

with the Viking face, but he just winks at me and carries on with his silent assault.

"So, I just have to sign this stuff and then everything my dad left me is officially mine?"

"Uh, yes," he confirms, "except full access to the money of course, but I should probably head over to see your mother now."

I half-smile, irritated, and walk him back to the door.

"Well, thanks, I guess. I'll sign the forms and leave them with Natasha if that's cool."

"Sure, that works, and can I ask what happened here?" he finishes, inspecting the dried blood on my head.

Before I can answer, Pax gets in between us and puts his arm in front of me as if he's shielding me.

"Gabe is it? I think it's time for you to leave."

His tone is so low and dark, it causes my skin to prickle. Gabe simply nod's and exits without another word said.

"What the fuck was that about?" I ask baffled.

I know Whiskey can be territorial and all, but I've never seen him like this.

"Are you serious, Vix? The guy is a total schmuck, and I don't like the way he looked at you."

"Yeah, okay, so he's a douche... I know that and I also know how you feel about lawyers. But he was only trying to be nice."

"So he can get in your pants."

"No, because I happen to have a gaping wound from Satan on my head."

"Don't be naïve, Vix. I'm a man and I fucking know what I saw."

I roll my eyes and sigh.

"Even if you're right, why would it matter? It's not like I'm gonna fuck a guy who slept with my mother... that's *her* gig. And besides, you are not my boyfriend so stop acting like you own me."

I turn to walk away but he grabs my arm and spins me back toward him. His eyes are filled with an angered hunger, the expression that says I've provoked him as his lips meet mine and he's even rougher about it than usual. He holds my face to his, controlling my tongue until he bites my bottom lip and stops.

"I may not be your boyfriend, Vixen, but just to be clear, I absolutely own you."

I gasp as he runs his hand forcefully between my legs and the other one grabs hold of my ass firmly. His nose is pressed to mine, and his eyes are piercing mine with a look of intended destruction.

"I also own this," he hisses, massaging my pussy, "and this," he continues, gripping my ass. He continues his methodical movements running his hands underneath my sweater onto my breasts. "And these, and also this," he finishes, kissing my lips again. "I'm the only one who can give you what you need, and you know it."

I'm wet and he understands it's what he does to me when he takes control. The way he is able to make me feel craved; as if he only breathes for me.

"Say it Vixen."

I swallow, lost in his touch.

"Only you can give me what I need."

"Say it again," he demands, slapping my ass.

"Ouch! Okay... only you can fuck me the way I need it."

"That's right... and if I tell you that some arrogant prick lawyer is looking at you funny, you should damn well listen to me," he states as he rips my sweater over my head. "Isn't that right?" he continues, now removing my shorts and panties in a seamless motion.

I nod, now standing completely naked and lost in his barbaric movements as he continues his rhythmic incursion against my pussy, my body shaking and begging for more.

He lets his hair down and it falls just below his shoulders in dark waves of unruliness and then he removes his shirt. He smiles wickedly and is deliberately slow about unbuttoning his pants because he knows he has my attention, but I can also see that I have his.

"Now," he whispers, pinning me against the wall and lifting my arms above my head. "Tell me it turns you on knowing that I own you."

I let out a moan as his fingers graze over my heat and push deep inside me.

"Ahhh, fuck Pax, you know it does."

"I want to hear you say it."

I ignore him, enjoying the rigid movements of his fingers penetrating me fiercely.

He stops, jerks me forward, smacks my ass and I yelp.

"Fucking say it, Vixen, or I'll just make you watch me jerk off instead."

As much as I love watching him masturbate, I'm far too turned on to let him.

"It makes me wet knowing you own me," I breathe out.

Resuming his hold on me against the wall, he smiles, kisses me deeply, and drops to his knees.

"Spread your legs," he commands, licking my inner thighs.

I do it, panting and trembling to the warmth of his tongue.

I feel like exploding as he laps it over my pussy, concentrating solely on my clit and I have no choice but to brace myself with his head as I moan and push against his face.

He holds my hips steady, growling and pleasuring me with exact precision as my body trembles, my heart pounds and I begin to climax into his mouth.

"Oh. My. God," I pant as the orgasm courses through my body.

When I can't possibly take any more, I push his head away and he stands, licking his lips.

"You've always tasted of such sweet sin, and you are the only thing that makes me feel alive. I might own your body, but you, Vixen, own my soul. Turn around," he commands.

I do, gripping my hands into the back cushions of the sofa, still reeling from the orgasm and trying to decipher his words. He takes no time and drives himself into me, stretching and filling my swollen pussy as I whimper.

"You had better brace yourself," he hisses. "This is about to get rough, Vix, *hate-fuck rough*."

He's solid in his plight, fucking me as hard and as fast as he can, it's how we both like it as I moan out in yearning.

My body is tensing, building toward release again. His presence is intense as he grips my hair and growls under his breath.

"This, Vixen, is. How. You. Affect. Me," he growls with each relentless movement. "There is no man on the planet who will worship you the way I do."

The lust in his tone and feel of his hand feverishly working my clit sends me over the edge into another orgasm.

"Holy shit, Whiskey," I gasp, riding it out, dazed by the force.

I feel his release begin, his body locking firmly against mine as he spills into me.

"Fuck," he grunts.

We stand motionless, catching our breath and I close my eyes, relishing in the feeling as his hand sweeps my hair to the side. He places gentle kisses down my neck, then my shoulder, his stubble amusing me as he does.

"Now that we've cleared that up," he teases, "I think we should talk about the incident with Helen this morning."

I turn and look at him, throwing my sweater and panties back on in the process.

"You want to talk about her walking in on us?"

"No… I want to talk about her nailing you with a fucking glass."

"Oh. Well whatever, it's nothing new, and she got lucky. Her aim usually sucks."

He pulls me close and cups my face, his gaze dead serious.

"This isn't a joke, Kirsten."

"I never said it was."

"Then tell me what the hell we are going to do about it. She's going to end up killing you one day."

"She's not," I say pulling away from him. "I have a plan and don't give me that stupid look as if it's going to be reckless, Pax. It's a good plan, but I haven't worked out all the kinks yet."

His eyes narrow and he sighs, taking a seat on the sofa. Patting his lap, he tells me to sit, so I do.

"And what are the kinks?" he asks raising his brows.

I shrug, not wanting to tell him. I know he's not going to like my idea of payback.

"How about I let you know once I've worked out all of the details?"

"Before you initiate the plan... right?"

"Sure."

"Good," he winks, "now you can sit and rest that bashed-in head of yours while I make us something to eat."

I smile and find my comfy spot on the sofa, feeling exhausted. He's right as usual. My head hurts like a motherfucker, probably because of the blood rushing around my body from the intense orgasms.

Sometimes I'm positive Pax knows me better than I know myself. He's the man I would marry if I was the marrying kind. But I'm not, and I don't think he is either, especially since I know it bothers him that he can't have kids, which is one of the biggest reasons people tend to get married. *Legitimacy, what a joke!*

I'd give my right hand not to be related to Satan, never mind the fact my father never should have married her.

But Pax is different, he's talked about the things he would do if he had kids, even mentioned wanting to adopt one day. I know he would be an outstanding father. He'd be *that* dad. The one that never missed a game or a recital, the one that taught the little shits how to ride a Harley before they were legal, and the kind of dad I had. Smart, strong, and fearless.

But legitimate baby Paxes can never happen though, not for Whiskey. He got screwed out of those hopes, literally.

He's only ever told me once about the night it happened. I knew after hanging out with him for less than three weeks, that he was the man I wanted to lose my virginity to, and he knew it as well. So, when the night came, he was hard into the whiskey and we were both desperate to fuck, I was worried about not being on birth control or having any condoms, and that's when he told me about the abduction. He thinks he was four when they snatched him, he's never been sure, just remembers living in an orphanage of some sort when they lured him from the park into the van. A man and a woman, he calls them The Imposters, and I'm not sure why.

What they did to him is unspeakable, and makes Helen look like an angel. The things they made him do for food, the way they beat him and tortured him and the others. They groomed and abused them until they gave in and did what they were told.

I cry every time I think about it. I'm crying now. Crying for him and crying for them. I can't even handle the images inside my head.

The only thing I know for certain is those sick sons of bitches permanently made sure there would be no pregnancies as a result of the crimes they were committing. They found a gruesomely twisted, inhumane way around having to worry about abortion costs, missed birth control pills, and the price of condoms.

My heart breaks for Pax, but he survived it and the minute he found a way out of that hellhole at seventeen, he took it and he's never looked back since.

I don't even know if he remembers telling me, so I've never brought it up and likely never will. It bothers me that he thinks my mother is abusive after knowing what he's survived, and whether he knows it or not, I'm in love with him. I just can't take the chance of giving him my heart when he could take off at any time.

It's the only thing that scares me.

Losing him.

Money can't buy Satan's sobriety and it sure as shit can't force Pax to stay, but when I get done crucifying my mother, it'll guarantee one thing: she won't be laying a filthy fucking finger on Whiskey. *My Whiskey, anyway.*

CHAPTER 4
Timing

T wo Weeks Later...

THEY SAY TIMING IS EVERYTHING. I think it's a crock. Time is a killer, it's the echoing sound of a ticking clock, and endless torture for those of us who want to get shit done yesterday, but instead have to wait patiently for the right time.

I woke up four days ago to an empty sofa. Pax is gone, again. Off on one of his skewed sabbaticals, I suppose, slaying his demons or whatever, but I see this as a good thing for once. It's time to put my plan in motion to slay my own demon.

I've invited the douchebag lawyer over, and he'll be here in a few minutes... seems he and Lucifer have spent the last two weeks soiling her sheets but at least he won't have far to walk. If I didn't know better, I'd have to say Lucifer is quite smitten with Wall-street. He's well off, not bad looking, and I can't say I blame her. I also can't say I'm cool with it either. Pax was right as far as I can tell. Gabe is into me. I've noticed his eyes on me a few times when I've been in the main house, although I've ignored it. Pax was quick to make his presence known when he noticed it once or twice as well, but I ignored that too. But now, since there is no genie in a bottle of Whiskey to interfere, with my strategy, I'm going all in.

Gabe thinks I have questions about the will, which I do, just not the ones he believes I will ask. I glance in the mirror, adjust my breasts, and check myself out, just as the bell rings. *Showtime.*

"Gabe," I say, welcoming him in. "Please have a seat."

"Good morning, Kirsten."

I smile and close the door behind him, taking in the way he scans the room first and then his eyes hover over my appearance.

It's safe to assume he was trying to see if Pax was here. He's clearly attracted to me by the way his eyes dart away from my exposed stomach and lack of attire.

I'm purposely dressed in my thigh high boots, jean shorts, and braless underneath my sheer lace crop top, precisely to garner this exact reaction.

"So, Gabe," I say taking a seat beside him. "Did you get the papers I left with Natasha last week?"

He clears his throat and moves several inches to his left, seemingly uncomfortable with how close I am.

"I did and I filed them with the clerk's office."

"Fascinating," I say, crossing my legs.

I watch his eyes wander down to check me out briefly before he crosses his arms and pins me with a stern look.

"Did you invite me here to ask me something important, or is this one of the games your mother warned me about?"

He gestures all around me, his vibrant green eyes narrowed.

"That depends," I laugh, "what is it she told you?"

He shrugs, "Just that you have a tendency to try to seduce her partners."

"Interesting," I say sarcastically as I lean in and whisper in his ear; "This would be my first attempt. Usually it's her who fucks all of my friends first."

He sighs, his breathing deepens, and I can tell he's reacting to my presence, so I back off and give him some room.

"Can I offer you a drink?"

"That won't be necessary. I think I should go."

"Why? What are you afraid of Wallstreet? Pax or Satan? Because Whiskey isn't here, and I had the locks changed. There is nothing to worry about," I assure, lightly running my fingers up his thigh.

He doesn't move, just sits staring at me, tempted I assume. His breathing is visibly faster, and I can tell he's contemplating.

"What is this about? Are you trying to get back at your mother?"

"Maybe… or maybe I'm just lonely."

Adjusting his position, he runs his hand through his thick hair and sighs.

"Look, you are a very attractive young woman, Kirsten, but I don't think this is a good idea."

"Well, your dick seems to think it is," I point out, noting he's hard and straining against his pants.

I grip it firmly and stroke it, climbing onto his lap as I do, and I press my chest against his, listening to him moan quietly.

"You like me… I can tell," I whisper, "and there are so many things I can do for you that Helen can't. It can be our little secret; I won't tell Pax if you don't tell Satan."

I feel his dick grow even stiffer as I trace my tongue over the soft edge of his ear and begin to lay rough kisses down his neck.

"We have to stop," he breathes out.

With my wrists in his hand, he pushes me onto my back, rendering me useless and for a brief moment, he stares at me with angst until he gives in and his lips collide with mine.

I can't get enough of his delicate tongue as his hand makes its way south and into my shorts.

I moan into his mouth and he lets go of my wrists so he can undress in a flurry as I work quickly to rid myself of my clothing as well.

In the heat of the moment, the only person I can seem to think about is Pax, so I decide I should keep this oral for the time being.

Gabe has a generously sized dick, although it's not quite what I'm used to, but I drop to my knees and lick the length of it, before stopping.

"Did you fuck my mother last night? Please tell me you washed this thing."

"What? No! And I showered this morning."

"Good," I gargle out as I swirl my tongue around the tip of his dick.

Just the thought of Satan fucking this guy turned me off completely, but I'm going to finish the job just in case I need ammo for later.

I take him into my mouth slowly, studying his length with my tongue, before I start to suck him hard.

"Ahhh, that feels fucking incredible," he mumbles. His hands are planted firmly on my shoulders as I begin to ease him in and out of my mouth at a steady pace. He's not overly lengthy like Pax, and I can take him all the way to the back of my throat.

I can feel the back of his thighs starting to tense as he rocks himself to the same rhythm I'm using.

His dick is pulsating in my mouth as his hand finds its way into my hair, tugging at it, so I quicken my pace realizing he's close.

"Yes, like that, right there."

"Mmm-hmmm," I hum.

My lips are becoming numb as I continue sucking and moaning; guys like it when they think it's turning you on, at least I know Pax does. He loves when I moan and slobber during a blowjob.

Gripping my hair, Gabe stops abruptly.

"You need to stop now if you don't want me to cum in your mouth," he warns.

I hum uh-uh and keep my rapid pace as I smack his ass, hoping he will get the idea and understand I plan to swallow.

He thrusts into my mouth hard, pressing my face into his pubic hair and I begin to feel the warm liquid pulse of his liberation.

"Fuck... holy fuck, God yes," he moans.

Swallowing the continuous spilling of his cum, he finishes, and I release his dick, kissing it lightly before I get to my feet.

"That was incredible," he says, pulling up his pants. "Now it's my turn to pleasure you."

"I'm good," I smile, throwing my sweater on. "Kind of lost my mojo thinking of you fucking Satan. But let me pour us a drink."

"Well, that doesn't seem fair, at least let me try to get you hot and bothered again."

"It's fine. Really, I'm not in the mood right now, but maybe later," I lie, taking in his unhappy expression.

"Right, okay. I'll have a scotch if you've got any then."

I pour us both a glass over ice and take a seat at the table watching as he eyeballs an abstract that hangs above the love seat. He's got a nice physique, he's in shape, but not nearly as toned as Pax; nothing about him is anything like Pax. A sudden flush of guilt runs through me as Gabe takes a seat, sipping his drink.

"So, you really aren't going to tell your mother about this are you?"

His eyes scan my face, likely searching for honesty.

"Of course not. I don't think another martini glass to the head sounds particularly inviting. Besides, she would tell Pax just to get me back since he's always refused her advances."

"I thought he was your roommate. Is he your boyfriend?"

"No, but he's a tad protective of me and he hates lawyers, and when I say hate, I mean he won't hesitate to tear you apart limb from limb and dump your body in a hole somewhere."

"Jesus! I could tell he didn't like me, but I figured it was because I'm seeing your mom. Now I have to worry about that fucking animal finding out I let you blow me. Thanks for the warning," he gripes.

"Oh, stop overreacting. Whiskey isn't going to find out. He's not even here; he's been gone since Saturday on one of his Lone Ranger missions. Now drink up and go crawl back to the Devil."

"Wow, you really are something sweet, aren't you?" he asks rhetorically. "What is the deal with you and Helen anyway?"

"I already told you... she's a twisted cunt. My father's downfall in life, an infection. She's like a poison that taints you over time, slowly doing enough damage to hurt you but never enough to kill you. I'm sure you'll find that out all on your own though."

I slam my drink and pour another, wondering why he wants to discuss my stained existence.

"Has she always been an alcoholic? I can't believe the way she can drink."

"Yep," I say, pouring him another, "she's also always had an addiction to throwing tantrums and breaking shit my whole life. My head didn't become a target until I found out she was fucking one of my boyfriends... walked in on them actually."

He cringes, looking shocked.

"Shit! I'm sorry... and Pax?" he asks, raising a brow.

"What about him?"

"Is he your one? The one that your mother can't take from you."

I half-nod and half-shrug.

"I guess."

"You guess?" he repeats. "I've seen the way you two are together, you guys move like water; you're in sync. And the way he looks at you, I mean that has to be worth something, right?"

"What are you? A fucking shrink?"

"No," he laughs, "just a guy who cares. I want to help your mother, and I also want to help you."

"Who says I need help? And why the fuck would you entertain the idea of burdening yourself with Lucifer's sins?"

He must be absolutely insane.

I pour myself another drink as he covers his glass.

"None for me, thanks, and you should slow down a bit."

"Answer my questions please," I prompt, ignoring his attempt to father me.

He smiles genuinely. He's got a gorgeous smile to match his emerald eyes and for an instant, I'm attracted to him again, but I shut it off.

"It's not that I think you need help up here," he says, pointing to his head, "I just think you need someone to intervene so that you aren't in harm's way whenever you enter the main house."

"You mean hell's kitchen."

"Exactly," he laughs. "I think I can get your mother into a program eventually. It might take some time, but I think it would give you some space to heal, and her some well-needed addiction control."

"You're playing with fire," I warn, "you do realize that monster has money, correct? Not to mention claws, sharp teeth, and a tail she could probably strangle you with."

"Now, now," he chuckles, "I'm not entirely worried, I have connections. I've got money too, and over the last couple of weeks, I do believe I've managed to tame some of her demonic spirit if you haven't noticed."

"Sure, you have," I laugh. "If you are referring to the plastic cup you gave her to drink from that she shoved in the garburator, I wouldn't call that helpful."

"No... I am referring to the two times I stood in front of her so you could get away unscathed."

He lifts his brows twice as if he's some kind of hero, and I sigh.

"Oh, those times... well don't get used to trying to defend me, that's what Pax is for. And if he sees you doing it while he's around, he will take it as an act of war."

"Take what as an act of war?"

My heart pounds to the sound of Pax's voice behind me and I glance quickly at Gabe before I turn in my chair to see Pax's venomous expression.

"I think I should leave," Gabe states, standing up.

"Sit the fuck down," Pax growls. "Answer the question, Vixen. What will I take as an act of war?"

His eyes are cold, like blue ice as he stands there with his arms crossed, his tattoos practically moving with how tense his muscles are.

"It's nice to see you too," I say dryly. "We were discussing Satan's attempts to send me to the underworld if you must know. You were gone, so, Gabe stepped in twice and botched her plan. That's all Pax, it's not a big deal."

"I suppose not," he says, still unhappy in his tone. "But what the fuck is the lawyer doing here now? Not saving you, I'm assuming."

I can tell by his tone he's gritting his teeth, growling, which makes me nervous. He only does that when he's holding back his desire to either fuck me or kill something.

"No... Gabe came by because I asked him to. I had some questions and I wanted to avoid the bitch at all costs. Now can you please drop the angry man attitude, Gabe was just leaving."

Pax eyes him over wearily, and then juts his head toward the door.

"Go then, you fucking weasel, and learn to talk on the goddamn phone!"

I watch Gabe make his way to the door swiftly, stopping once he's there.

"Thanks for the drink, Kirsten. You know how to reach me if you need anything."

"Stop talking and get the fuck out!" Pax snarls before I can say anything.

The sound of the door slamming startles me as I stand and shake my head with an exaggerated sigh.

"You are a lunatic sometimes, Whiskey, you know that? The guy is half descent." I say it feeling slightly guilty and then add; "He actually has good intentions when it comes to Satan."

"Yeah right," he barks, "I'll be the judge of that, Vixen."

"No, I'll be the fucking judge of it. What is with you? You can't just show up here after four days of radio silence and behave like a complete barbarian because you're in a mood."

"A mood?" he mocks, "I just came home to that smug bastard sitting in our kitchen, drinking with *my* girl."

"Oh, so, *now* this is your home? Because the last four days it didn't seem to be when I woke up to you being AWOL. And since when am I *your* girl?"

"Since fucking always, Kirsten! And don't pretend you didn't know who I was when you asked me to stay here with you. I've always hated lawyers, and so what if I take off sometimes? I always come back, Vix, always."

I hate that he's so damn gorgeous and that he's right. It makes me feel guilty, but it's not like I know where he goes or what he does on these stupid trips, never mind with who.

"Fine, Whiskey, let's just drop it. Gabe won't be a problem, I'll make sure of it."

"Yeah, you'd better or else I will," he warns. "Now close your eyes... I have something for you."

"What?" I ask, shocked.

"You heard me. Close them, please."

I shut my eyes, listening to the sound of him rummaging through his duffel, wondering *what the fuck?* Pax isn't a romancer, and he's never surprised me before. Maybe with some fresh wildflowers while we were laying in a field drunk once or twice, but he's not the kind of guy who shows a soft side. *Shit, I don't think he even has one, and if he does, I've never seen it, except when my father died.* But that was an exception.

"Lift your hair, Vixen."

I lift it and feel him slip something cool to the touch around my neck; I can tell it's a necklace and my heart begins to beat rapidly.

"Okay, you can open your eyes."

I open them and look down as Pax moves in front of me to check out my expression.

"A cross?" I question, studying the pendant that is embedded with diamonds.

"Uh-huh, it's to protect you when I'm not around."

"It's beautiful, Pax, but you know I'm not religious right?"

"No kidding," he laughs. "You live with Satan."

"Then why the cross? I don't get it."

"Come," he says, dragging me to the sofa.

Pulling me onto his lap, he runs his thumb over the pendant and smiles as he flips it over. Engraved on the back are the words, 'For my saint, -Pax.'

Then he rolls up his sleeve and lifts the edge of a bandage so that I can see his freshly inked inner forearm. There are two snakes tangled together on his arm with some writing that says, 'Kirsten's Sinner.' I'm unsure whether to smile or cry at the gesture as a loose tear escapes my eye without warning.

"What's wrong, Vix? I'm not asking for a commitment, just wanted to show you that you will always be a part of me."

"It's not that," I mumble. "I love it, Pax, I really do. I just don't understand why you called me your saint, yet you always call me, Vixen."

"Because you're both. The bratty little badass I met three years ago who needed me to keep her out of trouble, and you're also my savior. My home, Kirsten. The place I can just be myself and not have to worry about you judging me or asking questions."

"That's because you wouldn't answer them if I did, and I don't judge you because, seriously, have you seen my life?"

"Well it won't be like this forever, Vix. As soon as you turn twenty-four, I'll take you wherever you want to go."

"Sure, you will," I say, rolling my eyes.

"What the fuck is up with that attitude? Haven't I proven myself? What do I need to do to prove it's always going to be you and me no matter what?"

"It's not that, Pax. I know I whine sometimes about the way you screw off on me, but I get it, it's your thing."

"Then what's the problem?"

He jerks my face closer to his and kisses me roughly, the way he always does when he wants to get me going.

I place my fingers over his lips and stop him.

"The problem, Whiskey, is still the same one it has been since we met. I can't give my heart to you until we get out of this place. If I say the three stupid little words out loud and commit to a relationship with you, then that makes us real. And being real terrifies me, because the minute I find you in bed with her... fuck, I swear, Pax, it will kill me."

He growls angrily under his breath.

"Oh, for fuck's sake, Kirsten, don't you know me at all? For three years we've been going over this shit. I would never do that to you. Don't you get it? I never even liked sex until I met you!"

I instantly feel shameful seeing his face now flooded with the pain of his past, the things he never wants to talk about, not that I blame him. My chest hurts as I work to hold in the tears that want to come.

"I'm sorry, Whiskey, I didn't mean to—"

"Just save it," he whispers, "I'm going to go for a ride... and yes, I will be back tonight," he adds, noticing my concerned expression.

I say nothing and watch him grab his helmet and leave, feeling the ache in my chest grow and I can't hold back anymore.

I wipe the tears as they fall, struggling to think of anything other than what he must have gone through for all of those years, but my vivid imagination won't stop torturing me with evil thoughts. My only resolve is to drink them down and I know it, so I swig from the bottle of whiskey, trying to embrace the burn as I swallow.

Image after image of a young boy's soul being shattered just keep flashing through my mind and I keep downing the numbing agent with no resolution.

I slam my fists on my thighs as hard as I can, hating the way I just fucked up his romantic gesture, despising myself for being such a loser, wishing I could take it back and just tell him I love him. But I am what I am, a Vixen, a stupid rich girl who has no clue what hell really is and no clue what love should be.

All I seem to know is revenge, and how to mess shit up.

I take the bottle with me and wobble my way to the bed; the world is finally spinning as I lay down thinking about Pax's last statement. I am the only girl he's ever liked having sex with. I smile thinking about it and begin to laugh, because it's not like we make love. If anything, we make *hate*, deep, dirty, angry sex with the purpose of letting off steam. Hate-fucking as Pax calls it. It's the one connection we both seem to thrive off, *me and my Whiskey*. We are soulmates whether I say it out loud or not.

CHAPTER 5

High Expectations

Pax ended up coming in the door late last night. I can't be sure what time because I'd already passed out. I felt better when I woke up with him beside me but left him sleeping because he looked far too comfortable to wake. I get that he loves me, I get that he wants me to trust him, but he doesn't know my mother the way I do. He doesn't know the lengths she's gone through to get what she wants.

I knew about the affairs she was having while Dad was away on business, and I kept her secrets for years because I knew it would destroy Dad. Eventually it did. I remember the exact look on Dad's face when he found out I knew about it and never said anything. It was the same week Pax took off on one of his glory rides, and I will never forget the sound of Natasha's blood-curdling screams when she found him dead in the garage, hanging from the rafters.

The Marron brothers' parents were driving by just as I was walking home from the Club before sunrise that morning. We all heard Natasha's screams and the garage door was wide open. If

Jack and Jimmy hadn't jumped out of the vehicle to stop me... I'm just glad they did.

"Good morning," Pax greets, taking a seat at the table. "You were snoring by the time I got in last night, so I decided to watch you sleep for a bit... and I guess I dozed off."

I turn with my mug of coffee and take in his annoyingly perfect morning face.

"I don't mind if you sleep in my bed, Pax. Do you want a cup of coffee?"

"No, I'm good thanks, and since when? You made it clear that we are roommates to the schmuck next door... doesn't that mean I should take the sofa?"

The bad boy smirk on his face almost makes me crack a smile.

"I know what you're doing right now, so you can cut it out."

"What am I doing?"

Now laughing at his stupid dimpled proud smile, I take a seat.

"You're trying to cause an argument so we can hate-fuck, and it's not happening."

"Is that what I'm doing?" he shrugs, acting innocent.

"Yes... but it won't work because I'm not mad at you. I feel like I owe you an apology and an explanation."

His brows furrow and he crosses his arms, seemingly intrigued.

"An apology and explanation for what?"

"Last night," I sigh, trying not to look too long at his blessedly ripped body and all of his ink. "I love that you got a tattoo with my name, I really do, and I love the necklace, Pax. I wasn't trying to be ungrateful."

"I know," he smiles. "I have a knack for being able to read you, Vix, and I threw you for a minute I'm sure."

"That's an understatement."

He leans forward and traces the pendant with his finger.

"You know I love you don't you? Even when we are visiting the dark city of Hate-fuck, right?"

I nod.

"Yeah, I know... but last night when I mentioned Satan—"

"Shhh," he hums, placing his fingers over my lips. "We don't need to rehash last night. What we need to do is correct the situation growing in my pants."

His wicked smile makes my heart pick up before I glance down at the swelling erection pressing against the crotch of his jeans.

"I have to go up to the house. I promised Natasha a couple of days ago that I would go through my closet with her and start sorting what clothing I want to bring out here," I white lie.

Truthfully, there's nothing I want to do more than fuck him right now, but I can't. Not while knowing I gave Wallstreet a B.J. yesterday and how much that would destroy Pax. The whole "he hates lawyers" shit is really messing with me, because I know if Gabe were in any other profession, my transgression wouldn't matter. It's the fact I did it to one of his arch nemesis's that has me guilt ridden.

"Alright," Pax sighs, "then I'll head over with you, just let me shower quickly."

I lift a shoulder and cringe.

"Why don't you just meet me there when you're done showering?"

"Because you might get nailed with a flying statue. Fuck, Vix, we've been over this and I don't give a shit if the hotshot lawyer is there or not. I'm going with you."

"It isn't even nine yet. Satan doesn't rise before noon, I'll be fine."

"Are you seriously going to debate this with me?"

The growl in his tone is setting us right back into hate-fuck territory, so I back down.

"Nope, I'll wait for you, shower away bodyguard."

"There's my saint," he says mockingly. "I won't be long, I promise."

I smile, aggravated, as he kisses my cheek and heads to the washroom.

My heart is pounding to the knowledge that I will likely come face to face with Gabe in front of Pax again and its freaking me out.

God, I really am a Vixen, but if Gabe isn't able to get my mother into rehab, then at least I have some leverage on him that should keep him motivated to keep trying. Either that or I may have to blackmail him into making her sign everything over to me. I don't care either way. I just want her out of my life and away from Whiskey. No pun intended.

I pour myself a glass of orange juice and add a splash of vodka in hopes to kill my nerves.

"I don't think so," Pax declares, taking the glass from my hand. "You are not turning into your mother on my watch."

There are a ton of things I could say back, but the truth is, he's probably right and I can't afford to argue with him right now.

"Fine, have it your way," I smile.

I take in the way his damp hair drips from the loose ends he missed when he tied it back and how his muscles make his torn, almost see-through t-shirt look way too small. He's gorgeous, and I can't help but stare at his ass in his jeans while he crouches to tuck his laces into his shoes.

"Are you ready?" he laughs. "Or are you just gonna stand there staring at me like usual?"

"I can't help it; you are way too fucking hot for your own good... no wonder Satan wants you so badly."

"Well that's too bad," he emphasises, his eyes glistening. "Satan can't possibly hate-fuck me the way I know you can, so she's shit out of luck. Now, if I were you, I'd get that sexy ass moving before it ends up bent over the sofa and at the mercy of this dick."

I take that as a solid warning, slip on my sandals, and make my way out the door.

Passing one of the Azalea bushes, Pax stops and picks one of the flowers, and I shake my head at him.

"Are you trying to get murdered? You know she'll kill you if she catches you messing with her prized Azalea's."

"No," he laughs, "she only chucks shit at your head, not mine... but don't worry, I'll protect you!"

I roll my eyes as he tucks my hair behind my ear and places the flower in the fold.

"You know, Whiskey, if you weren't so easy to love, I'd slap you right now," I mutter. "Now get in there and check if the coast is clear please."

He smiles his *you said you love me* smile, all proud as he enters through the kitchen and waves me in.

"It's clear, there's no sign of the demon or her hellhound," he teases.

I scan the kitchen, tell him to keep quiet, and grab his hand, dragging him behind me through the sitting room, past the front foyer, and up the stairs to my room.

Not seeing Natasha along the way, I shut the door behind us and open the closet. There is literally over five hundred outfits, plus my shoe collection, belt collection, and purse collection. I feel like an idiot for having all of this crap, knowing I haven't worn even a quarter of it.

"Grab that backpack from the coat hook," I tell Pax, pointing to it.

He does and holds it open as I pull a few things off the hangars and shove them inside.

"Remember the night you snuck me in, and I slept in this closet?" he whispers.

"I do... we weren't sleeping," I retell, "and my dad busted us because you kept pounding me so hard, I ripped the shelf down."

"I know," he says, all pleased with himself. "Want to do it again?"

"No... we need to get my stuff and get out of here."

"That would be a good plan," Mother interrupts. "I'll be turning this room into a gym. Good morning, Pax. I'd say it's nice to see you with your clothes on, but I'd be lying."

I shove the bag into his arms and push him out of the closet.

"Just take it downstairs while I talk with her."

He looks at me and then at her, presumably noting she doesn't have a glass in her hand.

"I'll wait in the hall."

Satan checks out his ass as he leaves, and shuts the door behind him.

"So, dear, I have news," she's states. "Gabe is planning to take me on a little trip next week. I think he might propose."

I laugh and tilt my head.

"That's doubtful, Mother. You've only been together for a couple of weeks."

"Long enough to know he's a good man, wouldn't you say?"

Her arrogant face makes me want to barf, and I'd love to tell her how her "good man" let me suck his dick.

"Sure, whatever you say... I just came to get a few things though, so if you wouldn't mind..."

She opens the door and gestures at me to walk ahead of her, and then my heart stops as I exchange stares with Gabe.

"Whiskey and I were just leaving," I mention, grabbing Pax's arm.

"Nonsense," Mother says, "Natasha is about to start breakfast; why don't the two of you join us?"

"What? Why?" I swallow.

"So, we can chat about the trip of course... right, Gabe?"

I glance at Gabe and he nods.

"Right... I'm taking your mother somewhere very special," Gabe confirms.

"Interesting," I mumble, turning to Pax. As usual, he says nothing and just stands there monitoring the situation.

"Pax and I are busy we have prior engagements," I blabber out.

"No we don't. Breakfast sounds good... we'll be down in a few minutes."

My mouth parts, and I frown at Pax, appalled.

"Well don't take your time," Mother says. "You know I hate it when the food sits uncovered for too long."

She takes Gabe's offered arm and they head downstairs.

"What the fuck, Pax?" I hiss, smacking him on the bicep.

"What?" he smiles. "I'm hungry and I want to hear about the trip."

"Cut the crap. Why do you want to suffer through a meal with those two?"

"Why not? I thought you said the lawyer schmuck is a decent person."

"He is! But it doesn't mean I want to sit down to breakfast with them and act like we are a family for shit's sake!"

"Oh, come on, if we are going to stick around here for another three and a half years, we might as well try to make the best of it. And I promise, if anything comes flying at your head, I will catch it," he teases.

I roll my eyes and sigh, annoyed.

"It's not funny, and this is a very bad idea."

"Vixen..." he says with concern, "why do I get the feeling there is something you aren't telling me?"

My chest floods with guilt as I study the distress on his face.

"I don't know, Pax, maybe it's because you have a guilty conscience for whatever it is you do on all those glory rides you keep taking."

"Why are you bringing that up right now? I think your deflecting. What is this really about?"

Great, now I've set off his red flag alert.

"Stop looking at me like that, you know what this is about. I just don't want to sit through a breakfast with Satan, that's it!"

"Alright," he sighs, "I'll drop it for now, but we *are* going to eat with them, so move your ass."

I'm fuming inside, knowing that I have to give in, or he will become more suspicious if I keep fighting him on it.

I take a seat at the dining table, unhappy that Gabe is sitting in my father's seat at the head of the table while making disgusting googly eyes at my mother sitting directly across from him. Pax takes a seat to my right, likely so that he can catch whatever Satan decides to launch at me before this event is through. I know it's not a matter of *if*, but a matter of *when*.

"So, Helen," Pax pipes up, "tell us about this trip you're taking... Kirsten told me once how much you loved your time in Rio when Robert used to take you there. Is that where you and the schmuck are heading?"

I choke down a slice of bacon, trying not to laugh as Natasha fills my glass with orange juice.

"No, we are heading to a beautiful villa on the sands of Morocco actually, and darling, please address my lover as Gabe, will you?"

Pax nods and I roll my eyes to the fact she called him her lover. *Gross! And Morocco my ass. I hope that's code for rehab.*

"It's fine, Helen," Gabe states. "I'm not easily offended by men who can't seem to hold down a job or get an education, let alone enter into a committed relationship with a woman."

Every hair on my body rises as I take in his statement, watching Pax's face do nothing more than smile and nod in Gabe's direction.

"Schmuck still about covers it," Pax says nonchalantly.

"What in the fuck is wrong with you, Gabe?" I ask, deadpanning with him. "You don't even know Pax, let alone Satan over there and you think you have a fucking right to an opinion at this table? Well, guess what, Wallstreet, you don't."

Gabe shrugs and says nothing back, just bites into a slice of toast with his eyes bolted to Pax's.

"Alright, boys, let's try to be civil," Mother intervenes. "Kirsten, what is that you are wearing around your neck? Have you taken up religion recently?"

"No, Mother, I haven't, it's a gift from Pax if you have to know."

"Good, because I have to say there is no God that will look upon your faults and forgive you for being such a disappointment to this family."

"Well, then it's a good thing I don't need God's approval. Besides I'm pretty sure that being born to you instantly disqualified me from ever being blessed by God's good graces."

Mother laughs, pleased with herself as she takes a sip of wine and I feel Pax squeeze my thigh as if to let me know he's got my back.

"You know," Mother starts in, again, "I remember a time not so long ago when I felt the exact same way about my mother, God, she was a wretched thing. You ought to consider yourself fortunate that she passed before you were born, Kirsten. That woman..." she pauses in thought, "if you think I am the devil, well, let me tell you, she must have been the Antichrist. It makes me wonder what your daughter will think of you one day."

I glare at her and shake my head with a smirk, knowing she's trying to curse me.

"I won't be having kids, Mother, so I guess we'll never know."

"Whatever do you mean? Don't you think you should consider that Pax might want children even if you don't?"

"Seriously, Satan!" I shout, standing instantly enraged. "What me or Pax want is none of your business, and if you were half the mother you should have been, you would fucking know that we aren't even dating, you contrite, self-centered cunt!"

Mother stands just as quickly, her eyes narrowed, and her fist white-knuckled from gripping her fork.

Pax stands saying nothing but blocking me with his body.

"Drop the fork please, Helen," Gabe states, now standing as well.

"Yeah, Helen, please do. It would be greatly appreciated," Pax adds.

I peek around Pax's body at my mother's hostile expression and watch her hesitantly place the fork down on the table.

"Fine, you win for now, Kirsten, seeing as how these two always come to your aide as if I'm some kind of monster."

She covers her face and begins to cry, but I can tell its fake, one of her spot on dramatic performances.

Falling for it, Gabe makes his way over, wraps his arm around her shoulder, and then leads her out to the sitting room as I roll my eyes and cram another piece of bacon into my mouth.

"Never a dull moment is there?" Pax asks, taking his seat.

"Nope."

"Why have you never told her that I can't have kids?"

His question catches me off guard and I stare at him, lost in the man who seems to be an imposter, not the Pax I know who never talks about his inability to bear children.

"Why would I tell her that? She would ask questions, and how exactly would I explain it to her? I don't even understand all of it myself."

"You could have just told her I was born sterile; it happens you know."

"Yeah, well with my luck, she would have labelled your dick as an absolute must-try... the way she always flirts with you is bad enough as it is, thanks."

He takes my hand and holds it in his lap.

"You know I think we should adopt one day, right? I mean as soon as you get over the whole we aren't together shit and actually believe I'm not going anywhere, and I'm not interested in hate-fucking your mom."

I smile at his beautiful grin that emits nothing but genuine honesty.

"I still can't believe you want kids after everything you've been through."

He shrugs and nods, completely confident.

"Of course. Little badass Vixens and Whiskeys, we could love the hell out of and show them the awesome parts of who we are. Don't you want that?"

I lift a shoulder, unable to look him in the eyes any longer. It's too much, seeing him so excited while I feel so guilty about so many things.

"I don't know, Pax. I'm on the fence about it. I'm not feeling well, so I think I'll head back to the guesthouse and nap," I say as I stand.

"Is it because I mentioned kids?"

"No... I'm just still feeling the effects of my hangover," I lie. "Meet me there when you're finished?"

"You know it," he says kissing my hand.

When I think about the kind of man Pax is, I know I have got to be the luckiest person on the planet to be loved by him. And if I am completely honest with myself, I know either way, if he screwed Satan or not, I would still be in love with him, and I'd probably forgive him. I can also admit that every time he leaves, in my heart, I know he's coming back.

The thing that terrifies me about giving in and making us official has nothing to do with who he is, but it has everything to do with who I am.

CHAPTER 6

The Secrets We Keep

The tension between Pax and Gabe has continued to grow over the last week, and it is at an all-time high. They literally can't pass by each other without having a verbal pissing match and it's infuriating. It's gotten to the point where I can't even enter the main house because Pax refuses to let me go alone, and Gabe, the fucking dickwad, is always walking around shirtless as if he owns the place and tries to make small talk with me about the upcoming trip.

Thank God they are leaving tonight.

I haven't even been able to find out if it's a *real* trip to Morocco or an actual plan to throw Satan's ass in rehab, because there is no getting Pax off of my ass long enough to ask Gabe.

I guess it really doesn't matter though... I'll gladly take a week or two away from Mother.

As for me and Pax, it's Friday, so we are preparing for another kegger down at the Club.

Jack and Jimmy are hosting which is nice because it means I'm free to drink and destress while they hold down the fort and holy hell do, I need this.

It's been insane trying to avoid Pax's hate-fuck advances all week. I can tell he knows something's up, so I figure once I'm drunk my conscience won't be an issue anymore because fuck am I horny.

I glance over at Pax, watching as he sets up the folding chairs around the tables. I'm excited because tonight we get to test out the new sound system Jimmy installed, and I know what song is going on full blast first. Tonight is going to be a bash we will never forget.

"Are you daydreaming right now?" Pax asks, tossing his shirt at me.

"Yep! I totally was... and why may I ask, are you stripping?"

"I'm hot."

I laugh at his childish grin.

"I can see that, but you make my job difficult when you force me to stare at all of those uncaged creatures," I admit, continuing to apply new drip spouts to the liquor bottles.

"Well, I can easily correct the issue for you, Vix. My anaconda has definitely been feeling a bit neglected lately, and the sight of you in that skin-tight dress is also quite distracting."

"Too bad," I mutter, trying to ignore him, "we have less than an hour to get this place ready and I haven't even started polishing the glasses yet."

"Excuses..." he states, jerking the bottle from my hand. "I'm getting tired of them," he says, pressing his nose to mine. "It's been a week of this shit already, and either you are going to tell me what's up, or I'm just going to have to hate-fuck it out of you."

The warning growl, great.

His scent alone is intoxicating, but it's his hand underneath my skirt and in between my legs that has my attention and forces me to swallow.

"Nothing's up, Pax."

"Then stop pretending you don't want this," he says, continuing to taunt me with his hand. "You're already damp which means you want this dick... so will you please stop avoiding me and let me do what I do best?"

"I fucking can't!" I snap. "Now just go and finish setting up the chairs already!"

He raises his hands in the air and backs off, his face riddled with concern.

"Fuck, Kirsten, I don't get you right now. It's like you have all of this pent-up emotion, yet you refuse to let me in on the issue, let alone ease you down, and I just want you to talk to me."

"Well I can't because there is nothing to talk about, now just drop it please."

I watch him set up the last of the chairs before he grabs his jacket and heads toward the door.

"I need some air, so I'm going for a ride."

"Fine... I guess I don't need to ask if you plan to come back or not."

"I'm not leaving the Hill if that's what you mean... and even if I was—"

"Yeah I know," I bark, cutting him off, "you always come back."

He stalks toward me and slams his helmet on the countertop, startling me.

"Is that what this is about? You still think I'm going to just up and leave you, never to return?"

"No, I don't think that," I hiss, exasperated. "I just have other things on my mind, okay?"

"Then what? Just fucking tell me! Is it because I mentioned wanting kids? Christ, Kirsten! You used to tell me everything."

"And you still never tell me anything," I undertone. He's trying to back me into a corner, and I hate feeling like this.

"Then tell me what you want to know, and I'll answer."

"Really?" I ask, studying his face. I can tell he's completely serious.

"Mmm-hmmm," he nods, "but I can't promise you will like the answers."

"I don't need to like them, Pax, I just don't want to feel shut out anymore."

"Neither does my anaconda," he teases, taking a seat. "So, what's on your mind?"

I shrug, knowing the things I want to ask are private, so I pour him a glass of whiskey and slide it to him.

"Where do you go when you leave?"

He takes a mouthful and swallows as his old-world blue eyes meet mine, and he takes a deep breath.

"Fairmount, it's a small town about a six-hour ride from here. I visit with a few friends, check up on them, and make sure they're doing okay. They are the closest thing I have to family besides you."

"Are they the same people you grew up with from when you were—"

I can't even say it, but I can see he understands what topic I'm pursuing.

He nods.

"We don't talk about it though, not since the imposters got caught, tried, and convicted. But somehow they were only sentenced to ten years plus time served. It's a slap in the fucking face really, but I guess that's what happens when you're a sick fuck with a powerful defense attorney."

My mouth parts and I stare at him, shocked and wondering why he never told me they'd been caught. I have so many questions, and I need a drink now.

"How long until they get out, Pax?"

The question comes out before I can stop it and I'm not sure I even want the answer.

He swirls the glass of whiskey before he swallows it back and slams the glass down on the table.

"They got released last year. I have no clue where they went but if they're smart, they had better be in hiding," he warns. "But the lawyer on the other hand, I know exactly where that fucking smug prick lives. I've paid him a few visits too." His tone is filled with sinister vibes.

"What do you mean *visits*?"

"Let's just say that the less you know, the better. I was doing what I had to. Can we be done with the questions for now?"

I nod, taking in the way his hand trembles as he lifts his glass gesturing for a refill.

"I'll leave it alone for tonight, but I still have questions. Thank you for letting me in," I say, planting a kiss on his whiskey lined lips.

"You're welcome," he winks, "but now it's your turn."

"My turn for what?"

"To tell me why you've been so off lately."

I glance up to the sound of the door creak open and see Jimmy enter, instantly relieved.

"We will talk about this later, I promise," I whisper. "Hey, Jimmy! Where's your clone?" I ask, noticing his brother isn't with him.

"What's up you two? Jack had a few errands to run, but he should be here by the time the party is in full swing. Did you have a chance to check out the sound system?"

"Not yet," Pax says, giving him the brotherly embrace. "Vixen's been too busy maintaining the liquor spouts and I've been setting up chairs for two hours."

"Well, it is work before play as they say," Jimmy states, "I'll go turn it up and test it out while you two finish up with the bar."

"Thanks, Jimmy," I say, handing him a beer.

The bass from the music is strong, causing the walls to rattle as

Jimmy cranks the tunes and people start to pile in, including Jack. I let the two brothers take over doling out the drinks while Pax collects his regular fees at the door and I start to wind down, drink in hand, swaying to the music.

I can't help but think about the last three years, knowing Pax has not only been trying to keep an eye on his makeshift family, but that he's been dealing with knowing those sick fucks would be getting out of jail and yet he never said a word to me. It hurts, knowing he didn't want to confide in me, or maybe he didn't want to worry me. Either way, I feel like there are still things he's not telling me, but I'm glad we've finally opened a line of communication, and at least I now know where his avid hate for lawyers stems from.

Now I'm even more terrified to tell him about Gabe, but I know I have to.

"Want to dance?" Pax asks, a long while and a few too many whiskeys later.

I nod, slam the rest of my drink and follow him onto the dance floor. He has no clue how to dance, but I enjoy watching him try; especially when he gets all hot and sweaty from trying to do the Running Man and removes his shirt. I could stare at him all night under the blacklight, watching his reptile tattoos practically come alive, gleaming underneath his streaming beads of sweat as if they've just exited the pond.

"Come on, Vix, you can move these hips better than this, I know you can," Pax taunts.

He jerks me closer, spins me the other way, and begins to grind himself against me from behind with slow and deliberate movements as I take in the way his hands grip me only the way he can. It's like nobody else exists when he touches me, and I close my eyes, feeling the effects of the alcohol kick in.

"That's it, girl," he whispers down my neck.

I lift my arms above my head, blindly searching for and finding his hair, weaving my fingers through it as our bodies move together to the rhythm of the music. Gabe was right, the way Pax and I move together is harmonious, mirroring each other. I feel his hands shift, one down and in between my legs and the other onto my breasts.

I know I'm buzzing, but it feels like I am weightless when we dance like this, and fuck am I turned on... and boy is his dick letting my tailbone know he is too.

My body is reacting to him as always, to the persistence of his hand massaging me with a determination that only Pax has, and I know if I let him continue, I'm going to orgasm right on the dance floor.

I stop his hand and open my eyes as the music stops, noticing the place is damn near empty as I turn to look at Pax.

"Where is everybody going? The party is just getting started, I swear it's only been like four hours since we opened."

"Don't worry," he says smiling wickedly, "I gave Jack and Jimmy the kill the party signal, I'd rather be alone with you tonight."

I glance over at the twins as they salute us with a bottle of Grey I can only assume they are taking home as payment and I watch them make their way out the door. The place is a giant mess, but it's empty, and my heart starts to pound, realizing why Pax wants to be alone.

"I need another drink," I say dragging him over to the bar. I pour him his regular and slam back a double, trying to regain both my buzz and my balls, knowing I have to tell him.

"Listen, Whiskey... there's something I have to tell you that I know you aren't going to like, and by not like," I pause to gain my composure, "I mean you are probably going to want to get on your bike and either do something really stupid, or never come back."

Pax locks his fingers together and leans forward, his eyes tapered and brows strained at the center.

"You went and fucked the lawyer, didn't you?"

"What? No, I didn't," I pause, stunned. "I sucked his dick."

My confession comes out so inaudibly I'm not sure if he heard me until he starts to laugh uncontrollably. I stand there, feeling tipsy, watching him laugh until he stops and shakes his head.

"Was it a 'hate blow' or an 'I'm going to fuck with Satan's day' blow?"

"The second one," I admit, feeling the guilt rise in my chest.

"And you seriously thought I would leave you over it?"

He starts laughing again and pulls me onto his lap.

"Ummm, yes, I know how you feel about lawyers, Whiskey, and I'm really sorry. I just thought that maybe if she knew how it felt... or if—"

"Shhh," he whispers, "I told you, Vixen. I know you, and I already know what you thought. It serves me right for always letting you take matters into your own hands. But I get it, and to be honest, I expected it."

"You did?" I cringe, wondering how the fuck he isn't angry.

My eyes are welling with tears because I have no clue how he is being so fucking rational right now.

"Of course I did. You were born to handle your own, you're a badass. Truthfully, it's no different than the way I leave sometimes to take care of things I don't want to burden you with. I love you far too much to drag you through my mud, and I know you feel the same way about me."

Now the tears are running down my face, so I close my eyes tight, willing them to stop. Between them, the alcohol, and the warmth of his fingers wiping my face, I swear he is an angel.

I open my eyes and take a staggering breath.

"I love you, Whiskey. I always have."

"I know."

He lifts my chin and our lips crash together like a storm as our tongues melt against one another's in waves. I taste the salt of my tears crossed with the whiskey on his tongue and moan needfully as he slips my panties down and growls that growl, the one that makes me weak in the knees.

"I need you, Kirsten," he hisses against my neck, "but I'm taking you in the bed, so move that ass and ditch the dress."

Knowing I need him too, I slip the dress off and follow him to his old room in the back. I take a seat on the bed, watching as he removes his shirt and walks around lighting a few candles before he shuts off the light.

All I can see is his beautiful silhouette in the darkness as he stands in front of me, stopping to remove his pants and let down his hair.

"Say the words again," he whispers, straddling his body over mine. "Tell me that you love me."

My pulse picks up instantly to his tone and his presence, the kindness in his voice.

"I love you, Pax."

He laughs quietly to himself as he leans down, gently laying soft kisses over my stomach, his hair tickling me as he does. I'm aroused by the scent of him as he imprints his soft lips up my body before he stops to lay himself against me and focus on his hand that skilfully taunts me.

"Hey, Vix," he whispers.

"Yeah?"

"You realize I am still going to beat the living hell out of the schmuck the second he's back, right?"

"What?" I ask, half moaning.

"You heard me; I'm going to make sure the mother fucker never comes near you again."

Unable to concentrate on his hand, I sit up and cover myself.

"Why are we talking about him right now? I thought you weren't mad about it."

Jerking me by the hips back down the bed, he growls. "Stay the fuck still."

He puts all of his weight on me, resuming his finger massage over the folds of my pussy. It feels incredible but I'm irritated that he just mentioned Gabe while he's touching me.

"Pax," I moan in frustration, "What the hell are you doing? I asked you a question!"

"I'm doing my goddamn job!" he barks, continuing his methodical assault.

I moan even louder as my body betrays me. My mind is angry, but his hand is even angrier as he begins to fuck me with his fingers.

"Jesus fuck, Pax! Will you just slow down for a second?"

He ignores me, knowing full well I'm pissed but past the point of being able to ignore the building climax as his thumb works my clit only the way he knows how. I press myself harder into his hand, matching his movements and rhythm as my heart throbs in my chest.

Running his tongue up my neck to my ear, he stops to whisper.

"Do you still want me to stop, Vixen? Because I think you are enjoying my wrath and you're about to spill your hate all over my fingers."

"Holy fuck!" I whimper, gripping the sheets. My entire body shudders as my orgasm rips through every nerve ending I have leaving me breathless. "How the hell do you do this to me every time?"

I look over at him smiling wickedly as he licks his fingers and winks.

"I just know you climax better when you're angry; you've been like this forever and fuck do you taste good."

I smile at him, loving the way he looks at me and how hard his dick is against my thigh. I grab it and stroke it, leaning down to take him into my mouth but he stops me.

"Uh-uh, I don't think so," he cautions.

"Why the hell not?"

He grabs my wrists and in one swift movement, he flips me face down and smacks my ass.

"Because I'm about to hate-fuck the sin out of you," he seethes, "and when I'm done, we are going to have a chat about the schmuck once I'm not so fucking angry!"

"Fine, Pax, fuck away then!"

"I'm not asking for your permission. I'm warning you," he advises. "Better bite down on the pillow, this is going to be intense."

As always, my pussy reacts to his tone and begins to ache in need again just from the way he talks to me and controls me with his man-beast temper.

"Lift that fucking ass so I can see that pussy, Vixen, and take a deep breath."

I do, knowing that he's pissed at Gabe, and this is how he's going to calm himself, so I inhale sharply knowing he is going to be more physical than usual. *Not that I mind. I like that my body is his temple.*

He's forceful and rough as he drives himself into me and I grip the bars in the headboard for stability, listening to his carnal sounds of appreciation. There is no slack in is impaling movements that feel like I'm being slammed by a freight train as he runs one hand onto my breast and squeezes it hard and his other onto my pussy to assault my clit again.

I give in to the feeling, closing my eyes, loving every dirty second of it and he knows it. I can't help but push myself back to meet his every thrust, which is both pleasure and pain against my pussy and inside my stomach.

The harsher I moan, the louder he growls and the stricter his penetration becomes.

"Fuck yes," he groans. "Maybe fucking you like this will teach you not to make hasty decisions without me."

"Not likely," I grunt, trying to bear down and accept his aggression.

"Is. That. Right?"

His tone is more destructive than I've ever heard from him as he lets go of my breast and wraps my hair around his fist, jerking my head back hard as he continues on pounding into me.

"You might be a fucking masochist, Vixen, but I've got you beat," he hisses into my ear. "I'm trained not to give a fuck what you think, how you feel, or what you want. So, I can keep this up for hours, but if you come for me, *again*, I'll stop and return the favor."

"What did you just say?"

I stop moving to his tempo and drop to my stomach, waiting for him to realize I'm done.

"What the fuck, Vix?" he asks, letting go of my hair. "I almost had you right where I wanted you."

"Get the fuck off me, Pax."

He does as I roll over and look up at him trying to breathe, but his words keep playing in my head on a loop.

"What happened?" he asks, "Why do you look so upset?"

"Are you fucking kidding me right now?" I sit up and punch him in the peck so hard I groan in pain.

"Well don't hurt yourself, shit," he laughs, seemingly confused.

"It's not funny, you big dummy! God! Did you even hear what you just said to me?"

He shrugs and shakes his head as if he isn't even from the same planet.

"No, I was kind of in the moment."

I can tell by his sweet face he really has no clue what he just admitted to me, and it's taking everything in me not to cry.

"Whatever I said... I'm sorry, I take it back... Let's just start over, I can do better," he pleads.

The disappointment on his face breaks my heart as the tears start to flow from my eyes. I can't stop them as I cover my face and don't know whether to throw up or hide. The man I love not only thinks he is a trained rapist; he thinks he can do it better... and I made him feel like he was sucking at something he clearly thinks he's good at. What is wrong with me? What the fuck is wrong with him?

My God, how did I not see how broken he is?

"Vixen, are you okay? Fuck, will you talk to me, please? At least tell me where this is coming from. I've never seen you cry."

"I just need you to stop talking for a minute," I undertone.

I feel like I'm stuck in quicksand, sinking, afraid to do or say the wrong thing and he just keeps making it worse because all he can do is worry about me crying!

I mean, what the fuck?

I wipe the tears away and take a deep breath.

"Come here," I tell him.

He moves closer and I guide his conflicted face onto my stomach, so he is looking up at me as I run my fingers through the lengths of his hair.

"You know you're a good person, right?"

I ask it not knowing what else to say as he stares up at me like I've lost my mind.

"Some days, yeah, I guess," he shrugs. "Why? What does it have to do with anything?"

"First of all, you are a good person *every day*, Whiskey, and second," I pause to kiss his forehead, "it has everything to do with us. You and me... the way we work together. The way we fuck to get out of our headspace."

"Okay... I'm still not sure what you are getting at, so can we just go back to the fucking?"

He smiles that stupid grin he does when he's not listening to me because he's still horny and I roll my eyes.

"No, Pax," I say, smacking him lightly. "I'm being serious right now; I don't think you understand how much your childhood affected who you are. And I want you to know that I love you and no matter what you say it will never change that, but I want you to get some help."

His eyes narrow as he crosses his arms and scoffs.

"What the fuck, Vixen? Are you serious? I don't need help, and I sure as fuck don't need you treating me like I'm a goddamn victim of some kind or looking at me like I'm weak."

"You know that's not what I'm doing, you are the strongest pigheaded person I know, you are anything but weak. I just think you need to get some of your story off of your chest, talk about the abduction with a professional so you can start to heal, that's all."

"That's all, huh?" he gripes as he gets up and throws his clothing on. "Well fuck that, I don't need to take this shit... least of all from you Vixen. When's the last time you talked to a fucking shrink about Satan and the way she uses your head like a carnival game of Smash the Bottles? Fucking hypocrite."

I say nothing knowing he's right as he slams on the light and searches for his keys.

"I'm going for a ride; I'll see you when I see you."

"Wait, Pax!" I beg, "You've been drinking, I'll leave and go home if you need space."

He looks at me and shakes his head in disappointment.

"See you around."

CHAPTER 7
Loud Silence

The main house is empty, the guesthouse is empty, and my fucking bed is empty. I've been sitting here in radio silence for five days going insane wondering how far I pushed Pax past his breaking point, wishing I had said or done something differently. He said he loved me because I felt like home, never judged him, and never asked questions. I guess I screwed all of it up and I wonder if he still loves me, or if he's ever coming back.

I've spent the last five agonizing days trying to do anything and everything not to hit the bottle to numb the throbbing in my chest and stuff down the tears, but there are only so many things I can do to keep busy.

It's gotten so bad that whenever I hear the roar of an engine, I run onto the street like a lunatic hoping it's Pax, only to find out it's one of the twins or both of them, or some other fucker that makes me realize how much I love him and need him to come home. By Wednesday, I was so stir crazy I took a cab down to the tattoo parlor and spent three excruciating hours in the chair getting my first and last tattoo, it fucking stings but it reminds me that I am alive, that I am deserving of love, and in a way, seeing it define my hip, I realize how much I can't bear to be without Pax. I'd hoped getting a tattoo might set me on common ground with him and get him to tell me the story of how he got all of his. I've asked a billion times, but he's always shut me down. If he won't talk to a shrink I figured maybe he could learn to talk to me.

Then when I woke up this morning to an empty bed again, I promised myself I wouldn't do what I've been considering since the night he left, but now that I'm sitting here staring at a bottle of whiskey, I know what I have to do.

Like Pax says, I'm not allowed to turn into my mother.

I grab my backpack, my keys, and my helmet and head out to the main garage. I haven't been in it since Dad's death, but I have no choice now. I need the Harley he left me. I'm going to Fairmount to find Pax and bring him home.

I take a deep breath as I hit the key code on the panel on the wall and wait for the door to open. Stepping inside I take a quick glance around and ignore my inner hurt that tells me to either cry or break some shit as I spot the bike, climb on, flip the kick stand, and start the engine.

The bike is hella heavy, but the rumble between my legs is so powerful my heart begins to race as I rev the engine and tell myself that no matter what I see when I get there, this is my only option.

Here I come, Pax.

I've never driven a bike, let alone left the Hill to go any further than the liquor store, so a six-hour ride on this beast should be interesting.

On the highway, I feel nothing but freedom as I squeeze the clutch, pop it into fifth gear, and turn the throttle, speeding up to 65mph; this motherfucker is badass. I've never felt more alive than I do right now, and I think I've found a new love for driving motorbikes.

By the time I pass the junkyard in the middle of nowhere, it's been close to two hours and according to the map I downloaded from Google, I know there is a rest stop ahead in the next forty-five minutes.

I pull into the station a while later to refuel and clean the bug guts off of my visor. My legs are sore as shit and I'm walking as if I've just been fucked for days, so I decide to stop in at the diner to rest.

I take a seat and check the map for my next landmarks, wondering where I will start looking once I get to Fairmount. I guess I could show his picture around and ask the locals.

"Coffee for you, hun?" the waitress asks.

"Please," I say, pushing the mug toward her. "Would you happen to remember if this man came through here last Friday?"

I hold up my phone as she glances over the picture of Pax.

"No, sorry, hun. I don't recognize him."

"It's fine," I shrug, "just thought it was worth a shot."

I hand her a ten and tell her to keep the change for the coffee as I fold up the map.

I'm antsy to get there because it's getting dark quickly, so I take a few sips and make my way back out to the bike.

It's close to eleven by the time I see the sign welcoming me to the town of Fairmount, population 720. I pull over and dig through my bag for the town map I printed.

The sign looks as old as all of the buildings I can see on what looks to be the main street. Everything is weathered and decayed with the paint and letters missing from the bar, motel, and homes I pass as I idle down the road until I find a spot to park the bike.

I enter the convenience store that doubles as the town motel. It's shady as shit and creepy too, so I head right to the weird looking guy behind the till, and I smile.

He's pale and super skinny, maybe forty with dark eyes and hair, and he doesn't seem too friendly.

"Hi," I say, holding up my phone, "have you seen this guy around by any chance?"

He leans in closer as he pulls a pair of glasses from his pocket and slips them on.

"Yeah, I've seen him around… question is, what's a young thing like you doing looking for a dirtbag like Pax for?"

My first instinct is to swallow down my excitement because this guy doesn't seem to like my runaway drifter.

"I have business with him," I lie. "Any chance you could point me in the right direction of where he might be staying?"

I don't take any chances and slip him a hundred, hoping it'll give him incentive to answer honestly.

"What kind of business?" he asks, taking the money.

"Repairs… on my bike, he told me to meet him by the sign just outside town, but I waited for a while and he didn't show."

"Yeah well, you shouldn't be out this late in this town, and you definitely don't want to walk into the mess of a crowd that guy hangs out with, so I'll tell you what…" he says, reaching behind him for a key, "take room twenty, last door down the hall on the left, and I'll see if I can't track him down for you in the morning."

I take the key as my heart pounds in my chest.

"Are there cockroaches?" I blurt unintentionally.

He laughs and shakes his head.

"Honey, in this town it ain't the cockroaches you need to be worried about… the sheets are clean and the TV works. Just smack the side of it if it's fuzzy."

I nod and slip my phone in my pocket as I turn toward the hallway that leads to the rooms.

"I didn't catch your name, sweetheart," he calls out from behind me.

"Vixen," I say back, waving the keys in the air, "and thanks for the room."

He mutters something but I just keep walking until I reach the last room on the left. The place is decked out in wood paneling board and unnerving wall sconces that flicker as I pass.

If ever there was a time, I didn't want to be handling shit on my own, this is it.

I enter the room and lock the door behind me as I scan the place. It smells like musty old mothballs, but the bed looks clean as far as I can tell. I set my bag down on the wood chair and pull out my bottle of whiskey, knowing it is the only thing that will help calm my nerves. I'm curious as to what the guy at the counter meant when he said Pax's friends are a bad crowd.

I take a swig of whiskey and let the liquor sit on my tongue, hoping the familiar flavor of Pax will etch into my taste buds if I just don't swallow. Man do I miss him, but one more night won't kill me even though I'm not positive that's true in this place.

Startled by the roaring sound of bike engines, I choke down the whiskey and fly toward the window to check it out.

Seems the bar across the street is a midnight hot spot.

Thankful I came prepared for anything, I tie my hair back, grab my purse, bear spray, and keys before I make my way out of the room and exit through the back entrance of the motel.

The bar looks like a shithole and as I cross the street, I feel the panic erupt in my stomach that says maybe I shouldn't go in there, but I shove it down and tell myself to stop overreacting. Pax looks mean on the outside but really, he's harmless and sweet... maybe everyone else is too.

I step inside the bar and take a look around before I make my way up to the counter, seeing no sign of Pax, just a few burley looking dudes and their girlfriends shooting pool on the far end of the place.

"Evening," the bartender nods. "What can I get for you?"

I take a seat, trying not to stare at all of the skull tattoos down his arms as I pull out my phone to show him the picture of Pax.

"I'll have a whiskey, make it a double, no ice, and have you seen this guy by chance?"

He glances me over, his dark brown eyes narrowing before he pours me the drink and places it on a napkin.

"That'll be five bucks, and sorry, hun, never seen him."

I don't buy it for a second, but hand him a twenty.

"Are you sure?"

"Yep, I'm sure," he says, as a woman enters the bar from the back room. "Hey, Verna, you ever seen this guy?"

He hands the stocky, bright orange-haired woman my phone as she scans it over quickly.

"Nah, never seen him, sorry, sweetie... so, what's a pretty girl like you doing looking for a guy like that in a shithole like Fairmount?"

"I have business with him," I say finishing my drink. "I'm staying across the street at the motel, so if you see him can you please tell him Vixen is looking for him?"

I write my name and room number on a napkin and she takes it from me.

"Sure thing... and hey," she pauses, eyeing over the people in the corner playing pool. "Not everyone around is friendly, so watch your back when you cross the street."

I swallow as my heart pounds, and I nod in appreciation of her warning.

Note to self, never travel to butt fuck Fairmount alone again.

Taking no chances, I pull out the bear spray and pretty much jog my ass back to the motel, making sure no one followed me and then I double-check the locks once I'm back inside the room.

How the hell Pax lives in a place like this is beyond me. I undress into my panties, throw on one of Pax's old t-shirts and climb into bed, with the mace and the bottle of whiskey. All I can smell is his scent and all I know is that tonight is going to be one of the longest nights of my life, but if I get to see Whiskey tomorrow then it's worth it. He's worth anything this eerie shithole town wants to throw at me.

* * *

A loud knock at the door jolts me awake as I look around, hungover, remembering where I am.

Fuck, my head hurts.

I stand and stagger my way to the door and peek through the peephole and instantly swing the door wide open to Pax's angered expression.

Ignoring it, I jump and throw my arms around his neck and my legs around his waist and hug him tight as he carries me into the room, kicking the door closed with his foot.

He lets me down and grabs my waist, seemingly inspecting me as I cringe to the pain of his hand gripping my freshly inked tattoo.

"Why in the fuck did you come here, Vix? This isn't a nice place for you to be," he growls.

I inhale sharply to his angered tone.

"So, you're not happy to see me?"

He jerks me closer and wraps his arms around me as I take in his intoxicating scent.

"Of course, I am, I just don't know what made you think coming here was a good idea. How did you get here anyway?"

"My dad's Harley," I mutter into his chest.

"You drove a fucking hog out here?"

Now his tone is even angrier with a hint of shock mixed in.

"Yeah, and it was fun as fuck," I laugh. "But I think the Kawasaki is more my style if I'm being honest."

"You are such a naughty little vixen," he says with a growl. "I should hate-fuck you right now just to show you how you make me feel."

"Don't threaten me with a good time, Whiskey," I wink.

He laughs as he takes a seat at the table.

"I was planning on coming home today. I just needed to clear my head for a while."

"Mmm, sure," I mumble. "Could have fooled me... you do know that the words *I'll see you around* can be taken many different ways, right?"

I lift the bandage under my t-shirt to check on my tattoo that's now stinging.

"Not really," he argues, "not when they come from me... I always come back and I wish you would trust me on that already."

He clears his throat to get my attention and I look up at his probing expression.

"What the fuck happened? Did you wipe out?"

"Of course not! I'm pretty sure I'd be dead, not standing here listening to you lecture me."

"Then what's with the bandage?"

I smile, feeling a little nervous about showing him now that I know he's not still pissed at me.

"I got restless while you were gone, and I went to the tattoo parlor... figured it would keep my mind off the liquor."

He stands and walks closer to me.

"You got a tattoo? I mean, don't get me wrong, it's hot that you're into it, but fuck, Kirsten, I was only gone five days and now you're riding hogs and getting inked! Lift your shirt, I want to see it."

I roll the bottom of the t-shirt up to my navel as he gently peels the bandage down my hip and smiles proudly.

"Whiskey and Vixen," he mumbles, kissing the fresh wounds. "And what is this?" he asks tracing the outline of the tattoo lightly. "A magic lamp," he continues, "I love it, almost as much as I love you... but does this mean I owe you three wishes?"

"Way more than three," I laugh, "but enough about the tattoo, I want to meet your family Pax."

He sighs, carefully reapplying the bandage and pulling my t-shirt back down before he takes a seat at the table again.

I can tell he's hesitant as he pours us both a shot of whiskey and hands me one, raising his glass.

"To Whiskey and Vixen," he toasts, "and to taking my hog riding, ink-inspired girlfriend to meet the fam."

I raise my glass grinning like a moron.

"Your girlfriend huh? Yeah, okay, I'll go with that... but I want to trade bikes with you. The Kawasaki is much lighter than the Harley."

He glares at me and pushes the glass toward my lips, shaking his head.

"Let's celebrate first, and hate-fuck over the bikes later," he growls.

We both down our shot and stare at each other for a few seconds, me biting my lip and Pax looking at me as if I'm breakfast.

I determine it's *now* officially *later*, and lunge at him, jerking him up by the belt as I unbuckle it and whip his pants down, exposing his erection. I nudge him back onto the chair as he tears my panties off, lifts me like I'm nothing, and slides my already wet pussy onto his dick, his mating call leaving his throat in a low groan.

"Fuck," he moans, trying to get deeper, "it's like you were built to ride this dick."

"I was," I tell him, panting as I work to find my pace. His hands are gripping my hips, driving me up and down his length in support, and between the pain of him rubbing my tattoo and the pleasure of having him inside me, I'm already about to climax.

"Let me see those tits," he demands.

I'm panting and moaning as I tug the shirt over my head and toss it behind me.

Letting me take control, Pax slides one hand up my back, into my hair and onto the base of my skull and the other under my breast as he takes my nipple into his mouth and nips down on it.

"Holy fuck, Pax," I moan, "I'm going to cum."

"That's the fucking point, Vixen, show me the hate, baby, and fuck me like you mean it."

I grip the back of his hair as my body begins to seize and shake, my release exploding through me like fireworks as I drop my head onto his shoulder until it subsides. He holds me tight against him, now back to controlling the severity of my movements as he brings himself to his own climax. I can't help but bite his neck to the sound of the growling he does when he's releasing inside me.

"Ouch! Fuck, Vix, not so hard," he gripes.

"Sorry, it's a bad habit, and also its payback for the pain you inflicted on my magic lamp."

He laughs and kisses the tip of my nose as I sit straddling him, admiring his compassionate gaze and the way he always makes me feel tough like I don't have to answer to anybody for anything.

He lets me handle my own shit even when I know it scares him.

"So, now that you're my girlfriend, I suppose it means I need to take care of you better... especially since you're becoming an ink junky and riding a Harley now."

I kiss his sweet face and climb off of him so we can get dressed.

"No... it's you who needs to ride the Harley, Pax. I'm surprised I even made it here in one piece. It's fun, for real, but the damn thing weighs a fuck-ton, so trade bikes with me please."

I cross my arms and squint at him, tapping my foot on the floor, waiting for his answer as he works on tying his hair back in thought.

"Okay, I'll agree to ride the Harley but only on one condition."

"Which is?"

"You agree not to ask me questions when I tell you that you cannot offer my family a place to stay on the Hill."

"What?" I cringe, not fully understanding.

"You heard me... we are not taking them back with us, Vixen... I know you, so just shake on it, and I'll commandeer the Hog."

I shake, not even thinking about it. I just know that the beast of a bike is hard as shit to lift so I cave.

I pack my bag and check the room over to make sure I haven't forgotten anything as Pax hands me his jacket.

"You have to wear it until you have one of your own."

"Fuck that, you said one condition and I'm good in my sweater, thanks, now let's get moving... I want to meet your family so bad!"

He grabs my wrist and stops me abruptly.

"Wear it, or I am not taking you to meet them, it's that simple."

I can tell by his tone he means it, so I snatch the jacket from his hand, throw it on and follow him out to the bikes.

"Just be careful on the back roads and ride behind me... oh and make sure you don't hit the throttle too hard, the Ninja has a strong kickback to it, unlike the Hog."

I lift my visor and stick out my tongue.

"I'm sure I'll be fine. I've ridden on the back a million times."

"That's not the same and you know it. And you'd better not get the urge to try to race me either, Vix, understand?"

I nod and roll my eyes, not that he can see me through the tinted visor as I climb on the Ninja and start the engine. Pax looks hella hot on the Harley, his tattered t-shirt and inked sleeves make him look like even more of a man-beast than usual.

I wait for him to pull out in front of me and then hit the

clutch and ease up on the throttle as the bike jolts forward scaring the shit out of me, and I slam hard on the brake. Stopping, Pax walks the Harley backward, gets off, and removes his helmet.

"See... I told you, and I think you need a lesson."

"I don't need a damn lesson. Just get on the Harley before I make you walk!"

He growls and knocks on the side of my helmet like an ass but finally gets back on his bike as I follow him very slowly. He's doing less than 20mph, and it annoys me, so I rev the engine, hoping he'll pick up the pace.

I feel like he's screwing with me, testing my patience, so I speed up and go around him, flipping him the bird as I do.

He speeds up, his engine's deep rumbling vibrates through my head as he passes and wags his finger at me.

I give in and let him take the lead, satisfied he's going 50mph now as we head down a heavily tree-lined road. I wonder what his family will be like and hope they will like me. I have no clue what to expect, although it's crossed my mind that they could live in tents since that's how Pax used to live. I'm fine with whatever I'm heading into; as long as I'm with Pax I'm sure it will be okay. At least that's my story and I'm sticking to it.

I watch the right signal on Pax's bike come on as he turns onto a dirt road barely visible from the street. It's thick dense bush all around us and if I'm honest, it's kind of creepy. We travel another forty minutes until we hit a field and up ahead, I see a cabin just as weathered as everything else in this town.

It's small and looks abandoned, with tarps half covering the windows and sleeping bags hanging on a clothesline. I'm positive it's straight out of a horror movie, but then again, so was his childhood. All of theirs was.

CHAPTER 8
Welcome Home

Pax pulls over just outside the fence and hops off his bike as I park mine and remove my helmet. My heart is pounding with excitement. Or fear... could be both as I take in the smell of the campfire smoke that rises from behind the cabin.

"Are you ready?" Pax asks, offering his hand.

"Am I ever not ready? As long as I don't have to dodge liquor bottles or vases, I think I can handle meeting your family."

He smiles as if I'm in for a surprise and drags me through the field until we reach the entrance and then he stops and pulls my lips to his. The kiss is like nothing I've ever felt; he's gentle and controlled with his tongue. It's a different connection with him almost as if he's showing me a different side of him.

I inhale sharply when he stops and he smiles wide. I can tell he's proud. I don't know if it's me that makes him proud or his family, but seeing him so happy is riveting.

He opens the door and glances around as I step in behind him and take in the surroundings. It's small and scattered with mismatched furnishings, blankets, and décor. To the left is the kitchen. It's falling apart, literally. The cupboards are hanging off the hinges and the stove looks like it's from 1950 and rusted badly. The living room is to the right, but it also seems to serve as a bedroom with a curtain dividing it down the center, and straight back is a hallway with two rooms.

"They must be out back cooking breakfast. Come," he says, dragging me down the hall. "This is the washroom," he informs, nudging one door open, "and this is Ken and Verna's room."

I peek inside and hold my composure, trying not to cringe at the mattress that sits on the floor. It too is surrounded by old worn-down furnishings that look like they were hauled from the dump.

"It's lovely... antique-ish," I say, trying not to sound judgmental.

"We both know it's a pile of shit," he laughs, "just be honest around them, Vix. No one here holds any judgment."

"Good to know."

I smile at his humorous face as he shows me to the back door, and we step out onto the deck. There are four chairs seated around a fire pit, three of them occupied by two men and a woman. I happen to recognize two of them from the bar last night and smile politely.

"This is Kirsten a.k.a Vixen," Pax says. "Vixen, meet Ken, his wife Verna, and Ken's mute brother, Cliff. He doesn't talk, but he's not deaf so don't piss him off."

I nod at Cliff and he smiles before I turn my attention to Ken and Verna.

"Hello, it's nice to see you again."

Verna smiles and stands to hug me.

"You too, dear. I'm glad to see you made it back to the motel in one-piece last night."

"Yeah, me too. This town is a little unnerving at night."

"It's really not that bad if you stay away from the Harlowe

brothers. They own the land across the way that serves as the town cemetery, and they aren't too polite to drifters or newcomers."

"Oh, you mean the other people from the bar last night?"

Ken nods. "Yep, that's them. They own the motel too. But just stick with Pax and you'll be fine. Can I offer you something to drink? A double shot of Jack perhaps?"

I laugh and nod. "You remembered. How sweet."

"I work in a bar, remembering what people drink comes with the job."

He asks Pax for a hand and I watch them head inside and turn my attention to Verna.

"So, I don't mean to be rude, but I'd like to know how come you lied last night when I asked if you knew Pax?"

She smiles and flushes slightly.

"He's like a brother, and in this town, we don't tend to give out information on each other's whereabouts. We all sort of stick to our own, if you catch my drift. Besides, even if I had recognized you, there are no phones out here and the bar didn't close until after two, so I had no way to contact him here at the house."

"I guess that makes sense, but what did you mean by recognize me?"

Verna laughs gruffly and crosses her arms.

"Pax showed us some pictures of you a few times, but your hair was blond, and you said your name was Vixen, but we only knew you as Kirsten. You add that up with the fact we ain't never met you in three dang years, just thought it'd be safer to get Pax's permission before we brought you out here."

Verna hands me a bowl of beans and a spoon as I glance over in Cliff's direction. He looks like a younger version of Ken, dark hair, dark eyes, and a moustache to match.

"Don't mind him, he may not be much of a talker, but he's one hell of a listener! Especially when we get him to man the jukebox down at the bar, he's a real music fan," Verna states. "Now eat up before it gets cold."

I take a bite as I notice the strange scars that line Verna's arms, they look like thicker versions of cat scratches as if she was mauled by a tiger.

"Pax tells us you live six hours from here in someplace nice called the Hill, what's that like?"

"Pardon?" I ask, trying to focus.

My mind is a ball of torture wondering who the hell did that shit to her unless she did it herself, but I can't imagine that's the case.

"The Hill..." she repeats, "What's that like?"

"It's okay, it's full of douchebags and spoiled jerks, but I can't complain. The neighborhood is secure and me and Pax run a bar on Friday nights."

"Oh, yes, I remember him telling me something about that. He's been bringing his earnings back here to help us keep the heat and power on. He's such a good man."

I nod and smile at her knowing she's right. The guy has practically nothing, yet he gives what little he has away regardless.

"The night I met him, I was sloshed," I laugh, recalling the event. "I'm pretty sure if he didn't stop me, I would have peed on his tent. Anyway, he was sweet enough to carry my ass up the giant hill and all the way home. I just remember loving the way he smelled, and the way I felt like nothing bad could happen whenever he was around."

"Well don't worry, darling, you aren't the only one who feels that way," she laughs. "Pax has always been that way, trying to save other people from things no one cares to speak of. Him and Ken, both of them took severe punishments when they were kids trying to look out for Cliff and me."

Her eyes well up with tears and I can't imagine what she must be thinking or feeling, nor do I want to.

"I'm sorry... I didn't mean to—"

"Oh, hush now," she says, "it's all in the past. Long done. We try to remember the good times and be thankful we still have each other."

"The good times?" I ask curiously.

She nods and winks.

"Did he ever tell you why he fell in love with snakes?"

I shake my head and smile, excited to find out the story.

"Your drink," Pax interrupts. "You wouldn't happen to be talking about me behind my back, would you?"

He looks straight at Verna with his *you're in deep shit* stare as I sip the drink.

"Oh, come on now, I was just gonna tell her the story about the snake. I won't get into the dark parts, just the funny stuff, I promise."

Pax laughs and crosses his arms.

"Tell away then, but you had better skip the part—"

"Please don't leave anything out," I blurt, covering his mouth with my hand. "I want the whole story!"

Pax slobbers on and licks my fingers like a pig and then bites them lightly before I rip my hand away laughing.

"You are so nasty," I say shaking my head. "Now, Verna, please continue with the snake story."

I sit back and sip my drink as she proceeds to tell me a story about when they were kids, all of them around eight except Cliff who was six. They'd been living in a basement of a house on a secluded piece of land in the middle of fields of wheat as far as their eyes could see. Verna told Pax she had a plan to escape from 'the imposters' and that when she did, she would live at the zoo, but Pax had no clue what a zoo was, so Verna explained it to him.

"Now hold on a second," Pax interjects, "in my defence, you were not very clear about what kinds of things lived in the zoo."

"Yes, I was," she laughs, "I said donkeys and goats... but what did you come back with? A freaking garden snake that you shoved in your pants to sneak inside without them seeing."

"It was a gift!" Pax hisses, "and he would have made a great pet if Ken didn't stomp on him to death."

We all bust out laughing at Pax's attempt to remain mad about it.

"That was the only time I ever saw Pax cry," Verna adds, "and it wasn't long after that he decided that one day, he would own a mansion full of snakes... well that was his goal anyway. But instead, as you can see, he only ended up with a bunch of tattoos and no mansion."

Pax scoffs and shakes his head.

"I asked you not to tell her that I cried, that was really uncool of you," he gripes, failing to mention that he kind of does live in a mansion. "Now," he adds, "I may just have to tell her about the time you, Ken, and Cliff over there, burned down the tree fort I built us."

"Whoa now!" Ken laughs. "I had nothin' to do with that, it was all these two," he says, pointing at Verna and Cliff.

"Oh my God, you have to tell me the story! Please," I laugh, watching Verna and Cliff simultaneously shake their heads, pleading.

"Nah, I think I'll save that story for another time since it was the first place we ever called home. I'll show it to you on the way back to the Hill... if you're lucky."

"If I'm lucky?" I repeat. "I'm pretty sure I am, but I have to pee, so please excuse me."

"I'll join you and get us some refills," Verna says, following me inside.

I shut the washroom door behind me and can't help but hold

my breath. It smells like mold and looks even filthier than it smells. The bathtub is rusting and the tiles that surround it are cracked and covered in grime. *Living like this can't possibly be healthy*, I think to myself as I wash and dry my hands.

"I could use a hand," Verna calls out.

"Not a problem," I say as I head to the kitchen. I grab two of the glasses from the countertop as Verna places her hand on my shoulder and locks eyes with me.

"I know what you must think of us," she undertones. "We were just kids doing what we had to, to survive on the cards we were dealt."

I shake my head and open my mouth to say something, but she squeezes my shoulder firmly.

"He did what he was told to do, what they forced him too, we all did. We had no choice, not one of us, but Pax took the brunt of what he could. I don't hold any grudges toward any of them, nor do they me," she continues, her eyes dancing with grief. "Pax is a dang hero the way I see it... he came back for us, took care of us, and loved us when no one else did." She pauses to wipe the stray tears that stream down her face and she inhales sharply. My heart is breaking at the pain in her voice, but I suck down my urge to cry because it isn't my pain.

"Those monsters didn't get nowhere close to what they deserved for the things they did to us, but there's no sense in staying angry about it. We all chose to move on... we needed to. Now... I'm only gonna say this once," she says sternly, "that boy needs to move on with his life just like we have. He doesn't owe us anything, not a goddamn thing, do you hear me?"

I nod, not fully understanding as her eyes blaze into mine with fury.

"Good, then make sure he understands by Monday, that we ain't gonna be here no more. We are moving on too. We don't need this dirty, haunted past lingering between us no more. Pax has you, and I got them two. Tell me you're going to help him move on so he can start to heal. Can you do that for me?"

I swallow and wipe the one tear I couldn't hold in and I clear my throat, knowing by her tone there is nothing I can say to change her mind.

"I will, Verna, I'll tell him, but only on one condition."

She glares at me suspiciously and crosses her arms.

"And what would that be?"

"You have to let me leave you some money, *no* questions asked. It's the only way," I pause to take a deep breath. "It's the only way that I can handle justifying lying to Pax, and it's also the only way he will know that you're all okay."

She nods steadfastly, as I hold out my hand to shake on it, but instead, she grapples me with her stocky body, bear hugs me, and whispers in my ear.

"He was right about you... you're a saint, just like he is. Now, wipe them tears and serve the drinks, we need to end this visit on a happy note."

I laugh at her brusque tone and follow her back outside where Pax pulls me onto his lap with a growl.

"What were the two of you up to in there?" he asks shiftily.

"Girl talk. So, you just never mind and don't hassle the lady," Verna bosses, "now lift them glasses and toast with us before we head back into town to open the bar."

We raise our glasses, even Cliff who sits smiling, contented by the warmth of the midday sun shining on all of us, almost as if this is what a family should feel like.

"To good memories, good women, and a life full of driftin'," Ken hollers.

We all clink glasses and swig back the whiskey as we say our goodbyes.

The ones that I know don't mean I'll see you later, or next

time, but instead it means Pax can try to move on from a life of pain.

I stand on the porch and watch from a distance as Pax hugs them and sends them on their way. I'm quick about writing a check and slipping it through the mail slot of the door just as I told Verna I would when she hugged me goodbye.

I came out here wanting nothing more than to find my drifter and bring him home, but instead what I was filled with was an understanding of his unspoken horrific past, and what the man would do for his family. A family that loves him and forgives him for the things he had no control over, and a family that carries secrets so dark, that in the end, it's easier to drift apart. It isn't my place to judge them or ask questions, I know in my heart Verna is doing what she thinks is best for everyone, and I'm okay with it. The question I don't know the answer to, is will Whiskey be okay with it too?

"Heads up," Pax yells.

I catch the deflated football he tosses at me and laughs as he takes a seat on the porch beside me.

"Never owned one of those fucking things when it was full of air, and probably couldn't catch it if it was... So," he pauses eyeing me over, "what did you think of my mysterious family?"

I move closer to him and rest my head on his shoulder.

"I think they are really amazing. Sweet, kind, honest... the sort of people I'd be honored to call family."

He lifts my head and stares at me questionably.

"You aren't considering dragging them back to the Hill with us, are you?"

"No," I laugh, "you already warned me not to. Besides, I still have Satan to face and I don't think she would take too kindly to me bringing home any more drifters."

Pax laughs quietly, seemingly amused with something.

"What's so funny?"

"Nothing... it was just a stupid thought," he says passively.

"Tell me!"

I give him the eyes; the ones that warn him I'm about to pull his hair if I have to just to get it out of him.

He stays silent, staring at me with his deep blue gaze holding mine as he twirls my hair around his finger, and then he sighs.

"This is the first time I can look at your sexy face without getting the urge to cause an argument so that we can hate-fuck. Do you think that means there is something wrong with me?"

"Are you kidding me?" I laugh. "You are such a big dummy sometimes, Pax, and no, there is nothing wrong with you. Maybe it just means you are at peace with yourself because you're realizing you are a good man... just. Like. I. Said."

He traces his fingers lightly down my face and smiles mischievously.

"You wouldn't be trying to purposely cause an argument with me right now, would you?"

"Me? Of course not," I feign innocence. "We do need to get going though if we are going to make it back to the Hill before dark."

"Your wish is my command."

He kisses my forehead and takes off running through the field toward the bikes and I start to chase him, laughing because his pants are falling down. God, I love that man.

It's funny to me that he doesn't even realize yet that I only have one wish.

For us to stay like this forever, Whiskey and me.

The two of us laughing and happy, fulfilled by each other's presence just like a real family. But that isn't possible just yet, at least not until I cut ties with Satan... while I pray to God that come Monday, Pax will still love me enough to forgive me once he finds out that I helped his other family split.

CHAPTER 9
When it Rains

It's Tuesday morning and I still haven't said a word to Pax about Verna skipping town with his family. It's been on my mind for days, but I can't bring myself to tell him yet, not when he seems so happy and content with life. We still haven't fucked either, but that's only because I've been lying and saying I'm on my period since I can't seem to bring myself to do *that* with Pax either.

The only thing I have going for me at the moment is that Satan still isn't back from her trip which has me thinking she's not in rehab or I would have heard something about it from Gabe by now. Whatever... at least it's still nice and quiet around here.

Logging into my bank account, I check my balance and see Verna still hasn't cashed the check I left her. I mean fuck, what is she waiting for? How am I supposed to tell Pax I made sure they would be okay when she still hasn't accepted the money?

I slam the lid closed and run my hands through my hair, aggravated.

"What's got you all pent up this morning?" Pax asks. "You need me to get you some Midol or something?"

"Yeah... that or a new conscience would be great!" I mutter inaudibly.

"Want to go for a ride down to the Club?"

"Sure, why not? Sitting around here isn't exactly entertaining at the fucking moment."

"Yeah, well if you prefer, I can definitely find a way to entertain your sassy little mouth instead," he offers.

I flip him the bird and rip the leather jacket he forced me to buy down from the hook and head out to the garage. I'm miserable and I know it's unfair to him, but still, it's better me than him.

I follow behind him as he pulls onto the street, watching as loose wisps of his hair sway in the wind because he's decided that riding the Hog means it's safe enough for him to not wear a helmet; yet another argument we had over the weekend that didn't end in hate-fucking... only a yelling match. He won.

It is what it is though, he's a grown man I figure, so, if he wants to ride without protection, who am I to say otherwise? Seems riding things without protection is his specialty, pun intended.

He's deliberately slow with his speed this morning... *probably because he's not wearing a helmet, fucking brat.*

Annoyed, I pull out ahead of him and engage the clutch and grip the throttle until I hit eighty, feeling the intense pressure of the wind against my chest. I feel free, no longer angry or guilty; it's just me and the bike navigating together, and I love it.

I pull in behind the Club and hop off the bike, turning to wait for Pax to enter the lot. I can hear his bike less than thirty feet away as I remove my helmet and stretch. He comes barreling in beside me and comes to a screeching stop, and I can tell he is pissed as he hops off the Harley and fucks with his wind tousled hair.

"What the fucking fuck, Kirsten? You had to be doing eighty back there! Do you have a fucking death wish?"

His attitude is complete bullshit... *Mr. I don't have to wear a helmet.*

"No..." I say, crossing my arms, "I was simply trying to have a bonding moment with the bike."

"That's not what that was, and you know it," he says, yanking the helmet from my hands. "If you can't be responsible when you ride, you can't fucking ride, Vix."

I scoff and follow him into the Club as he slams the door behind us, pushes me into the wall, and begins searching my pockets.

"What the fuck, Pax? You're being an asshole!"

"And you're being a brat!"

"A brat?" I yell. "Oh, I can show you a brat!"

I bite his arm that's pressed against my chest holding me in place, but he doesn't even flinch as he finds my bike keys, waves them in front of my face, and smiles.

"You are officially grounded," he says as he shoves them in his pocket.

"You can't fucking ground me! They're my bikes... now give me the keys back."

"Or what? You gonna bite me again?"

I stare at his cocky face, feeling my blood boil and decide to walk away. He is such a dick right now.

I pour myself a drink and sit at the bar, watching as he pulls out a book and starts to read at one of the tables.

Seriously? What the fuck? Since when does he read?

Now I know he's just being a douchebag and trying to teach me some sort of *Pax is boss* lesson. He's probably going through hate-fuck withdrawal, and this is my punishment.

Without thinking, I launch a beer mug across the room and nail the wall with it, the sound of it shattering on impact startling us both.

"Are you insane?" Pax growls, slamming his book on the table.

"I should record you right now so that you can see how much you look like your crazy mother!"

Instantly, my hand grabs another mug and I smash it exactly where I stand, as every nerve in my body twitches.

"Say it again, Whiskey, I fucking dare you!"

"I don't think I need to," he says shaking his head. "I'll see you later, when you're done behaving like a lunatic."

I watch as he walks toward the door and it takes everything in me not to throw another mug straight at his head.

When I hear the Harley pull away, my heart sinks in my chest, and I can't help but feel stupid and pathetic, I'm behaving exactly like my mother, and I know it.

By the time I get the shards of glass swept up, I feel much calmer and pour myself a drink while I sit, thinking. I know I need to get this burden off of my chest already. I have to tell Pax the truth so we can move on and I can stop being such a bitch.

I start the long ass walk up the Hill, thinking of all the ways I can break the news to Pax, also contemplating all of the various ways I can apologize. Not just for lying either, or for supporting Verna financially in her decision to cut ties with a part of their past. What I really need to apologize for is losing my temper and treating him the way I did, but I'm not sorry about speeding on the bike, that was absolutely on purpose.

I finally reach the house after an hour of walking and I head to the back. Not finding Pax in the guesthouse I wander over to the main house, knowing he's probably hounding Natasha for something to eat. I enter through the kitchen, spotting both sets of bike keys on the countertop. I shove them in my pocket and head into the sitting room.

"Pax, what the fuck are you up to?" I call out. "We need to talk about a few things."

He isn't answering me as I make my way through the foyer and head upstairs. I can hear the sound of the shower running in the washroom and laugh to myself; he totally would want to shower in the main house. It's like a spa in there and so much more luxurious than the guesthouse.

I turn the corner and see Pax as my heart stops dead. I inch my way closer and stare at his ink covered arms wrapped around what appears to be my mother's naked frame through the fog of the shower door. I take yet another step closer, feeling dizzy, but I shake my head and I'm not damn well leaving until I know it's her... and *motherfucker*, it's her all right, I couldn't possibly mistake those bleach-blonde locks.

You've seen enough, I tell myself, as I back away and stagger into the hall trying to find my composure. I breathe in deep, begging myself not to overreact, not to cry, *just put one foot in front of the other.*

Escaping out the back door, I stop in the middle of the yard, my heart pounding in my chest, and the tears streaming down my face.

Kings don't fucking cry, stop crying!

It hurts to breathe, and I'm caught in a moment of madness wondering if I should grab a fucking butcher knife and kill that cunt. *God knows I want to. Fuck it.*

I glance over at the lawn tractor and smile as I wipe my face on my sleeve and swallow. I can't help but laugh as I crash the thing through the patio doors and straight into the sitting room as glass falls all around me, and I don't give a single fuck as I hit the lever and turn on the blade. The sound of it grinding up the rug under the tires is fascinating, and I can't help but continue to drive it into every table and piece of furniture, cursing Satan's name until I look around and see that the entire room is now just as scratched and broken as I feel.

I leave the thing running and hop off before I saunter my way into the garage and key the fuck out of the Beamer and Mother's Cadillac, making good and sure I leave my name where she can see it. Then I start that shit with fingerprint command and back it the fuck right through the garage door. The impact sends wood chunks flying all around me, nailing the roof, and landing all over the driveway.

I put it in park, storm back inside, and straddle the Hog before I start and rev the engine as the exhaust billows in while I walk it backward as far as it will go until I hit the wall. I watch the gauge until the RPM's hit max and then I punch it out of the garage as I hit the throttle again and open her up. *Fuck you guys!* I think to myself; I'm seething inside.

Those fucks are so lucky I don't have a goddamn gun. The tears just keep coming, making it hard to see, making me more livid. The angrier I get, the harder I turn the throttle as the pounding in my mind and chest fill me with nothing but rage.

I barrel through the stop sign and keep the bike pinned to the max as I see the Club approach up ahead. I'm not sure if the Harley can take out a wall but I'm about to find out. I laugh to myself. I glance at the speedometer, happy as fuck to see it redlining as I shut my eyes and let the bike take me through the tin wall. The sound is extremely loud as I slam down as hard as I can on both brakes, the tires screeching as I blow through the bar counter and come to a hard stop. Bottles of liquor smash all around me and the rush is like nothing I've ever felt. I shakily dismount the bike and look behind me at the damage, stunned I'm still alive.

I guess it helps being the daughter of Satan.

I'm positive it's the adrenaline coursing through me that's keeping me going as I chug from the bottle of Jack and slide down the wall to the floor.

Think, Kirsten, what are you doing... what's next?

My hands are trembling as I try to get a grip on myself, wondering where to go from here. Angered that my lips taste like

Pax, I smash the bottle against the floor as hard as I can and reach for the gin.

My world is a fucking sham and I realize that no matter how much money I have, it's useless when I have nowhere to go when it falls apart.

I feel my phone buzz in my jacket and squint my eyes to see it's Pax on Satan's phone. I don't care what his excuse is, I always knew this would happen. I ignore his messages, dump the bottle of gin over the phone, and pick up my helmet that rolled its way over to the wall and I smile.

That which doesn't kill me only makes me stronger, right, Satan?

I pull myself to my feet, shove my helmet on, and make my way out to the Ninja, happy I took both sets of keys.

Fuck you, Pax, if you think you're ever gonna find me. Hearing sirens in the distance, it's safe to assume I've been ratted on, so I take one last look around and leave the Hill, knowing there is nothing left for me here.

I don't know where I'm going but I plan to drive this bike until it runs out of gas and then figure it out from there. Maybe I'll become a drifter, who the fuck knows… I mean shit, who needs a home that feels like the pit of hell. Who needs a boyfriend either? Not me goddamn it. Not me.

I continue to tell myself it'll all be fine, I'll be okay if I just keep driving, embrace the spirit of the highway and the road that will lead me away from the pain.

Away from the truth.

Away from hell.

I make it another eighty miles before I have to pull over to fuel at the rest stop. It's dark and I'm literally exhausted, no longer running on adrenaline and heartache.

After I fill the gas tank and park the bike behind a motel *just in case that piece of dick is looking for me*, I wander inside and pay for a room. It's a shoddy looking place but what does it matter? I'm not on vacation, I'm on the run.

Inside the room, I toss the keys onto the table, march straight for the minibar, and chug back the first airplane bottle I see, trying to stuff down my urge to cry. The only person I want to talk with about this is Whiskey, God, why the fuck is that? UGH!!!

Who was I kidding anyway? Me and Pax… as if we would have made it anywhere great together in this life. I'm a liar and he's a cheat. We come from two different worlds and I was an idiot to think I could ever outdo my mother's tactics. God! I was so stupid!

I savagely twist off another plastic bottle cap and slam the contents, exhaling the burn of the alcohol, but it sure as shit isn't helping me right now. There is only one thing that will help me at this point, and I know it.

I grab my purse and head outside; the air is cool as I scan the dark street for anything that resembles a bar. Up ahead, I see a flickering sign and start walking in its direction until I get close enough to see it's some kind of biker hang out.

It'll have to do. I walk closer and study a solid row of motorcycles lined up in the parking lot and instantly feel unnerved about what I'm doing, until Pax's face floods my mind and the pain in my chest reminds me why I'm here.

I lean against the brick wall, debating if I should go in or just wait out here as the faint sound of classic rock music echoes through the wall. I'm cold and tired but I know I won't be able to sleep with these horrible feelings of hate weighing down on me like this.

The bell chime on the bar door makes me jump as I take in three men exiting. Two of them look mean and burley, kind of like Pax except bigger with long dark hair and less tattoos. The other is shorter than the first two, his hair blond, also long, and they are all wearing matching leather vests.

The blond one stops to light a cigarette and drops his lighter. As he turns around to pick it up, he halts and his green eyes lock solid on mine. Then he crosses his arms, looks me over from head to toe, and taps his buddy on the shoulder.

"What do we have here?" he asks, smiling waywardly. "You lookin' for a ride somewhere honey?"

I shrug, my heart pounding as the other two men stand there smirking and light up cigarettes as well.

The first one bends down to pick up his lighter and then walks closer to me, inhaling and then blowing the smoke from his cigarette in my direction. He's not more than four feet from me as he reaches out his hand and offers me the cigarette.

"The names Chiv," he says bluntly, "and there's no need to be shy, sweetheart, what's your name?"

I take the cigarette and smile.

"Vixen... and I'm not shy," I inform as I take a drag. "I'm horny."

"Is that right?" he asks cunningly. "I think I can help you out with that... in fact, I think the three of us could take you on a wild ride if you're down for some group action."

I look behind him at his friends and take another drag, thinking about it. It would absolutely fuck with my bleak reality and I'm always down for a good fuck, but this is a tad over the top, even for me.

Shit, how am I going to get myself out of this one?

I flick an ash on the ground and exhale the smoke into Chiv's face, doubting his name is short for Chivalry.

"Just you, not your friends, and only if you have protection on you... do you?" I ask, trying to hide the crack in my voice.

"No... but I sure as fuck do!" Pax growls.

I hear the click of what I think is a shotgun being cocked as my heart jumps into my throat. I turn slowly, my eyes wide as I take in his angered expression as he stands to my right aiming the gun at the three of them.

"Get the fuck in the car, Vixen."

I look behind him and sure as shit, he drove the Beamer here, *great*.

"Fuck you, Pax. I'm about to have a really nice time with Chiv here, so if you'd kindly fuck off with that thing it'd be greatly appreciated."

"Yeah, man, you heard the lady," Chiv echoes.

I jolt as Pax fires a warning shot into the air, and the sound rattles through my head as the shell casing hits the ground.

"Next one's gonna blow your fucking dick off, *man*, so I'd suggest you get a fucking move on and take your weasel friends with you."

Chiv raises his hands in surrender and begins to back away slowly.

"Whatever, you nut-job. The bitch came down here looking for us, but you can fucking have her."

"I know I can, and I will," he says still pointing the gun at them. "Now get your ass in the fucking car, Vix, before you make me shoot someone goddamn it!"

I look at him and shake my head.

"I don't give two fucks what you do anymore, so you can take that thing and shove it up Satan's ass for all I care."

I walk away, fuming inside. I'm so angry my nails are digging into my palms and I feel like I'm going to unleash the wrath of fury on his ass.

Hearing the car door slam and lock behind me, I keep walking, listening to his footsteps trailing behind.

"Will you please just stop and talk to me, Vixen?"

"No, just fuck off and go back to the Hill, Pax."

"I'm not going back there until you hear me out. I don't know what you think you saw—"

I turn instantly and backhand him so hard in his face, I grunt from the fleet of pain it shoots through my knuckles.

"Stop fucking following me! I can't listen to this bullshit! You fucking wrecked everything, Pax. You are a stupid drifter and I hate you for destroying us!" I yell, pounding my fists on his chest. "And you know what else? I paid your fucking family to disappear because even they can't fucking stand you! You're a liar, a cheat, and a fucked-up degenerate and the only thing you were ever good for was hate-fucking and bootlegging, now stay the fuck. Out. Of. My Way!"

He grabs my wrists, shakes me hard, and growls, completely unnerving me.

"Are you fucking done now?"

His eyes are raging into mine and his face is riddled with hurt as I work to recover my breathing, holding back my pooling tears and my urge to bite him.

"Let go of me."

"No. Not until you listen."

I try to pull my wrists from his grip, but I can't.

"Ugh! God, I hate you! And I need a fucking drink. Just let go so I can walk back to the motel and get one... okay?"

"Fine," he says letting go, "I need one too."

"Fuck you if you think I'm sharing, asshole."

"Fuck you if you think you're not," he undertones.

"Shut up and stop trying to talk to me."

He mutters something under his breath as I keep walking, taking strides as big as I can trying to put distance between us. He smells so fucking good; it's annoying and I hate being near him.

I know I can't outrun him and I know whatever he has to say is probably going to destroy me even worse than he already has... but what really sucks the most is that somehow, even with all of this pain, I still love the stupid asshole.

CHAPTER 10
What The Fuck?

I rummage through my pocket for the key card to the room as Pax stands leaning against the wall by the door, watching me silently with his stupid sad face.

Fucking douchebag.

Why does being so angry with him always seem to make him more appealing to me?

I can't believe he fucked my mother and yet the only thing I want to do right now is grab him by the ponytail and hate-fuck the hell out of *him* as a punishment.

What is wrong with me? Fuck!

And to make things even more awkward, I swear he damn well knows it with the way he's standing there all sexy with his inked arms crossed like he's done nothing wrong at all.

I push the door open and show him in, pointing at the table. The further he stays away the better.

He clears his throat and flips the chair around so he can straddle the seat, a total Pax move that says he wants to have a serious talk.

I roll my eyes and ignore him as I dig through the bar fridge and toss a handful of mini bottles onto the bed, before I take a seat beside them all and slam the first one.

"Are you at least gonna pass me one of those?"

I slam another one and then shake my head.

"Get your own booze, asshole. I'm sure Satan has a nice collection you can choose from."

"She doesn't actually," he says standing up, "she's going through withdrawal and there is no alcohol in your house."

"Yeah, right," I snort half-laughing, "Satan would kill anyone who fucked with her poison."

"I'm serious," he says, reaching for a bottle, "she's in pretty bad shape."

I smack his hand, but he snatches it and takes a seat beside me.

"What the fuck, Pax? This isn't a friendly visit, you fuck. God you are relentless, sitting here lying to my face like I'm an idiot. I fucking saw you guys, you stupid shit!"

He slams back the shot of whiskey and growls like he always does when he's mad.

"You're wrong about what you think you saw, Kirsten. Just think about it for a second."

"Fuck you Pax, I don't want to think about it for a second! I've been thinking about it my whole fucking life already... don't you fucking get it? You gave her exactly what she wanted."

I unscrew the lid off another bottle and slam it, starting to feel the anger come back tenfold as I picture them in the shower, together, his hands all over her, and it makes me want to puke.

"Oh, for fuck's sake already! Stop drinking and just listen to me for once! I did not sleep with your mother; I was helping her, goddammit!"

"Helping her what? Get you off because I never put out all weekend? That's classy Pax, really fucking classy!"

"Not even close... she was covered in vomit and piss for shit's sake! Gabe dropped her off with Natasha and left to go and get her prescription filled at the pharmacy. That's the fucking truth! I walked in there to Natasha refusing to help her, so I did. I love you, and I told you I would never fuck your mom, and I didn't!"

I stare at his enraged face for a long minute, wishing I could buy his story, but I saw what I saw, and I know my mother. It was probably one of her schemes to get him to give in to her.

"I wish I could believe you," I mutter, looking away. "But I can't Pax... I just... I can't."

Now my stupid fucking girl tears are pouring out and I have nowhere to fucking hide!

"Holy shit... are you crying?"

"What the fuck does it look like?" I snarl, feeling stupid. Kings aren't supposed to cry.

"It's going to be okay, Vix," he whispers.

I'm half-cut and defenceless as he pulls me into his man-beast arms, the smell of him making my chest throb even worse as I sob uncontrollably. I don't want to be crying *about him on him* for fuck's sake, but God does he feel nice.

"Kirsten," he whispers a long while later.

I'm emotionally drained and feel like dead weight, I don't want to move, because if I don't maybe it won't be real.

"Kirsten," he repeats, "remember when we argued last time and I told you that I never even liked sex until I met you?"

"Uh-huh, yeah, sort of," I snivel, not really listening.

"Well there's a lot more to it..." he says softly. "Things I'm not sure you will understand, but I'm willing to try to explain it if it will clarify my position for you."

I take a deep, quivering breath, trying to focus on what he is saying as I wipe my eyes and sit up.

I can tell by his face he is really digging deep to tell me something that isn't easy for him, and I know he wouldn't bother putting himself through it if he wasn't telling the truth.

I look into his pained eyes and take a solemn breath.

"Christ, Pax, you really didn't fuck her, did you?"

He shakes his head no.

"There is no way I could have even if I wanted to, Vix. She isn't you. No one else is *you*. This dick..." he says, pointing to his pants, "it only comes alive for one woman. It's broken or something... I couldn't even get it up for that hot waitress I tried to fuck back in December... and boy was it embarrassing. I don't know, but I think it's a side effect of the sinister shit I did as a kid, or maybe I'm just getting old, but either way I don't care. I just need us to be Whiskey and Vixen again."

I half-smile at him and roll my eyes to his sweet but serious face, feeling relieved.

"I still have questions though."

"About my dick?"

"No, you big dummy... about the gun and how the hell you found me out here."

"Oh," he laughs, "I got the gun from the lawyer schmuck's trunk... thought I might need it depending on where you were headed. As for finding you, I used a tracking app on your mother's cell phone. There's a chip inside your helmet."

"What the fuck? Are you serious? Since when?"

"Since always. It came like that... it's for riders who travel long distances, just in case they get lost or stranded. I didn't put it in there if that's what you're thinking."

"Oh... okay... well that explains how you tracked me to the motel, but how did you find me up the street at the bar?"

"What do you take me for?" he growls. "I know you Vixen, I know what happens when you are upset: *Hate-Fuck city*! I knew the bar was the first place you'd go to ease the tension."

I shrug and laugh, knowing he's right.

"And about your family," I mumble, feeling guilty. "I get if you're mad, but I didn't actually pay them to leave, I just offered Verna a hand with a plan she already had set in motion."

"I figured as much. She's been telling me for the last year to stop visiting and to stop giving her money. I think looking at me just made shit worse for her." He pauses for a moment. His eyes meet mine, gleaming with a sense of support. "Thank you, Vix. You really are a saint."

"Thanks for what? And I am not a saint."

"For making sure they would be okay. You didn't have to. And yes, you are, you're as fucking sweet as it gets."

"They are your family. I did what anyone would have done. You don't need to thank me... and I am not going to argue with you about the saint shit."

"Good," he growls, "because I'd rather spend the rest of this night making love to you."

I bust out laughing at his sly smile and climb on top of him.

"I don't think either of us even know how to 'make love'," I admit as I remove my shirt. "But we can practice."

He rolls me off of him swiftly and begins to undress, so I follow suit, watching him peel off his shirt and then his pants. This man has the most beautiful body and the stories of strength to go with it, and he's mine.

I push him onto the bed, straddle him and trace my fingers up his stomach, following them with my tongue, until my lips reach his, tasting his sweet whiskey flavour.

His hands grip my hips as we kiss in a slow, deliberate rhythm, our tongues exploring each other's as if for the first time.

It's a profounder connection between us, one I never knew could get any fiercer, but here I am taking in the way he is gently stroking my back and teasing my hair. His hands are patient and calm, his moans quiet, not a growl coming from him as I leisurely rub my dampness over his erection.

I moan into his mouth and shut my eyes, relished in the sensual nature of our bodies becoming one as I push myself onto him.

"Fuck yes, Vixen. I swear you were so built for this dick," Pax utters into my mouth.

"Shh, no talking, just feel."

He glides his hands onto my breasts as I ride him as unhurried and deep as I can, denying my desire to move faster.

I can feel his body beginning to tense, his muscles flexing all around me and I think he too is fighting his urge to get rowdy.

I'm so wet, so needy and I can tell he is on the verge of cumming as he entertains his tongue with my nipple and slips his hands down onto my hips to help me keep the pace.

"Fuck, Pax," I moan.

"I know," he growls, his hips starting to buck.

I grip his arms and tilt my head back, and I can no longer hold the pace, I need to fuck this man damn it!

"It's okay, Vixen, let go and just hate-fuck me already," he hisses.

I take that as a checkered flag and start to ride him hard and fast, the way I need to. The way I know we both need it.

My climax is close as I dig my nails into his arms, taking in the way he slams me down so hard against him I can feel his dick sentencing my insides.

"Holy fuck, Whiskey."

"I know, Vix, I know," he says, breathless.

I begin to come apart, arching my back as he growls, his dick spilling into me as my body convulses in his hands and our intense moans fill the room.

"Shit!" I pant, "So much for making love. I really tried for a bit there, but it was just weird."

"It's fine," Pax laughs, "it was weird for me too. We just have to keep practicing."

"Nah... screw practicing, I like the way we are, and I already love whatever the fuck it is you are!"

I kiss his sweaty forehead and lay my head on his chest,

listening to the sound of his heartbeat as I draw lazy circles over his tatted abs.

My eyes are closing to the warmth and comfort of his body, the way he's weaving his fingers through my hair. I could lay right here forever with him, just like this, until the end of time.

"Vixen?" he murmurs.

"Yeah?"

"You do realize your mother is innocent and that you left a running lawn tractor in her living room, right?"

"Yes," I laugh, not feeling guilty. "But she's only innocent *this* time, so, she can just accept that and all the other shit I terrorized as payback for all of the other times she messed with me."

"Yeah, I'm sure that ought to teach her," he laughs, kissing the top of my head. "But something tells me she's already learned her lesson."

"I doubt it," I say, yawning. "The last time Satan learned a lesson was um... never."

"I'm being serious, Vix, she's different."

"Don't be dumb. You spent a little over an hour with her trying to help her sorry ass, I hardly think that qualifies you as an expert in the field of Lucifer and her practices."

"I've been paying attention for three years," he points out. "All I'm saying is that you should give her a chance."

I roll the other way and sigh, unable to think anymore.

"Fine Pax, I'll go back with you to the underworld in the morning, but can we please just go to sleep now?"

He shifts his body around mine and the weight of his arms around me is contenting.

"I love you, Vix," he whispers.

I pull his arm around me tighter.

"Goodnight, Whiskey. I love-hate you more."

CHAPTER 11
My Mother's Daughter

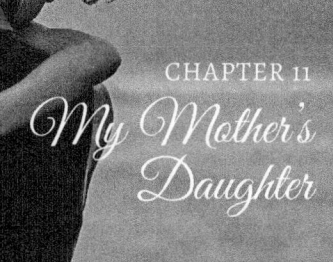

We are heading back to the Hill to face Helen King, the ruler of hell herself, and the very woman who birthed and taught me the golden rule: Kings don't cry. This is going to be a literal shit show.

My mother has always been madder than the devil, and despite what Pax chooses to believe, I know this is a bad idea. I can feel it in my soul.

I stare at the back of the Ninja as the sun rises while I tail Pax down the highway with the Beamer. The one I so angrily etched my cursed name onto the side of. Even after all of the darkness that man has seen between his own fucked up life and my dysfunctional joke for a family, he's still optimistic. I love it about him but at the same time, it kills me that he thinks people change. People don't change, we are what we are. *I proved it last night with the whole hate-fuck scenario.*

Regardless, I would follow Whiskey anywhere, to the ends of the earth and back. He's my ride or die, my *tainted love*, and in the end, he is the only family I will ever need.

He taps on the car window, gesturing for me to roll it down as

I sit idling in front of the house staring at the blown-out hole in the garage door.

"It's going to be fine, just come inside. I'll be right beside you."

His reassuring smile fills me with a sense of strength, and I shut off the engine and exit the car.

"How did I ever get so lucky?"

"You didn't get lucky," he laughs, "you got drunk… and then you almost pissed on my tent in Dellwood Park."

I cross my arms and lean against the car thinking about it.

"I'd still say that was lucky, who else can say they met their man-beast drifter boyfriend in the middle of a park in a gated community for rich schmucks?"

"Well when you put it that way," he says with a wink. "You do know I was scoping out the neighborhood to rob it though, right?"

I laugh and shake my head.

"And how exactly did you plan to transport the stolen goods? Nice try… but you never really did tell me why you were actually camped in the park that night," I say, squinting at him.

He leans against the car beside me, both of us staring out at the quiet, empty streets as the sun hits it's mid-morning position over the peak of the Hill. A beautiful sight, but one I would have preferred to skip this morning when I awoke in Pax's arms to a cup of coffee while he insisted we head back at the crack of ass to face the music.

"Well?" I ask, nudging him. "Why were you tenting it in Dellwood the night we met?"

"If I tell you, do you promise we will go inside and check on your mother?"

"Fuck, fine," I whine, "but don't skimp out on the details."

I kind of hope his story lasts all day. I do not want to go in the house at all.

"You remember the lawyer I told you about?"

I nod.

"Yeah, the stupid prick that defended the ped—"

"Yes!" he hisses cutting me off.

He grips my hand and squeezes it and I know he's telling me he doesn't want to talk about them, just the lawyer.

I squeeze it back and kiss him on the cheek.

"Anyways, the lawyer..." I prod.

"He lives in your neighborhood."

"Oh?"

My heart begins to pound, my mind filling with questions.

"I was here that night to finish what I had planned for the schmuck; I'd been stalking him for months."

I turn and look him in the eyes, knowing he's not being completely honest, but one day I'll get the truth out of him.

"And did you?" I ask, "end up finishing what you had planned that night?"

He laughs a sincere laugh and shakes his head.

"Nope... I ended up carrying a drunk seventeen-year-old up a giant fucking hill home to her daddy."

"You rescued me," I blush, taking in his deep loving gaze.

"Wrong again, Vixen," he pauses running his fingers over my necklace, "it was you who saved me, my saint. Had I not met you, I would have done something I'd be regretting for the rest of my life."

"See... it was luck, just. Like. I. Said."

"No, it was fate, and stop trying to start an argument. You promised we would go inside if I told you."

"Yeah but if we hate-fuck first it'll get me in the mood to deal with the Devil," I say, raising my brows up and down.

"It's not happening!" Pax states, smacking my ass. "Now get moving."

I growl at him to the best of my ability, but he ignores me and follows me inside. The sitting room is still completely destroyed and there is no sign of Mother or Gabe.

"Maybe they fucked off?" I tell Pax.

"Maybe they're still in bed," he retorts, smacking my ass, *again*, and jutting his head toward the stairs.

I roll my eyes and drag him up the staircase and all the way down the hallway until we reach Mother's room where I tap on the door.

"One sec," I hear Gabe say.

He opens the door, eyes us over, and waves us in as I look at my mother, noting she is out of it and looks like absolute shit.

"Maybe we should give them a minute," Gabe tells Pax.

"Sure thing, schmuck, I'll be in the hall if you need me, Vix."

"I'll be fine."

I walk closer and take a seat on the edge of the bed.

"After you, hobo," I hear Gabe gripe.

"Nah, you can go first, minion, I'm a gentleman," Pax replies.

"What the fuck you guys? Just get out already!" I hiss, annoyed.

Jesus! They aren't in the room twelve seconds together and they are already bickering.

I take a confounding breath to calm myself as I hear the door close and I return to studying my mother's pale face. She looks old somehow, weathered and worn. I've never seen her like this, and it's almost sad. Is this what detox looks like? The nightstand is riddled with medications and used tissue, and there is a pail on the floor. I can't help but feel kind of sorry for her as I grab her hand and skim over her warm knuckles with my thumb.

"Kirsten," she says, stirring, "you're home."

Her voice is weak, but caring, a tone I have never heard from her. Ever.

"Yeah, Pax dragged me back this morning. He said you've been sick."

"Was," she says sternly. "Was sick... for a very long time, but I'm trying to fight it. I have a sponsor now; her name is Claire. She says alcoholism is the work of Satan... I laughed and told her my daughter would agree."

I look at her genuine smile in disbelief.

"You talked about me?"

"Yes," she nods, "and about your father too. I have a counselor as well; he gave me some medications and a book he wants me to read."

"A book?" I laugh, confused.

"The Bible," she says proudly. "He says it'll give me strength and bring peace to me."

"Well, *he*, sounds like a fucking whack job!"

"I thought so too," she laughs, "but if it might help me repair the horrible things I've done, then I'm willing to read it."

I look away, not wanting to see the guilt in her eyes, the pooling tears, it's weird and I'm not sure I can trust it.

"Kirsten," she says softly, "I know I can't make up for most of it, I can't undo it or take it all back, but I can apologize. Will you please look at me?"

Her pleading breaks my heart, yet it angers me at the same time.

"No, Mother, Kings don't cry, you taught me that."

"I was wrong. God was I wrong. I'm sorry, Kirsten, but I understand if you can't forgive me."

"Forgive you?" I hiss. "For which part?"

I cringe at her remorseful expression and shake my head in disappointment.

"I don't know... maybe just one thing at a time. I'm trying here, doesn't that count for something?"

"You have got to be fucking kidding me! Did I count for something for the last twenty years while I watched you drink and cheat your life away? Did I count when I was pegged in the fucking head with countless objects? Or how about when Dad killed himself and you went to the funeral drunk? When the fuck did I count?"

I watch her wipe the tears that run down her tired, beaten face as she sits there trembling. I don't know if it's what I said or the withdrawals that are causing her to shake, but I've seen enough. I want out of here.

"Where are you going?" she whimpers. "At least take this with you."

I turn and stop to eye over the folder she has in her unsteady hand.

"Why? What is it?"

"Everything. His company, his house, his bank accounts, all of it. I'm giving it to you."

"What the fuck? Why?"

"Because it's the only way I know how to start over... and because he should have left it to you. I've made too many mistakes, and the truth is, underneath it all I loved your father, but I was also addicted to hurting him. I don't know why, but when he took his life, he took everything I loved with him... except you."

I understand it all too well, the addiction of wanting to hurt the person you love, and hearing her say it tells me I'm not much different then she is.

"I don't want this stuff," I say, handing her the folder. "I never wanted any of it. All I've ever wanted is to leave this place. Just get on the back of Pax's bike and go."

"Then at least take the money, Kirsten. Bless the world with your spirit and your compassion. Buy a seaside cottage somewhere and start a family with Pax, or open a bar that isn't hidden in a shed."

"Really?" I ask, both shocked by her genuine tone and the fact she knows about the Club.

"Yes, Kirsten, really... I want you to do what makes you happy."

I laugh at the irony of her words.

"That's just it, Mom... I already am, I have Pax. But maybe I'll visit from time to time, and we can look back and laugh about the time I sucked Gabe's dick."

Her face goes cold and her jaw drops as she fumbles, reaching for her glass of water and I cover my head.

Some things will never change.

CHAPTER 12
Untainted Love

T wo Years Later...

THE SMELL OF THE OCEAN IS STRONG AS I SIT ON THE PORCH taking in the morning breeze.

Our house is small but it's ours, it's a fixer-upper because we wanted to build something, we could be proud of, that plus it has a wicked view. A sight that never fails to take my breath away.

"Put your arms out, hold them up like this, so you can catch the ball," Pax babbles, showing Liv what he means.

Liv lifts her stubby arms above her head and giggles, not yet quite understanding what she's supposed to do.

"Not up in the air, silly," Pax laughs. "Like this, see, so Daddy can throw the ball to you."

"She's only two, Pax, maybe give it another year... I don't think Olivia wants to be a football player just yet," I point out.

"And why not?" he asks, now spinning her in the air. "This

little monkey can be anything she wants, isn't that right?" he finishes, now pretending to bite her porky little belly as she squeals in his arms.

I love watching them together, and I don't think I've put the camera down once in the last year since we adopted Liv. She's beautiful and full of life, reminds me of her daddy. Especially with the way he's already got her little paws hooked on learning the ins and outs of the motorcycle.

The look on her pudgy face is priceless when her big blue eyes become all fascinated with the sound the bike makes when Pax starts it up. It's the first thing she wants to explore in the morning, not that I blame her. She's a thrill seeker. *Like her momma.*

I'm positive he's only distracting her with the ball as a way to make sure today goes smoothly, no tantrums when he shuts the bike off.

"Okay, you two, times up!" I remind. "Help your daddy put the deflated football away and hop in the van. We still have a forty-minute drive ahead of us."

"Yes, Mommy!" Pax says in his sweetest Liv impression. "Grab the ball, monkey, that's it," he praises, making airplane sounds pretending she's flying over the ball.

I load the last of the luggage into the trunk and slide the side door open for Pax. He has a slight obsession about making sure she's properly strapped into her car seat.

I climb in the passenger side, laughing to myself about the conversation we had last year just before the adoption was finalized.

I'd come home from a shift one night from the beachside bar Pax and I opened when we first moved out here. It's not far from our counsellors office in the center of town.

The bar has become a hotspot, and it's so happening we ended up having to hire extra hands to help us maintain it on the weekends.

I could tell Pax was antsy one night, not quite into it, so he'd left early. I remember him mumbling something about wanting to make sure we had everything in place for the then one-year-old girl we'd fallen in love with at the local orphanage.

Needless to say, I walked home along the beach when my shift was over to find Pax growling and beside himself, stressed, trying to attach the car seat to the back of his bike.

I'll never forget his reaction when I told him he'd be driving a minivan, as I explained that we would not be carting our daughter around on the back of his Hog.

He walked straight into the house, took a pair of scissors, cut all of his hair off, and then threw on a baseball cap. At first, I was shocked until I saw the look of pride on his face. I knew right then that there was nothing he wouldn't do to be the best father to her.

"There we go," Pax says excitedly, "Liv's all buckled in, and ready to ride!"

I smile at him and roll my eyes as he starts the car and I reach behind his seat to hand her a granola bar. She looks adorable with her headphones on and her eyes are lit up by whatever Pax has playing on the movie screen. I'm sure it's some National Geographic special about snakes or lizards, his idea of teaching her to love what he does.

"What's so funny, Vix?" he asks, noting the smirk on my face.

"You," I say handing him his own granola bar. "I was thinking about the time I came home from the bar and you were hellbent on strapping her baby seat to your bike."

"You promised you would stop bringing that up," he says as we hit the highway. "And I'd really appreciate it if you didn't mention it to your mother."

"Why not?" I shrug. "Even if she actually does show up to meet us at the cemetery to visit Dad's gravesite, it's not like she was the perfect parent. She can't possibly judge you, because you are an incredible father and husband," I say, kissing his hand. "And if she does," I whisper, "I can always make it up to you in the cemetery washroom."

I watch his eyes glance in the rear-view, likely trying to make sure Liv's headphones are still in place.

"As much as I'd thoroughly enjoy that, I'd still prefer you not mention the car seat incident, but feel free to brag about what an awesome husband I am, because we both know I look like a complete nerd driving a minivan."

"You do not look like a nerd, Whiskey! You look hot and stop worrying, please, I'm already freaking out inside about taking Liv to the Hill. I mean, what if she ends up cursed and hates me by the time she's twelve. I don't think we should do this, maybe we should just turn around," I say, feeling the panic set in.

Pax gives me the *fuck that* eyes and pulls onto the shoulder of the road.

"I know you're worried, Vix, but you have me," he says, gripping my hand. "It doesn't matter what happens today. You are not your mother and you never will be, just like I am not Carl or Dana. We are good people, just like you told me once, and that little girl behind us will understand what being loved is supposed to feel like the same way you've always shown me."

I look into his eyes that glisten with both hope and pain, still not used to the fact he can say their foul names out loud now.

Carl and Dana, the predators. It turns my stomach to hear him mention them, but I'll never tell Whiskey that.

He's come to terms with what they did to him, and I don't think I will ever be able to repeat the things he's told me, even though our shrink says we should talk about it.

Pax and I wanted to make sure we were free of our afflictions when we decided to adopt, so we agreed to go to counseling together. Doctor Dell is nice, but I think he takes my not-so-perfect childhood far too seriously. He asked me once how I deal with the reality of it, but I wanted to keep just one thing between

Pax and I sacred, so I never told him about our hate-fuck therapy sessions. Instead I told him that the easiest way to tame my demons is simply to look at Pax; he makes everything bad disappear. That was the same day he asked me to marry him and I didn't need to think twice.

"Earth to Vixen," Pax murmurs into my ear. "You know I'll pull over at the next motel we see to fix that look on your face if you don't put a smile on it," he growls.

I snap out of it and take a deep breath before I glance back at our sleeping angel and smile, instantly filling with more affection than I knew was possible.

"No, I'll be okay, just keep driving... let's hold off on the therapy, at least until we reach Hate-Fuck City. If it goes really bad today, at least we can get Jimmy and Jack to watch Liv."

"That's my girl, always planning ahead... just like a good mommy."

I shake my head at his corny tone.

"Just get driving again, please, before I change my mind."

He nods and refastens his seatbelt as I sit wondering what mother will look like. I haven't spoken to her directly since we left the Hill, and I've only talked with Gabe a couple of times. Last I heard, he mentioned she'd gotten her five-month sobriety chip, and that he was planning to marry her. I guess he's forgiven her for smashing the glass on his head and chucking the Bible at him the day Pax and I left.

It still cracks me up when I think about the look on Pax's face as Gabe cried like a pussy, I think the words that left Whiskey's mouth were: *That about makes up for you letting Vixen suck your dick, schmuck.*

"Heads up," Pax states, turning into the Hill. "Do you want to do some sightseeing first?"

I shake my head no.

"I don't think reminiscing about the stupid things we did

before we became parents seems appropriate with our little monkey in the car."

"Good call," he says as we pass the Club.

It doesn't even look the same, seems the rebuild of the wall I took out made the Marron brothers decide to rebuild the entire thing. It looks like an actual bar now, complete with a patio and a parking lot.

It's not even half as fucking cool as the one we run on the beach.

We pull into the cemetery lot behind Dellwood Park, and I glance around, panicked for a second, questioning why we came back.

"It's good, Vix," Pax says shutting the car off. "I'll be right beside you, and so will she."

For a second, I think he's talking about Liv, until I realize he's staring out my window as I turn my head and see my mother standing there with a bouquet of orchids.

I smile politely but feel my motherly instincts take over and all I want to do is shield Liv from her as my heart drums mercilessly in my chest.

Pax rolls down my window and grabs my hand firmly as I squish my eyes closed tight, trying to calm my nerves.

"Hi, Helen... Gabe," he greets warmly, "I think we need a minute to recover from the drive, would you guys mind if we met you at Robert's plot? We won't be long."

"Oh, of course, dear," Mother states. Her voice sounds almost as nervous as I feel, and the sound of Pax rolling the window back up tells me it's safe to open my eyes.

I peek back at Liv, relieved she's still out of it, dreaming of amphibians or pythons, not demons and devils.

"She's going to be fine, I promise, just take a deep breath, like Dr. Dell showed you."

"Easy for you to say," I undertone. "Just don't let Olivia out of your sight, in fact, don't even put her down... if something gets chucked, I'll protect my own head."

Pax sighs and kisses my cheek.

"I hardly think she's going to beat you with a bouquet of flowers, but fine, I'll keep the little princess safe, same as I will you," he pauses to kiss me. "Nobody messes with my girls."

The slight growl in his tone hits me square in the stomach as I lean in and grip his hair, forcing his lips to mine. I want him so badly, and I know we've both been so focused on Liv, sex has been on the back burner.

Just kissing this man gets my body fired up lately, and I can't help but run my hand over the thickness in his pants, wanting to hear him growl the words.

"Bad Mommy! Yuck!" Liv squeals in her playful tone. "Bad, Bad, Bad!"

That wasn't even close, my little angel.

"Well, I think that's our cue, you heard the lady," Pax shrugs and laughs. "Now stop being a bad mommy like your daughter said and get your sweet ass out of the car."

I stick my tongue out at both of them and stretch as Pax grabs Liv from her seat and sits her up on his shoulders.

I haven't been back to my father's gravesite since the day of the funeral, and as we approach, I'm thrown off by the memorial statue that now stands at the head of his plot. It's a massive angel, at least fifteen feet high, made of grey stone that sits weeping over a rock.

I watch mother place her bouquet on the ground just beneath it, as she pulls out a flower and turns to me.

"He would have wanted you to weep for him," she says, handing me the flower. "He loved you more than anything," she pauses, staring at Pax and smiling as he yelps playfully, trying to remove his hair from Liv's fists. Her eyes meet mine again as she runs her withered hands up and down my arms. "Wow! Look at you, you are so beautiful, Kirsten, so grown up," she continues, "And look at her, she's precious... oh my goodness, is she yours?"

I nod and smile.

"Not just mine... she's ours, mine and Pax's... her name is Olivia, Liv for short."

"Olivia... what a beautiful name... can I hold her?"

Her eyes meet mine, pleading, as I take in her spirited tone that tells me she isn't the mother I used to know.

She's caring and kind, no hostility in her whatsoever.

I turn to Pax and nod, giving him permission.

I watch contentedly as Mother takes Liv into her arms, studying her precious little face and taking in the same magic we saw the minute we met her too.

"She's perfect... absolutely perfect," Mother coos. "Isn't she Gabe?"

"She is," he confirms, quickly looking in Pax's direction.

I almost want to laugh but hold it in as Pax steps forward and extends his hand.

"I think we should try to be civil and let our differences go for my daughter's sake."

"Yes, of course," Gabe agrees, "I'd like that very much."

They get to talking as I stand in front of the weeping angel, running my fingers through Liv's dark brown curls.

"I thought she looked like Pax the second I laid eyes on her; I fell in love with her even quicker than I did when I met Pax. She's a King now, and I will teach this little girl to cry whenever the hell she wants too. Well at least when it comes to her emotional well-being anyway," I add.

"I can see this little angel has an amazing mother already. She's blessed. But how is it that she's a King? I thought the two of you were married."

"We are, but Pax took my name since he doesn't know his."

"I'm sorry, I'm not following... how does the man not know his surname?"

"It's a really long story, Mom, one that will take all afternoon and a giant box of tissue to explain. And in my family, Kings are allowed to cry, so I'm not sure you want to witness that."

She grabs my hand, squeezes it, and brings it to her lips, her eyes lined with tears.

"I do, sweetheart, I really do. I'm ready to listen if you'd like to tell me."

I shake my head and smile, knowing our story is one that I never want Olivia to hear, unless it's the good parts. The good pieces of Pax and me that won't cause her to drive a lawn tractor through our window or have her building a secret club behind our backs.

Or hate-fucking in the bathroom of a cemetery.

Scratch that, that part isn't so bad is it?

I look over at Pax eyeballing me with that look that says he wants to eat me, and I realize I want him badly too.

"Hey, Mom?" I ask, watching as she fake nibbles on Liv's tiny fingers, making her giggle uncontrollably.

"Yes, dear?" she says, lost in my precious cargo.

"Will you watch her for a few minutes?"

"Sure, take as long as you want, I'll just be here telling her stories about her granddaddy, won't I? Won't I, you little darling?" she chants away in baby talk.

I give Pax the once over and bite my lip to the sweet smile plastered over his bad-boy face as he juts his head toward the funeral home and mouths the words, *Come over here and get on this dick.*

We are going straight into Hate-fuck territory, God yes!

No hate required.

CHAPTER 13
Introduction to Pax

Dr. Dell's office has a rustic, calming feel to it, almost as comforting as the doctor's voice when he gives Vix and me homework. It's a safe place where we can just be ourselves. He doesn't judge us for the way we are or who we used to be.

Not that we've ever mentioned our hate-fuck sessions.

The doctor is a short weighty man, mid-fifties if I had to guess, with eyeglasses almost as thick as the glass awards that line his bookshelves. Vixen and I came to him in agreement that we needed to become our best selves in order to be good parents to Liv.

We adopted her last year from the local orphanage when she had just turned one, after we'd spent the year prior in therapy preparing.

I never doubted us once; I didn't need to, not even for a second the day we met our little girl. I knew the moment I saw her, same as I did Vixen, that she would become the other half of our world, the same way Vix is the other half of mine.

Liv or 'Monkey' as we call her, just turned two. She has these great big wild blue eyes that are always curious and a sassy attitude almost as bold as her mommies.

We have a quiet little place on the beach, only forty minutes from the Hill, but somehow, it's far enough from Helen to make Vix feel content, yet close enough to bring Liv back and forth every few months to work on a relationship with 'Bama', *Liv's current pronunciation of grandma.*

Doctor Dell asked me once, two years ago when we'd decided to adopt Liv, to work on a personal project that would help me discover myself.

Not who I am now, but who I was before I met Kirsten. His way of helping me sort out the memories of my past I'm still trying to let go of, or at least forgive myself for.

He asked me to answer a series of ten questions with as much detail as possible, and to write the answers down no matter how long they were and even if they make no sense. He even typed and printed them out for me on a piece of his fancy doctor paper, *letter head Vix calls it*, but she's had to help me with some of the words. I'm not the strongest at reading even though I've tried to teach myself.

I've been working on the answers daily in the self-love journal he gave us while Vix helps me with my spelling, and if I'm honest, it fucking blows. I'm still on the first question, been trying to finish it but I'm not sure there is an end to any of my answers.

It's frustrating sometimes, and I'd rather be hanging out with Vixen and Liv, not dredging up the pain, but at the same time I understand that this is a part of the healing process.

The ten questions he wants me to answer are as follows:

1. How would you describe yourself as a person before you met Kirsten?
2. What is your earliest memory before the abduction?

3. Would you want to know what your real full name is if you were given the chance?
4. Can you describe what your idea of family was with respect to Ken, Cliff, and Verna?
5. At what age did you start to entertain the idea of escaping your captors?
6. At what age did you follow through with the idea and did you have a plan? If yes, please list the details.
7. Did Ken, Cliff, and Verna attempt to locate their families once they were free? If yes, how did that make you feel?
8. What brought you into Kirsten's life the night you met?
9. Describe the day you and Kirsten decided to move to the beach and what you hoped to gain from it.
10. If you looked back upon your life at all of the good, bad, and indifferent moments, what would you change?

I've read them over at least a thousand times, but Dr. Dell specifically instructed me to answer each one in order.

So that's what I'm doing, working out the riddles of my life one by one, so that I can tell my story. At least that's what Vix says I'm doing.

Olivia and Vixen, this books for you, and for every other fucked up soul who doesn't have a voice and suffered at the hands of life's monsters.

BOOK II
TAINTED LOVE
The Complete Trilogy

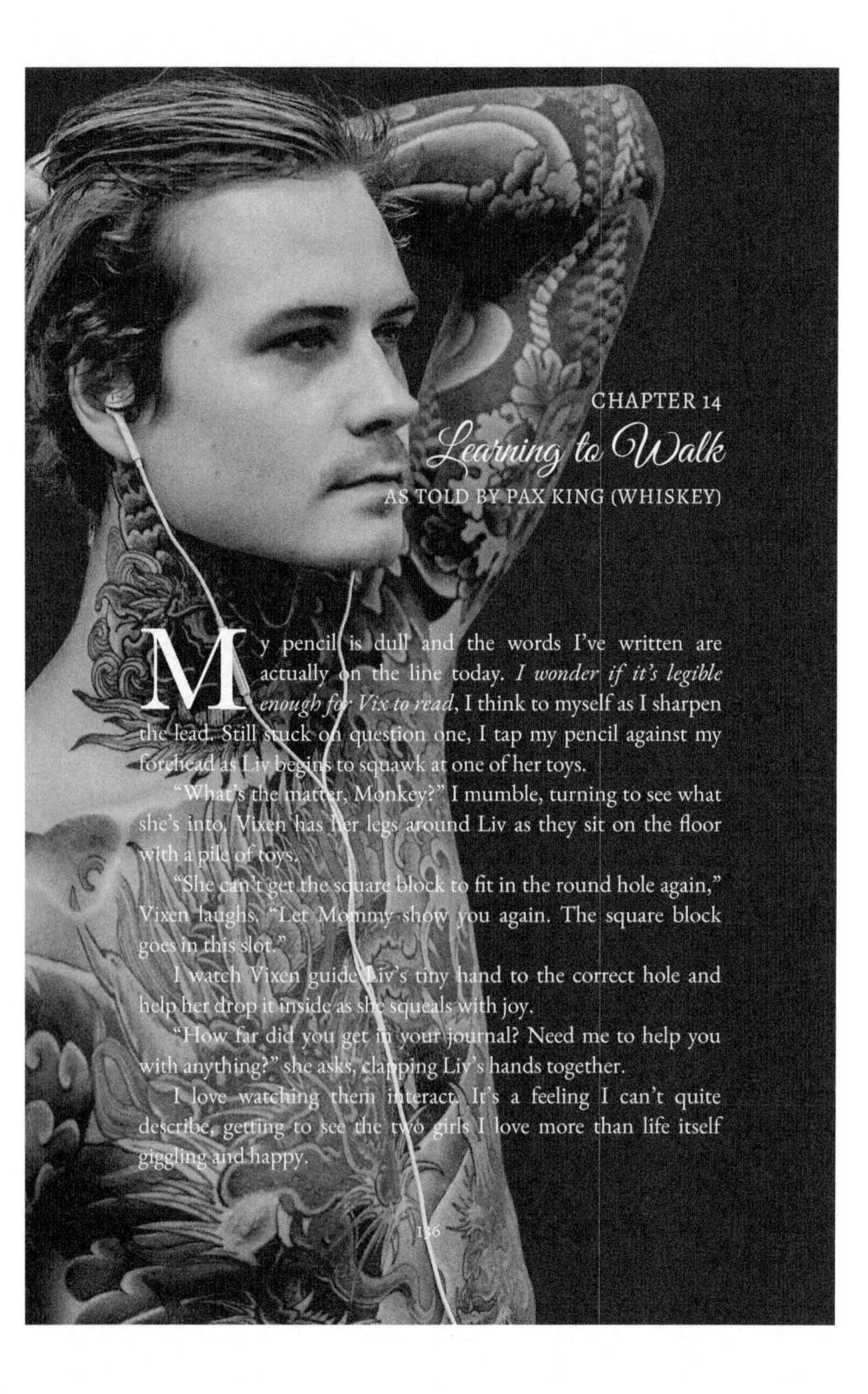

CHAPTER 14
Learning to Walk
AS TOLD BY PAX KING (WHISKEY)

My pencil is dull and the words I've written are actually on the line today. *I wonder if it's legible enough for Vix to read*, I think to myself as I sharpen the lead. Still stuck on question one, I tap my pencil against my forehead as Liv begins to squawk at one of her toys.

"What's the matter, Monkey?" I mumble, turning to see what she's into. Vixen has her legs around Liv as they sit on the floor with a pile of toys.

"She can't get the square block to fit in the round hole again," Vixen laughs. "Let Mommy show you again. The square block goes in this slot."

I watch Vixen guide Liv's tiny hand to the correct hole and help her drop it inside as she squeals with joy.

"How far did you get in your journal? Need me to help you with anything?" she asks, clapping Liv's hands together.

I love watching them interact. It's a feeling I can't quite describe, getting to see the two girls I love more than life itself giggling and happy.

"I'm not sure yet. I managed to stay on the line this time, but I'm not convinced my writing is entirely legible."

"Just let me put this monkey down for a nap and then I'll have a look at it, I'm sure it's not as bad as you think."

I smile at her praise. She's the best teacher I could have asked for, and co-parent too for that matter. She's come a long way from the mess she was when we first got here. We both have.

She used to tell me all of the reasons she thought we shouldn't adopt which were mainly her internal fears about ending up like Helen. But the second she laid eyes on Liv, everything changed.

Sometimes it makes me wonder if the same thing had happened to me, if someone would have shown up to the orphanage that day, the day Carl and Dana took me from the park… or any day before it, how different would my life be? And if it had happened, where would I be now?

* * *

"How old even are you," Ken asked, poking me in the chest. "Did they steal you from the supermarket too? That's where they took Verna from," he said in a hush.

I shrugged unsure of where I came from or how old I was, so I stood on the tips of my toes trying to feel taller like Ken was. Him, Verna, and Cliff had been quiet for the first few days we'd spent together until then, but it seemed Ken was like their leader. Not knowing how long I'd been there alone before they arrived, it felt good to have them to talk to and in a way, look up to.

"I don't know how old I am just yet, why, how old are you, and what is a supermarket?" I asked him back.

Ken laughed and leaned in close, sniffing me and pinching my cheeks before he answered.

"I'm eight and Cliffy here is six, but since you are bigger than

him and smaller than me, I'm gonna guess you are seven," he stated proudly.

"Okay, seven sounds good," I said wiping my face. Ken was missing his two front teeth so when he talked, he would spit unintentionally. "And the supermarket place, does it have snakes in it?" I asked him.

"No, stupid, the supermarket only has food in it. Really good food. Things like chocolate and candies that parents buy when kids be good."

"Oh," I said, wondering what those were too, but didn't ask.

His dark eyes were big, and he licked his lips as he began to list them out loud, so I knew they must've been something incredible.

When he was done, I sat down in the corner on my mat. We all had one that sat on the cement floor of the basement they kept us in. There were no lights except for what came through the cracks of wood that had been boarded over the two tiny windows, but we did have a flashlight. It was Cliff's and for some reason, he was allowed to keep it and we knew better than to ask why.

"What is parents?" I finally asked.

Ken looked over at me and shook his head as if he was annoyed with my never-ending questions.

"Parents," Verna piped up, "are the people who made you. The imposters upstairs aren't parents; that's why they stole us," she said, squinting her eyes in anger. "But my parents are the best and I bet they are still looking for me. At least I hope they are. Don't you remember who your parents are?"

Her face made me think I should have but I didn't. I only remembered the big grey building with the yellow door. The one that so many other kids lived in with me and the small park that was behind it.

"Nah," I said, picking at the hole in my pants. "I don't think I had any of those, but if we ever get out of here, maybe you guys can share yours with me."

"Sure we will," Ken said as Cliff and Verna nodded in agreement. "You'll like our dad and our house. It's like a mansion compared to this place."

"Mine too," Verna added, her face plastered with joy. "And at my mansion, we have a cat. I don't really like him too much, so I think one day when we exscape we should go live at the zoo for a while first because they have really cute animals that do more than just meow."

Feeling stupid, I sat listening to them talk about their mansions which I assumed was code for a house with lights in it. It sounded exciting to me, but like usual, I had a more important question on the tip of my tongue.

"What's a zoo?"

They all looked at me like I was crazy and then Verna came and sat beside me. She took my hand and linked her fingers with mine, and I remember the feel of her hand being different than anything I was used to. She felt warmer and it was as if all of the bad things we had done or would be told to do didn't matter just then.

"The zoo, Pax, is where goats and donkeys live. I went there once, and I petted them and fed them. It was my favorite day because it was my birthday."

I felt like I'd asked too many questions and didn't want to ask what a birthday was, so I focused on the goats and donkeys. Whatever they were, I told myself that very day, that I was going to get her one someday, and until then I had an idea.

"Shhh, be quiet... Cliffy get in the corner, you to Verna," Ken said in a startled whisper.

We could hear the jingle of the keys at the top of the stairs and it stopped us dead in our tracks. It was a sound we knew all too well.

The 'imposters' as Verna called them were about to come down and no matter what they would tell us to do, me and Ken had the pact. The one he set in place since he was the biggest out of us. The *promise that meant him and me would try to make them turn the focus onto ourselves.*

* * *

"I'm sorry it took me so long to get liv down for her nap."

The sound of Vixen's voice hits me hard and I take a deep breath as I feel her warm hand massage the nape of my neck.

"You're sweating, Pax. Are you okay? Where were you just now?"

I turn my chair and pull her down onto my lap, taking in the scent of her as she wraps her arms around my neck.

"It doesn't matter where I was. It only matters where I am," I tell her as I kiss the tip of her nose. "And now, I'm right here with you."

"Smooth answer, Whiskey... we can go with that, for now. But let's go over what you've written today, I'll mark it with the red pen you love so much."

"I only love it because you said it's how teachers used to mark your work in school, and you told me to pretend this was schoolwork," I say, tapping my finger on my journal.

"I know I did, and you are the best student a teacher could ever ask for."

She kisses my lips long and hard, it's her way of letting me know I'll be rewarded if I've done well. As expected, she teases my mouth, parting my lips with her tongue and running her hands hard into my hair.

She sparks something in my soul—she has since the moment we met. It's like we are two shattered souls, repairing each other day by day, sad story by sad story, and then replacing them with the good moments we create.

I growl, fully aroused as her tongue continues to tangle with mine and her hand slides its way down my body and onto my dick.

"Save the warning sound," she whispers into my mouth. "I have marking to do first."

I give her my best sad face, but she wags her finger at me and tells me to grab another chair so that I can pay attention to the lesson.

"Nice job staying on the line," she says, placing a red smiley face beside my sentence.

"Aren't you gonna put hearts for the eyes?" I ask, pulling my chair in and leaning closer. She smells like the salt of the ocean and fuck do I want to inhale more of her right now.

I watch her color in the eyes with tiny hearts and smile, feeling better because those heart eyes are how I feel every time I look at her.

"Okay... what is this word?" she asks, sounding it out the same way she's been teaching me. "Ob... ob... obstruction, is that what this is?"

"Abduction," I correct, pointing to the word.

"A-b-d-u-c-t-i-o-n-s," she spells out slowly, writing it above mine. "Ab-duc-tions," she then sounds out. "The t-i-o-n makes a shhh sound. I know it's dumb, but you were pretty close," she praises.

I laugh and look at my own spelling. O-b-d-u-c-r-s-h-i-n-z.

Sometimes I screw up, but she never gets mad. She just shows me the right way to do it and then makes me re-write it.

"Your turn," she says handing me the pen.

I take it from her along with the journal and copy the word letter for letter as nicely as I can and then slide it back to her.

"Nicely done. You get another smiley face!"

She draws them so quickly and always makes curls on top of their little round heads just like Liv's hair. It always makes me smile.

"Next, Pax, I want you to read the entire question Dr. Dell asked and then the sentence you wrote, out loud for me."

I clear my throat and read it word for word.

"He asked me, 'How would you describe yourself as a person before you met Kirsten?' I answered with, 'I was a lost soul and I was angry and looking to hurt someone as payment for the abductions.'"

Vixen smiles and then takes my hand into hers, turning it face up so she can color on my palm. It tickles like a motherfucker as I watch in complete anticipation.

"There! Now you have a smiley on your hand because this is really good, Pax. This is the strongest sentence you've written yet, and I think Dr. Dell is going to be so proud of you. But not nearly as proud as I am."

I glance at my hand, feeling accomplished as she closes the journal and tucks it inside the drawer with hers.

"Wait a second... aren't you going to do your homework now?"

"I can do it later; Liv is only going to be asleep for an hour if we're lucky."

"That's plenty of time, Vix, come on, I'll help you and we can get it done fast."

"I don't want to get it done right now. I can do it tonight before bed."

"That's not fair, you got to play with Liv the whole time I was working on this and now you don't have to do your homework until you feel like it?"

"Mine is less important, and also I'm horny if you can't tell, so can we please just work it out the way we always do?"

"Maybe."

"What do you mean by *maybe*?"

I take in the way her voice drops low and husk, and how her eyes light up with flames, it's her mating call. Seems I've still got it in me to push her buttons.

"What I mean is that I *might* be willing to let you get on this dick *if* you tell me why you think your homework is less important than mine."

Now she's fuming and giving me the evil eye. She hates it when I pry because Dr. Dell always gives her harder homework than me. She's jealous that I've been working on the same ten questions for over two years because I'm technically only in the third grade, and I always get gummy bears when I hand mine in. Vix gets nothing but a lecture on how she could put more effort into her work.

"Fine, Pax, I'll tell you why but only because I'm positive you just want to start an argument, which by the way isn't healthy according to the parenting books."

"You always bring that up," I laugh. "And you know the book is only referring to parents who argue about dumb shit like money or sex, which we have no problems in either area," I point out. "So, let's get back on topic here. Why do you think your homework is less important than mine?"

She crosses her arms and gives me the *whatever, you suck up* face.

"You'd better pay up after I tell you, Whiskey," she hisses.

"I will. Trust me," I growl.

"My homework is bullshit. Dell expects me to write some dumb before and after list on Helen's traits before she became a Bible thumper. It's stupid because I'm not sure which Helen I could stand more. There... are you happy? Can we get on with the fucking now?"

Hate-fuck city, here we come!

I smile at her scrunched up angry face, with no hearts for eyes, as I pick her up swiftly and toss her over my shoulder.

"Time to drag you to my cave," I say in my grizzly caveman voice.

"This isn't dragging, Pax, this is more like tackling," she grunts unhappily.

I drop her onto the bed and close the door, holding my finger over my lips so she'll lower her voice.

"We do not want to wake up the beautiful little badass, do we?"

"Hell no," she whispers, quickly ripping all of her clothing off.

I smile at her as I slowly begin to unbutton my shirt. I know she wants me to release the exhibit of ink so she can have at it with her tongue, but I like to taunt her because it makes her madder.

"Are you wet, Vixen?" I ask, knowing she is as I unhurriedly drop my shirt on the floor. "Do you want me to take my pants off so you can have at my dick and undo that anger building in your chest?"

"You already damn well know that's what I want, you big dummy, now hurry the fuck up!"

"I like it when you're ordery," I tease.

"The word is *ornery*, now get a move on or I'll hate-fuck myself right in front of you."

"You wouldn't."

"I will."

"Seriously?"

"Uh-huh."

"Show me."

"What? No, now get over here."

Deciding not to push my luck considering she's pretty mad, I start to remove my pants just as I hear Liv start to cry.

"Now look what you did, you dork! I told you we were on a time limit."

I throw my hands in the air and shrug.

"You were the one grunting while I carried you in here!"

Her eyes bolt down onto my shirt on the floor and mine dart over to her pile of clothes. Neither of us move as Olivia's cries get louder.

"Momma? Dadda?" she breathes out in between her precious squeals for love.

With that, Vixen and I both scramble to get dressed, racing to see which of us is faster and can get to Liv first.

I've almost got my buttons fastened as I glance over at Vix, still working on securing her bra. I'm about to win the race as I walk toward the door, but then I feel something tug on the bottom of my pants, so I look down as my jeans pool at my ankles.

"What the shit? You're a cheater," I say, pulling them back up.

"Maybe..." she says boldly, "but you're messing with a badass from the Hill named Vixen, so all's fair. In love. And. War."

That said, she smiles wickedly and slips past me as I watch her fly down the hall to Liv's room.

"That was completely unfair," I call out, still trying to re-buckle my belt.

"So is my homework compared to yours," she challenges, "and also the fact you get gummy bears, and what do I get?"

When I'm finally face to face with my girls, I smile and kiss them both.

"You get me and Liv," I say, pinching Liv's pudgy cheek.

"Yeah and Liv is much sweeter than Gummy Bears," she admits. Vixen kisses her little face until she giggles and then hands her over to me.

"I'll tell you what, Mr. King, I'll do my homework tonight and cook dinner while you show Monkey Face which hole the circle block goes in, on one condition."

I can tell by her mischievous smile that her offer is going to be a tough one, considering she never cooks dinner. In fact, she despises cooking and has begged several times for us to hire a cook. I always say no because I want Liv to grow up in as 'normal' of a household as she can.

"Really, Vixen? Baiting me with dinner and an entire hour with this angel... alright, ante up." I laugh.

This night is gonna be awesome!

Vixen's face turns serious and she takes a deep breath.

"All you have to do is promise me that tomorrow when you start your homework, you will move past question one and try to answer question two."

My heart pounds as I think about the questions I have memorized in my head.

What is your earliest memory before the abduction? A-b-d-u-c-t-i-o-n.

CHAPTER 15
Learning to Tie

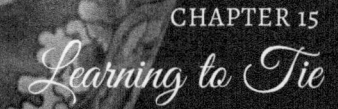

Last night while lying in bed, Vix and I finally came up with a name for the motorcycle-themed beach bar we opened. We run it on weekends only at present, but it's kind of like a second child to us. It took some compromising, but we both agreed on The Olive King. It's a play on words she tells me, Olive being short for Olivia and King, well, it's our last name. *Surname*, as Vixen likes to point out.

We ended up cutting our working hours so we can spend more time at home with Liv. Vix was smart and convinced Jack and Jimmy Marron to move here from the Hill. They got bored in about twelve seconds, so she offered them a job running the bar during the weekdays and then they take shifts babysitting Liv while we run it on weekends. The assortment of girls they manage to bring home every weekend absolutely love her, *not that anybody couldn't*, but I'm pretty sure it's why they love having Liv over.

They bought a place that's just three doors down from us—although their place is classified as an actual mansion—which I now know means large, full of luxuries, and not in need of repairs or updates.

I appreciate having them so close by, especially when Vix shows up with a new contraption for Liv that I can't figure out how to put together solely based on the diagrams. Jack's a whiz at figuring that kind of stuff out and Jimmy, he's pretty handy with the other stuff I sometimes find trying. Like how to remove a jumbo crayon that's been lodged inside the slot of one of Liv's favorite toys. Vix figures she's gonna grow up to be a parts fitter, maybe working on motorbikes with the way she's able to get her tiny hands into tight places.

"Say good morning, Daddy," Vix says as she enters the kitchen with Liv.

"Good Daddy," she repeats.

"You hear that Vix? She says I'm a good daddy!"

I pick her up and twirl her around. It makes her laugh.

"She would be correct... most of the time anyway," Vix winks. "Can you please help her get her shoes on?"

"Sure, I can. Where are you two off to this morning?"

I dig in the closet and scan the mass pile of tiny shoes and pick the pair with the flowers on them, knowing they are Liv's favorite.

"I'm taking her with me to the grocery store," Vix says, watching me try to get Liv's fat foot into the shoe. "You know the Velcro ones are so much easier to get onto her feet, right?"

I look up at her curious expression and shrug.

"But Liv likes these ones the best, right Monkey?" She nods her head up and down and claps. "Can I come to the grocery store too?"

"No... you are still grounded from there, remember?" Vixen says, wagging her finger at me.

"What if I promise not to step foot in aisle four today?"

"Grounded is grounded, Pax. Besides, you said that the last three times we went, but you lied and stood there with your 'I'm completely mesmerized' face on the entire time. Meanwhile I was forced to handle Liv's shrieking cries every time she saw something that was pink."

"Okay, first of all," I say as I tuck the laces inside Liv's sneaker, "I can't help the fact the store has an entire aisle dedicated to goodies. Second of all, you're the one who taught Liv about the color pink. And third of all, I don't think it's fair that you can ground me."

Vixen laughs sarcastically and gets down on her knees beside me to help with Liv's shoes.

"First of all," Vix copies, "you need to learn to tie her laces, not shove them inside her shoes like you always do to yours. Second of all, I've told you we can just buy aisle four and bring it home if you want to stare at it all day. I'll throw the whole shelf in the garage for you if it makes you happy. And third of all," she says tying a bow on Liv's shoe, "I specifically remember you grounding me from driving the motorcycles once, so just call this payback."

I chuckle at the memory, wondering how *this* equates to *that*.

"Yeah, but you were speeding on the bike. I was just looking out for your safety," I remind.

"Is that right?" she asks doubtfully. "And if I remember correctly, you chose *not* to wear a helmet that day, but you're implying that I was the one being unsafe, nice try."

"I was driving the speed *limit*, Vix. You were being a brat and testing the *limits*."

She looks over at me and sticks out her tongue and then Liv copies her.

"Hey, now, don't you teach her to be a brat too!" I say, feigning shock.

"Maybe I should tell our daughter that the only brat that day was you... pretending to read a book that you had no clue how to read. That and the whole shower incident with her Bible thumping grandmother."

I laugh at how good her recollection is and clap. Liv follows suit and copies me.

"That's right, Liv, clap for Mommy, she seems to remember everything... except how that day ended."

"Don't you dare tell her that story!" Vix warns.

"Which part?"

"Any of it!"

"How about just the part with the lawn tractor, the hole in the garage door, and the wall you took out with the Hog?" I tease.

"Don't listen to him, Olivia, Daddy's just mad that I busted him fake reading *Romeo and Juliet* once," she whispers satirically into Liv's ear, making her giggle.

"I was not fake reading!" I say, quickly untying one of Liv's shoelaces.

"Were too!" Vix says, smacking my hand. "And now you have to practice tying that yourself."

"Okay...fine, but if I do a good job, then can I *please* come to the grocery store?"

I give her the *pretty please* face, the one I use when she's really trying to make a point that I don't like.

"You know you are so bad sometimes, right?" she asks with one brow raised. "You're too innocent for your own good. Fine... you can come, but you're still going to learn how to tie her shoe."

Yesss! That face never fails me.

I watch closely as Vixen shows me how to make the bunny ears, as she calls them, and then I try to copy. My attempt once again ends up in a knot as Liv kicks her feet at us.

"Go car?" she squeals.

"Yes, Liv," Vix tells her, "one more second and then Mommy will fix Daddy's bad shoe tying lesson. But he gets a B for effort."

"Only a B?" I ask, confused. "But I did the bunny ears."

"I might upgrade it to an A if Liv makes it out of the store with both shoes still on today."

I'm not sure why Liv losing her shoes all of the time is always my fault, but I smile happily and follow my girls out to the van.

I stand behind Vix, checking out her perfect ass as she fiddles with buckling Liv into her baby seat. Once she finishes, I double-check that everything is secure on Liv, kick all four tires, and I hop into the driver's seat.

The store is a few blocks away, in the center of town. It's not overly populated here which is nice, and everyone is friendly, except for Riva, the lady that runs the daycare center. Vixen and I went to check it out before Jack and Jimmy moved down here and took over our shifts at the bar.

Vixen says Riva doesn't like me because she's turned on by my tattoos and that she's jealous she can't have me for herself, but I really don't think that explains the woman's attitude. Riva's a nice-looking woman, late twenties I'd guess—she's closer to my age than Vixen's—with nicely tanned skin and long dark hair. Kind of reminds me of Vixen's hair before she let her natural blond color grow back in.

Anyway, the Riva lady, she looks at me funny sometimes, stares at me actually, almost as if she thinks I'm going to steal from her or something.

All I know is that I'm glad we didn't have to put Liv in her care. I don't need her disapproving looks messing with my daughter's head.

By the time we finish in the grocery store, I'm pleased to say I managed to skip aisle four entirely *and would you look at that?*

"Liv still has both shoes on!" I cheer as I kiss her and buckle her into her seat.

"Yeah, only because I tied them," Vix chimes in. "But since you stayed out of the candy aisle, I'll upgrade you to an A as promised."

She leans in and kisses me which makes Liv cringe.

"Bad Mommy! Bad, bad, bad. Yuck!" Liv scolds.

"Yeah, you tell her, Monkey," I say as I slide the door closed.

Vix rolls her eyes at me and gets in the van, leaving me to put the cart full of groceries into the back by myself. *Totally unfair.*

I catch the last few words of a phone conversation between Vixen and someone as I shut the hatch, return the cart, and then climb in the car.

"Is everything okay?" I ask, noticing Vixen's less than happy expression.

She shrugs and sighs as I hit the main road.

"I'm not sure. I just got off the phone with my mother."

"How's Helen? Is she still lodging it up with the schmuck? Let me guess, they are finally getting married?"

"Nope, they broke up according to her. She doesn't sound so good."

"Shit! I mean shoot," I say, glancing back at Liv, happy I remembered to put her headphones on. "I'm sorry, Vixen. Maybe we should go and see her this weekend. Liv would be the perfect girl to cheer her up."

"I don't think that's a good idea."

"Why not?" I ask as I turn onto our street.

I look over at Vixen, staring out the window, ignoring me.

I know better than to push her when she's thinking so I pull into the driveway and get the now sleeping Liv tucked into her bed. Car rides are like gold when it comes to getting kids to nap.

Heading back to the car, I start to unload the groceries as Vix finally exits the vehicle. I can tell something's off with her as I follow her inside.

"Do you want to go for a ride and clear your head?" I offer. It's the only thing I can think of because she doesn't seem mad which is hate-fuck curable. But this... this is new.

"Nah, I'm gonna do my homework now, and you should probably start yours too."

She must be ill. She never wants to do her homework.

I say nothing and finish getting the *perishables*, as Vix would call them into the fridge. I like to call them milk, yogurt, and eggs… but that's just me.

I grab a chair from the dining table and set it down beside Vixen at the desk in the corner of the great room. It's impossible not to take in the way she's covering her journal with her arm so I can't see it, so I try to peek at what she's working on.

"Keep your eyes on your own book please," she whispers. "And don't forget our deal. You're moving on to question two."

"I know… a deal is a deal. What are you working on today? Maybe I can help."

Sometimes, *rarely mind you*, but sometimes I'm able to help her put some of her past with Helen into perspective because I was a witness to the carnage.

"Nope, you can focus on question two and I'll sort this one out on my own."

She turns her body away from mine which makes me want to look even more than I already did, but instead I read out number two aloud.

"What is your earliest memory before the abduction? Shit, Vix, I totally could have cheated and looked at the letterhead to spell it yesterday!"

"Shhh, please. I'm trying to focus, and I already told you, cheating doesn't teach you anything, Pax. When we finish our assignments we can trade, okay?"

She looks over at me and I can tell she's upset, so I nod and smile. Maybe I need to draw her some little red smiley faces with hearts for eyes today.

I return my focus back to the question and tap my pencil on the desk in thought. *My earliest memory.*

* * *

There are long wooden tables in the large room. Three tables that I see. The chairs were orange and arranged around each one, maybe ten or twelve at each. It was hard to get up on the chair, my pants were too big and started to fall down as I tried to climb on, until someone helped me with warm hands. A lady in a long black dress with a weird hat, but she smelled nice, like the cinnamon in the oatmeal that sat on the table in front of me.

"There you go, now eat up," she said in a kind voice. "When you are finished, I'll take you and the others to the park to play with the ball."

The red ball! I remembered it, it's the big rubber one that always rolled around beside the yellow door.

The lady in black took my hand and walked with me and the other kids to the park. The big park behind the grey building with the yellow door. There were tires to climb in and sand that was hot on my naked feet. Some kids had sticks and they were waving them at each other. Others had dolls and they were burying them in the sand. All I wanted was the big red ball, and there it was rolling down the grass toward the street. I chased it. Running fast, through the hot sand until I felt my scorched feet cool down when they touched the grass that tickled as the ball kept rolling.

I was so close, I almost had it, and my heart was racing and then the ball stopped.

I reached to grab it with my dirty hands, and my chest filled with excitement because the man in the shiny shoes stopped it for me. I hugged the ball. I could smell the rubber; it made me happy.

Then I looked up as far as I could at the man and then I saw the lady standing beside him. She smiled and I dropped the ball, because I wanted to reach for the teddy bear, and then out of nowhere a door slammed behind me and the memory goes black.

* * *

THEY WERE 'THE IMPOSTERS.' I KNOW THAT NOW, but that is my earliest memory, the day of the abduction.

I close the book and turn to Vix who is looking at me with tears in her eyes, as one escapes and slides down her saddened face.

"What's wrong? Was your homework that bad?" I ask, realizing my own face is wet too. I bring my hands to my face and wipe away my own tears, feeling stupid.

"You were smiling as you wrote, Pax. A smile I only see when you look at Liv while she's sleeping, or she says your name," she pauses, taking a deep breath. "Then I watched that smile turn to an intense fear that I haven't seen from you ever. Not in five years. Am I a bad wife if I tell you that the tears that came after were a relief?"

I grab her hand and shake my head, hating myself for seeing her so hurt.

"No, Vixen, you can never be bad at anything in my eyes. I love you too much, come here," I say, pulling her closer.

I wrap my arms around her, holding in my tears as my chest crushes painfully inside. I think this is why I was supposed to do this project by myself, but I'm so stupid because I'm a thirty-year-old man who can't read, and I made Vix promise not to tell Doctor Dell.

"I love-hate you more," she breathes into my chest. "I'm proud of you, Pax, no matter what you wrote in your journal. You *know* that, right?"

"Yeah," I force out, "I know that. But maybe we shouldn't trade today."

Pushing herself off of me, she looks at me oddly for a second.

"But we always trade. I need to mark yours, remember? No smileys if you start holding out on me now."

I lick my dry lips, tasting the salt of my own tears.

"What if you can't handle the answers in my journal? I don't want to be the reason you're crying, Vixen. Maybe I should tell Dell the truth, that I can't read good because it's his job to sort through my fucked-up past."

She shakes her head in confusion.

"Don't you dare quit on me now, Pax. I can, have, and will handle anything you write in the journal. Even if it makes me cry. I'm tougher than you think, and yes Dell can help us get through this, but we are not telling him you can't read. Because you can. I'm teaching you."

I can tell by the fierceness in her tone she isn't going to back down, and she's right. She's always been tougher than I've given her credit for. She's taken glasses off the skull, a wall out with a Harley, I know my girl can handle this.

I reach for my journal and hand it to her as she grabs hers and offers it to me in exchange.

"Red pen please," she requests, holding out her hand. I give it to her and then dig in the drawer to get one for myself.

I open her journal to the last entry and read the two lists she made out loud.

"Helen's traits before she was a bi.. a bib—"

"A Bible thumper," Vixen corrects, "the bi in the word Bible makes an I sound. Bi—ble."

"Right, Bible thumper. Helen's traits before she was a Bible thumper and Helen's traits after."

"Nicely done, Whiskey, you get a smiley face."

"You can't give me a smiley face for reading your journal," I laugh. "And what does this say?"

I point to the middle of the page where she wrote only one sentence that entire time and spent the rest doodling a picture of an ugly goat man with crooked teeth.

"Sound it out, you tell me what it says," she nudges.

"Sure, I'll give it a try," I say, not feeling too confident. "Luck... luckif... luckyfur is back, once an alc... alcho—"

"Lucifer is back," she buds in, "once an alcoholic always an alcoholic."

Well, that explains the screwed up looking devil goat with the crooked teeth.

CHAPTER 16
Learning to React

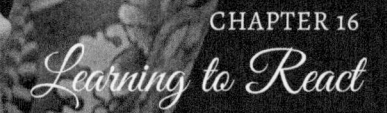

My wife is officially a basket case. She's been losing her ever-loving mind for the last two weeks and I swear if she cleans out Liv's closet one more time, I'm going to have to take her on a serious date to the only place that will cure this. *Hate-fuck city.*

It's not even just her constant need to clean, reorganize, and label things in alphabetical order and on every item in Liv's room, *including Liv's forehead*, it's the fact she refuses to talk about the upcoming weekend I'm trying to plan. We need to check on Helen, but Vixen's too busy with her post-it notes as if they can ease her worry.

And as if that's not bad enough, poor Olivia's been walking around with a sticky note stamped to her head that says 'Olivia's ham' because she wouldn't let her mommy finish writing the word hamper. Now our Monkey is toddling around pointing to her head and repeating 'Olif's ham' everywhere she goes.

It's the cutest thing I think I've ever seen, but seriously, I need to save my wife from herself. This thing with Helen, whether she's drinking again or not, it has to get resolved. I'm thinking Vix and I need to take a trip, just me and her, on the bikes. If I take her back to the Hill to confront her mother, it might be good for her. I just need to make sure she'll be okay with us leaving our *'ham'* with Jack and Jimmy.

I lean against the door frame of Liv's bedroom and knock lightly.

"Want some help? You've been at this for days, Vixen. I can start moving furniture around if you really want to go *ham*."

I almost laugh at my own joke as she turns to look at me, *and boy is her face angry.*

"It's not funny, Whiskey. This is important to me."

"Labeling Liv's entire room is important? Why?"

"Because it will help both of you learn to read at the same time."

I never really thought of that, but still, this seems nuts to me.

I enter the room peeking inside the playpen at Liv. She's consumed with a baby doll and package of sticky notes, so I take a seat on the floor beside Vixen. She's really great at folding tiny clothes. She always makes them fit in the drawers perfectly. I usually just shove them in and pray the drawer will shut.

"Can I label some stuff while you put her clothes away?" I ask.

"I'm done with the labeling, unless you see something I've missed."

I glance around the room slowly, noting that the dresser, bookshelves, wall art, playpen, toddler bed, lamp, baby monitor, door, door handle, toy shelf and every drawer on it, dollhouse, garbage can, window, curtains, change table, piggy bank, rocking chair, and the hardwood flooring have all been labeled. Then I move my eyes upward to the bright pink ceiling fan and Benji!

"You did miss something," I say excitedly. "Pass me the sticky notes and the marker please."

Vixen looks around as if I'm pulling her leg, but hands them over.

I write the words on the paper and stand, getting up on the rocking chair to stick it on.

"What the heck, Pax! Don't teach her to stand on the rocking chair to reach stuff! You know it's hard enough to keep her tiny fingers out of trouble," Vix gripes.

"She didn't even see me, look at her, she's gone into zombie mode all consumed with her new addiction to sticky notes," I point out. "So now that everything is officially labeled, can we talk about the weekend now?"

I figure it's safe enough to bring it up now that Vix seems less stressed.

"What does that even say?" she asks, squinting up at the fan.

"Ceiling fan."

"No, it doesn't."

"Yes, it does, I even sounded it out in my head."

"Well it was a good try, but that says sealing fan, as in the mammal kind of seal. The one you need to spell is c-e-i-l-i-n-g."

"Fine, I'll re-write it then," I say getting back up on the rocking chair.

"No! Just leave it, she'll see you!"

Without warning, Vixen yanks me away from the chair and I lose my balance and teeter my way backward toward the tiny bed, dragging Vixen with me. The sound of us crashing onto it is loud, but the sound of it snapping in half even louder as Vixen lands on top of me and we both start to laugh.

"Bad Mommy! Bad, bad, bad," Olivia says, now standing to check out the commotion. She shakes her head and points to it. "Olif's ham!"

"My lord," I say, unable to stop laughing, "what did you teach our daughter?"

"That she's just like her daddy," Vixen retorts. "A big old ham head."

"What did you just call us? That's it!"

I watch in amusement as Vix scrambles to her feet and bolts out the door and down the stairs. It takes me a minute to get up from the lopsided baby mattress, but I manage and then I pick Liv up out of her playpen.

Her eyes are wide with surprise as she assesses the damage.

"Bad! Momma break Olif's ham bed!"

I could die laughing at her face—it's priceless—and I can't help but shout out the fact our daughter just said her first entire sentence as we chase after Vixen.

"Did you hear me?" I ask, finding her in the kitchen armed with a spatula.

"No, but if you come any closer in an attempt to get me back for name-calling, I swear I will not go easy."

"You wouldn't hit a baby with a spatula! Especially one as cute as this who just spoke her first full sentence, would you?"

Vixen's face lights up, glowing as bright as a star.

"Oh, my goodness! What did you say Liv?"

"She said, 'Bad! Momma break Olive's ham bed!'"

We both start laughing again as Liv reaches her arms out toward Vixen, so I hand her over.

"I'm so proud of you, Olivia. You are the sweetest thing to ever walk this planet," Vixen says, as she kisses her all over.

"I beg to differ. There are two of you that walk this planet, covered in sugar."

Vixen smiles at my genius flirting skills as Liv yawns and rubs her eyes.

"Nap time, then homework time," Vixen says, "I'll meet you at the desk in ten."

"But we broke her bed," I remind.

"I guess it's a good thing Jimmy's picking her up tonight for a sleepover then, at the request of his girlfriend no less! But for now, I'm sure she'll be fine in the playpen and then we can get her a new bed when she wakes up, right Monkey?"

Olivia nods, rubbing her face on Vixen's shoulder.

Agreeing, I kiss Liv and watch the girls leave to go do their singing thing as I pull out my journal and sit down. I know I need to answer question three today, and I don't need to unfold Dell's paper to read what it is.

"Would you want to know what your full name is if given the chance?" I say out loud.

I start to print it on the page, thinking I already know the answer, but then again, sometimes I'm not sure, would it even change anything if I knew?

* * *

"Pax, come here boy," I hear the man say. The man with the hair all over his face, the one who always sounds mean and angry. My heart pounds as I climb the stairs, unsure if it's me he is calling for. The steps creak so loud underneath my feet and I feel scared, cold, and entirely alone, as I reach my shaking hand toward the door handle, afraid of the man on the other side. "Pax," he shouts again, "I called ur name, boy, get your ass up here, now!"

* * *

"Pax, she's asleep now—"

I jump at the feeling of a hand on my shoulder and react instantly with my elbow.

When I look down, I see Vixen on the floor, holding her hand over her mouth, her eyes filled with the same fear still beating in my chest.

I reach my hand out and she takes it as I pull her to her feet.

"I—I—I'm sorry Kirsten."

I pull her into my chest feeling like I'm not even inside my own body as I hold her tight, and as close as I can, not understanding what the fuck just happened.

I feel her quickened breathing, her chest rising and falling against mine and I know she must be as confused as I am.

"Pax, please let go," she pleads, "you're squishing me."

I let go, with no clue what to say and I'm terrified to look at her, so I cast my eyes to the floor. What will I say if I hurt her?

"Pax, sit down," she says so calmly, lifting my chin so our eyes meet. "I'm okay, and it was an accident."

I wipe the small pool of blood forming at the corner of her lips before I stumble backward and fall onto the chair, trying to snap myself out of this awful feeling.

"I'm fine, really, you barely clipped the side of my lip. Just sit for a minute, let me get you a glass of water, and then we can talk about it, okay?"

I nod, taking in her serene tone as if all I just did was spill a glass of milk, the same way she talks to Liv when she's having a hard time with one of her toys.

I'm confounded by her calm and caring reaction; I feel undeserving of it as I work to steady my breathing.

"Here, drink this," she smiles, handing me a glass of water.

I take it from her and slam it back.

"Sometimes, Vixen, I wish we had whiskey in the house... just for times like this when I don't feel like myself."

"Me too," she admits, cringing. "I could have used a drink the other day when Satan called, but we agreed for Liv's sake that we would never drink when she is home."

I nod and take a deep and painful breath.

"I think I thought you were Carl when you put your hand on me. I know how stupid that must sound, but—"

"It's not stupid, Pax. And you'd better not be working up another apology."

She takes a seat on my lap and wraps her arms around my neck, placing her smooth forehead against mine.

"You are working through things I'm sure neither of us will ever comprehend, and things I'm positive your mind doesn't want to remember. Doctor Dell warned us that this was going to be exceedingly hard. So, listen to me when I tell you, Whiskey, I know you would *never* hurt me intentionally."

I exhale the breath I was holding in, relieved she isn't afraid of me, even though I'm officially afraid of myself.

Her eyes gleam with a deep sense of love, the kind of connection I've only ever felt with her. I weave my fingers carefully through her silky hair, guiding my thumb gently over the small scar that sits at her hairline and then I pull her face to mine kissing the rest of my apology onto her lips.

"I was thinking about question three, if I would want to know my full name," I pause, spinning her hair around my finger. "Sometimes I think I do, but then other times I think it's a bad idea. I mean, what if it turns out to be something appalling, or worse, it changes who I am?"

"Well, I'm not gonna lie," Vix states with a shrug, "there are some pretty grotesque names out there, so I understand where you're coming from. But I do know that no matter what name anybody calls you, it can't change who you are. And if a name did hold that kind of power, it better at minimum, turn my husband into a better handyman, because I'm not calling Jack over here to build Liv's new bed."

I laugh at her attempt to be funny.

"Alright, Vix, I hear you. I can be this so-called handy ass husband you desire. I'll build Monkey's entire bed, from scratch, and by myself. Just you wait."

She raises a brow and crosses her arms.

"Is that so Mr. King?"

"It is. But I will need you to refer to me by my new handyman name which is... Gus."

"Gus?" she laughs.

"Yeah, Gus. It sounds like the perfect badass handyman name to me," I tell her in my serious tone.

"Sure... okay... *Gus*, since you are willing to boldly attempt to harness your inner handyman, knowing full well, you will likely fail, and probably end up building our daughters bed upside down, I'm willing to make you a deal."

"Ohhh, a deal? I like the sound of this already," I say, ignoring her attempt to mock me. *She knows not how well I've been paying attention to all of Jack's wise teachings.*

"Stop looking so excited, you don't even know what I'm about to offer you."

"No, but I do know *you*, and the way that mind of yours works. Therefore, I know it'll be something I want more than you do."

"That's true, but... you actually have to earn the prize this time. There will be no more of *me* letting *you* off easy," she warns.

"You never let me off easy, wait, do you?"

"Yes," she laughs, "pretty much every time, except this time. So, tonight, if you build Liv's bed with no help, which means no phoning anyone, or googling the words *'how to put Liv's everything together,'* then I will agree to take a trip on the bikes with you back to the Hill this weekend."

"Fuck yes!" I shout, way too loud out of sheer excitement. "This is going to be a piece of cake, and then guess what?"

"Dare I ask?" Vix laughs.

"I'mma take my girl back to where it all started! Hate-fuck city, here we come!"

I watch Vixen's beautiful face flush red and she shakes her head as if I'm off base about what exactly this trip is for. *Which I'm not*, I know we are going there to check on Helen for the most part, but I *also* know that the cure Vixen will require for whatever Helen is or isn't up to will be in order no matter what. This is totally going to be the best weekend ever!

"I'm going to go check on Liv in a sec, but I was thinking that maybe I can ask Jack to take me to grab the new bed while Liv's still napping. Unless you want to go with him to pick it out?"

It crosses my mind that if I went, I could probably sneak the entire bed back already built. Then again, Vix does always tell me that cheating doesn't teach me anything.

"Nope, you go ahead and pick it, I'll just sit and work on the rest of my answer to question three."

"Okay, *Gus*, I'll walk over to Jack's and see if he has time to help me before The Olive King opens. I won't be long and remember, no cheating."

"I'm still Whiskey right now, and he ain't no cheater, and neither are you. So, you better come back over here and kiss me before you go and come back to Gus the handyman Goldstein."

She half-laughs as she kisses me and says, "Are you seriously giving your alter ego a last name too now?"

"Surname," I correct, "and yes, I think he needs to sound professional because my girls deserve only the best! Now get going, you sexy little vixen, before I tell you to get on my dick which will force me to cancel my very important date with the handyman."

Blowing me a kiss, I tilt my head and lean my chair all the way back to watch her fine ass as she leaves the room.

I open my journal and stare down at question three that I've managed to write out impressively. It's got to be my nicest printing yet, so I draw myself a smiley face, leaving out the hearts for eyes, but I add extra curls for the hair, as I sit thinking.

Pax isn't my name, but did I ever have one before it?

It sucks that yesterday's question didn't help jog my memory either, I keep hearing the nuns voice in my head when I think about that memory. Maybe she did say my 'real' name that day and I just don't remember. The most fucked-up thing about all of it is that I never really thought about it at all until the doctor brought it up. I was fine being Pax, Kirsten's Pax. I'm cool with Whiskey too, even though I hardly drink at all anymore, and then there's Vixen. The nickname I came up with that used to describe my wife's naughty side. It almost doesn't suit her anymore either, except for when she has to deal with some of the drunken beach brats on the weekends. *Who am I kidding? She's totally still a vixen.*

But am I really a Pax?

* * *

"What even is a Pax?" Verna asked with her face all contorted. "How did you get a name if you don't remember your parents?"

"I dunno." I shrugged. "The imposters call me it, what do you think a Pax is?"

Verna lifted a shoulder and clicked the button on Cliff's flashlight, shining it right in my face.

"Stop that!" I whispered, covering my eyes. "Your gonna die the batteries."

"Shhh," Ken hissed, "they told us to go to sleep, now turn it off, Verna!"

"Fine! I looked enough at Pax's head and now I know what a Pax is."

"What is it?" I asked, feeling all over my head with my hands for a clue.

"I'll tell you tomorrow after we bury the dead snake like we planned."

"But I want to know what I am now."

I felt something hard hit my leg and I growled knowing Ken threw something at me. I searched frantically in the dark with my hands, patting the area around my mat to see what it was.

"What the hell, Ken!" I growled quietly as I hugged the dead snake.

"You deserved it!" he lisped. "You're always asking too many questions and girls don't like snakes for presents, now go to sleep!"

I stayed quiet for a very long time while running my fingers over his cold, scaly body, sad that Ken squished his head off and killed him, and not wanting to ask what a present was. I kissed the snake and placed him on the cold floor beside my mat, still wondering what Verna would tell me in the morning. It wasn't often we got to go outside, except when the imposters needed us to get water from the well. The next day I knew we would get to while Carl watched us with his rifle. The well was far enough away that we could quickly bury the snake in the same place I found him; under the rocks in the field. The Big Golden Field, Verna called it, the one that went on forever and ever, as far as our eyes could see.

"Pax," Verna whispered.

"Yeah?"

"I like snakes. He was the nicest present I ever got."

"Really?" I asked, smiling big but so happy she couldn't see me.

"Yes, really, he was even better than the dazzling Deborah doll I got at my last birthday when I turned eight. I'm sorry Ken stomped on him."

"It's okay," I told her. "I'll get you an even nicer one when we make it to the supermarket one day."

"Zoo," she revised. "Goodnight Pax."

"Night Verna."

* * *

The sound of Liv's high-pitched cry startles me back to reality as I stand from the chair knowing I now have my answer to question three.

"Daddy's coming, Monkey," I call out.

"Sit, I'll go up and grab her," Vix says as she enters the door. "You just keep working on your homework, *Gus.*"

She winks as I sit back down and write my answer underneath my stupidly awesome smiley face.

No, I would not want to know what my real full name is if I was given the chance. I am a Pax. A Pax that Verna once told me was a boy with a head that resembled a helmet the same as a warrior's, and now, I am the same Pax that wears that same suit of armor for Vixen and Liv.

I sure think this answer will earn me some hearts for eyes, and I can only hope Gus will earn me a weekend away with my wife.

CHAPTER 17

Learning to Ask

I'm not sure what it is about Doctor Dell's award collection that draws me to it every time I'm in his office, but it never fails. I always end up waiting for him to finish up with his last patient as he walks them out or writes them a prescription and then I end up standing here. Right in front of the trophy shelf I've memorized almost as well as the ten questions he gave me.

There isn't even a speck of dust on any of them and there are fifty-two, I've counted, twice. My favorite one is the smallest, and I could be wrong, but I'm pretty sure it was given to him for 'outstanding practices working with victims and survivors of booze and trauma.' It really is eye catching, sparkling more than any other award up here and it's also pink... Liv's favorite.

"Good late afternoon, Pax," Doctor Dell says, closing the door behind him.

"Doctor," I greet, "please don't sit, I'm not here for therapy today. I just came by to drop me and Vix's journals off before I head to work and then out of town for the weekend."

"I won't keep you long today, I promise," he says, taking a seat anyway. He gestures at me to take a seat on his sofa and opens my journal, glancing through it quickly. Sometimes I wish he didn't know that we owned a bar and can technically make our own hours, therefore allowing him to never listen when I tell him I have to get to work.

"So, Pax," he says, rubbing his chin, "where are you and the Mrs. headed this weekend?"

Hate-Fuck city is what I want to say, but refrain.

"Just up to the Hill to visit Helen and also to take our first holiday since we adopted Liv."

"And Vixen is okay with leaving her for an entire weekend?" he asks curiously.

"Yep, she sure is, and all because I owned that fucking bed, built it like a carpenter, and it's as sturdy as hell!"

"Wow!" he says, leaning forward. "You built something did you? Right on!"

I smile, feeling proud. I had told Doctor Dell one time when he asked me what one thing I wished I could do better was, that I wanted to work on being able to build stuff.

"It was all Vixen's doing really. I mean I built Liv's new bed, but it was Vix who gave me the incentive."

"That doesn't surprise me. She always has your best interests at heart."

"That she does, sir."

"How are things at home besides bed building? Any major breakthroughs you want to talk about? I see you've both been working really hard in these journals."

"Well," I pause, thinking about it, "I did have kind of a small breakthrough last week when I accidentally hit my wife."

His face turns serious and I realize immediately how bad that must have sounded.

"Uh, please, continue Pax," he says now flipping through the journal, again.

"I was trying to answer question two, about my earliest

memory and somehow I thought Vixen was Carl... I didn't mean to hit her."

His eyes meet mine again and he smiles as he closes the journal.

God, I hope I'm not in trouble.

"I know you would never hurt your wife on purpose, but with that said, Pax, I'm wondering why you aren't following my instructions. I specifically stated that I wanted you to answer all of the questions in order, but you haven't finished question one."

Should I tell him it's Vixen's fault for bribing me with a cute baby and a night off from cooking?

I shrug and remove my ball cap to scratch my head.

"I skipped ahead because I thought I was ready. Two years searching for an answer I can't find was starting to seem pointless. I don't know who I was before Vixen. I only know who I am with her, sir."

"Okay, Pax," he sighs, "I can understand that, so, here's what we are going to do. I see you've made it through question three, which I want to discuss in a minute, but you are not to answer any more questions unless we are all together in this office from here on out. Got it?"

I nod happily. "Absolutely, sir!"

Oh man, Vix is gonna be so pissed, no more homework at home for me!

I feel like celebrating but hold my composure.

"Good, because I think the emotions that will start to surface are going to be excruciatingly hard on both of you. And listen," he says, locking his hands together, "I know that you and Vixen are tough. The two of you are incredible. You are survivors. I've been working with you long enough to know that where one goes, the other follows, and what demon one battles the other also draws their sword. But I need you both to trust that it is no longer the two of you against the world, it's the two of you against yourselves, and that's where I come in."

His face and tone are serious, and I get what he's saying for the most part.

"Is this the speech that got you the award over there?" I ask, jutting my head toward the bookcase.

"Which one?" he laughs curiously.

"The tiny pink one that you got for having 'outstanding practices while working with victims and survivors of booze and trauma.'"

He looks at me funny for a minute and shakes his head.

"What would make you think the A in abuse is silent, Pax?"

Fuck me! The word is abuse, not booze. I knew I should have asked Vixen what that said!

I look at the all-knowing grin across his face and shake my head in wonder. "You already knew, didn't you?" I ask him.

"What? That your wife is teaching you how to read?"

"Mmm-hmmm," I nod.

"Of course I knew. What kind of good head doctor would I be if I didn't? I could tell from day one when she was filling out all your paperwork for you."

"That's some sneaky shit, Doctor, I'll hand it to you. But you have to admit the 'survivors of booze and trauma' makes total sense when you look at Vixen and me."

He nods. "Sure, that makes complete sense, and it also explains all of the smiley faces in your journal, even though Vixen was never supposed to be reading, let alone marking yours."

"You try saying no to her," I retort. "She's a real bossy badass most days and don't even get me started on what happens when she's mad."

"I concur," he says with a wink, "I've heard the stories, but speaking of Vixen," he says, eyeing his watch, "I think I've over kept you and I'm sure she'll be needing your help at the bar."

"The Olive King," I say proudly. "We finally named it. The Olive is for Liv and the King is—"

"Your family name, I like it!"

"Our *surname*," I correct politely as I follow him out.

"Thanks for coming in, Pax. I hope you two have an incredible weekend away. You both deserve it."

I shake his hand and laugh because it's jammed full of gummy bears, so I shove them in my pocket. "Thanks, doc. We'll see you next week."

I cross the street and head back down the walkway that leads to the beach. It's crazy to think that only two years ago when Vix mentioned the idea of therapy that one time, it made me want to get on my bike and never look back. I never told her that because I knew it was just my fear talking, not my heart. She's *always* had my heart. Now that we see Dell and talk about the old us, I can't imagine *not* having him in our lives. Sure, he's funny looking to an extent, but shit does he help with things I never thought anyone would understand, except for Vixen. She's a given, although understanding her is damn near impossible.

Dell has tried to get her to talk about her father, and his suicide, but she'd always get mad and by the end of the session, we'd end up in hate-fuck territory instead of dealing with the actual problem. Same thing with the countless times I picked glass out of her skull or caught a toaster before it nailed her in the back of her head. The stories we've had to confide in Dell are countless.

This thing with Helen presumably slurring the other day when she called Vix, it scares me. I don't want to watch Vixen go through that shit again, but I also don't want her to have any regrets either, especially when it comes to raising Liv.

Helen and Liv have grown close over the last few months. In a way I think it makes Vix jealous that her mother never loved her the way she loves Liv, *not that I blame her*. I'm sure no matter what happens Doctor Dell will be able to help us through it, and if things do get thrown by Helen, I'll be there to make sure they don't hit my gorgeous wife... *who looks fine as hell tonight, by the way.*

"Hey, Vix, toss me a rag and I'll start polishing some of these glasses," I say as I step behind the counter.

She turns to me and smiles, the naughty smile I only see when she's manning the bar. The place is packed, there's a line-up of people down and around the entire thing, and the classic rock is cranked as usual.

"What took you so long? Did you and the doctor end up polishing his awards again?" she shouts over the music.

"You're funny," I shout back sarcastically. "We did not... *but* I did learn something new today."

"What's that?" she asks as she starts mixing a drink.

I watch, intrigued, as she flips a cocktail shaker in the air, it always distracts me because it looks awesome. I swear its why our patrons keep coming back, Vix perspires an atmosphere about her that people can't get enough of.

Including me.

"Earth to Whiskey," she says, tugging on my shirt. "What were you gonna say a minute ago?"

"I was gonna tell you about the word I learned from the tiny trophy."

"Which one, the tiny pink one that mesmerizes you because it's all shiny and shit?"

"Yep! That's the one," I laugh. "One sec, I think that's the angry Riva woman and she want's your attention."

She glances behind her at Riva waving as if she's dehydrated and in desperate need of a drink.

"Uh-uh I'm not serving that bitch, I refuse, she was such a dick to you."

"That was like an entire year ago and you can't refuse a paying customer, dick or not," I say smacking her ass. "Now get going."

I can swear she just tried to growl at me, but the music makes it hard to tell as I watch her pour Riva a drink and they seem to be talking. *Girl stuff, I guess.*

Starting to polish another glass, I check the time, noting it's almost eight. I want to be on the road by nine at the latest and Vix and I still have to get the bikes and say goodbye to Jimmy and Liv, once Jack shows up here to take over the bar.

"Hey, Vix," I say, looking up.

Realizing she's gone, I scan over the line-up of people and then the beachfront directly behind them, but I don't see her. I figure the music was too loud for her to hear Riva and they probably went for a walk.

Barely managing to keep up with the barrage of Friday night party animals, the hour passes quickly and I'm happy to see Jack's arrived.

"Hey, Pax, what the heck are you still doing here?" he asks, sounding confused. "I thought you and Vix left for the Hill already."

I give Jack a high five, and hand him the key to the till.

"Thanks for coming...Vix and I are leaving soon, now that you're here, but I seem to have lost my wife at the moment. She left with that Riva lady and hasn't been back."

"What are you talking about? Vix came by the house forty-five minutes ago. She said you guys were taking off and that you guys closed the bar until I could come down here."

I shake my head wondering what he's talking about.

"Okay, wait, Vixen said *we* were leaving, as in me and her? Or did she say *she* was leaving?"

Jack shrugs as he cracks the lids off three bottles of beer, in one hand and passes them out like a pro.

"I can't be sure what she said, she seemed off and kind of mumbled, but I figured it was because she was sad. She was saying bye to Liv."

"What the fuck, Jack? I need a better answer than that," I say, slamming my fist on the bar. "Did you see her bike parked by the house when you passed it on your way here?"

"Sorry, man, I didn't really look," he says still pouring drinks left and right.

The music, the people and the pulsing in my head are really beginning to light a fuse in me, because I'm starting to worry that my wife left without me. I clench my fists, now panicking inside, wondering what the hell is going on and Jack doesn't even seem phased by the fact I'm interrogating him.

"Oh, for FUCK'S SAKE!" I holler. "THIS FUCKING BAR IS NOW CLOSED FOR THE NEXT THIRTY MINUTES, NOW WOULD YOU ALL PLEASE, JUST SHUT THE FUCK UP?"

The place goes dead quiet as I turn the volume for the speakers down and turn my attention back to Jack, who looks like he may have shit himself.

"Christ, man," he says, startled, "I haven't seen you shut down a party that fast since you ran the Club. What am I missing here, bud?"

"My wife, Jack, that's what the fuck is missing here! Tell me again, word for word, very slowly what she said to you."

My hands are shaking as I wait for his explanation and all I can think about is the fact she left here with Riva, the day-care lady neither of us really know who looked at me funny the only time we met her.

Jack cracks two beers and hands me one.

"All I can tell you is that when Vix came over she seemed, I dunno, upset. She was a bit shaky, not really her cheery usual self. She handed Jimmy an extra diaper bag, your house keys, hugged and kissed Liv, and then she said she would see us soon. Does that help at all?"

"No, Jack, it doesn't, I'll try her on her phone and run back to check the house, so in the meantime please hold down the fort and I'll keep in touch."

I make the jog to the house as fast as I can, seeing that her bike is gone and I'm not getting an answer through calling or texting her, as I sit breathless on the step.

I suck at forming messages and usually spell half of what I'm trying to say with 'emojis' as she calls them, but I don't have time for that right now. Instead I type:

Are you okay?

Where are you?

Can we please talk?

I try to think of reasons why she wouldn't take off on me.

She loves me, and Liv, and the bar. We have a life, a home, and a family here.

Then I try to think of reasons why she would leave, and then for a second I wonder if she knows about—*nah, she can't*, I tell myself as Riva's cold stare pops into my head.

That's it! Maybe she's with Riva.

I head over to Jimmy's and bang on the door before I let myself in, seeing him and Liv in the kitchen.

"Daddy!" Liv squeals from in the highchair, "Num-num's in Olif's ham!"

"Bedtime snack," Jimmy confirms. "What did you guys forget? Or did you change your mind because you can't leave this little angel behind?"

"Neither," I say, kissing Liv on top of her head, "I need my house keys so I can grab my bike keys. Seems my wife started the holiday without me."

"What? No way, Vix wouldn't."

"She would, and she did. Lawn tractor incident," I remind.

"Yeah, but didn't she only do that because she thought you were screw—"

"Yes," I confirm, quickly covering Liv's ears.

"Sorry, sometimes I forget," Jimmy says. "The keys are on the table by the front door."

I nod and kiss Liv again before I head back toward the door.

"Let me know when you find her please, so me and Livy don't worry too much."

"Will do," I say halfway out the door, "and if she shows up back here, call me."

"You got it!"

I head back to the house and climb the stairs, skipping two in between until I make it to the top and enter our bedroom. Finding my keys, I grab my jacket from the closet and head out to the garage. I have no clue where Riva lives, only where she works so I'll drive past there first. If it doesn't pan out, I'll call Helen and ask her how to use the tracker app she had on her phone and then I'll find Vix through the chip in her helmet.

Seems like a smart plan, I tell myself, just as my phone rings.

Oh, thank fuck!

"Are you okay, Vix? Where are you?"

"I'm already at the Hill," she says, sounding unlike herself.

"Why? We were supposed to do this together. I wanted to be there with you."

She says nothing but I can tell she's still on the line because I can hear her breathing. I hate that her tone is distant and solemn, she's upset, and it hurts that I can't fix the fear I sense in her voice. I need to know what's happening, so I muster up and ask.

"Have you seen Helen yet? How bad is it, Kirsten? I can head down there now and be there in thirty if I speed."

"No, Pax, you can't come here right now. I need some time alone; I need to think."

"Think about what?" I ask, puzzled. "If Helen needs meds, or rehab... whatever it is I can help. You don't have to do this by yourself."

"This isn't about my mother, Pax. I haven't even gone inside to see her yet."

Even more baffled, my already thumping heart begins to beat harder inside my chest and my head is swarming with uncertainty.

"Then what is this about?" I ask, feeling completely shut out.

The silence between us lingers and I feel like we are a lifetime apart as I sit waiting, hoping she will say something... anything at all.

"Riva," she finally whispers. "She knows you, Pax. She says she remembers the tattoos on your arms."

A chill rips down my spine as I study my arms, trying to grasp what she's telling me. *Where does she remember me from? I've never met Riva besides the day at the day care, I'm sure of it. And even if I did, I would remember... wouldn't I?*

"Pax, are you still there?"

"Yeah, uh, fuck. I swear I don't know what she is talking about, Vix. Can you maybe, just, give me a little more detail?"

"I'm working on it," she pauses. I can tell she's crying and trying to hide it. "I have to go. I'll call you once I've figured out how to handle this," she swallows. "I love you, Whiskey."

The line goes dead.

CHAPTER 18

Learning to Compromise

It's dark on the highway as I watch the lights twinkle in the distance, trying to keep my speed in check. My mind is a mess of jumbled thoughts and all I can think to do is head toward where my wife is. If she's on the Hill already I'm assuming she's either at one of three places: at the Club, the guesthouse, or the graveyard, so finding her shouldn't be too hard.

I know Vixen almost as well as I know myself, and if she hasn't been to the main house to see Helen yet, there is a reason, so I haven't bothered asking Helen about the tracking app. I will cross that bridge when I come to it.

The rumble of my bike is strong, *I've missed the feeling*, I think to myself, trying to keep my hand from turning the throttle.

Glancing between the speedometer, the road, and my arms, I keep trying to place Riva anywhere around me between the time I had them inked and now.

I was fifteen the first time the needle pierced my flesh. It was done by an elderly friend of the imposters with a makeshift tattoo gun and a flashlight in the basement.

A story Vixen has asked me so many times to tell her, but I

couldn't. I've always felt like it's wrong that my time in that basement wasn't always as bad as the boy I was. I didn't know how to explain to her that there were times I didn't care that I was there, that I'd grown used to it, to my friends and the way life was.

The night we met the tattoo guy, me and Ken had already told Verna and Cliff to get in the corner when we heard the keys jingle, because no matter whose name got called, it was gonna be me and Ken going up those stairs first; that was the deal. But that night, no one got called. Instead, we came face to face with someone who wasn't the imposters and in our underground hole of all places.

He looked scary at first. He had this scruffy grey beard and long hair to match, but it was the tattoos that covered his arms, neck, and face that really made him look mean as fuck.

The guy said his name was Graff, which Verna said was short for graffiti, a word she learned from an old magazine she found under her mat. Since she and Ken could read, they told me that graffiti was colorful paint people used on the outsides of buildings to make them look nicer and they showed me the pictures.

It wasn't until later that we learned *Graff* was actually short for skin graph, because by the time he would get done inking someone, they would need one if they ever decided they wanted the ink gone.

As time went on, me and Ken thought Graff was pretty cool. He was the only person who even took the time to come into the basement and hang out with us with no expectations at all. He would come every couple of weeks. It always seemed to be when the imposters were leaving, likely to get food and supplies which we were positive had to be thousands of miles from our location. Sometimes Graff would end up staying for two or three days, which felt like weeks to us, and it was such a relief.

It was during those small moments in time when the four of us didn't need to say it out loud; we knew just looking at each other that we were safe. Safe and free to be loud, or laugh, and just breathe, unafraid of hearing the keys jingle against the door for at least one day.

He never said it, but I could see it in his eyes that Graff knew he brought us a sense of peace.

What I've never known, is if Graff knew who we were or why we were there, but I never asked because I was too afraid of the answer. Too afraid to rock the boat and lose the only potential ally we had who brought us altered versions of time, a ceasefire from our regular days, and he was the one person any of us knew wasn't there to cause us any pain. *Besides the tattooing that is.*

Come to think of it, Graff was the only person we'd ever met who was ever actually nice to us, even though it took months and many visits before Verna would trust him enough to go near him or the tattoo gun, she hated needles.

But for me, his skill was a blessing. It was the kind of pain I could take if it meant covering up every fucked-up thing I did and felt while we were there. Truthfully, I never gave a shit what he colored on my body, as long as it meant I could escape my own head as I took in the buzzing sound and feeling of a different type of pain. By the time I was seventeen, *according to Ken's aging calculations*, I'd allowed Graff to cover every inch of my torso, neck and arms with 'the exhibit' as Vixen calls it. Except for the spot where I had hers and my name added back before she finally gave her heart to me.

Now I'm about to find out if I still have that heart of hers.

I pull into the Hill, and idle slowly past the Club, and then I circle it. The place looks packed and I don't see Vixen's bike parked so I head toward Helen's house.

I keep the bike idling, wondering if I should get off and walk, because if Vix hears the hum of the Hog, I know she might bolt since she doesn't want to see me tonight.

Turning off onto the road beside Dellwood Park, I cut the

engine and start on foot toward the cemetery because its closer than Helen's place.

When Vix and I first met over five years ago, she was just a kid. She still is in some ways, I guess. But I remember how she used to take off from home all of the time, and if I couldn't find her at Jack and Jimmy's or the Club, I knew she'd be at the cemetery. Even before her father killed himself, it was the place she used to go because she said it brought her peace. She even showed me the spot where she'd picked out her own plot under an apple tree in the far back corner. I knew by her tone that she was contemplating taking her life, and it echoed in her words when she explained how the tree would represent her existence and the way her mother was hell-bent on destroying her family. She referenced some passage from the Bible, about a woman who ate fruit from a sacred tree which spawned a devil in return for her sin. She said that devil was Helen. The same thing I'd once heard her father say, and even though I never fully understood what she was going through, I knew she needed to feel something other than pain.

That's the night I gave in against my better judgment and the art of our hate-fucking was born. We ended up at the Club she was letting me live in, and I'd told her some things about my past that night knowing she was apprehensive about neither of us having protection. I let her into my world of pain, and she didn't even flinch at the horrific things I told her I'd done, nor the things I'd admitted were done to me.

Vixen simply poured us both another drink, slammed hers, and then threw the glass as hard as she could against the bare floor. Then she looked over at me and said, *"That felt fucking awesome. Try it, Pax. Break something. Let your anger out. It's how Satan does it."*

"I know," I said, surprised, "but I don't think acting like your mother is going to change the things that are bothering you."

"I don't need them to change. I need to not feel them," she stated.

She was about to smash another one, but I stopped her hand and growled at her in warning. The same growl I'd always used as a kid when I was mad or in protective mode, which was most of the time.

"This is not going to make the feelings disappear, trust me," I said, taking the glass from her.

"Then show me something that God damned well will."

The fire in her eyes and the way she had no fear of me or what I was, turned me on in a way I had never felt. It was like she awoke something in me, something I'd forgotten existed, or thought no longer worked. She aroused me, made me want her.

"Oh, I can fucking show you all right, but I don't think you're going to like it."

"Like what? This," she said, grabbing my dick that was pressed hard against my pants.

"Yeah, that," I told her, not stopping her hand.

"If it's going to make me not want to destroy this entire building then I'm pretty sure I'll like it just fine."

The taunt in her tone was it for me. I fucked the hell out of Vixen so hard and so long that night she couldn't walk straight for two days, but the smile on her face from that day forward when we fucked taught me something. She was the one person in the world that didn't make me feel like a monster when we were together, and I was the only monster in the world who could make her smile.

* * *

I glance up at the funeral home, blinded by the motion sensor lights as I enter the cemetery. The plot in the far back corner is too far for the light to reach so I head in its direction, hoping to find Vixen.

Sure, as shit, my hell bound wife is sprawled out on the ground using her jacket as a pillow and hugging her helmet as she lay there.

"I found you," I say, as I take a seat on the grass beside her.

"Figured you would," she says, grabbing my hand. "You're like a tracker, except you cheat and use apps."

"I didn't cheat, I just know you. Vix. I know the way you think. Always have, always will."

She rolls toward me and shines the flashlight of her phone at my body, leaning it against her thigh. Then she begins to study my fingers, my hands, and my arms, the way she's done a thousand times before, slowly grazing her fingertips over every tattoo. I sit, just watching her hands, taking in the comforting feeling and listening to the sounds of the crickets in the field.

"Tell me about Graff," she finally whispers. "I know his name from Riva, but not the story. I *need* to hear the story, Pax. Please."

Her eyes meet mine and I swallow, stunned by the fact Riva knows Graff's name, but even more dazed by the way my wife is begging me to tell her how, yet I don't even know.

"Why is this important? I'd rather talk about whatever that Riva woman told you. How does she know me? How does she know who Graff is?"

"I asked you first," she states pointedly, "and I will tell you who she says she is after you tell me the story."

"Well, what if the story makes you see me differently?"

"*Nothing*, Pax, could *ever* make me see or love you differently. I just need to hear it because then I'll know if she's telling me the truth."

"The truth about what? I don't even know that woman for fuck's sake. Did I do something to her? Just tell me what she told you."

I feel like my head is going to explode because I'm terrified of not knowing what this is about.

She grips my hands hard and squeezes them.

"You didn't do anything wrong; I promise. God, I'm so sorry if I made you think you had."

I close my eyes and exhale, relieved.

"Thank fuck," I mumble, gaining my composure. "Then who the hell is she?"

"The story first, or I'm not telling you, Pax. That's the deal."

I growl, annoyed, and squint my eyes at her.

"Fine. But only because I want to get this issue dealt with so we can focus on your mother. She is supposed to be the reason we are even here."

"Well then it's too bad I love you more than I love her. Now lay down so I can listen to you talk and smell you at the same time."

She passes me her jacket and I prop it underneath my head before I lay back and guide her head onto my chest. I like being able to smell her too, she smells like the cedar of the bar mixed with the ocean, and she feels like home no matter where we are.

I start off slowly and explain the night Verna, Ken, Cliff, and I met Graff, filling her in on all of the details as I run my hands through the back of her hair the entire time. As I'm talking, she doesn't say or ask anything, she just draws circles over my stomach with her fingertips and listens quietly until I finish.

"So, he was nice to you guys?" she asks hesitantly.

"Yeah, he wasn't like the imposters if that's what you're asking. I think he was sort of babysitting us I guess because he only ever came down when we would hear the van pull away."

"What about a cell phone? Did he have one with him when he was with you guys?"

I think about it for a second and nod my head.

"Yeah, he used to let Verna fuck around with it because she always hid in the corner as far away as she could get from the tattoo gun. Why do you ask?"

It occurs to me that she must think we were absolute idiots for not calling 911.

"And before you say anything, I want you to know that the

others had been in the basement for a very long time before we met Graff. When you get used to living a certain way, reality doesn't really kick in like it should. None of us thought to call the cops at any point, and the truth is his phone probably wouldn't have had reception where we were."

"I wasn't going to question you," she says sincerely. "I didn't live it, Pax, so I don't have the right to ask why you did or didn't do anything."

"Sure you do. I mean fuck, I question myself all of the time about the things I wish I'd done differently."

"That's not the same thing. You will always question yourself, but no one has the right to question you," she says, poking me in the chest.

I smile and nod, knowing she's saying she holds no judgement.

"Next topic please... what does the phone have to do with anything?"

She kisses my lips long and hard before she answers.

"This might be hard to hear, but I think Verna must have snapped a few pictures with the phone unintentionally," she admits. "Riva said that the photos were used at the trials as evidence. I know you said you turned them in anonymously before you went back and freed the others, and that you couldn't stomach watching the trial, but Riva did. She was there through both of them, from the opening argument right through to their sentencing."

"How the fuck is that possible?" I ask, now sitting up, as my heart beats rapidly.

Vix grabs my hand again, linking her fingers with mine, and she takes a deep breath.

"Graff is dead, Pax. He killed himself, and Riva is his daughter."

CHAPTER 19
Learning to Accept

I never knew anyone that died before except for Robert, Vix's father. A man who had just as many demons as I do, and a man with a secret as dark as the one I harbor.

Last night when Vixen told me about Graff killing himself, it was weird. I didn't know how to feel about it. I wasn't sad, and I didn't cry or curse at the top of my lungs like Vix did when her father died. I don't think I felt any emotion over the news at all.

Maybe it's because he wasn't important to me in any real way. Sure, he was nice, snuck each of us a candy bar once when we fake celebrated Verna turning sixteen. We never knew what day it was but went off of the temperature to guess when it was September. He even took us outside one night so we could see what the stars looked like. He never talked much, always just listened to us ramble on about unimportant things. Perhaps I'm a freak for not caring, but the only thing that affects me in any way whatsoever is knowing that he had a daughter that was close to our age the entire time he'd been visiting us down there.

I don't know why it bothers me, but it does. It makes me question so many things and I can't write them down fast enough like Vixen wants me too. She says it will help if I take a list back home with us on Sunday night for Doctor Dell to look at.

She also thinks it would be good if I sit down with Riva one day to get her side of the story, which she told Vix she'd be willing to do, I'm just not so sure if I am.

"Do you need another piece of paper?" Vix asks.

I shake my head as she takes a seat beside me and slips me a mug of fresh coffee. It's not yet nine in the morning on the first day of what was supposed to be our holiday and here we are doing stupid homework in our old stomping ground, the guest house.

"Thanks for the coffee," I say as I stare at the overrun page. "How do you spell disappointing? Is it with two s's or two p's?"

"Two p's," she confirms with a smile. "I like it when you try to use big words to describe what you're feeling. It means you're probably closer to being in the fourth or fifth grade now, and you know what that means, don't you?"

I look over at her as she raises her brows tauntingly up and down, full well knowing the answer she wants to hear, but too taken by her beauty this morning to answer just yet.

She looks incredibly sexy with her messy bed hair and she's dressed in nothing but my ripped Harley t-shirt.

I lean over, grab her soft face, and kiss her. It feels like déjà vu and then I pull away.

"We are not having a fake grade school graduation party again, Vix. I refuse."

"And why not?" she asks, crossing her arms.

"Because," I say firmly, "it's embarrassing."

"There is nothing embarrassing about you celebrating your achievements, Pax. We celebrate all of Liv's and you never say that she's embarrassing."

"That's because she's two and cute."

"Yes, well you're thirty and *cute*," she argues.

"I'm not cute... I'm *disappointing*," I say, circling the word.

"And so is the fact we are now doing homework on what is supposed to be a holiday slash check-in on Helen weekend."

Jerking the pencil from my hand, Vixen tosses it behind her blindly into the kitchen and shakes her head disapprovingly.

"You are not a disappointment, Pax, and neither is your homework or this weekend," she says sternly. "Meeting Riva and listening to her talk," she continues, "it was weird. She talked about knowing who you were before I ever knew you. She said that Graff had told her about all four of you after she found the pictures on his phone. She had this look in her eyes when she spoke, Pax, I don't know how to describe it."

I take a shallow breath and lean forward placing my hands on top of hers.

"Did she seem mad? Maybe she blames me for her father blowing his brains out."

"Jesus, Pax, do you have to put it like that?"

"Like what? That is what you said Graff did, isn't it? And I'm pretty sure I can guess why."

"Yeah, well you and me both. The guy was an asshole. How the fuck could he leave you guys down there like that? Why didn't he let you out and tell you to run for fuck's sake? Or take you with him one of the how many times he got to leave that fucking rotten place? I just can't fathom how—I can't understand how he could —I just fucking hate him for not saving you!" she roars.

A single tear runs down her face and I strengthen my grip on her shaking hands as I watch her try so hard to hold back the rest that are pooling in her eyes.

"It's fine, Vix, you've made your point. Don't be afraid to cry in front of me," I pause, wishing I had a drink to numb the pain written on her face. "Crying is a good thing," I continue. "At least the doc says it is, so let the tears flow. I won't judge."

"Right," she says sarcastically as she wipes her face with her collar. "It isn't me who should be crying here."

"You want me to cry?" I ask, puzzled. "Over what? I don't really care that he's dead."

"No, you big dummy," she hisses, slamming her fist on my page full of questions. "I want you to cry and get angry over the fucking fact he could have helped you all. He had every fucking chance to, but the selfish coward didn't!"

I swallow, feeling stupid.

"I'm sorry, Vixen, maybe I'm too much of an idiot to know how to cry properly. But I just don't see the point. Graff may not have done the right thing in the situation, but at least he gave us something good when everything else was so bad," I say, shrugging.

"What then Pax? Tell me what that spineless prick could have possibly given you that was any fucking good? A body full of tattoos and two more years of misery rotting in that basement waiting for someone else to come along and f—"

She stops herself from saying it as the tears stream down her anger reddened face.

"Fuccckkkk!" I holler, running my hands angrily into my hair. I pull on it hard, madder than I think I've been in years.

Not wanting to discuss it anymore, I stand and walk over to the bar, pour myself a glass of whiskey, and slam it before I refill the glass and take my seat at the table.

All I can do is watch my wife struggle to stop crying and it hurts. I know why she sees it the way she does, and I feel stupid wanting to defend the only person who gave me a moment's peace in that hell hole. I can't win no matter what I say.

Her eyes meet mine and they look damn near green instead of blue because of the tears. They're beautiful, she's beautiful, but this part of me is dark and ugly.

"I'm sorry," she whispers, her tone shaky. "I know I wasn't there, and I know I have no right to tell you how to feel," she says, jerking the glass from my hand.

Drinking it back, she wipes her lips and then continues.

"Okay, Pax, I've said my piece. Now I want to hear yours. Tell me why it doesn't make you want to find his grave and spit on it. Tell me why you aren't fuming at the seams so that I can try comprehending where you are coming from. Please. I need to understand."

I lament inaudibly before I stand and spin the chair backwards and straddle it, and then I rub my hands hard all over my face, trying to concentrate.

"I'm not sure how to explain it other than to tell you that at the time, Graff seemed like a blessing to us. At least to me he did. I can imagine the others felt the same way." I stop, wanting to correct my defensive tone. "It's hard to explain Vixen. I can't hate someone who brought me moments of solace during some of the darkest times of my life. I can't hate him because he was good to us... can you try to understand how much we needed that?"

She nods, her eyes glistening in the tears she's no longer trying to hold back.

"You are the strongest person I have ever known," she whispers.

I watch as she wipes her face mesmerized by her ability to somehow smile while she's crying.

Until now, I have only seen this response from her once; the night we brought Liv home and stood in the doorway of her room watching her sleep.

I have no clue at this minute how or why she thinks I am any stronger than she is because I am not. But I won't argue because she couldn't possibly hold my soul in her hands any clearer than she is right now.

I take a staggered breath and steady my heart rate as I lean across the table and wipe the tears from her face.

"You are every bit as strong as I am, Kirsten, don't kid yourself. I have removed more glass from that perfect fucking head of yours than either of us should have to admit. Yet here we are, trying to check on and support the woman who once spent her life trying to kill you."

Vixen laughs and rolls her eyes. Her trademark reaction that tells me she doesn't feel the same way.

"My life with Helen doesn't even touch the hell you survived. But I'll tell you the truth, Whiskey," she says licking her lips. "The taste of your mouth is something I can guarantee has kept me breathing. I've never understood it, the way I love how you can be so rough with me, so brutal sometimes when we are intimate, you are the one person who has *always* made me feel alive."

"I have no issue with bringing this party to the bedroom if that's what you need," I say, gesturing at the crotch of my pants.

"If you only knew how long I've been waiting to hear you say *the* words."

"What words would those be?" I ask knowing exactly which ones she's referring too.

"Are you really going to make me say it after I've been crying?"

Her face tells me she isn't interested in my humor, just my ability to pleasure her and make the pain disappear.

"I know what you want me to do, Vix, but I'm sorry... I will do no such thing, but only because you aren't just angry anymore. You are emotional, and you've been drinking."

"It was only one shot," she points out.

"That doesn't matter, Vixen. neither of us have a tolerance for liquor thanks to our beautiful little 'ham.' Speaking of whom, you did call to check on her right?"

Her face turns angry and she crosses her arms.

"Yes, I did."

"I had to ask. You did manage to take off on her fairly quickly last night. Almost like leaving her behind wasn't a big deal for you."

"Are you being serious right now? What the fuck, Pax? Of

course it was difficult to leave Liv. I can't believe you would think it wasn't."

"Fine," I shrug, "as long as you called to make sure she's good, then we're good."

"I already told you I did, Pax, I called the second we fucking got here last night."

"And... how is she?" I ask, watching her face become madder by the second.

"How the fuck do you think she is? She's with Jimmy and Jack for shit's sake! If you're so worried then why don't you give them a call, instead of standing there judging me like I've abandoned our daughter?"

I wink at her knowing I've just tipped her over the edge into hate-fuck territory. *Exactly where I want her, and where she needs to be.*

"Well then, that's all you had to say," I taunt. "If you want me to abolish the anger from you, then I would suggest you take my t-shirt off and get ready to get on this dick."

Her angered face floods eagerly with a darkness I can only describe as sheer Vixen as she removes and drops her t- shirt to the floor.

My eyes travel over her completely exposed body as she stands before me silently daring me to take her. To turn her world upside down and inside out with pleasure, because I can, and she knows it.

"How angry are you Mrs. King?" I ask walking closer to her, dropping my pants and exposing my hard-on.

"Pretty fucking angry," she hisses, not moving an inch. Her eyes are bolted to mine as if she's silently telling me off.

"Good," I say taking another step toward her, "I like it when you're mad. But, do you think you are so angry that you can withstand me fucking you up against this table mercilessly?"

She takes no time as she closes the distance between us so that we are mere inches apart and then she runs her hand firmly over my erection and tugs me toward her.

"I'm so fucking heated right now," she whispers, tightening her grip. "I'll let you fuck me into next week if you think you can make it happen."

I smile and flex my dick in her hand. I want to fuck her almost as badly as my mind wants to inhabit her pain so that I can bring her resolve.

With her breath hot on my lips, she glides her other hand up my body, begging me with her eyes to give in.

"Next week it is, Vix," I growl, gripping her hips.

I'm not careful as I spin her away from me and push her up against the table, spreading her legs apart with my foot. She moans quietly as I press my body against the side of hers and graze my fingers lightly over her pussy. She's slick and wanting as I taunt her, moving my fingers back and forth over her heat.

"Ah, God," she whimpers. Her body is trembling with desire and the more it mounts the harder she tries to push herself against my hand.

"I'm still not God, Vix," I whisper. "And stop moving. You're making this difficult."

"Then stop with the foreplay, I'm already wet and *you're* making me crazy," she gasps breathlessly.

"Your wish is my command."

I shove my dick inside her slowly, feeling her body shake in reaction, as mine fills with a sense of urgency. The feeling of her warm flesh around my dick is mind-bending, and it provokes something in me. Something carnal and raw that impulses me to lose control, but I hold steady.

I bury myself as deep inside her as I can go and she moans, tilting her head and arching her back, accepting everything I offer.

"Jesus fuck, Pax..." she breathes out, "stop stalling and be a freight train already. Fuck me into oblivion."

Her words erupt inside my head as I grab a fistful of her hair in one hand and clutch the table with the other.

I'm in no way gentle as I begin to impale her body with my own losing myself in the sounds that escape her lips.

Flashes of every horrible thing I've ever done and seen flood my mind as I continue to fuck her.

"Holy Christ," she wails.

I watch her hand grip the table beside mine and I move mine over top of hers, locking our fingers together as the table relentlessly nails the wall with my movements.

"Still. Not. Jesus. Or. God," I grunt with every thrust.

"Fuck. Yes. You. Are," she groans back.

I can feel her entire body tightening and with every thrust, I can feel mine ridding my evil memories into her.

Thrust after thrust, moan after moan, I can feel myself becoming whole.

All of my hate.

All of my fear.

All of my anger.

It's as if the darkest parts inside me are disappearing in this one act of complete selfishness.

Her hate and my hate weaving together like two snakes

"Are you still doing okay?" I ask.

"Oh, fuck yeah," she whimpers, "pull my hair harder and say some dirty shit to me, I'm about to climax."

I jerk her head back and run my tongue from the dip of her shoulder up to her ear and then I whisper.

"Let go of your anger and come for me."

Her moans become louder as my assault on her body pushes her to the brink.

"Yes, oh God, yes," she cries out.

Her body is beginning to shake and seize everywhere, her pussy tightening around my dick as I hold steady in my movements, still pounding in and out of her as she breathes through the wave of her orgasm.

I can't stop, I don't want too, because the feeling of freedom in my soul is one, I only have in this moment.

"Are you getting close yet, Pax? Fuck me harder if you have to."

Her gasps of pleasure crossed with pain tell me she's working to regain control of her breathing. Sometimes I wonder if I'm too rough or if she even realizes the way I'm using her, but it feels so good I almost don't care.

She takes my hand and guides it onto her breast, presses her ass up against me, and wraps her arm around my neck.

"Come on, Whiskey, it's all you now," she moans. "Hate-fuck me like you mean it. Let go of all of the hate you feel and transfer it to me."

"Fuck Vixen," I growl.

My balls tighten as her words spur on my release and with each thrust, I ejaculate inside her until there is nothing left in my head but her satisfied sobs of praise.

"Are you good?" she asks huskily.

"Oh, yeah, I'm fucking great," I say, pushing myself into her hard one last time. "How about you? Was I too much?" I ask, rubbing her shoulders.

"You will never be too much, and I'm perfect... not angry anymore, so I'd say it's mission accomplished. Now," she says unenthusiastically, "we need to head over to hell and see what's up with Satan."

"Maybe you shouldn't call her that until you know if she's really back to her old ways again."

She turns and kisses me all over my face a bunch of times before she picks up her shirt from the floor.

"And maybe you should get yourself prepared for the worst. It'll make the sting of it a little less painful. Then we can march right back in here and repeat what we just did so that I can get over it before we have to haul her drunk ass to rehab."

I nod and throw my hands in the air, knowing arguing at this point is useless, *unless we plan to re-enter Hate-fuck city.*

I ignore her, get my pants back on, and help her pull the t-shirt on with a satisfied smile.

She half-smiles back and says;

"I'm going to wash up and change and then grin at myself in the mirror for a few minutes—while I think about the orgasm you just gave me—and then the one you are going to end up owing me. After that, we'll walk over to the Underworld. Sound good?"

"I'll be waiting," I say with a wink.

That beautiful woman is a force to be reckoned with.

I can honestly say, she's usually right even though I don't want her to be.

I've thought about our history together over the years, and how many times we've had to visit the dark city of hate-fuck. With those thoughts, I've always asked myself the same question. *How is it that she and I are able to connect on this level?*

Eventually it had occurred to me that we've both been through some hardcore shit in this life, but Vixen is something else entirely, something euphoric or unworldly, something I've never been able to put into words. *And words I know I'd definitely never be able to spell.*

I throw on a clean shirt and tidy up the kitchen, pulling the table away from the wall that is now crumbling bits of aqua-blue drywall onto the floor compliments of our hate-fuck session.

I look over at Vixen as she enters the room looking gorgeous as ever, with her hair pulled back and sporting a black cotton summer dress.

"Wow! You look stunning," I say, slightly surprised, "not that you don't look perfect all of the time, but I don't think I have ever seen you in a dress besides at our wedding."

"That's because dresses are for special occasions, Pax. Like weddings and funerals."

"Well then why are you wearing one now?"

"Because chances are that heading up to the main house is likely going to be comparable to a funeral. Satan's anyway... if she's back on the booze and deliberately fucking with Liv's chance of ever experiencing what a grandmother is supposed to be."

She walks toward the door notably irritated.

Grabbing her hand, I stop her in her tracks and pull her up against my chest so that her back is to me.

Her hair smells wicked good, like the flowers they use to age the shampoo with before they package it inside the bottle. I breathe her in just for a moment, holding her until I feel her start to relax.

"Alright, Vixen," I say calmly. "How many times have we faced Helen and survived?"

"I don't know," she shrugs, "at least two thousand, give or take a Martini glass or fifty to my head."

"Well I wasn't here on some of those days," I remind, "but I'm here right now. I just want you to know that Liv will be fine no matter what because she has you, and you have me. Alright?"

"Yeah, alright, Pax."

"Say it out loud like you mean it. Like Liv's little ham head grin is smiling at you with her tiny teeth begging for a hug."

"Liv has me," she laughs, "and I have you."

"That's right, and don't ever forget it," I say kissing the top of her head. "Now move that ass and let's go see if we need to exorcise the grandma back into Helen."

"Yeah, that or the spirit of Doctor Dell's pep talks out of you," she teases.

"God, do I love you, Vixen."

"Hell do I love-hate you more, Pax."

CHAPTER 20
Learning to Knock

S tanding at the back door of the main house, I look over at my wife as she nervously stands on her tip toes trying to peek through the windows of Helen's house.

"Take a deep breath, Vixen, it's going to be fine," I tell her.

"Would you stop saying that and just go first, please."

I enter through the door that leads to the kitchen and take a quick look around.

"It's clear... a little unkept but clear," I say waving her inside.

Vix enters and calls out Helen's name, as I take a look around.

I can honestly say the place doesn't appear it's been cleaned in at least two weeks. Not at all indicative of the way Natasha has always maintained it.

There are dishes piled in the sink, I don't think the place has been dusted in a while.

"Mom? Natasha? Anybody?" Vixen hollers.

The place is dead quiet as we head into the great room.

"Hey! Look at that... it looks like your mom finally replaced the rug you chewed up with the lawn tractor that one time," I point out.

"Why do you always bring that up?" she laughs, "stop stalling and take the lead, she's probably half-cut and dragging herself off the bathroom floor at this minute preparing to chuck something at us."

"I doubt that," I say walking toward the front foyer. "I haven't seen any indication that there is even alcohol around here, let alone a drunk Helen."

"Oh no?" she asks. "Well if she isn't drunk then she must be senile. Look at this."

I turn back and eye over the bright purple bra Vix is swinging back and forth like a pendulum.

"I don't think Helen's choice in undergarments makes her senile, Vixen."

"No, maybe not, but unless she just got breast implants, the fact that this bra appears to be at least four cup sizes too big for my mom says something's off for sure," she says flinging it at me.

I catch it and place it neatly on the entry way table laughing at her disgusted expression.

"You really need to stop assuming things and just ask her. Let's go upstairs, she's probably still sleeping considering it's not even ten yet."

"Oh, I will ask her alright, once we find her," she says storming past me. "Most likely naked and drunk in whatever corner of hell she's hiding in and probably using her Bible as a pillow."

Her sarcasm makes me smile as I follow her up the steps and down the hall to Helen's bedroom.

Vixen stops and turns to me, closing her eyes and inhaling deeply.

"Just knock," I say in a hushed tone. "I'll be right here no matter what we find on the other side of the door."

"You knock," she whispers back. "You're the one who insisted on this stupid trip in the first place."

"What? No, I'm not. You made a bet that I couldn't build Liv's bed and I did."

"That was after you wouldn't stop mentioning that my post-it habit was driving you crazy," she says, crossing her arms.

Hearing a loud whimper come from the bedroom, we stop dead and stare at each other. I can tell we are both thinking the same thing; *Helen's drunk as a skunk and probably in bad shape.*

Vixen gives me the *I told you so* eyes and juts her head at the door.

I lift my hand, hesitating, but then knock lightly before I turn the handle and peek my head inside.

"Jesus fuck!" I mutter.

I try to back up, but Vixen shoves me forward and sees what I see.

"Oh, my fucking God!" she screams, covering her eyes.

"Kirsten? Shit! Fuck! One second!" Helen reacts. "Let me and Claire cover ourselves!"

The woman that is with her, naked, says nothing as I turn and leave the room immediately.

Well, it's safe to assume that I've just officially now met Claire, Helen's A.A. sponsor, as I stand now frozen in the hallway wondering if there is a correct way to react to what I just witnessed.

Claire has an ass. A slightly heavy, dimpled, stark white ass, that unfortunately caught both me and Vix's attention when we entered.

Note to self; knock fucking louder next time.

Trying to compose myself, I smile politely as Claire exits the bedroom and approaches me.

"Hi, I'm Claire... you must be Pax," she greets.

I nod and smile, wondering if my face is as red as hers is.

"So," Claire continues, "can I maybe offer you something to

drink? I think Helen has a little something she needs to discuss with her daughter."

No fucking kidding.

I shake my head no.

"I'm good. I think I should wait here just in case things go sideways in there," I say, nodding at the bedroom door.

"Yes, well, okay then... I'll just be downstairs," she mumbles.

I nod and watch her walk away sheepishly. I can tell Claire is still embarrassed about the way we met.

Now that I've seen her actual face, I can say she's a pretty decent looking woman, older, maybe mid to late forties with brown eyes and wavy auburn hair that sits just above her shoulders.

She seems nice enough and I'd have to say the upside of having just walked into a room to accidentally find out my mother-in-law is a lesbian, is the relief it brings to see at least that she's not drinking again.

I'm trying really hard not to listen through the wall, but the two of them are being kind of loud.

"So, let me get this straight," Vixen says, "Gabe left you because he walked in on you cheating on him with a woman. And not just any woman, your sponsor for shit's sake!"

"I'm sorry, Kirsten, I don't know what to tell you. It's new for me too."

"Oh, fucking hell. You were cheating on dad for years. This behaviour is not *new*."

"I wasn't talking about the cheating, I was talking about the whole, you know, fact that Claire is *female*," Helen undertones.

"Oh lord, Mom, who cares! You can be with whoever you want; male, female, or even a lamp if that's your thing. But what you can't do is cheat on whoever or whatever it is you plan to be with. *That*, or forget to lock the damn door when you're making out!"

"Well how was I supposed to know you were going to show up here like this?"

"Jeez, I dunno, Mom... you just finished telling me two weeks ago that Gabe left you and you sounded drunk! It took me the entire time to get the balls to bother even coming to check on you in person, just in case you traded in your obnoxious holy book of happiness for your old satanic horns and tail."

Ouch. That a girl, Vix, hold nothing back.

"Okay, maybe I deserved that, but come on, sweetheart. Haven't I proven myself at all? I go to church every Sunday, I go to my meetings every week, and I would never jeopardize my visits with Olivia. You have to know that."

Well played, Helen. Liv's the way to Vixen's heart.

"I wish I did, Mom, I really do," Vixen pauses briefly. "I'm just glad to see that you aren't drinking again, because I'm finally getting used to seeing you happy. But I'm telling you, if you fuck it up—"

"I know, Kirsten, and I won't. I love my granddaughter just as much as I love you. Speaking of the adorable little monster, where is she?"

"At home with Jack and Jimmy. I couldn't risk bringing her here if you were relapsing."

Another point for my amazing wife, although I can imagine that stung Helen a bit too.

"Right, that makes sense," Helen replies sombrely. "You know Kirsten, I have no clue how you turned out to be so strong, and maybe I don't deserve such an incredible daughter, but as the good Lord says, I'll count thy blessings."

"Gross, Mom, save the Bible talk for church please. And I'm not strong or incredible, I just know what I want for my daughter," Vixen says firmly, "and you need to figure out what it is you want for you, as long as it isn't liquid poison. I'll be in the guesthouse until tomorrow if you need anything."

"Alright, dear, I love you."

There is a pause of silence.

Say it back, Vix. Come on, she's trying.

Hearing her feet march toward the door, I step away from the wall.

"I love you too," Vixen finally says as she exits the room and closes the door behind her.

She wide eyes me over and grabs my arm.

"Come on, Pax, let's go, I need a stiff drink."

"It's not so bad," I say, following her downstairs. "I mean she does sound happy. Maybe this is a good thing for her."

"What is? Her Bible talk, or how she's coming out of the proverbial closet? And with her sponsor of all people! Because as far as I know, that is a huge, fat fucking no-no."

I shrug wondering what proverbial means as I tuck my laces inside my shoes and respond.

"I just mean that at least Claire is in full support of her sobriety. They could be really good for each other."

"Or really bad," she airs. "What if they both fall off the wagon together and then *we* are stuck trying to dodge twice as many martini glasses and *two* angry lesbians instead of one?"

I laugh and then hear Claire clear her throat as Vix and I turn our heads slowly toward her.

Grinning awkwardly she says, "I know this must be weird for you, but I can assure you that although I am completely out of the *proverbial closet* and totally comfortable with being labelled as an *angry lesbian*, that I would never, ever, throw anything at anyone, let alone waste a perfectly good martini."

I stare down at my feet hoping Vixen can come up with something that will make this feel way less uncomfortable.

"Right... okay then," Vixen undertones, kicking me in the foot. "Well I would be lying if I said that this whole thing wasn't right fucked and super weird for me. But as long as you manage to keep my mother sober, I'm positive I can sort myself out so that next time we meet, Pax and I will be better prepared."

"So... dinner tonight then?" Claire offers, her eyes meeting mine.

"No can do, sorry," Vix lies. "Pax and I have other plans, but maybe another time."

What? No, we don't.

Trying to ease the tension I grab her hand.

"Let me talk it over with my wife and maybe we can change our plans."

Vixen glares at me unhappily, but I ignore her.

"Sure, dinner's at six if you two change your minds."

"Perfect. It was good to meet you, Claire," I say hurriedly.

She smiles and I'm quick to take Vix and lead her out the door, knowing she's pissed I just agreed to discuss coming back for dinner.

"What the fuck?" she gripes, jerking her arm away.

"We are going to dinner and arguing will do you no good."

"It'll do me good if I want it to, Pax, and since when do you get to make decisions for me?"

"Since you became about seventeen again and are acting like you need to run away from home," I say smartly.

"Wow, Pax! You really are something aren't you?"

"Yep, I sure am."

I have no clue what it is she's saying I am, but I figure agreeing with her is a safe bet considering how angry her face is right now.

"First of all, I am not going to dinner. Second, even if I was acting 'seventeen' again and running away from home, I would still be a minimum of twelve years older than you maturity wise. Third of all, and most important, I'm still not going to dinner."

"You said that twice," I point out, "and yes you are."

"I know I did, because you're five and I need to say things twice to make sure you will listen. And no. I. Am. Not."

"Are you trying to make me growl? Because I'm not going to."

"Good because even if you did, I am not looking for a trip to hate-fuck city, nor am I going to dinner with those two lunatics."

"What the fuckidy fuck, Vixen?" I ask, slamming the door behind us. "Why are you being so difficult?"

"I'm not! I just don't feel like sitting down to dinner with a ticking fucking bomb underneath the table."

"Well what the shit does that even mean? Your mom doesn't even drink anymore, nothing bad is going to happen."

"Says you! I can smell the sulphur of Hell from a mile away. Those two are destined to explode. Think about it... two recovering alcoholics trying to find love... come on, let's be real. Helen is only using Claire to rebound from just losing Gabe."

I crack two beers and hand her one before I take a seat on the sofa.

"Fine, maybe that makes some sort of sense to you, Vix, but have you ever really thought that maybe your mom has always been gay? Maybe the reason she cheated on your dad so many times is because she's always secretly preferred women. And just maybe if you give her a chance to prove how happy Claire makes her you will see that. And if not, there is the off chance that she realized Gabe was a lawyer schmuck and maybe he's the one who turned her gay."

I give her the *how do you like them* oranges eyes and she starts busting up laughing.

"You are such a dork sometimes."

"Pardon me?" I ask, insulted.

She knows I hate it when she calls me a dork.

"I meant dick. I always mean dick," she says.

"Sure, you do... that's what you always say, but fine, I'll let it slide if you come over here and get on mine."

She shakes her head.

"It's not happening. I need to call our baby girl and see her pretty little head. Man, do I miss her."

"Yeah, me too," I say, patting the seat beside me. "Come sit and we can video chat with her together."

I wait for her to sit and then I yank the phone from her hand and shove it in my pocket fast as a thief.

"What the hell? Give it back, Pax."

"Not until you agree to go to dinner with me."

"Fine, I'll go to dinner with you."

"Really?" I ask apprehensively.

"Yes really! You're holding Olivia for ransom right now. It's dirty *and* shady but it worked."

She holds out her hand, waiting for me to give the phone back, so I pull it out and hand it to her.

"Dial Jimmy," she says. "I'll turn on the smart TV so we can see her on the big screen."

"Video call Jimmy," I tell her phone.

I like how it listens to me better than she does; makes me feel listened too.

Vix takes the phone from me and presses a few buttons and then just as Jimmy answers, his funny looking mug shows up on the big screen.

"Mr. and Mrs. King," Jimmy greets, "how's the weekend getaway going?"

"Great," I say, at the same time Vix answers, "puzzling."

"I'm sure you two will end up on the same page by the time you come back to this little boss," Jimmy says, turning the camera onto Liv.

Vix and I laugh as we watch our daughter wobble back and forth in front of Jimmy's TV with a video game controller in her hand.

"Are you seriously teaching Liv to play video games?" Vix asks.

"Teaching? No way, she's already mastered them. I think we

should put her on Youtube and get her a sponsor. Your kid can build the hell out of the colored blocks."

"Hey, Liv," I say, trying to get her to look at me. "Olivvvvi-iaaa... Monkey? Ham Head? Darn, Jimmy, what have you done to her? She won't even look at me!"

Vixen laughs. "Well we did sort of let her play with motorcycle parts, I think she's found her calling."

"Whoa!" Liv cheers, "Olif did it!"

"Did what?" Jimmy asks, walking us closer to Liv and the TV screen plastered with tiny gold blocks with animals and people on them.

"Olif fix it! Mommy, Daddy's bad, bad, bad, broke bed! Olif fix it!" she squeals, pointing at the blocks.

It looks nothing like a bed as far as I can see, but her excitement is by far the cutest thing ever. That and how big the controller looks in her tiny hands, yet our girl has already mastered it.

"I love you, Livy," Vix says, "Mommy and Daddy will be home in one more sleep."

Olivia turns to look at Vixen on the screen, her eyes wide and as blue as the ocean as she kisses Jimmy's phone, which on the TV looks hilarious. Her slobber is sliding down all one-hundred inches of the flat screen as me and Vix take turns kissing her back.

"Bye-bye, Mommy, Daddy, Bama," Liv says, returning her focus to Jimmy's TV.

"Bye, Monkey," we both say in unison.

"Jack and I have a surprise for you two when you get back," Jimmy says, wiping the slobber from the screen with his sleeve.

"Oh, yeah?" I say, excited. I love surprises, especially when it's from those two. They are like wizards when it comes to gift giving.

"It had better not be you telling us that you or Jack turned the bar into a strip club again," Vix warns.

"It was a wet t-shirt contest," Jimmy recaps. "That is not the same as a strip club, and no, Vixen, Jack and I have done an awesome job of behaving this time," he adds with a wink.

"I'll believe it when I see it," Vix declares. "So, everything's good there then? Are you sure you can handle another night of our little Ham?"

"Don't even answer that," I butt in. "Vixen is just trying to get out of going to dinner tonight with her two newly-happening awesome gay moms."

"Shit! What? No way! Helen 'the man-whore' King is gay?" Jimmy asks, astounded.

"Shhh! Watch your language," I remind as Vix hits me and shakes her head.

"Wow! You two are so girly sometimes with your gossiping. And for the record, we don't even know how gay she is. She could just be, I dunno, experimenting," Vix points out.

"It's still hot, I just gotta throw that out there," Jimmy states.

"And as usual I have to tell you that you're disgusting. Bye, Jimmy," Vixen says and disconnects.

She looks at me and scowls, saying nothing, just shaking her head.

"What? It's not like it's a secret... or is it?" I ask.

She looks slightly worried and I realize I should have asked her first.

"No, but I would have preferred to tell Jack and Jimmy myself in person... now the two of them are going to chat it up like sixth graders and I don't need people looking at my mom the wrong way once word starts to spread. You know how people can be."

"I'm sorry, I never thought about that... I just think it's kind of exciting news is all."

"I know, Pax, and it's okay," she says taking my hand. "You always think other people's love lives are exciting. Somehow you only see things from an optimistic perspective, but it's what I love about you."

"That's not all you love about me," I notify, placing her hand on the crotch of my pants.

She jerks her hand back and straddles me, sliding her fingers up and down the outside of my arms as her eyes travel with her fingers that study my ink.

"I love more things about you than I could possibly list, but I think we should save the dirty thoughts in your head for later."

"You mean for after dinner."

"I do," she nods.

She leans in and kisses my ear, sending warm sparks pulsing down my neck and into my stomach, before her hand finds its way onto my dick again.

And then in a whisper, as she parts my lips with her tongue, she says, "All I know, Pax, is that after we spend an entire meal with the two women in that house, I can guarantee you that one of us is going to need this dick to settle us down."

"Don't worry," I whisper, "this dick has your back. And this heart," I pause, pulling her free hand to my chest, "literally only beats to make sure your pretty face always stays smiling."

CHAPTER 21

Learning to Fit In

There have always been tell-tale signs I've noticed Vixen give off over the years. Little gestures with her hands or body, or a certain sigh, sometimes even a look, that told me what she was thinking.

They are the trademark reactions I've always watched for when things used to be unpredictable between her and Helen. When the possibility of having to protect my wife's head from becoming target practice for an enraged alcoholic was the only thing on my mind.

Now, however, I don't need to be as cautious. I can relax a bit and I only have to read the signs to make sure my wife is having fun. That she's comfortable and happy, because every ounce of beauty she possesses radiates tenfold when she's smiling.

And there it is, the smile that brings penance for my sins.

I wink back at Vixen from across the kitchen, admiring how she and Helen are flipping through memory books full of photos and old family memories, as I stir the sauce that Claire offered to share her recipe for.

"You know, Pax," Claire says, "in the last two years of being

Helen's sponsor, I can honestly say she is a changed woman. Not just because she no longer drinks, or has a relationship with God, but she's truly different. She's happy."

I glance back to take in the laughter coming from the two of them, and Claire is right. Helen does look incredibly happy.

"Why do you suppose that is?" I ask.

Claire leans over and tosses in the freshly chopped ingredients to the pot I'm stirring.

"If I had to guess," she says, now washing her hands, "I'd say it's that cute grandkid of hers. She loves the heck out of her. I must have seen a thousand photos," she pauses, now looking at them laughing for herself. Her eyes meet mine again and she continues. "I think Helen sees in Kirsten the kind of mother she wishes she had been when she had the chance. It changed her, seeing your family so blissful, connected, and strong."

"Yeah, we are pretty fucking awesome," I admit, "but it isn't always as easy as it looks."

I turn down the heat on the burner to let the sauce simmer as Claire pours me a glass of wine. I'm unable to hide my angered expression as I take it from her, wondering what she thinks she's doing.

"Whoa down there with the Frankenstein face," she laughs, "Helen and I are okay with being around a little wine without needing to drink it. We only bought it so that we could offer it to you and Kirsten."

Her tone tells me she's being genuine, so I take a sip and glance over at Vix. She winks at me as I hold the glass in the air and nod, understanding she's been told the same thing.

"Okay, well thanks, but Vix and me don't really drink much and this wasn't necessary. We usually have juice and sparkling cider at get togethers for future reference."

"Sure, no problem, I'll remember that for next time," she says, stirring the noodles.

"Is that one for me?" Vixen asks.

I nod and take the other glass of wine Claire poured and walk over to hand it to her.

"Thanks," she says, taking a sip. "Can you believe Claire talked Mom into letting Natasha go?"

"What? Really?" I ask surprised.

I look over at Helen and she shrugs.

"Natasha wouldn't let Claire take over the kitchen, and they bickered like kids," Helen states. "They kind of reminded me of you and Gabe way back when. One of them had to go, and since me and Claire had just started becoming romantic, I decided it had to be Natasha."

I hold my glass up and gesture in applause.

"Gabe was a fucking schmuck and you know it," I tell her.

She laughs and nods.

"Yep, he was... that bastard let my daughter suck his—"

"We know, Mom, Jeez," Vix says cutting her off. "I don't think any of us need to talk about all of the stupid things I did that year."

"Okay, dear," Helen agrees.

"Would you mind setting the table, Pax?" Claire asks.

"Not at all."

The four of us sit through the gratifying dinner talking, but I mainly stay quiet listening to Vixen chat it up about Liv and the 'video game prodigy playing Ham head,' as she retells the funny stories as they come up.

It's nice to be able to sit and watch her brag, even though I know it isn't her intention. Helen also brings up the details of the few good memories she and Vixen had once shared. It's sweet, and I have to say I enjoy watching the way Claire rubs Helen's arm in support, being that Claire doesn't have kids, but admits she'd love to get her hands on Liv sometime.

I leave them all to it, and begin to tidy up the dishes, laughing in my head because Vixen was wrong this morning.

There is no ticking time-bomb in this house, and neither of us will be in dire need to revisit hate-fuck city, as far as I can tell.

"Here, let me help you with these," Claire says, joining me at the sink. "You wash, I'll dry. The girls went out back onto the patio to take in the air for a bit."

"Sure, sounds good, thank you," I say appreciatively.

I hand her the plates one by one as I wash them, noticing how her eyes are more focused on my arms than the dishes. It unsettles me slightly, because it makes me feel as if either she's judging me, or maybe like Riva, she's recognizing me from somewhere.

I hand her another plate and it slips from her hands, but I'm quick to catch it with my foot before it hits the floor.

"Shit! You're fast!" she says grabbing her chest, "I'm so sorry, I wasn't paying very close attention."

"No worries, it happens."

I bend down to pick it up and wash it again before I hand it to her, making sure she has a good hold on it this time.

"Thanks... so, I've been wondering, does it hurt to get a tattoo? I've always wanted one, but I'm worried I'll chicken out partway through. I really don't want to end up with half of a permanent drawing on my body."

"Nah, it doesn't hurt, it's actually kind of peaceful. I fell asleep while mine were getting done most of the time."

"Really?" she asks, stunned.

I turn and hand her another plate.

"Really," I nod. "I wouldn't lie, but my sister was a lot like you and hated the buzzing sound and the thought of having a needle poking her anywhere thousands of times."

"Well I would have to agree with your sister, but maybe if you introduced me to the person who did yours, I'd see it differently. I mean the talent they must have to be able to do it while you sleep sounds incredible."

I shake my head and hand her the last plate.

"I'm sorry, Claire, but even if the man who did mine was still alive, I wouldn't know how to find Graff to introduce you."

"Oh, shoot, he's dead? My apologies, were you close?"

"Don't be sorry. I don't care that he's dead. I mean Vixen thinks I should be mad at him and desecrate his grave or something, but I thought the guy was alright. I try not to hold grudges."

She puts the plate in the cupboard, and I hand her a glass.

"It sounds like Vixen holds some strong animosity towards the man, mind if I enquire about her reasoning?" she asks, curiously. "Did he happen to mess up one of your tattoos or something?"

She winks and I laugh at her attempt to be funny.

"Nope, not a chance, these babies are all perfect," I say, handing her a glass. "Vix is just pissed that he left me, and my siblings locked in the basement for two years."

I start to wash the next glass and am not fast enough to catch the one I hear shatter on the floor.

I look over at Claire and her face is white as the refrigerator.

"Somebody locked you and your family in a basement for two years?" She asks, dumbfounded.

Her eyes are as wide as Liv's when she hears the sound of the motorbike's engine.

"No," I say thinking maybe I should clarify, "I was there first for a year or two, I'm not sure exactly, but eventually they just appeared and ended up stuck down there with me for the rest of the time."

I hand her the last glass and watch as she puts it down. Then she takes my hands into hers and oddly she looks like she's about to be sick.

"Jesus, Pax, what are you saying? Does Vixen know about this?"

"I'm just trying to answer your questions, and of course my wife knows... she's the one helping me sort it all out. Well, her and Doctor Dell anyway."

"Wow! Okay," she mumbles, "so whose basement did you say this was? Your parents' or the tattoo guy's?"

"Neither, the imposters were not my parents, they didn't make me. They stole me from an orphanage as far as I remember, but they stole my sister Verna from a supermarket, and Ken and Cliffy from a carnival."

Now her face is even more contorted.

"Oh my God, Pax, are you saying you were all abducted?"

Her eyes look even bigger which I never thought possible, and her hands are squeezing mine so tight I think she might be having a heart attack.

"Maybe we should change the topic," I offer, feeling weird about her reaction. "Doctor Dell told me once that some people might react the way you are now. I probably shouldn't have said anything."

She lets go of my hands and takes a deep breath, wiping her palms on her thighs.

"Okay, this is a lot to take in, but it's fine, really," she says in a calm tone. "Does Helen know any of this?"

I shrug.

"I don't think so, but it's not a secret."

"Well, I think maybe we should keep this quiet for now. I don't think telling Helen any of this will do her any good. But I want you to know that if you ever need to talk, you can call me. I am a very good listener."

"That's kind of you, Claire, but I think I'm good with just working through it with Vixen and my doctor."

She hands me a towel and smiles acceptingly.

"Of course, now come," she says, grabbing my arm, "let's go and join them on the patio. I can finish up in here later."

It's a beautiful evening as we step outside. My wife being the most beautiful part of it, fills me with pride as she banters back and forth with Helen about things that once made them want to kill each other.

I take a seat watching them, amazed by their laughter that fills the cool evening air. The only thing that could make this moment any better would be if Liv were here, snuggled on my lap and witnessing her mother and her grandmother getting along.

Their laughter dies down and Vixen grins at me, wrapping herself tighter in the blanket.

"Is everything okay?" she asks.

"Everything is perfect."

I smile at her inquisitive expression, knowing she can read me like a book.

"Actually," Claire chimes in, "Pax was just telling me that he was hoping to whisk you away for a night of alone time."

I glance over at her holding hands with Helen and they're grinning, then I look over at Vix's uncertain expression.

"Alone time, huh?" she asks, eyeing me over.

She knows me too well. Knows that I wouldn't want to cut her visit with Helen short, but I'm pretty sure the ladies want to be alone.

"Yeah, that's right," I confirm, "I was thinking maybe we could take a walk down to Dellwood Park for old times' sake."

I stand and stretch, hoping I'm being subtle enough.

"Alright, I'm in, which means we are out!" she says, now standing. "Goodnight, Mom and Claire, thanks for dinner. This was nice."

"It was, thanks for having us," I add.

They too stand and take turns hugging us, which is weird for me, but also relieving in a way. I've never been much into hugging people in general, but I let the strange feeling of it fade as we say our goodbyes.

Vix and I make our way hand in hand down the walkway surrounded by a calm breeze when something occurs to me. Question four on the list, describing what family meant to me when I was a kid when it comes to Ken, Cliff, and Verna.

I wasn't too far off base back then now that I think of it. There is nothing I wouldn't have done for my family back then, and nothing I won't do for the family I have now.

I recognize now that although the dynamics were different between the four of us when we were kids, the feelings of affection that come when I see the people I love laughing, that part feels the same.

I think that's what made us a family; even in the basement, we always had each other.

It reminds me of a time when we were around seventeen, the moment I understood what both love and family meant. We were fetching water from the well, the sun was hot, and the air smelled of humid wheat fields.

* * *

"Hurry up, will you? Sheesh, Pax, how come you're always so slow?" Verna asked. "I don't want them to yell at you every time you take your time getting back inside with the water."

"Well then plug your ears," I told her. "I like it out here, and I'm willing to take a whooping for an extra two minutes of fresh air."

Just then we heard the loud echo of the imposters whistle and Verna jumped. We looked over at the porch where Carl stood pointing his rifle in our direction as Ken and Cliff ducked past him with their pails and into the house.

"One day it won't be a whooping, Pax," Verna said cautiously, "it'll be a bullet."

"Just get moving. He ain't gonna kill us as long as we don't try to run," I told her.

Verna's pail hit the ground and I threw myself in front of her as the crack of a shot being fired rang through the air, followed by the repulsive sound of the imposter's laughter.

"What a fucking asshole," I said as I stood terrified and pulled her to her feet.

"Shit, the pail, Pax!" she said handing it to me. Her hand was trembling as I took it from her.

It was empty, but somehow mine was still full so I handed it to her. The dark fear in her eyes told me she didn't want to be the last one through the door. That was always my job anyway, and I knew it.

"Here just take mine," I told her, giving her a nudge toward the house.

I could tell she was torn between leaving me there and heeding Carl's warning, but I knew in my gut I'd be okay.

"I'll be right behind you, Verna, stop staring and go," I growled.

She stared at me with tears in her eyes just for a moment and then she said it.

The three words I'd never heard in my life.

"I love you, Pax."

I looked at her in confusion and then the fear of Carl's unpredictability kicked in.

"Just go, Verna, now," I hissed. "I'll be fine."

I picked up the pail and walked the other way toward the well with a new emotion I didn't fully understand.

Not until I met Kirsten, anyway.

* * *

"We're here, Pax," Vix says, taking a seat on the bench. "Do you want to tell me where you were just now?"

I sigh as I sit beside her and pull her close, wrapping my arms around her tight.

"I never said it back to Verna the first time she said it to me," I admit hesitantly.

"Never said what?"

"That I loved her too."

Pushing herself out of my grasp, Vixen eyes me over carefully.

"What kind of love are you talking about?"

Her tone is calm and curious, not mad like I thought she would be.

"I dunno," I shrug, "not the same kind I feel for you. More like the way I feel about Jack and Jimmy, I guess."

"So, you loved her like a sister, I already knew that," she winks. "Were you thinking about the day she spilled the bucket because of the gunshot?"

I nod enjoying the way she's tracing her fingers over my hands and relieved how she never forgets the things I tell her.

"Yeah, same day, but do you think it made me an asshole for not having said it back to her?"

"No, Pax, you're never an asshole intentionally. Why do you think she said it to you in the first place?"

I think back to the fear in Verna's eyes and I swallow.

"She was afraid, maybe she thought one of us was going to die that day. It was weird, the way she said it, but then I was even weirder because I ended up yelling at her to go back inside."

Vixen sighs and lays her head on my chest. She smells like the scented laundry soap that Helen always uses, and it brings me comfort.

"If you didn't say it back, it's okay," Vixen eases. "I'm sure you had a good reason."

"A good reason?" I repeat. "The only one I can think of is that

I must have been saving those words for you. Because," I pause to kiss her hand, "hearing them from her that day felt pretty fucking amazing, and I wanted to make someone else feel that way one day."

Vixen lifts her head and smiles.

"You're *pretty fucking amazing*," she says, pressing her lips to mine. "It blows my mind every time you tell me you love me. Gives me those freaky little butterflies in the pit of my stomach," she laughs. "But I'm telling you, Pax, Verna knew that you loved her without you having to say it."

"How do you know that?" I ask.

I tuck her stray strands of hair behind her ear, loving the way she looks at me as if she understands the way my mind works.

"I know it because she told me the same day I wrote her the check," she says simply. "Verna told me that not only are you a hero in her eyes for going back to get them, she said you were the only one who loved them when no one else did."

"She said that about me?"

Vixen nods.

"She sure the hell did. And I knew precisely how she felt, Pax, because I felt the exact same way when I met you."

"How do you mean?" I ask, not fully understanding.

"You made me feel loved and protected. Untouchable. Like I was guarded by a sexy ferocious beast with a heart made of gold, and a body that could dole out as much pain as it had once taken. I fell in love with you before I even knew what love was, right over there," she says proudly.

I look where she's pointing and scratch my head.

"Right over there, huh?"

"Yep."

I stand, take her hand and ask her to show the spot as she remembers it, and then she stops on a patch of grass and wraps her arms around my neck.

"Right here," she says firmly.

"No," I laugh, "but nice try."

I pick her up and throw her over my shoulder as she laughs, and I walk another twenty feet through the bushes and set her down.

"It was right here," I declare.

She looks around and shakes her head.

"No way, Pax, I don't remember it being this far into the park."

"That's because you were drunk, but I'm telling you this is it. My tent was right here," I explain, gesturing toward the small clearing.

I can tell she still doesn't believe me as she crosses her arms and narrows her eyes.

"I grew up here," she reminds, "I think I would know where you parked your tent that night, drunk or not."

"Then if that's the case, go and have a look at that tree."

I indicate toward the tall oak tree and watch her as she studies the trunk with her hands until she finds what I knew she would.

"Oh my God, I can't believe I never knew about this," she says in disbelief.

I smile watching her face light up as she reads what I carved there on the night we met.

P + K

"I came here to kill a lawyer schmuck that night and ended up falling in love with a badass instead," I remind.

My chest fills with a sense of guilt, but I dismiss it, as I do every time we discuss this knowing it's not why I was really here.

"That you did," she confirms, "and just so you know, I would have loved you even if you'd become a convicted felon."

"Shit! Really? You wait until now to tell me this?" I say, acting put off.

She nods.

"Yeah, well don't get any ideas, Mr. Bond. We have Liv to think about now."

I cross my arms and lean against the tree wondering who this Mr. Bond fellow is.

"Well, I don't know anything about a Mr. Bond," I confess, "but I do have the answers to questions four and five on my list," I pause to trace my fingers over the carvings in thought. "The day Verna told me she loved me, two things happened. I realized that she, Ken, and Cliff were my family, and I knew with uncertainty that I never wanted to see Verna look at me the way she did ever again. Making sure of it meant I needed to get them out of there. So, the answer to the other question is that I was seventeen as far as I know. And it was in that field, that very day when I started to plan my escape."

Vixen runs her hands through my hair and smiles up at me, one of the proudest smiles I've seen yet. It makes me want to do all kinds of crazy shit to her, but I'm holding out for her praise.

Her love is sweeter than every gummy bear on the planet.

"Wow!" she whistles. "This officially puts you at the halfway mark, five of ten questions answered, now that's impressive."

"How impressive?" I ask, biting my lip.

I try hard to hide my urge to smile, knowing Vixen actually likes all my dumb questions.

I think it makes her feel needed, and she always makes *me* feel wanted. Both things, plus seeing her in that sexy damn dress have given me an intense erection, and as usual, my wife has already noticed.

"Hmmm, that's a tough one to answer in the middle of the park," she taunts, as her hand studies my wood. "But," she continues, "I think we can rectify the situation if we head back to the guesthouse."

Unable to argue with that, I gesture at her to pave the way.

"Me and this dick just have one more question," I inform.

She sideways glares at me and winks.

"Ask away, Mr. King."

I cup my hand around her silky face as I take in her naughty smile, and I growl.

"Just how angry are you, Mrs. King?"

CHAPTER 22
Learning to Lie

It's good to be home.

Back in the place that smells of fresh ocean water, full of good recollections and the sound of Liv's unopposed squeals of joy. There is no stress here, except for my knowledge of Riva's existence, but since we are getting back into the routine of things today, which means stopping by Dell's office to grab our journals, I'm sure I'll end up throwing her name into the mix. It's probable Vix and I will get sucked into one of his therapy sessions anyway, so why not give the man another puzzle to sort out when I hand in my list of shit I want to confide in him about Riva. I just hope it doesn't mean he will add to the list of questions he's already given me.

I swear, sometimes it seems like the doc asks even more questions than I do, which brings me back to what I am supposed to be doing... question number six.

The escape plans.

"What are you working on?" Vix asks.

"Homework," I say as I look up and kiss her cheek.

"Yuck! Bad Daddy! Bad, bad, bad," Liv shouts.

I lean over and kiss her too as she swats at me and giggles from her saddled position on Vix's hip.

"You know you can take the morning off and wait until we get our journals back this afternoon, right?" Vixen asks.

"No can do," I tell her. "No homework means no gummy bears, so I need to bring something in there this afternoon."

"Is that really the only reason you're doing homework right now?"

I sense a hint of doubt in her tone as she puts Liv in the playpen and turns on the TV to the kid shows.

"It's the majority of the reason," I confirm.

"And the minority of said reason would be what?"

I slide my chair over as she takes a seat beside me and eyes me over skeptically.

"Well... I just feel like it's important to prove to Dell that we can handle answering the questions together."

"Oh, well, why? Did he say something last week that would suggest he thought otherwise?"

I nod, not wanting to tell her that he technically terminated all of my homework assignments and specifically said not to go any further without being in his presence.

"He might have said some things," I mutter, "but I wasn't paying too much attention once his hand went into the candy bin."

"Pax Whiskey King," she hisses in her firm tone. "What *things* did he tell you?"

Her eyes are locked hard on mine, glistening a vivid shade of the sky and I can tell she's concerned.

I shake my head and sigh.

"All he said was that I'm not allowed to do any more homework at home."

"And?" she asks, squinting. "Why would he say that?"

I knew she was gonna be so pissed about this.

I scratch my scalp with the pencil feeling unnerved by how she's tapping her nails on the desk, seemingly waiting for my answer.

"I kind of told him about how I hit you after question three," I whisper.

"You did what? Why Pax? That was none of his business and you and I handled it."

"It just slipped out, I didn't mean for it to," I profess, "but he wasn't mad… he just said he wants us to do my homework during therapy from now on."

Vixen shakes her head unhappily and kisses my forehead.

"Okay, it's fine… but you have got to learn to stop feeling guilty about it, and you really need to stop being so damn honest all of the time," she advises.

I agree with a subtle nod even though I wonder why she wants me to lie, but at least I've told her about the dilemma.

She slides the piece of paper I was working on closer to me as Liv starts to make a ruckus tossing her toys around.

"Keep writing," Vixen says. "I'll go and make her a snack and then put her down for her nap."

"But Dr. Dell said not—"

"Zip it, Pax. I don't care what he said, now do as you're told, or you won't be getting any smileys today."

Fuck me she's evil!

I put my pencil to the paper and wait for her to carry on, deciding it's best if I just listen. Lord already knows what goes down between us when she's mad and I'm just horny.

Now, where was I?

Oh right, *question six, the escape plans.*

* * *

The sun was down, and I'd finally paid my dues for the day as I entered the basement and heard the loud click of the door lock behind me. I turned the corner and caught eyes with Verna, and I knew instantly she'd been worrying.

"I told you I'd be okay," *I said to her as I took the dry bread she was handing me.*

Her hand was shaky and I could only assume she'd told Ken about what happened earlier with the gunshot because he nodded at me as I sat down on the hard floor beside her.

I looked over at Cliff sitting directly behind Ken with his knees pulled to his chest and his light long-matted hair half covering his eyes. He looked paler and more sickly than usual. He always looked smaller and weaker than the rest of us, but I could tell this was something different.

"Maybe he should eat this too," *I said.*

I tossed my slice of bread at Ken and he looked behind him at Cliff.

"He ain't hungry," *Ken said, moving Cliff's hair away from his eyes.* "He's just tired, right Cliffy?" *Ken asked pulling Cliff's head hard to his, so they knocked together.*

Cliff nodded, and then Ken let go of his head and threw the bread back at me.

"You eat it," *Ken said,* "and let me worry about Cliffy."

I caught it and took a bite as I stared down at Verna's dirty naked feet, wanting to avoid her eyes. Her big brown eyes that were highlighted by her mangy orange hair that resembled the color and texture of the carpet upstairs. I didn't want to see the face I knew would've been questioning why I never said the words back to her.

"Ken says it to me, you know," *Verna stated.*

"Yeah, well Cliffy doesn't," *I pointed out with my mouth full.*

"That's because he can't talk, stupid."

She smacked me in the back of the head just as I was removing the dry bread from the roof of my mouth.

"What the hell was that for?" I growled.

Ken laughed and shook his head side to side.

"That, Pax, was Verna showin' you she has feelin's. Dumb, gross ones that I only say back cause she's mean otherwise."

"You're lying, Ken," Verna hissed. "Take it back. You love me and you know it!"

Ken laughed and shrugged.

"Graff needs to stop bringing you those stupid fairy-tale books, they're fillin' your head with nonsense," he declared.

"They are not!"

"Are too!" Ken insisted.

Verna raised her arm to throw one of the books at him, but I grabbed her wrist and shook my head.

"Thank you, Pax," Ken said. "The last thing we need is to listen to her cry again when I rip that stupid book apart and finally get it through to her that love can't exist in this place."

Verna tried jerking her hand away, so, I took the book with my other hand and let go of her wrist.

"I hate you both," Verna shouted, her voice filled with hurt. "I hate you guys almost as much as I hate this place," she then added.

I swallowed, feeling bad and knowing she was about to cry and all over three meaningless words in a bottomless hell.

I was about to say it to her just to ease her sadness but then we heard the keys against the door and assumed our positions.

Ken and I stood and waited silently near the bottom of the stairs, listening as Verna climbed onto Ken's mat beside Cliff.

Then we heard Graff clear his throat.

"Guess what I brought tonight?"

I could almost hear all four of us sigh in relief as he shut the door behind him, turned on his flashlight, and made his way down.

We already knew it was the tattoo gun, but what we didn't expect was the telescope. Graff handed it to Cliff, probably *wondering if it would get him to talk, but he said nothing, just studied it with his hands.*

Seeing as though we never knew what day it was, and time was based off Ken's seasonal observations I'd decided to mark that night in the field as my birthday. I'd never had one before and figured that was as good a day as any and that being outside was the greatest gift I could have asked for. Graff had mentioned that it was the 31st of August, so, that was the day I considered myself to be officially seventeen as we laid underneath the stars not questioning why we were there, just happy to see them for once. It was also the night Verna tried to take her life with a splintered chunk of wood. She'd have done better if she would have tried to ram it through her chest though because all she really did was mess up her arms to the point of scarring. When I'd asked her what she was thinking the next morning as Ken and I cleaned the wounds the best we could, she said she refused to spend another birthday in that place. Seemed it was my fault for being stupid and wanting a fake one since her actual one was right around the corner, on the 9th of September. I knew it right then and there, that I needed to get all of us out before it was too late, because she wasn't going to last, and neither was Cliffy with how fragile he'd gotten.

As for the plan, it was simple, I'd wait for the next time Graff showed up. But what I wasn't so sure about was if any of us could survive beyond that point, or even make it out alive in order to find out.

✱ ✱ ✱

"Nice work," Vix says, rubbing my shoulders as she looks at how much I've written. "I think Dell just might give you the entire candy jar for your efforts."

"I doubt it," I sigh. "He's more likely to throw the thing at me because I didn't listen."

"He's not the old, drunken Helen's replica, Pax," Vixen laughs. "Besides I promise to catch it if he tries. Now get your shoes on. We have to be there in twenty minutes."

Well that totally just felt like Déjà vu.

I hand Vixen the red pen and all four pages I managed to scribble most of my answer on before I begin to search for my shoes. Liv, the little Ham Head, has been on a terror relocating our shoes to some of her more devious hiding spots since we returned. I like to think it means she never wants us to leave again.

I lift the sofa cushions one by one, but only find some pocket change and a hair elastic. Then I search under the sofa but come up empty, wondering where else she could have stuffed the darn things.

Concluding I need to ask Vix for help, I sneak up behind her in the chair but stop short of pranking her because I can see she's upset.

"Is it my spelling again?" I ask hovering over her shoulder.

She shakes her head and turns in the chair slowly.

"I never knew she tried to kill herself," she whispers.

I can see the pain written across her face, and it sucks; I can't stand to see her hurting.

"Yeah, but she survived. It was so long ago," I remind. "She's happy now, Vix. They have a trailer and a full acre of land now because of you."

The year after we moved here, Vix got a call from a bank manager somewhere over 2500 miles from here in a town called Clancy, Montana. He asked if Vixen knew Verna personally and wanted her to verify the substantial check. Then he asked if it was okay to pass along our address to Verna because she wanted to send us something. We received a letter not too long after with a picture of their place and a very heartfelt thank you. I was impressed with how neat Verna's printing was, but Vix was more concentrated on wanting to visit them, but I said no, and for good reason. I won't be the brother who flashes both our jaded past and my perfect future in her face. If it weren't for Vixen, I wouldn't have our amazing daughter. The second light of my life that I probably don't deserve but thank my lucky stars for every single day. And seriously, the only thing harder than dealing with a pissed off Verna is trying to console a crying one that recognizes what she and Ken may never have, a child. Like me, they have no proof of who they are, so adoption is out of the question. I have a happy life. I'm spoiled with love, family, we own a bar, and I'm even learning to read. These are not things I would want to brag about. I refuse to do that to Ken, Cliff, and Verna, let alone Vixen and Liv. Looking into the eyes of someone who sees only pain, loss, and how imbalanced the world is, would be unfair to all of us, and that is all our presence would do. Make Verna suffer because of my happiness, and I won't do it.

Vixen hands me the papers back without looking at me and I can tell she still has questions beyond what I've written.

I kneel down in front of her chair and lift her chin until her eyes meet mine.

"What is bothering you this time? I thought you'd be happy… we got to see the stars for the first time in what really felt like forever," I grin as goofily as I can.

She doesn't bat a lash at my attempt to lighten the agony in her eyes.

"We've been celebrating a fake birthday for you for five years and I didn't even know it," she mumbles almost inaudibly. "I feel like such an idiot, Pax. And not only that, why would you think Verna wanting to end her life was your fault for simply wanting a birthday?"

My heart sinks to the damaged tone in her words.

"First off, I like my *fake* birthday. You always make sure it's fun!" I point out. "And second, and more importantly, it doesn't matter whose fault any of it was, it's done now."

"Yeah, but—"

"But nothing, Vix," I say, covering her mouth. "If you can't read my confessionals without getting upset, then you can't read them at all."

She cringes and shoots me a pissy look.

"The word is confessions... and fuck that, Whiskey, I can, and *will* be reading and marking *all* of your homework."

I hold in the urge to laugh at her heated face, and the fact she just called me Whiskey. I like her angry face so much more than her sad face.

"Alright, Mrs. Confessions, have it your way then. But can you please help me find my shoes?"

"Liv hid them again?" she asks cracking a smile.

"Yes, ma'am," I nod. I'm cheering inside at how quickly I was able to change her mood. I deserve at least three smile faces alone for this feat!

"Check inside the heat register and the fridge too. She likes to hide things in the drawers."

"I'm on it," I say, pecking her on the cheek. "And don't forget the smiley faces."

Correct as usual, I find my running shoes, both of them in the fridge with cheese slices stuffed inside. I consider leaving them, thinking they might add comfort but change my mind when I notice Jack eyeballing me through the screen door.

"Don't just stand there, bud, come on in," I tell him as I tuck my laces inside my shoes.

"The good old cheese in the shoe trick," he laughs, stepping inside. "Where is the little Ham? Vix asked me to come and get her early today."

"She's still napping, but she should be up soon."

Handing me my homework Vixen then hugs Jack.

"Thanks for coming early, we'll pick Liv up from your place once the bar closes."

"Sure, no prob," Jack says with an odd smile on his face. "I've been dying to ask if the rumor is true."

"What rumor?" Vix asks as we head to the door.

"The one about Helen, you know, being into women now."

"You are so immature," Vixen says, laughing. "I'm not even going to bother answering that and tell Jimmy to zip it, will you. We are leaving now, bye Jack."

"I'll take that as a yes then," Jack declares with a wave.

I nod my head to confirm the rumor as Vixen shoves me out the door, shaking her head, unimpressed.

She always walks fast when she's mad. I pick up the pace and listen to my shoes make flapping noises since I never tied them, trying to keep up with her. Most days, I wish she'd have just let me have the biker boots that don't require shoelaces, but she insisted these were better for my foot health, whatever that means.

Her pace keeps getting faster and faster, it's as if she's walking to the speed her mind is spinning or something. I'm not even sure why she's so bothered by Jack's inquiry or Helen's gayness, so I decide to ask.

"Want to talk about it?"

She hits the button at the crosswalk and shakes her head.

"Not really."

"Well are you at least going to tell Dell about it? I'm sure he can shed some light on it."

"I doubt that," she gripes, slamming the button again. "It feels like the more stuff we tell him, the harder it gets."

"Yeah, but isn't that the point?" I ask.

"No, Pax, he's supposed to be helping, not making me feel like a stupid idiot."

I scratch my head and jog across the street to her pace.

"Does Helen's interest in Claire really bother you that much?"

"What?" she asks, stopping. "Why are we discussing my mother right now?"

"Well isn't that why your speed walking?" I ask, confused.

"Of course not! I was talking about your *confessional* from earlier," she hisses.

"Con-fess-ion," I correct, smartly. "And why are we back on that topic again?"

"Because it fucking bothers me, Pax! I want to know what day your *real* birthday is on... and I also want to go and visit Verna, Ken, and Cliff, but you always say no!"

I can see how much it means to her, but I can't help with a birth date and I don't think visiting Verna is a good idea.

"Too bad neither of those things are possible," I state. "Now can we please take this inside Dell's office? People are starting to stare at us."

Vixen glances around, taking note of the onlookers eyeing us over as I walk a few steps passed her and hold the door open. Stunned, Vixen's face turns awkward as Riva and Dell come out looking equally as uncomfortable.

Clearing his throat, Dell says, "It was a pleasure to talk with you Riva, I'll see you next week."

"I'll be here," she mumbles, quickly walking away.

"Well that was weird," I say as me and Vix follow Dell inside. "I sure hope you didn't give her all of the candy I planned on earning today."

Vixen smacks me in the arm.

"You need to stop giving Pax candy, Dell," she mocks, "and can I ask how long you've been counseling that woman?"

"You may not, because that information is confidential. But please have a seat." He gestures at the sofa. His tone is firm and unusually serious as he continues. "I'm fairly certain that what I am about to share with you both will be an enormous shock and I don't want you to react, just breathe and think about it once I've told you. Alright?"

I look at Vix as she looks at me, our eyes wide and my heart pounding to the importance in his tone. We both nod and take a seat in our usual places, and I grab Vixen's hand, squeezing it, unsure why I'm feeling so nervous.

"Okay, Dell, we're listening," Vix presses, "just rip the band-aid off. There is nothing Whiskey and I can't handle."

He studies our faces looking back and forth between us before he takes a deep breath.

"Pax, it's about your childhood, before the abduction, son. I have confirmation that this is accurate... I know what your given birth name is."

CHAPTER 23

Learning to Be Angry

Breathing. You'd think it should be the most natural thing in the world. For me, it isn't. I spent a huge part of my life holding my breath, listening to the sound of my heart pound in my chest with my eyes closed tight, wishing I were somewhere else. Wishing we all were.

But now I sit here trying to breathe and to fathom what it would mean to know my name. It was different when the existence of it wasn't actually sitting in a folder on Dell's desk, when it wasn't even a possibility. Now I sit here realizing that my answer to question three on the day I hit Vixen, all of it was for nothing. I glance over at Vix hoping she will give me a sign on what she's thinking, maybe she would want to know. I understand her well enough to guarantee she does, but that she would never make the decision for me. She has far too much empathy when it comes to holding no judgments.

She smiles at me, saying nothing, but in her eyes, I can tell she's thinking, likely weighing the pros and cons of the decision.

I glance over at Dell, his expression reserved as he rocks patiently in his wheely chair, the only thing making a quiet squeaking sound in the otherwise silent room. If it were his choice would he want to know?

Unable to come up with a conclusive answer, I fish my homework and my list of Riva questions out of my pocket instead and hand them over to Dell.

"What are these?" he asks, unfolding the crumpled papers.

"One is a list of questions I came up with about Riva over the weekend, and the other four pages are homework related to question six."

He scans them over with a perturbed look on his face and then rubs his eyes underneath his glasses.

"Considering the circumstances regarding Miss Paulson, I'm willing to—"

"Miss who?" I ask, recognizing her surname instantly as all of my hairs stand on end.

"Riva," he confirms as my chest crushes, sucking the air out of my lungs. Vix squeezes my hand as I sit feeling totally blindsided, questioning everything I know before I try to get verification.

"But that's the imposters' last names," I manage to push out. Trying to make sense of how it's possible, I look over at Vixen, hoping she can tell me it's just a coincidence.

"I'm sorry I didn't tell you," she whispers, no longer holding my hand or looking at me.

Fuck me, she's in on whatever this is.

"Didn't tell me what, Vixen?" I growl.

"Pax, anger is a normal reaction to—"

"Shut the fuck up Dell, and let my wife answer the damn question," I snarl, trying everything to control my brewing temper.

I look at Vixen, and never have I seen her look so vulnerable, or weak. It's surreal to me and confusing, seeing the tears run down her face. Kirsten King rarely cries. I no longer see the woman I married, the one who has no fear, no, the person who now sits crying next to me is unrecognizable.

"Pax," she whispers, "I wanted to tell you, I really did... but I couldn't. I didn't know how to."

"Well then tell me now for fuck's sake! How the hell does that woman bare the same name as the imposters?"

Dell stands and hands Vixen a box of tissue.

"Pax, none of this is your wife's fault, so please take a deep breath and calm down. This is the reaction she feared you might have which is why she couldn't tell you that Riva is Carl and Dana Paulson's niece."

I look over at him, clenching my fists into balls of anger.

"Are you fucking telling me that Graff was related to one of them?"

Dell nods. "Yes, he was Carl's brother."

"Wow! Okay, well this is just fucked. If you'll both excuse me, I'm just going to take a walk."

I turn to leave, my mind flooding with questions and I don't ever remember feeling so entirely betrayed or angry. How could she not tell me this? How the fuck did I ever think Graff was just some ignorant man with a tattoo gun... an innocent bystander not knowing what was happening in that place? This means everything I ever thought was wrong. And most fucked of all is that we ended up moving here to get away from Vixen's past and ended up colliding with my own. Digging up stupid shit that belonged to stay buried, but instead I'm left with the knowledge that me, my wife, and our daughter live in a town that harbors a blood relative to a pair of child molesters.

Fucking Christ!

Being so livid and lost in thought, I realize I've walked all the way back home and into the garage. I stare at the Hog, trying to think of any reason not to grab Liv, get on it, and just drive the fuck away. God am I angry. Angry and fucking tired. Tired of the unrelenting emotions and questions that never seem to end and completely lost as to why my wife felt she needed to keep this from me.

"Please don't do it," Vixen whispers. "Don't go, Pax. If you need some time alone, I'll go stay with Jack and Jimmy."

I take a seat on the steps and try to focus on her appearance, but all I see is the face of a liar.

"It's fine. You can stay and I'll go."

"Go where?"

"To work, where else?"

I hate that my tone with her is so harsh, but at the same time, I feel like she deserves it.

"Do you want me to come with you?" she asks.

"Not particularly, no."

"Look, Pax, I get that you're pissed and need some time to process everything. Why don't I ask Jimmy or Jack to go in with you tonight?"

"Why you don't trust me to run the fucking bar alone?"

"I never said that."

"That's right you didn't. You fail to say a lot of things lately, don't you?"

"That's not fair," she says, looking hurt. "Don't you see that it was this exact reaction I was hoping to avoid?"

I grit my teeth and smirk.

"Fuck off that's what you were doing. You were covering your own ass because you knew I would have moved as far the fuck away from that sick bitch the second I knew they were all related."

"That isn't true."

"Isn't it though? You love this place, the house, the bar, the ocean... the distance between you and Helen. So, it makes perfect sense to me."

"Fuck that, Pax, I'd give it all up for you and you know it."

I can't take the hurt in her eyes, nor can I trust anything she says, I need to get out of here.

"I have to go open the bar," I say, walking past her. "And please, do not send me a fucking babysitter, I'll figure out which bottle is what on my own, and I'll see you when I see you."

I walk away feeling even more damaged which I never thought possible. If this is what the 'healing process' is supposed to feel like then I'd rather stay broken. What does any of it have to do with the reason we even started the stupid therapy? I'm a great dad to Liv, that's the one thing I am absolutely sure of, but everything else is a jumbled mess of go fuck myself.

I'd seriously need to hate-fuck myself into the next millennium just to rid myself of all these feelings.

Approaching the bar, I dig in my pocket for the keys and notice the newly installed sign attached to the veranda.

Jimmy and Jack, I think to myself, realizing I'm now smiling.

The thing looks like its hand-carved with lights mounted all the way around it that showcase the giant letters that spell The Olive King. It's even got Liv's perfect tiny footprint showcased in the center of the O. I pull out my phone and snap a few pics, impulsively sending them to Vix, realizing she should be here to see this with me. Also, I'm comprehending how proud her father would have been to see this. He loved her more than I think she knows. I'd met the man once, just days before I ever met Vixen. It's a secret I can never disclose to her or Dell, one that will remain on my conscience so long as I live.

I enter the bar and begin to set up the bar chairs in front of the counter before I glance at the cheat sheet on how to make each drink. I've got another thirty minutes before the bar officially opens for the day, so I slam a shot of whiskey and get to work on polishing the glasses. I look around, feeling at ease because everything about this place is calming and inviting, it's all Vixen inspired. Every detail has been thought of with care from the motorcycle artwork on the walls to the road sign decals that cover the countertop and right down to the ash vault flooring that looks like the highway. My wife thought of everything we loved and brought it to life, the same way she brought me to life.

"Nice sign, it's classy," Dell says from the doorway. "Are you open for business?"

"Thanks," I nod, "and not for another twenty-five more minutes, but you're free to sit."

I gesture at the chairs and continue to stack the glasses.

"Okay," he mutters, seemingly nervous. He takes a seat and slips a folder onto the counter.

"What can I get you, Doc?"

"I'll have whatever's on tap, and for the purpose of my visit, let's just say I am not your therapist right now."

I toss the towel over my shoulder and slide him a pint of Bud.

"Did Vix send you in here to check on me?"

"No, I came of my own volition. You left my office pretty heated earlier and I thought I might be able to ease your mind."

"I thought you just said you weren't here as my doctor."

I eye him over skeptically as he opens the folder and slips me an old newspaper clipping.

"I'm here as your friend, Pax, and also as Vixen's ally. She was hurt when you left, so we got to talking and it became clear."

"What did?"

I look at the article and study the photo of the large grey building with the yellow door. It surges something in me, my heart picking up speed as old memories flood my mind.

"In the two years I've been working with you, I knew you didn't know your name, but it didn't occur to me that you may not have known your birthdate either."

I look up at his confounded expression and then back down at the article. Some of the words are blacked out but the date is clear as day and the headline says, '4-Year-Old Boy Goes Missing from Local Orphanage.'

I swallow and push the page back toward him. I'm not too strong in the math department but I can add and subtract.

"That can't be talking about me, Dell, the date doesn't add up. I would have been two that year, not four."

Dell takes a long gulp of his beer as if to collect himself.

"I thought you might say that, so I did a little digging and a lot of thinking after Vixen told me about your fake birthday. How old do you think you are?"

I look at him like he's off his rocker.

"You already know I turned thirty last August... what are you getting at?"

"Just bear with me," he comforts. "I read in your journal that it was Ken who guessed your age, but he was wrong, Pax. You lived in a place that had no calendars, no celebrations to mark events, and no concept of time. Correct?"

I think back to the cold floor of the basement and in my mind, I search the dark room and then I nod and say nothing.

"And you thought you were seventeen when you escaped, right?"

I nod again, waiting for the shoe to drop.

"According to the information I got from the orphanage, son, you lost track of time in there. I know your given name, and now I know your birthdate. You are not thirty, Pax, you are twenty-eight."

I rub my temples as a wave of dizziness comes over me.

"I know it's a lot to take in, just breathe, son. Try to look at it as a positive thing... you're technically aging backwards."

"I don't see much of a point to celebrating this considering whether I'm thirty or twenty-eight. I'm technically still only in the third grade."

Dell laughs and pats my hand.

"I beg to differ; I think Vixen would be me more than ecstatic with the news."

"I'm sure you're right, Doc, but I'm still undecided on anything at the moment."

I look up as a couple locals enter the bar and take a seat.

"You got a cheat sheet?" Dell asks.

"Yep. Why?"

"Give it here," he whispers, "I'll go ask them what they want while you sit and think about things."

I hand it to him, surprised he wants to do my job and I watch as he asks the two gentlemen what their poison is.

Then he joins me behind the bar and starts measuring out the liquor for each drink as he makes them. If I didn't know better, I'd say my therapist has an alter ego that enjoys playing with booze. I make my way to the front window and take a seat, watching as the sun begins to set over the ocean. The view is incredible, and I get why Vixen loves it here the way she does. I probably shouldn't have said the shitty things I did. She's never been anything but supportive of me, so if she didn't tell me, I know she had a good reason. And if I'm honest, it's no different than me keeping quiet about how I knew Robert before I ever met her. The only thing I do know right now is that I can't make any decision this important without knowing things are good between us.

"Hey, bartender?" I ask.

I take a seat at the bar counter as Dell grins proudly.

"What can I get you, son?"

"How about a doctor's note so I can go home and patch things up with my wife?"

"That's a tall order, apologies are never easy," he says in his doctorly tone. "Go, I'm good here, just leave me a key and tell me when to close her down."

If I were the hugging type, I would hug the man, but instead, I hand him my key and settle for a handshake.

"Thanks, Doc, just call me if you have any issues, last call is at eleven."

I head down the beach kicking the sand, thinking about how to approach Vixen. There is so much I want to say to her, mostly about how I shouldn't have reacted the way I did.

I cannot believe I am two years younger than I thought, *shit*, how old would that make the others? Did they lose track of time too? Maybe this is why Verna was never able to locate her family. If the cops were trying to find them based on her age and what little detail she could remember it makes sense why they failed. Ken and Cliffy too; they never did find their dad either. It was almost as if their families simply vanished the way we all did.

Or maybe they just gave up looking the same way we gave up fighting and did what we had too.

I shrug off the memories as I catch sight of the most beautiful human I've ever seen. There, sprawled across the sand is my incredible wife, with a telescope in hand and studying the stars.

"It's a nice night to lay below the stars," I say as I stretch out beside her.

"I just wanted to try and understand what it felt like to have been in your shoes, but I couldn't imagine never having seen them. I'm so sorry I never told you—"

"Shhh, you have nothing to be sorry for, Vixen. I'm the one who needs to apologize, and for so many things."

She turns onto her side and rests her head in the crook of her arm, shaking her head.

"You are learning to be angry, Pax, do not ever apologize to me for that."

She sounds so firm in her tone I decide not to list all of the reasons I still feel guilty, and instead I kiss her. A long, dirty kiss, with my tongue inside her soft lips as I stare into her loving eyes. She moans quietly and then pulls away as I savor the sweet taste of her.

"If you want to move, then we will. I've thought about it and there is nowhere on this planet I won't follow you. As long as it's you, me, and Liv, I don't care where we end up."

"Well I love you for saying so, but I think you might reconsider that when you have to plan my party," I warn.

"What party would that be?"

"The one when we officially celebrate my... hold on a sec," I say counting on my fingers. "Oh, right, it will be on the real day of my twenty-ninth birthday, although I haven't asked when it is yet."

She laughs as if I'm fucking with her.

"Why are you messing with me? And why do you think you're getting younger?"

I tell her how I left Dell in charge at the bar, and how he legitimately now seems to know everything about me, and her mouth drops open.

"Oh my God! Are you serious? Wow, Pax! This is incredible news and you bet your ass I'll be throwing you a party! Wait... does this mean you want to know your real name too?"

Her smile is undoing, it's brighter than every star in the sky.

"I'm considering it, but I have to say if it turns out to be Gus, we're legally changing that shit to Whiskey."

She laughs and hands me the telescope.

"Lay back and enjoy the moment because it doesn't matter how old you are or what your name ends up being... because, Pax," she whispers mischievously, "you will always be a dork."

With that, she takes off running down the beach knowing I'm full tilt behind her, as she laughs. Unable to catch up, I stop and kick my shoes off, and remove my socks.

Note to self, learn how to tie the damn things already!

By the time I catch up to Vix, she's standing outside the bar staring up at the new sign.

"Holy shit that's cool! Did Jack and Jimmy make it?"

"Yeah, it's pretty great. I'm assuming you didn't get my pictures?"

"Nope, I was laying in the sand from the minute you left, hiding from the world. I didn't have the heart to see Liv's adorable face that reminds me of you, knowing you were mad with me."

"Who says I'm not still mad?" I growl quietly, "You did just call me a dork, and do *not* say you meant dick either or else you will be getting on mine."

Biting her lip, she takes a step back.

"There you go trying to threaten me with a good time... When. Will. You. Learn?"

"Learn what?" I ask, entirely curious.

She smiles that one smile, the one that says she's up to no fucking good.

"In order to take me to hate-fuck city, not only do you need to piss me off, you need to catch me first."

"What the fuck?" I holler, now chasing her back the other way. "When I catch you, and I will, I hope you're mad as hell!"

I don't know what it is about her that makes my dick react in ways I've never understood. Ways that make me fall in love with her all over again, even though I'm downright nuts in my head. Sometimes I think she was made solely for me, like she's my reward for the few things I've done right in this life. And thank fuck that woman is made of steel when it comes to sex because her evil little monster and my angry giant one are about to tango in the land of Hate-Fuck.

CHAPTER 24
Learning to Run

Intimacy, as Dell says, is a part of human nature, the basic human need to feel loved and nurtured. He once asked me how I performed in the area, sexually speaking, but me and Vix avoided answering out of fear he would view us as sex-crazed animals. We knew if that were the case, he wouldn't have written the strong recommendation letter of support to the orphanage when we adopted Liv.

What I held back was that there is this place I go in my head when we are intimate, it's dark. It's a place full of twisted thoughts and malicious intent, a place where I am no longer me, I no longer see Vixen, and I am a machine doing what I was programmed to. *To fuck relentlessly and without emotion.*

To the imposters, it was our 'job,' and our lives concretely depended upon it. None of us wanted to end up buried in the field, forgotten. We'd been warned enough to know it was a possibility.

So, whether we ate or drank, or got to avoid the torture of having to watch each other get beaten, they made sure we knew the 'choice' was ours. There had come a point where I felt like a robot, doing whatever I was told out of fear not of what would happen to myself but to the others. I needed to get into a murky place in my head to get through doing the vile things I was instructed. I think we all had to become something else, something maddening and soul-consuming to do to each other and the imposters what they demanded. Sexual things, physical things, demoralizing things. Practices that were so wrong and unforgiving they left me hating myself and full of questions I knew the others couldn't answer, because they too must have been feeling the same things. Constantly questioning if we were good or bad, if we were strong or weak, or if we could ever apologize to each other. And most of all if the dark, the hate, and the pain were worth the air we breathed.

But somehow, we survived, and for me, sex has become nothing more than a way to release my pent-up hate. I think it's why me and Vix are so compatible; she makes me feel vindicated when I'm with her. The way she can endure the darkest parts of me that are only fuelled during sex. I'm driven by the way she's able to love and accept my inability to be gentle, and the way she uses her own madness to withstand what I do to her. It's her anger that shields her from me and mine that ends up pleasuring her, at least it's what I tell myself. Regardless, she is able to take the sinful parts of me and turn them into euphoric moments of ecstasy, in turn fulfilling me with a sense of accomplishment.

I've thought about it, us together, a lot. I wanted to gain perspective, but the actual truth of our connection didn't hit me until the night I called her a masochist. The same night I told her what I was trained to do.

When Vixen asked me to stop that night, it was the *first* and *only* time in my life that I didn't hesitate. I stopped. It was also the first time in my life that someone told me I was a good person and I believed it. But only because I *stopped*. I knew in that moment not only how much I loved her, but that I could also absolve my sins through our bond.

"What are you thinking about right now?" Vix whispers.

I roll from my back to my side to take in her beautiful naked frame in the darkness of our room. I graze my fingers down her silk-like arm and link my fingers over hers.

"How beautiful and faultless you are."

"You call this beautiful?" she asks, pointing to her messy hair.

"Hell yes I do. The just hate-fucked hairstyle is my favorite look on you."

"Is that right?" she smiles. "Remind me again what it was you did to piss me off."

Foreplay at its finest.

I run my hand down and in between her legs. The warmth of her sex is inviting as a discreet whimper seeps from her lips.

"Are you saying you're up for another round?" I taunt.

"What do you think, Mr. Benjamin Button?"

"Mr. who?" I ask, having no clue who the fuck she's referring to.

She laughs and raises a brow.

"I'll add it to the list of movies you need to watch, the guy ages backwards in it. Kind of like you... and since your two years younger, I think it means your dick can totally handle more work."

"In that case, maybe we can name my dick Benjamin Buttons."

She laugh-snorts and covers her mouth.

"You're doing a horrible job at making me mad, you know."

I stare at her, taking in the beauty that fades from my vision when I'm fucking her. She's captivating to me, the way her hair flows in every direction and her eyes seem to look inside my soul. It makes this part of my 'job' hard, knowing I have to give up what I see and trade it for an angered version of her. It's safer that way.

I conjure up the only thing I can think of that will get her going, knowing it's sure as fuck what I'm going to do.

"I'm planning on having Riva fired from the daycare. She doesn't belong near our family, let alone anyone's children."

"What? But you don't even know her, Pax, how do you know she's anything like those sick fucks?"

"How do *you know* she's not?"

I continue to knead her sex with my hand as she resumes defending Riva.

"I don't know, but at least give her a chance first," she half pants/half pleads.

"Like how her family gave me a chance? Not. Fucking. Happening."

I'm strong in my tone, not willing to budge as I return to my deliberate movements to arouse her.

"Jesus, Pax! Why would you throw that in the mix?"

She's now fuming which is exactly where I want her to be.

"I said it knowing it would piss us both off. Do you want me to stop?"

"Fuck that! I'm already too angry now. God you are revoltingly good at this!"

"I know."

I grin slyly, feeling her body tense up with anger and stimulation as her hips begin to move to my pace. Pressing my erection against her, I run my tongue over her breast, then up her neck and I stop at her ear. She tastes like a firestorm of sin and feels like damp silk against my hand as my need to occupy her grows stronger.

"Tell me you want this Vixen," I murmur. "Give me permission to violate every faultless part of you, mind, body, and soul."

I can feel her breathing elevate, the pulse in her neck throbbing against my lips.

"Please," she begs, "you have my permission."

I plunge my fingers inside her, feeling her body surrender to me, her whines crossed between imploring and yearning. I would do anything to be able to etch this moment into my mind, the way she looks at me with greed and desire, how her body reacts with every movement I make. If only this pristine account of her was what I'd see when I fuck her, I'd be an unfractured man.

But I'm not. I'm a tattered man about to take what I can from her, and then give it all back ten times harder.

"Tell me again," I demand.

Her body continues to keep rhythm with my fingers, her clit rising to the sense of my thumb as I tease her in an inflexible pattern.

"Yes! Goddamn it, Whiskey! I need you now," she appeals.

I can no longer hold off my urge as I grip her roughly and pull her on top of me.

"Fuck me then, show this dick what you want and take it from me," I challenge.

She smiles viciously, happy to oblige as she glides herself onto me with a slow precision so leisurely it causes me to growl.

"Do not tease me," I warn, jerking her lips to mine. She grunts to the feeling of me pulling her hair and kisses me back with a raw and carnal need.

I bite her bottom lip and set her upright as she licks the tiny pool of blood I drew and then she shakes her head at me.

"Now I'm going to have to hate-fuck this dick as payback," she taunts.

"Don't threaten me with a good time," I mock. "Show me what you're made of."

With that, she grabs my hands and places them on her hips as she begins to move her tight, wet pussy up and down my dick with calculated movements.

I close my eyes, trying to concentrate on the connection of our bodies, willing my thoughts to stay focused on her. On this instant in time.

My hands are planted harshly on her hips, and the harder I try to stay with the image I want to see, the stronger my grip on her becomes. I can feel my nails piercing her skin as I help her keep the pace that is now an inferno of rage. She moans out vulgarly, still slamming herself down against me and I refuse to open my eyes. Her pleasure and my pain are colliding together as husk mumbles of her impending orgasm fill the room. It's at a point now that I'm holding back my urge to get even stricter in my grip and tempo. This is the longest she's ever taken, and I can't tell if she's making it last on purpose or if I'm doing something wrong.

"Jesus, Vix," I grunt. "Get rougher, girl, and fucking come already."

Saying nothing, her moans become more distinct and even louder. I have no choice but to open my eyes, I need to gauge her expression.

She looks down at me and winks as my heart does flips in relief.

"Are you fucking with me?" I ask, heatedly.

"Nope! I'm just fucking you in general," she says with a cocky smile.

"Well not anymore you're not."

I flip her off me onto her stomach, pin her hands behind her back, and tell her to put her ass in the air.

"Yes, sir," she says trying to sound cute.

"I really hope you aren't laughing right now. Because you won't be in about half a second."

With no leniency, I shove myself inside her, jerk her wrists back and grab a fistful of her hair.

"Holy shit, Whiskey," she groans.

"I warned you, and I have no plan on stopping."

"Please don't then," she breathes.

"You do this shit on purpose don't you?"

"Shit yes I do."

It takes me less than fifty seconds to fuck my wife and her mocking tone so hard, we both end up releasing in a heated sweat of hell-flames and debauchery. Breathless and exhausted we both flop onto the bed reeling in the unspoken glory of our gratification. I pull her closer to me and she lays her head on my sweat-soaked chest as we listen to each other's breathing. I take in the sweet scent of Vixen and close my eyes lost in her comforting presence and in the warmth of her breath on my chest. My mind drifts to question seven: *Did Ken, Cliff, and Verna attempt to locate their families once they were free? If yes, how did that make you feel?*

* * *

"The cops are really useless, you know; them bastards can't even find the imposters, let alone help me find my parents," Verna vented.

I was seated on the curb outside the old worn looking cop shop picking at the grass. I shrugged at her comment, feeling a sense of relief.

"Maybe it's not their fault, maybe your parents stopped looking, or maybe they never started," I said, feeling unwanted. "But you always got me, Ken, and Cliffy," I added in, hoping she would realize she didn't need a family, not when I could be her family, and I didn't want to be alone.

I looked at her sad expression, knowing I wasn't good enough to make up for the family she thought she lost, and I felt guilty for not wanting her to find them.

"Maybe you should have left us there," she said, kicking at some stones. "Living like this, in a world where nobody remembers us, where people don't care, it sucks."

I growled at her and stood up.

"That's not true, and you better not say that shit to Ken, because he cares, and I wouldn't have gone back to get you if I didn't."

She was about to say something until we saw Ken dragging Cliffy toward us from the cop shop.

"Them fucks is stupid as all hell. They showed Cliff and me a bunch of pictures of missin' kids and we weren't in any of 'em. How about you, Verna? You find your parents?"

"Uh-uh, same thing for me, they said to come back if I could remember more details, like my last name, birthplace, dumb stuff I can't remember. All I could tell them was my mother's hair color, that we had a cat, and that my dad was really tall."

Ken grabbed Verna and hugged her before he held something up in the air and spun in a circle.

"Don't worry about them idiots, they probably don't even believe us anyway," he said as he stopped and waved the green paper in front of Verna's face. "Let's go celebrate our freedom and see what the diner down the road has for breakfast."

I snatched the paper from him and studied it.

"Where did you get this from?"

I'd only ever seen money a handful of times when the imposters would have people over who sold them tiny bags of sugar, but I knew that what I held was important.

"There you go as usual, always askin' me stupid questions! I stole it off the cop when he left the room to get the books full of pictures. He left his wallet on the desk... like I said, idiots."

Me and Verna laughed as Cliffy stared at his feet like he always did.

That morning was the first time I'd ever eaten a pancake, and it was the best thing in the world. That and the freedom we'd gained as we sat in the diner eating and laughing, even while knowing none of us had anything to return to, but at least we had each other.

* * *

"Let's go, Monkey, Uncle Jack's waiting for you," Vix says as she leads Liv to the door.

"No go!" Liv hollers. "Olif no go Unca Jack!"

Vixen picks her up and kisses her angry face all over as Liv kicks and thrashes while laughing in her arms.

"Mommy and Daddy will be back to get you soon, and then we will go and see the big sign!" Vix baits.

"Olif go to big sign?"

"That's right, but not until after Mommy and Daddy see Dell."

I watch in amusement still trying to undo the knot I made in my lace, starting to get frustrated with myself.

"Thanks, Jack, we shouldn't be more than a couple of hours and then Pax and I have some news to share with you," she says handing Liv over.

"Come on, you little badass, Uncle Jimmy is making your favorite... bananas in milk! Have a good session," Jack says as he leaves.

I jerk my shoe off, discouraged, and throw it back in the closet and start looking for my sandals instead.

"Do you want me to show you again?" Vix asks, hip checking me out of the way. "You can't learn if you don't try," she reminds.

"I don't want to try anymore. Shoelaces are pointless, and I wish Jack would stop calling Liv a badass out loud. She's going to start repeating it."

"Don't change the subject, Pax," Vix says, untying the knot like it was nothing. "Sit. I'll show you again, and don't worry about Jack's bad habits. Worry about your own."

Worry about your own, I mimic in my head, annoyed that Jack gets away with murder and I can't even get away with wearing sandals. I watch closely as Vixen shows me the bunny ears for the thousandth time and I copy her with my other shoe.

"Holy smackdown, I did it!" I shout. "Move over, let me do this one too."

"Nice job!" she praises.

"Why thank you," I say, proud I tied them both perfectly. "Now let me tie yours."

She laughs and unties one of her laces as I kneel below her. I take her foot and place it on my thigh, and again, I'm able to tie the lace with perfect accuracy. *If this doesn't get me five smiley faces today, I'll be damned.*

"You are officially a pro," Vixen says, "now let's see how fast you can run now that they're tied securely."

I laugh and chase her out the door and actually beat her by a mile by the time I reach Dell's office. Okay, maybe not a whole mile, but definitely a block.

I hunch over, resting my hands on my thighs, catching my breath as I wait for her, eyeing a couple of parents dropping their kids off at the daycare. Instantly, everything in me wants to go over there and warn them about Riva's shady connection to Carl and Dana. I look back at Vix, and she shakes her head, seemingly knowing exactly what I'm thinking.

"Dell's waiting. Let's go," Vix orders.

I look over one more time at the small blond-haired boy that can't be older than five and I imagine all of the terrible things she could be doing to him. For a moment I'm filled with an intense fear and it feels like I'm drowning as the door closes behind him.

Vixen grabs my hand and steps in front of me, her head tilted with a look of concern.

"That little boy is not you, Pax," she whispers.

I look into her genuine eyes as she runs her hand down my face, and she smiles. "He will be fine, and if it will ease your worry, I will go in there and check on every kid in that place personally while you head in to see Dell. Okay?"

I swallow and nod.

"Thank you, Vix."

She kisses my hand and squeezes it before she gestures to Dell's door and then jogs back across the street. If ever there was a time that I knew my wife was not just my saint, but my hero, it's now.

I head inside Dell's office and take a seat in his waiting room. It's small and has three chairs, a cabinet, a table with a half-dead plant and two magazines on it, and a poster of a supposedly blissful family on the wall. I've looked at the picture so many times I can tell you how many pearls are on the mother's necklace, the father's smile isn't proud enough, and that the two kids are both faking their smiles. I've hated everything about it since the first time I saw it. If Dell wants to promote a happy family, it should be me, Liv, and Vixen on the wall.

Without thinking, I grab the poster and slip it behind the cabinet and return to my seat as Dell's door swings open.

"I'll see you next week," he says to the couple.

I glance them over and smile, but I can tell they hate my tattooed appearance, and don't reciprocate, so I shrug it off and follow Dell into his office.

"Good morning. Where is Vixen?" he asks, taking a seat. "Did it not go well with the apology last night?"

Deciding not to tell him she's on a mission to *save the kids*, I take a seat before I answer.

"Uh, she'll be here soon, and the apology was good, great actually," I say, not mentioning the sex or my newfound hate for Riva.

"That's good to hear. I'm happy to report I'm quite the bartender," he boasts. "I now know how to make drinks with some very kinky names."

I raise my brows and nod as he slides the bar key across his desk.

"I hope this doesn't mean you want to replace your awards with bottles of liquor now."

"Not a chance, son," he winks. "I have too much work here to finish," he says, handing me my journal. "I think while we wait for Vixen, you should work on finishing your answer to question six."

Not the escape again, I hate remembering that night.

I sigh and take the journal and the pencil from him. Closing my eyes, I listen to the sound of his wall clock ticking as I think back to what I thought was thirteen years of time yesterday, but only eleven today.

* * *

It was raining that night, pouring hard and I'd decided not to tell the others I was leaving. I knew chances were that if Graff had a gun, or new where the imposters kept one, it'd be harder for him to hit one person than four. I waited quietly looking back and forth between Ken, Cliff, and Verna as Graff worked on the skulls Ken wanted on his arms. The sound of the thunder was loud, and water was seeping in through the cracks in the cement under the tiny boarded windows.

Verna hated it when it stormed so she moved closer to me and sat reading one of the books Graff had given her. I realize now the bastard was likely stealing them from Riva.

I take another difficult breath and let the thought fade, knowing it doesn't matter now.

I begin to write again, remembering how I told myself that Graff trusted me.

* * *

He'd been around enough times that he knew we all thought there was nowhere to run to which is why he took us outside the week before. I based my plan on that knowledge alone and told him I wasn't feeling well, that I didn't want to puke in the bucket we were given for bodily excrement. When the buzzing of the tattoo gun stopped and Graff looked at me with his muddy grey eyes, I prayed so hard to whatever God was listening to help me.

"Here, take the keys," *Graff said, digging in his pocket.* "Take the pail too and empty it while you're up there, kid."

My hand shook as I reached for the keys and I swallowed.

"Yes, sir," *I said as coolly as I could muster.*

I took one last look at the three people I loved most in the world, picked up the pail, and climbed the stairs.

It was dark and the rain was coming down hard as I counted my steps as I ran. The feeling of my feet slapping the wet ground and the cold rain was terrifying as streaks of light lit up the sky. At first, I felt like I was a thousand pounds, so heavy and weighed down. The faster I tried to run, the harder it became, like a magnet trying to pull me back the other way. It was as if my mind wanted to find freedom, but my body wanted to go back and take them with me. It wasn't until the loud crack of sound snapped through the air that I couldn't be sure whether it was a gunshot or actual thunder. Then my legs were set free to carry me as far and as fast as I could go, all the while counting as I went. I don't know how many fields I ran through, or for how long, but by the time I made it to anywhere that had power, my feet were raw and bleeding from running. But I counted 1233 strides. That was my marker, that's what I reported to the payphone operator, and that's how I found my way back to get my family.

* * *

"It was never much of a plan, but here's the answer," I say, handing Dell the journal.

Dell shakes his head and his face becomes serious.

"It was obviously the perfect plan, you got them out after all. Don't sell yourself short."

I take a seat wondering how one sells them self short as Vixen taps on the door and then enters.

"All seven boys and five girls are in the middle of snack and story time, including Riva's daughter, Zoe," Vix says in her matter-of-fact tone. "She's the same age as Liv, I think you should check it out for yourself. You have Riva's unconditional support."

Her face is sober, but her tone is reassuring.

"She has a daughter?" I ask, conflicted.

Vixen nods and I try to imagine Graff as a grandfather, which is stupid. The fucker is dead and deserves to be, yet it's all I can think of. I shake it off.

"If I can just intervene here for a second," Dell states, "would either of you care to fill me in on what it is you two are carrying on about?"

I cross my arms, not feeling guilty at all for judging Riva and I still want to see it for myself that the kids are safe. I decide to leave the explaining of it to Vixen, because I know if I get in trouble from Dell, there will be no candy for me today, and I'd have to wait for the next question to get any.

Question eight, what brought me into Vix's life the night we met?

The answer is simple, *I was supposed to kill Helen King.*

CHAPTER 25
Learning to Repent

I watch my wife and our daughter dancing in the warmth of the sun, laughing and celebrating something as simple as the bar sign, and it makes me smile. This is what life is supposed to be, moments of happiness and recognition for the good things in life.

These are the specs of time I count as victories, unlike the way Verna and Ken celebrated when they heard the news of Carl and Dana's imprisonment. It wasn't a victory to me; it was a punishment. It was a repetitive shot to the gut with a sledgehammer, knowing they had gotten away with most of their crimes.

The night I went back to get the others, I made it just as I heard the sounds of dogs barking and sirens in the distance. Graff had clearly heard them too and I'd hid in the field as he fled in his truck, my heart pounding as I wondered if he'd killed them first. When I stood up and looked at the porch, the three of them were standing there, Verna in Ken's arms and Cliffy staring at his feet.

One-thousand-two-hundred and thirty-three steps to freedom. I should multiply it by two, but math isn't my strong suit.

Whatever that number is, that's what it took to smile at my family the same way I am now.

I'd heard months later how the cops searched the house that night collecting evidence that amounted to a handful of charges. Riva had also handed over Graff's phone with the few faceless pictures of us and the living conditions we endured. When it was all said and done, they were caught several years later, and the charges had come down to the three that could be proven.

Child endangerment, child neglect, and some charge for drug possession. All of us knew we it would have been their word against ours. We had no proof, and no evidence we had ever been taken, so there was no reason to go forward with our stories. Instead, we'd simply decided to stick together until Verna and Ken could at least try to locate their families.

And for it all, what did those bastards get? Ten fucking years, *that's what*, all thanks to their lawyer and a lack of fucking evidence. No mention of the abductions, abuse, torture, or any of the horrific shit that went down in that place. No electric chair or lethal injection like I'd imagined they deserved. To me, ten measly years was no fucking victory to celebrate, not when they would have edible food, electricity, and a bed to sleep in, unlike us who'd spent longer in the basement with none of those things. But at the time, Verna and Ken felt differently which drove me nuts. They said the sentence brought them a sense of closure. It meant they could be done with it all, as if it never happened. I never understood it and it made me angry to the core. What I felt they deserved was to burn in hell eternally, and I was so mad one night after listening to them talk about it constantly, I walked out of the abandoned house we were living in and hitched a ride. I ended up hours away at some diner by a private rich community.

The same diner I met one very wealthy, Mr. Robert King in, the man I later learned was Vixen's father.

*　*　*

"Daddy, look big sign!" Liv squeals.

I take her from Vixen's arms and spin her around as the sun begins to set.

"Are you sure Jack doesn't mind taking over our shift?" I ask, setting Liv on my shoulders.

"Nope, he's good with it. He's also keen on the idea of throwing a birthday bash, but he wants you to invite Dell."

I told Vixen she could look inside the folder and find out my actual birthdate since she'd covered my ass with the whole 'go check on Riva' plot.

It happens to be in two weeks, on the thirteenth of November.

"Why does Jack want our therapist there?" I ask, twirling Liv around every few steps.

"If I had to guess, I'd say he wants to fish for your real name too. He keeps asking if I looked at that as well."

"And did you?" I ask, wondering the same thing.

She shrugs and smiles wickedly as Liv makes growling sounds noticing a stray dog further up the beach.

"Good girl, puppies say grrr and woof!" Vix tells Liv. "And instead of asking me what I *may* or *may* not have seen, you should ask the man *yourself*," she finishes with emphasis.

I growl at her as I set Liv down on the sand so she can pet the dog.

Her ham head is far too large for her little body, and watching her run is hilarious, as if her head is helping her gain speed. Vix and I laugh as she makes it to the dog and claps at it, refusing to touch it even though the scruffy thing is heeled at her feet.

"Puppy!" she shouts. "Olif's puppy!"

"Great," Vix mutters, "now she thinks it's hers. You go be the bad daddy and tell her we are not bringing that thing home."

"Why not?" I ask examining it. "So he looks like he needs a

serious bath and a haircut, but he could make a great addition to the fam."

Vixen cringes as me and Liv take turns petting his head. He's sweet really, with his dark grey fur and black patches that surround his eyes. He smells rancid, but I bet he just wants to be loved.

I look up at Vixen's unhappy expression, all hands on her hips and raring to say no, but I lock my hands together at my chest and stick out my bottom lip.

"Please can we take him home, Mommy?"

Liv jumps up and down clapping.

"Please, Mommy! Take Olif's puppy!" she mimics.

"Oh my Jesus, you two," she says, half smiling. "Fine, but I am not bathing that thing, nor am I teaching it how to spell, tie shoes, or shit outside!"

She covers her mouth as I laugh at how she swore in front of Liv.

"Puppy shit outside!" Liv repeats.

I turn my head to avoid laughing because then for sure Liv will keep saying it.

"No, Olivia, puppies poop outside," Vix corrects.

"Olif's puppy poop outside!"

"That's right, and he can take his bath outside too."

I gather my composure and stand, totally respecting how Vixen is always able to hold it together during funny moments like this.

I reach for Liv's hand and then Vix's as I tell the mangy little mutt to follow us as we head toward the house.

I knew my wife had a soft spot for strays. After all, she did fall in love with me. It's late when we reach the house, so, Vix tells me to stay outside and bathe the dog as she takes Liv inside to give her a bath too.

"Come here boy," I say unwinding the hose. "This is gonna be cold, but don't worry, you made it to safety."

The dog heels at my feet as I start to spray him down, washing away all of the misery I'm sure he endured. He reminds me of me, once lost to drift around, but now found and in need of a few lessons. *Like how good food tastes when it isn't spoiled or raw.*

I wait for him to shake most of the water off, noticing he's maybe all of six pounds. Then I let him follow me inside, also realizing he too is nameless and has no birthday.

"Come, let's see what we have for perishables, which by the way, is code for food not in a can. Maybe we can fill that skinny carcass of yours."

He makes a whining sound that strikes me hard, almost as if he understands I know what it feels like to be so hungry I could have eaten my own foot.

Finding last night's notoriously awful macaroni and red sauce concoction Vix poured her heart into, I remove the plastic wrap and set it down in front of him.

I watch as he sniffs it and begins to chow down.

Fuck yes! No crappy leftovers tonight!

"What the hell, Pax?" Vixen asks.

I step in front of the dog and cross my arms, unwilling to let her take his food away.

"He's hungry," I explain, "and look how clean he is! And don't worry, I'll cook tonight."

She eyes me over and sighs.

"It had better not be canned beans; your specialty sucks," she points out.

"Noted," I smile, "no beans for Vixen or Liv."

"Liv's asleep already. I think she's still full off of the pretzels and peanuts Jack fed her."

"Then in that case, why don't we order in and have a relaxing evening? You go and enjoy a hot bath and I'll meet you in there after I take our son for a potty break."

"Our son?" she asks trying not to smile.

I nod and raise my brows proudly.

"Yep, we just need to think of a name for him, and I want his birthday to be the same as mine."

"Sure, I'm good with that," she pauses. I watch as she looks him over, still slapping his food down like a Vulture and she shakes her head. "Name that thing whatever you want, but I will not refer to it as my son."

"Why not?" I ask, offended. "You refer to me as your husband."

"Pardon?" she asks, confused.

"I was even mangier then he is when we met, I probably smelled worse actually. But you loved me anyway," I say, gesturing at all of my tattoos. "If you could love me back then, you can love him now, and he is the perfect playmate for Liv, just like a brother."

She covers her mouth and laughs.

"Sometimes you are such a dor—"

Stopping herself from saying it. I growl in warning and tell her to get her ass moving to the bath. She doesn't delay and takes off up the stairs leaving me to hang out with my new buddy.

"Let's go, Mac," I tell him.

He follows me outside, and I take a seat on the step as he roams around checking everything out. It's a beautiful evening, the breeze is warm and the air humid. I sit thinking about question eight, knowing it's the one question I cannot answer truthfully. Vixen thinks I was on the Hill the night we met preparing to exact my revenge on the imposter's shady lawyer. Even if that were true, I wouldn't tell my therapist that. But the truth is so much worse. The truth would destroy my wife.

* * *

"How much are we talking?" I asked the man in the expensive suit.

"A hundred grand, in cash, and a boat. You can go anywhere you want when it's done. But I want that cheating bitch dead."

I studied the picture of Helen long and hard before he shut his phone off and took a sip of his coffee.

"I need a tent, the code for your alarm system, and a schedule for when you're out of town. Making it look like a home invasion will be tricky to pull off otherwise."

"Done," he said with a crooked smile. "You won't just be ridding me of an ungrateful wife, you'll be ridding the world of the Devil."

I took in the cold gleam his eyes gave off as he left a crisp hundred on the table for two pieces of pie and two coffees. I'd never seen that kind of money, and then he handed me two of my own.

"For the tent, kid, and stay away from the boathouse at the bottom of the Hill. If I catch you there, I'll kill you."

I nodded and took that as a solid warning that the man meant business, and all I cared about was the money. I could have taken my family anywhere on the boat and we could have restarted our lives like I felt we had earned.

Other than that, I didn't know much of anything at all, but the night I met Vixen and carried her home, I knew for certain I was fucked. It was then that I realized Vixen was the man's daughter and not long after why he'd told me to stay away from the boathouse. The look in his eyes every time we met wasn't that of anger or hate that I hadn't followed through with the plan, it was desperation. Sadness. Something I understood all too well from the years I'd spent in that basement. It's consuming, and it's an emotion that nothing can cure besides death or freedom.

* * *

Three years later, Robert chose death.

That is on me. That was my final sin.

The one thing I can't ever tell my wife. I am the reason her mother continued to hurt her. I am the reason her father is dead.

Fuck question number eight. I'll be skipping to nine.

Dropping a stick at my feet, I look down at Mac, realizing he wants to play, but I'm not in the mood.

"Come on, boy, let's go in and check on the girls."

I check on Liv first, nudging her door open just a crack. Her pink lamp that spins stars around her room barely highlights her sweet little face as she snores contentedly in the bed I built. I love the way her teeny foot dangles over the side and I know better than to try to move it onto her bed. Last time I did that she woke up and pulled my hair as hard as she could. I'm so proud that our daughter has the reflexes of a cat and takes no shit, just like her mother.

I back away quietly and head to the washroom, inching the door open ever so slightly. The candles flicker as I take in my wife's illuminated silhouette. Watching as her foot taps the wall to the beat of whatever she's listening to with her earbuds in. The room smells of vanilla wax as I take a seat on the floor, wanting to capture the beauty of this second. Seeing Vixen with her eyes closed and feeling blissful always brings me a sense of peace, as if I'm doing a good job at being her husband. Helps me remember I'm not just a horrible man keeping a secret from her.

I'm protecting her, and I'd give my life to make sure she never stops smiling.

I stand just as Mac finds me, coasts into the room without stopping, and jumps into the bathtub.

Unable to react fast enough, Vixen gets to her feet screaming bloody murder and swatting at the dog as the two of them splash around.

"Get, you mangy little bugger!" she scolds him. "And you,"

she says now looking at me, "stop laughing and help me you big dummy!"

I whistle and call him over, but he doesn't listen.

"Mac," I say again, "come let's go see what other food I can save Liv from having to eat. I bet you'll love Vixen's spaghetti casserole."

Vixen scoffs as she wraps herself in a towel.

"Hey, Mac," she says, placing the soaking dog in my arms. "I bet your daddy here can't even spell spaghetti or casserole, let alone make one."

I feign shock as she sticks her tongue out.

"S-p-...spa... s-p-u-g-e-t-y spells spaghetti," I say proudly.

"Not even close, now get out and go dry *Mac* off please," she says shaking her head. "And I can't believe you named him Mac."

I grin and shrug.

"Want to know why?" I goad.

"I already *know* why," she states. "You think it's funny to make fun of my Macaroni dish. Now get!"

Damn, how does she do it?

I close the door behind me as I take Mac downstairs and wrap him in a blanket. He looks more like a rat at this point but a cute one as I rock him like a baby.

"Don't worry, Mac," I assure him, "you'll grow on her, just give it time."

He whimpers and then licks my face as if he too knows I'm right.

I take a seat on the sofa comforting him and thinking about question nine.

The day we moved out here and what I'd hoped to gain from it.

It's one of the easier questions considering I gained more than I ever hoped for, between Vixen's hand in marriage, our perfect kid, and now this spunky little mutt.

I know Vixen's reason for wanting to come out here was to

start over away from Helen and the Hill in general. But my reason was simple. There is nowhere on or off this planet I won't go to be with Vixen. I'd follow her into the afterlife. I'd follow her into the darkest pits of hell, if it meant we would always be together. Hell, I'd even follow her back into that shithole of a basement if I knew she could forgive me for my part in Robert's death. But none of this is what I will write in the journal as my official answer. Instead, I'll write about how I'd hoped being here would help me heal, and that it has. That what I see when I don't close my eyes so tightly are images of a life not lost. I can now see the world in a way that makes me feel whole and important.

I'll write down that what I gained is far more than I ever lost.

"Hey, boys," Vix says, interrupting my thoughts. "It's weird to now have to pluralize the word boy."

I raise a brow as she takes a seat beside Mac and me.

"Does this mean you accept our new son now?"

I place Mac in her arms and pull her feet onto my lap.

"Son, not a chance, but as our new garburator, why not?"

I smile wide, knowing she's too stubborn to admit she'll fall in love with him eventually. It only took her three years to admit it to me way back when.

I watch as she puts Mac on the floor, tossing the soaked blanket down beside him. Then she gathers her hair and ties it back as she sits up, biting her lip in thought.

"What would you say if I said I wanted to adopt again?"

"I'd say h-e-l-l y-e-s!"

"Really?" she smiles. "Maybe we can get Liv that brother you're trying to fulfil with Mac over there."

"Hold on a sec, you're not suggesting we trade Mac in, are you?"

She laughs and rolls her eyes.

"No, Pax, we can keep the dog too," she reassures. "But I definitely want a little boy, and if we get to name him, I like the name Liam. It's Irish and means 'helmet of will.'"

"Well how big do you think his head is gonna be? He might get a complex if you name him that."

She slaps my thigh and laughs.

"So, you hate the name?" she questions.

"I don't hate it; I just think you shouldn't tell people you look at your kid as a 'helmet head.'"

"Why not? Liv already thinks she has a 'ham head.'"

I shrug and nod in agreement.

"Very true. I'm good with whatever name you want to call the little guy, big head or not."

"Yeah?"

"Yeah."

"What if I wanted to call you that instead?"

"Are you saying I have a big head?"

She moves closer and grips my hand, her eyes shrouded in mystery. For a second, my mind flashes back to the dark corner of the basement.

"What even is a Pax?" Verna asked with her face all contorted. *"How did you get a name if you don't remember your parents?"*

Then my mind flashes forward to my answer to question three.

No, I would not want to know what my real full name is if I was given the chance. I am a Pax. A Pax that Verna once told me was a boy with a big head that resembled a helmet the same as a warrior's, and now, I am the same Pax that wears that same suit of armour for Vixen and Liv.

I snap out of my thoughts as my heart races and Vixen runs her hand through my hair. I can tell by the way she's biting her lip that she's dying for me to confront her.

"You darn well looked, didn't you?" I ask, stunned. "My name was Liam?"

"Your name *is* Liam," she corrects, excitedly. "And you're Irish. Do you want to know your surname?"

If her smile wasn't lighting up the entire southern half of the hemisphere right now, I'm pretty sure I'd feel like I was falling off of the planet. *Me and my big head.*

I scratch my scalp, trying to unscramble my thoughts. I like being a King, I like knowing I'm keeping some small part of Robert alive in Vixen and our family. I would never change my surname for that reason alone, so it doesn't matter.

"I'm good with being called a helmet head or whatever, but I'd like to remain a King. So, no, Vix, don't tell me the surname. Those people never wanted me. You did."

"Okay! Then it's settled," she says kissing my hand. "You are officially now Mr. Liam Whiskey King, and we are going to see about getting Liv a brother who's every bit as special as you are."

I take in her excited nature before I really think about it.

"Special as in how? Are you calling me non-smart?"

"You mean un-smart, and of course not. If I was trying to do that, I'd use the word dork."

She totally means dick, and I'm all for telling her to get on mine, or Liam's whoever I am today.

CHAPTER 26
Learning to Forgive

I started this story with the intention to answer ten questions. The same ten questions that added on hundreds if not thousands more to the list in the process.

Some have been harder than others, but is there really such a thing as too many?

I know Vixen would say no, Dell would say never, and Ken, well I know what he would surely say, abso-fucking-lutely. My curiosity was always an annoyance to him, especially when I talked in the dark.

* * *

"Hey, Ken?" *I asked.*

It was hard to see him, but enough moonlight was streaming in through the tiny window that I could tell he was squinting his eyes at me.

"What is it now?" he then answered, heatedly slapping the flashlight out of Cliffy's hand.

Cliffy was always clicking it on and off like he was doing Chuck Norris Code, Verna once called it.

It rolled to me, so I picked it up and tucked it under my mat.

"If I'm supposed to be seven and your eight, but Cliffy's six, how come he don't never talk?"

"He's a mute," Verna piped up. "He got born like that."

"Oh," I said.

I laid back with my arms under my head and thought hard about how to word my next question. Sometimes I wished only Verna could hear me because Ken never liked my inquiries.

Finally, it came to me and I asked, "Did Cliffy get born without a tongue?"

"No, stupid," Ken grumbled, "he got born with a string around his neck and his head broke 'cause he couldn't get no air."

"Yeah, and then his momma lost her guts on the floor and died!" *Verna added.*

"That's gross," *I said.*

I wondered if Ken seen the guts or not but didn't want to ask.

"It's not gross, it's sad," *Verna whispered.* "None of you guys got to have a pretty mom like I did."

"Shut up, Verna, it ain't nice to brag," *Ken hissed.* "Besides me and Cliffy got a dad who's as big as a Goliath, and when he finds us, the imposters are gonna get squashed like that stupid snake!"

I could feel this anger in me, always festering up like a bomb waiting to detonate. I hated how Ken was always so rude, especially to Verna, and how he'd killed my snake. I wanted to yell at him, but they would hear me, which made me even madder.

Before I thought about what I was doing, the flashlight nailed Ken in the head and he hollered, muffling himself with his mat.

"That's what you get for telling Verna to shut up," *I told him,* "and for killin' my snake."

For as much as I wished he was right about whatever a Goliath was and it coming to squish the imposters, I knew it wasn't true.

Nobody was coming to save us and the only thing that pushed me forward was all the anger, hate, and darkness I felt for all of us, but most of all for Cliffy who never had a voice.

* * *

"No! Bad puppy!" Liv screams.

I look up from the stove as she scolds Mac for chewing on one of her dolls.

"Not num-num, bad, bad, bad, puppy!"

"Is Mac giving you a hard time?" I ask, trying not to laugh.

Liv shakes her head up and down, simultaneously growling as she tugs on the doll's legs. I can see she is so not going to win the war as Vixen steps in and kneels down.

"Drop it, Mac," Vix says in a scary tone. Impressively, he listens and lets go of the baby doll.

"There, see?" Vix tells Liv. "Just tell Mac to drop it, and he won't mess with your baby anymore."

"Drop it!" Liv copies, her face all scrunched up and stern.

"That's right," Vixen praises. "Now let's go wash up, lunch is almost ready."

She tickles Liv until she squeals and then runs toward the stairs.

"What is for lunch anyway?" Vixen stops to ask.

I block the stove and shake my head slowly.

"It's a surprise."

"Hmmm... well is surprise code for 'I have no clue what I'm making' by any chance?"

"Not at all," I lie. "You're going to love it, now stop trying to peek and go wash up."

She cringes doubtingly but listens.

I swear there is nothing I can get past that woman, it's like she always knows everything. I've been standing here throwing a bunch of different things together trying to make it both edible for us and Mac until we go to the grocery store to get him dog food. I dish out my invention, proud it has no canned beans whatsoever in it, as I set the table.

Not gonna lie, kind of makes me think we could open a restaurant next.

I pull out a chair for Vix as she gets Liv into her highchair, and then I pull out another chair and call Mac over.

"Uh-uh," Vix reprimands. "The dog eats on the floor like a dog."

"But he's a part—"

"The answer is no, Liam, and that's final."

Surprised to hear her use that name again, I accept defeat, take Mac's dish, and put it down beside my chair, feeling bad for the dog.

Sometimes I wonder if she knew how many times I sat and ate my food from the floor if she'd feel differently about saying it's where Mac belongs.

"Num-num!" Liv squeals.

"No kidding," Vixen says, "Wow, this is really good, what all did you put in here?"

"Wouldn't you like to know?" I say, pleased. "But too bad for you because this new me will spill no secrets! Now eat up, we have a date with Dell."

"Nope, you are on your own today, Liv and I have a party to plan and we will be doing what ladies do best... shopping for a present."

"Present!" Liv shouts and claps her hands.

"That's right, Daddy is having a birthday soon!"

I watch as Vix wipes Liv's face and begins to clear the table.

I'm not too keen on accepting gifts, but I won't try to talk Vixen out of it either. Last time I tried she finally told me how important it was to her. She has this ridiculous idea that she needs to make up for my years in the basement, which I find sweet, but totally unnecessary. Now I just let her because it makes her happy, and any wise guy knows *a happy wife is a happy life*.

"Do you want me to drop you off on the way?" Vixen asks as I finish buckling Liv in her seat.

"Nope, I like walking," I say, shutting the door. I stick my head in Vixen's window and add, "But I love you, and that little Monkey. Have fun and I will see you at the bar in a couple hours."

"I love-hate you more," she says, "and stay out of trouble, Liam."

The name hits me square in the solar plexus as I watch them drive away. I don't think I'll ever get used to it, but I have to admit I like it a lot more than the name that was never mine to begin with. It's strange but when I think about my earliest memory at the orphanage, I can now hear the nun's loving voice call me by my name. Maybe it's just my imagination, but it makes the memorial of the day feel not so dark, as if maybe someone did love me once before I became tainted to the world. And if the lady didn't love me, at least she knew my name which means I wasn't invisible to her and that she cared enough to report me missing.

And if that's true, it also means there was a time when I was good, which changes everything I ever thought. I wasn't being punished, I didn't deserve to be there, and I am deserving of the life I have now, even if I've done some bad things to get here. Including the plan I'd made with Vixen's father, Robert King.

★ ★ ★

"It's been almost three years since you met my daughter," Robert said as he sipped from his glass of brandy.

I looked around the room at all the books he'd acquired and wondered if he'd read them all.

"Yes, sir," I confirmed.

The pit of my stomach was on fire, and I was sure he wanted to scold me for not following through with the plan.

"You know she's damaged, don't you?"

The look in his eyes was cold and I couldn't believe he viewed Vixen of all people as nothing more than damaged.

I shrugged, wanting to tell him he should have protected her, but instead, I said nothing as he continued.

"Be that as it may, I love my daughter very much, fragmented or not. Kirsten is a King, my only child and as such, she could have had anything she wanted. Anything at all," he paused, seemingly trying to calm himself.

I could tell he was angry, maybe with himself, or maybe with me for not killing Helen when he'd asked.

"Now, Pax," he continued, "tell me why it is you think of all the things that girl was destined for, she picked you?"

I picked at my fingers knowing why but didn't want to admit it. Vixen hadn't even admitted it either, but I'd always known it. She found the other half of a broken soul and together we were whole. I looked up at the clock, unable to read the time because the numbers were weird looking symbols, but I knew it was late and that down the hall slept his wife, and the woman I loved.

"I'll tell you why," he finally said. "Whatever that pained look in your eyes is, she understands it, son. I've seen it in her own eyes more times than I can count."

I knew he wasn't finished speaking and I couldn't pry my eyes from his, or the depth of his tone and how he'd called me son. It made my heart race, as did every word he spoke.

"She doesn't think I know she never cries," he continued, "but I know—she also never used to smile either—but then she met you. The same fucked up kid I saw at the diner. Go figure." He then scoffed in disappointment. "My God-forsaken daughter fell in love with a drifter who's even more tainted than she is."

"She's not!" I growled. "Vixen is not tainted, sir."

His face became softer, almost as if he wanted to smile at my angered reaction. Then he gestured at me to continue, so I did.

"Your daughter, sir, is a fucking badass, stronger than any woman I've ever met. She's wild and spirited. She looks at me as if I exist. And I am in love with her too."

He laughed quietly to himself and slammed the rest of his drink.

"I know that," *he then said as he poured two glasses and handed me one.*

"The two of you are like a modern-day Romeo and Juliet. All ready and willing to go to battle for each other."

"Romeo and who?" *I asked, immediately regretting it.*

He looked dumbfounded for a moment and then he stood and plucked a book out from one of the alcoves.

"Romeo and Juliet," *he reiterated,* "were star-crossed lovers. They found love with all the odds against them and died trying to protect it. This is the story I used to read to Kirsten before bed. Here, take it, maybe you can read it to her one day."

I looked at the gold stitched, leather-bound book and grazed my fingers over the letters, wishing I could tell him I would. Instead, I thanked him and tucked it inside my jacket pocket praying he didn't know I couldn't read.

"So, Pax, besides walking around my house shielding my daughter from my wife, which I am grateful for, what else inspires you? I've learned that money is of no importance, and since you are the closest thing I'll ever have to a son, I'd like to be sure that you have goals."

I slammed my drink, trying to stuff down the fact this powerful man who could read, write, and run an empire called me his son, again, and then I answered.

"Vixen, sir. She's what inspires me. Whatever she wants, I want. Wherever she goes, I'll go. And whatever in the world it is that *makes her smile, I'll do it for her without hesitation, no matter the price."*

Robert King lifted his glass in the air, and with tears in his eyes, smiled the warmest smile I'd ever seen from him.

"Star-crossed lovers, indeed."

* * *

Those were the final words I ever heard from the man's mouth. He was dead and gone the very next morning, killed himself while I'd left to check on Ken, Cliff, and Verna. I think that was his way of making sure Vixen was in good hands, or at least capable ones even if he believed fate was against us.

Now I try to read that book every night to Liv, and I told Vixen that I stole it years ago because the cover was shiny. The book itself is mind-bogglingly confusing with how different the language is, but a promise made is a promise kept.

I arrive at Dell's office ten minutes early and take a seat in my usual chair. I'm not surprised to see that Dell found my hiding spot for the poster and hung it back on the wall. I stare at it wondering if I should try hiding it again, but then realize there's something else missing from the scene. A dog, which leads to my next thought. *Mac needs food.*

I text Vixen a quick message, using only smile faces. One that looks like a dog, one of a chicken's leg, and the last one of some hands praying. I hit send just as Dell's door opens and I stand to greet him as Riva exits. I force a smile as she looks away, the same disgusted look I swear she always gives me.

"Well fuck you too then," I say slipping passed her.

"Whoa, Pax," Dell says, "do not speak to my other patients that way."

"It's Liam now," I correct, "and why don't you tell her not to look at your other patients the way she just looked at me?"

"Wait... what?" he asks.

He gently takes Riva by the arm and turns her around, so she is facing me.

"Vixen peeked at my name when she was only supposed to find out my birthday," I notify.

"Well, alright then, Liam," he says as if it's the most natural thing in the world. "I think you and Riva should talk. I'll mediate if it's something you'd both be comfortable with."

I look over at Riva and she nods. Then I look at Dell's bald head and thick glasses before I shrug and nod also.

If I can figure out what her damn problem is with me it'll be a good start. How bad can it really be considering she's the one who's related to the imposters?

We take a seat in Dell's office, Riva on the sofa, and me in the chair beside Dell's desk as he raises his brow unhappily.

"What? You sit beside her," I tell him. "At least if she touches you, I'm sure you can legally drug her or something. Unless it's only little kids she's into."

"That's totally uncalled for, not to mention unfair," Dell starts in.

"No, it's fine. Let him talk," Riva says cutting him off. "I deserve whatever he has to say, and if it were my daughter, Zoe, I'd want her to get it off her chest."

Her eyes meet mine and, in the moment, as mad as I am, I also feel guilty. But predators are good at that. They make you think you're the sick one. They twist things up inside your head so you can't remember the truth anymore.

I swallow the pain in my chest, trying to think of what I want to say to her, wishing Vixen were here.

"Shit! I don't even know what to say to you. All I have are questions, and this anger that's building in the pit of my stomach."

"It's a good start," Dell praises. "Why don't you begin with whatever question comes to your mind first. I can grab your list from the drawer if you'd like."

"Those questions are baseless now," I argue. "They were from *before* I knew she was one of them."

"I am *nothing* like any of them if that's what you want to know. Not even my father, he was a spineless pig and I hate what he did to you," she hisses.

Well, welcome to my fucking world, lady.

I take in the way Riva's nerves are on end, she's shaky and her discomfort mirrors the way I feel inside.

"Vixen said Graff blew his head off, is that true?"

"All over our living room wall," she undertones. "I guess he hated what he did to you as well. I know an apology from me doesn't mean much, but I am so, so, sorry for your suffering."

I can't look at the guilt on her face, it's too much, so I mess around with Dell's candy jar, trying to guess how many candies are inside.

"What do you think of her apology?" Dell finally asks. "Riva is not her father, Liam, yet she's telling you that she's sorry for his behavior."

I shrug, counting eighteen green bears, before I look over at her.

"I'm madder at myself for thinking he was some kind of light in between the dark days. I wanted to like him, but now I just can't get over that he actually knew the truth and did nothing to help us."

Her face turns conflicted and she exhales a long breath. Her dark eyes seemingly searching my face for permission to ask or say something.

"It's fine, Riva," Dell comforts. "This is about putting it all in the open, so if you have something you need to say, feel free."

She rubs her hands on her thighs and sits up straight.

"I'm not sure I understand what my father's part in all of it was. I was under the impression he did things to you and—"

"What? No..." I say, stopping her there. "I mean besides coloring all over me and giving Verna a few books, Graff never crossed the line."

I watch her entire body fill with a sense of relief as if a boulder has been lifted from her chest.

"He didn't do all of the terrible things I imagined?" she mutters to herself. "I figured it was why he killed himself when I found the pictures on his phone."

"Well, it's not," I tell her. "I assumed it was because he felt guilty for not letting us out sooner. Either that or the coward didn't want to face his brother in court had he actually been charged for his crimes."

Now tearing up, Dell hands Riva a box of tissues and takes a seat beside her.

"I think this is a good place to stop for today. We can set up another appointment if either of you would like to continue this at some point."

I shrug, unsure if I want to. Maybe Riva feels better but I sure as fuck don't. She stands and thanks Dell before she approaches me with a kind expression.

"I've always admired your tattoos, knowing my father gave them to you. It was just hard to look at them thinking the things I did."

"I guess I can understand that since it is kind of how I've been looking at you."

She smiles a warm smile and grazes her thumb over the ink on my hand.

"You are a beautiful man tortured by a haunted past, and I just want you to know that I've prayed for you every single day since I was the young girl who found the pictures."

I say nothing as she checks her watch and leaves to get back to the daycare. Maybe she's not as bad as I thought she was. Maybe she too is a victim in all of this as well, and I'm misdirecting who the blame should be focused on. Losing her father the way she did couldn't have been easy, even if he did deserve it. The Paulson's really fucked up a lot of lives, Riva's included.

"How do you think that went?" Dell asks.

He removes the lid from the candy jar and holds it in front of me.

"I think she got a happier ending out of it than I did, that's what I think," I say unhappily.

I take as big a handful as I can get and shove them in my pocket, now feeling much happier.

"But your story is not over yet, son, and happy endings always come to him who has the most candy."

I laugh knowing he means me as we walk to the door.

"Oh yeah, Vix told me to tell you that the party starts at eight next Friday and not to be late."

"I'll be there not a second later," he says proudly. "And I will be expecting the answers to questions eight and ten."

I nod and jam my face full of bears, making sure I can't tell him eight is off-limits. And since that's the case, my happy ending probably is too.

CHAPTER 27
Learning to Co-parent

When I first told Vixen about the therapy session with Riva last week, she was pissed. Not because of the actual meeting itself, but because she said she would have been there to support me. She was so mad she swore twice, *out loud*, and while Liv was fighting with Mac again of all things. But then I mentioned how I felt a sense of peace when I'd walked home that day.

It occurred to me that Riva deserves my support and sympathy just as much as she'd offered me hers. I know being trapped and alone in the dark world we once lived that it didn't just affect me, Ken, Cliff, and Verna; it had damaged Riva as well. Maybe not in all of the same ways the rest of us felt it, but it impacted her in other ways. But knowing Dell, I'm sure he'll help her sort that shit out and, in the meantime, I've asked Vixen to invite Riva and her daughter to my party tonight, *because yay me*, it's my real birthday today, and I want to make sure bygones can be bygones. I'm actually pretty stoked about meeting Riva's kid. I'd love to see Liv play with another child her age and one that won't be inclined to chew on her baby dolls either.

"Drop it! You bad puppy!" Liv yells.

"Yeah, Mac, be a good boy," I tell him. "Come and I'll get you a toy of your own."

Mac growls at Liv, tugging on the doll as Liv pulls hard in the opposite direction, also growling, shaking and yanking the baby every which way.

"He so bad, Daddy! Fuck you, puppy!" Liv screeches.

I ram my face into my arm hard, busting out laughing and trying to control it.

"What did you just say, Olivia?" Vixen asks. "That is a very bad word, we don't talk like that. Drop it! Now Mac!"

Finally, he listens as I compose myself and look down at Vixen's serious face as she talks to Liv at eye level from her knees.

"Do you see this pretty little dolly with her pink dress and tiara?" Vix asks Liv.

Liv shakes her head up and down before she takes it from her mom and hugs the doll tight.

"That baby is a princess, just like *you* are a princess, and princesses *do not ever* say bad words," Vixen explains.

"Olif and baby princess!" Liv copies.

"That's right. Beautiful, sweet, smart princesses. Now no more bad words, please."

Liv shrieks happily as Vixen kisses her cheek relentlessly before she instructs Olivia to clean up some of her other toys.

"And you," Vixen then says looking at me with contempt.

"Me?" I ask, wondering how the heck I'm in trouble.

"Yes, you! Birthday or not, you have got to learn to stop laughing and hiding every time Liv does something bad but funny. Why do I always have to be the bad mom giving her trouble?"

"But you're not a bad mom. You're the best mom ever," I assure her. "Even if you did teach her a really bad word," I point out.

"Gee, thanks for mentioning that, you big jerk. Go and start your homework or something."

She walks away flustered and shaking her head.

I guess I shouldn't have told her that Dell expects me to do homework again.

I stick my tongue out at her back and Liv giggles, so I stick it out at her too as I head to the desk.

"Mommy not princess!" Liv says, tugging at my leg.

"Yes, your mommy most definitely *is* a princess," I correct.

"No! Mommy say bad word!" Liv growls.

I can tell she's confused by Vixen's explanation which isn't good considering my wife feels like the 'bad mommy.'

"You know the mean sister princesses from the movie with the pumpkin carriage?" I ask.

"Cinrella!" Liv hollers jumping up and down.

"Yeah, that one. Mommy is like one of the cranky sisters... she's still a beautiful princess, but sometimes she's bad. Mommy is a vixen princess."

Liv's tiny face twists up all cute as if she's thinking.

"Mommy fix it princess?" she asks.

"No, vix-en princess," I repeat.

"Oh! Mommy *fix* it princess!"

I nod my head a bunch of times and smile, knowing she'll get it soon enough, just as Vixen calls her over to the table for lunch.

Now staring at a blank page in my journal, I write down the number ten and circle it in a continuous pattern trying to think of an answer.

The only thing I know I would change besides the years I spent feeling dead inside, would be the secret I keep from my wife. If I could go back, I would tell her the truth, and maybe it would have altered time. Stopped Robert from killing himself in the garage that very morning after I left.

"Jesus!" I shout, startled by Vixen's appearance behind me.

"I hope you know you are going to burn a hole in that page if you keep circling that number, birthday boy."

I put the pen down and sigh.

"How would you answer question ten then? I feel like it's an impossible thing to ask somebody to answer."

"It's not impossible, Liam, it's just hard. Truthfully, I'd probably have an answer similar to yours."

"But I don't have an answer yet," I point out.

"Yes, you do. You just don't want to admit it."

"And how do you know that?"

"I know it," she pauses, dragging me to the sofa, "because," she continues, "it's the same thing that's bothered us both for years."

There's no way we are talking about the same thing.

She lays her head on my lap and looks up at me like an angel. Her face radiates the connection we've always shared. She doesn't need words to tell me how she feels, it's written in her eyes and the way she breathes. Right now, she's afraid to say what she's thinking.

"Tell me, Kirsten. What is it you think I'm afraid to admit?"

"Don't say my name in that tone," she gripes. "It's not going to help you get it out of me."

"Why not?" I laugh, "you do it to me all the time."

"Not true! You only got a real name a week ago! You've had all week to answer the question which means you would want to change something, but you're too afraid to say what it is."

Ignoring her accurate assumption, I say, "I'm not going to argue with you about this. Liv's down for her nap and we both know where anger gets us."

Vixen raises her brows twice.

"And what's wrong with a little trip to HFC if she's sleeping?"

"First off," I say in my mock Vixen voice, "we might wake her up. Second, we'd be arguing right through my entire party, and third, I don't know what kind of damage I'll do to you with how mad I'd be."

"Oh, please," she scoffs. "I don't sound like that and when have you ever actually 'damaged' me during sex?"

"Never. But this would be different."

"Different how?"

"Different, different."

"That is not computing for me, Liam, sound out the vowels and elaborate please."

I sigh, starting to feel annoyed, knowing full well that she is not going to drop this.

"I am not answering anymore of yours or Dell's stupid questions. I give up," I say, throwing my hands in the air.

"Fine… be a dork… see if I don't love you all the same either way."

"Did you seriously just—"

"Yes, I did. I called you a dork and look at how I am not running away either," she pushes.

I growl under my breath, now mad that she wants to get me riled like this, and for what? An answer she's going to damn well hate.

Taking a deep breath, I shut my eyes for a moment, willing myself to stop letting her get under my skin.

"Come on, dork, I'm waiting for a lesson in all things hate-fuck."

"Stop being an asshole, Kirsten."

"Then stop being a chicken shit, Liam. Either fuck me or tell me what I already know."

I throw my head back against the sofa and run my fingers hard over my face and into my hair.

"That's just it. You don't know, and I can't fucking tell you. So, please, I'm only going to ask you one more time. Stop."

There is a long pause of silence and for a few seconds I think she gets how trapped I feel which makes me so mad it literally hurts.

"Or. Else. What?" she then taunts, now standing. "What are you going to do if I don't stop?"

"Oh, it's fucking on," I warn her. "You want to push me into hate-fuck territory, well you got it, Vixen. You win, turn the fuck around."

She smiles like she's just won a bet against herself as I stand, remove my belt from my pants, and secure her wrists behind her back with it. I jerk it so damn hard and tight she lets out a gasp.

"Still smiling?" I ask as I whip my pants down. She says nothing as I pull hers down too and bend her over the arm of the sofa.

The things my body wants to do to her are unforgiving, but my mind is now on emergency mode and warning me to stop.

What am I doing? She's not even angry for fuck's sake.

This is not who I am, and I won't do it just because she thinks it will get her an answer or ease my discomfort. I unstrap her wrists and pull up my pants as she turns to face me, her face flushed with inquiry.

"I was enjoying that, you know," she whines.

"Don't lie, Vixen, we both know you wouldn't have liked anything about it. You're not even in the right mind frame."

"Why? Because I'm not seething or foaming at the mouth right now?"

"Benji! That's exactly right."

"You mean bingo, not Benji," she clarifies. "And I don't need to be angry to handle the way you release your hate, Liam. I'm tougher than you think. I'm also smarter to."

"What is that supposed to mean? Are you seriously poking fun at my third-grade mind and my destructive nature at the same time?"

"Never," she laughs. "I'm just saying that I can *not only* handle your roughness, I can also handle the motive that drives the need. I love you and I know you. I know that if I had said stop, you would have."

My heart pounds and I swallow, knowing she is right and with our eyes locked together, I take in this magnificent creature of knowledge and beauty. This woman who has no fear of me or what I am, but instead wants to take all of my burdens willingly.

Maybe she could still love me if I told her the truth.

I get up and walk to the shelf above the TV where a photo of Robert is prominently displayed along with Liv's bedtime book and I study his face as I grab the story.

"Star-crossed lovers *indeed*," I mutter under my breath.

Maybe her father was right, and if we really are star-crossed lovers as he once said, the stars have done a horrible job of keeping us apart, and that which hasn't killed us, makes us inseparable.

At least I think that's how the saying goes.

I hand the book to Vixen and kneel at her feet as she studies it.

"My dad used to read this to me every night from the time I was five until I was at least twelve," she recalls. "I miss him, and I love that you try to carry on his tradition with Liv. But I know you never stole this book like you told me, Liam," she pauses and takes my hand. "I know because I wasn't sleeping... so please, tell me the truth."

I lift my head from her lap and stare into the complexity of her conflicted eyes.

"Your father... he gave it to me," I pause searching my soul for the words.

I take a hidden breath and continue in a whisper.

"He said that me and you are like Romeo and Juliet. He told me that he knew why we were in love."

She runs her fingers through my hair the way she always does when she's intently listening to me confess my evils.

"Tell me what else he said."

I gnaw on my lip inspecting her face and I think maybe she does already know, but now she wants to hear it, out loud from me, like it's part of a storybook.

"He said that the pain he saw in your eyes, he saw in mine too, and that he loved you. He didn't seem to like that you loved me, however, and called me some names, but then he called me son."

"Because he did love you," she smiles with tears in her eyes. "And probably more so because you *didn't* go through with the plan."

My breath hitches and my heart stops.

"You know about the plan?" I ask almost inaudibly.

Vixen nods her head and takes a profound breath.

"Of course I know. It was my idea."

Motherfucker, is this for real?

I rub my eyes and look at her again, but her face is dead serious.

"Holy fuck. We are talking about the same 'plan' right?"

Again, she nods and smiles.

"I'm a vixen, what can I say?"

"No fucking kidding," I laugh still shocked. "Now I have questions, a lot of them."

"I would expect nothing less, but I need to ask you one first."

I gesture at her to go ahead as my mind swirls, completely disoriented.

"Does it change the way you look at me?"

I shake my head.

"Not a single bit."

"Really? Not even like this much?" she asks holding her finger and thumb just sixteenths apart.

"Still a big. Fat. No."

"But I plotted with my father to kill Satan, well my mother, but back when she behaved like the devil. And that changes nothing for you?"

"I accepted the fucking bounty on her head!" I laugh hysterically. "Wait... does that mean you look at me funny now?"

"Uh-uh, no way in hate-fuck city could I ever love you less than I always have."

I cup my hands around her face and kiss her foul little mouth, holding back the joyous relief in my chest that wants to explode into tears. Then I stop, knowing I have too many more questions I need to ask.

"So, did you know I met your father at a diner then?"

She nods.

"Was it random or were you both in on that too?"

"Random, of course, you big dummy," she says, smacking me. "Do you really think my dad would have taken me 'killer shopping?'"

I shrug, totally knowing it's possible but not likely.

"And what about the night at Dellwood Park? Was that random too?"

"No... that was luck," she emphasizes.

"Fate," I correct. "So, when did he tell you that I was supposed to be Helen's hitman?"

"The night he almost beat you with a baseball bat because we were hate-fucking in my closet," she smiles naughtily.

"Stop smiling like that. You do realize we are both guilty of conspiracy to commit murder, right?"

She scoffs.

"You can't even spell conspiracy, never mind the fact Helen's still alive and well, living it up with her sponsor as we speak."

"That doesn't change what we did, and for your information, I can so spell that word."

She shakes her head doubtfully.

"Alright, let's hear it then. Spell conspiracy."

"Are you serious? We are talking about our sins, not to

mention the fact your father took his life which I assumed was my fault for not offing your mother."

"No, Liam, my dad's death is still on my mother, not me or you. We might be tainted as all hell, but that woman is solely responsible for destroying my dad, even though I've forgiven her," she says heatedly, pausing to compose herself. "Now spell the damn word or you are not getting a party, never mind any red smileys I might have up my sleeve."

I give her the *fuck me you are evil* face and sound the word out in my head.

"C-o-n-s-p-e-a-r-a-s-s-y... conspiracy," I boast proudly.

"Nope, but it was a valiant effort," she applauds. "But you'd better go and finish your homework with the biggest lie you can think of while I get Liv up and dressed. We still need to head over to The Olive King to decorate."

I laugh to myself about her skewed way of thinking even though I admire how badass she is. I think Liv's right and her mother is a fix-it princess, because whether it's with lies, love, or spelling lessons, that woman does manage to fix absolutely everything, no matter how badly it's corrupted. I'm one of those things.

I take a seat at the desk and quickly scribble down the only thing I know I would change as I look back on my life, and then I shove the journal in the desk.

"Hey, Mac, come here boy."

I pat my leg and he runs over to me from his dog bed that Vixen bought when she picked up food for him. It looks a lot like the mat I used to sleep on and I hate it, but I never told her that. She thinks she did something good, something special for him and I don't want to wreck that. I scratch behind his ears and rub his head, hoping he feels as loved as I do.

As seen as I do.

As important as I do.

The mat he sleeps on does not define him. He's good and

loyal, just like me.

I'll make sure he knows that.

"I'll make sure you know it, Mac. The shitty bed is not permanent, I promise. And you're a good boy, *a really good boy*, but please stop chewing on Liv's baby dolls, bud. You're really bringing the vixen out in her."

"Are you talking to Mac like he actually understands you?" Vixen asks.

I look over at her and Liv, the two most beautiful women in the entire world, and I nod.

"He does understand me," I inform. "He knows he's the luckiest dog on the planet, as am I. Taking the two of you to the party will be the most unforgettable night of my life, of that I am sure."

"You are no dog, Liam King, and no person, or animal in the entire universe will ever understand you completely, but I'm willing to try. So please, let Mac be a dog, and let me worry about fulfilling your desire to be understood."

Her tone tells me she's either mad or insulted by my conversation with Mac, so I nod.

"Oh, Daddy so bad! Make Momma so mad!" Liv says from Vixen's hip. "Fuck you, Daddy! Momma haf to fix-it!"

Oh, for the love of God, why Liv? Mommy is so not happy right now.

I scratch my head as I swallow down my urge to hide while laughing as I take Liv from Vixen's arms and then set her on her feet.

My gosh, she is the cutest little thing in her light pink party dress with matching velvet shoes and a bow in her curly hair.

I kneel down like Vix does and take Liv's tiny hands into mine.

"Remember how I told you that Mommy is the vixen princess from the movie?"

"Cinrella movie!" Liv cheers.

"Yeah, exactly... well like I said, Mommy can be cranky sometimes like those evil sister vixen princesses, and guess what that means?"

Liv's eyes grow big and she growls as if she's mad.

"Mommy say bad word!"

"Yep! She sure did. But guess what else?" I ask in my super mysterious tone.

"Mommy fix-it?" she asks clapping.

If I knew how hard it would be to talk to a kid this adorable, I'd have adopted all of them and had an army of miniature swearing partygoers.

"No, Olivia, listen to Daddy. Vixen princesses are very bad girls. When they say bad words, puppies sometimes come and eat their baby dolls, just like Mac did to your baby. But since Mommy doesn't have a baby doll, Mac is going to chew her very favorite shoes instead."

Liv gasps and looks at her mom as do I, jutting my head toward the closet, hoping she'll get the idea.

Vixen's jaw drops and she squints at me but listens and calls Mac over as she finds and then gives him one of her shoes.

Happy as all hell, Mac lays down immediately and goes to town on it as Liv watches in horror.

"Bad puppy! You drop it!" Liv shouts.

"It's his now, because I said a horrible word," Vixen reiterates. "And next time you say one, Mac is going to eat one of your baby princesses."

Liv covers her eyes and shakes her head, devastated.

I feel bad, really bad, but at the same time, I hope this works.

"Olif no say bad word," she assures, peeking in between her fingers.

I stand and smile at Vixen who is smiling back at me, both of us holding in our laughter from our shameless parenting tactics.

I wink at her and mouth the words, *I am the coolest fucking dad there ever did was!*

CHAPTER 28
Learning to Seek Justice

I sit here in the warmth of the sand, outside the bar, and through the window, I watch Vixen feeling totally mesmerized. She's in there decorating for the party, always looking to get freaky on a Friday night that girl. Some things will never change. I love that about her. She is a complete and total badass, but still, I cannot believe she was in on the very plot that had me guilt-ridden for years. The last thing I ever expected was to tell her the truth, but then I did and once again she's managed to knock my shoes off. Are we really star-crossed lovers as Robert said? Nah, I think we are more like fate-crossed lovers, or tainted lovers. The kind of people who hold their own and at the drop of a pin would lay down their life for the other. I know I would.

It's surreal, getting to watch my new life unravel before my eyes. My name is Liam King, I was born on the thirteenth of November, and I'm alive to say it and live it. I take a swig of my celebratory beer and continue to watch in awe. The place is packed tonight and there are red balloons floating around and a banner with my name on it in gold writing. I look at Riva and her daughter playing with Liv and Mac, or more so harassing him, but he kind of deserves it; plus I think the attention is good for him. Then I look over at Jack and Jimmy running the counter like old times, the coolest friends a guy could have, and then there's Dell. The old wise guy is in there mingling and probably handing out business cards since my time with him is almost done.

These are the moments I could never have imagined as a kid, the feeling of a warm breeze on my skin on the day I was born and surrounded by people who make every day a day worth living.

God it's nice to be loved.

"What the heck are you doing out here, hobo? Party's inside," I hear from behind me.

What the shit?

My hand tightens into a fist.

"Who the fuck you callin' hobo?" I ask, turning to meet eyes with the jerk.

Gabe laughs and puts his hand out.

"Happy birthday, Liam, is it?"

I nod, relieved as I shake his hand.

"Yep that's me now. Wow! You're looking good, schmuck," I smile, adjusting his suit jacket.

Leave it to Vixen to invite this douche... makes me wonder if Helen and Claire are coming to liven my party too. I reach into the cooler beside me and hand him a beer.

"So, what brings you all the way down here?"

"Business," he says snapping the cap off. "But I'd like to step inside first and say hello to Kirsten and Liv if you don't mind."

I give him a once over and growl lightly under my breath.

"Be my guest, but I'll be watching you," I warn.

He laughs as if I'm messing with him, and heads inside. I'd be lying if I said I'm not still pissed about the time that arrogant fucker let my wife go down on him.

I sip my beer watching as Vixen hugs him and then picks Liv up to get one too.

Then I look over at Dell who's eyeing me over and heading to the door.

I pat the sand beside me as he makes his way over.

"It's quite the party in there," he says loosening his tie. "I see why you're out here, though. It's pretty crowded and so much cooler out here. Mind if I ask who the suit chatting with Vixen is?"

"You mean besides you?" I laugh. *They have got to be the only two people crazy enough to wear a suit to a bar.* "That's Gabe, he's Vixen's mother's ex and a lawyer schmuck from the Hill."

"Oh," he says scratching his head. "Nice of him to come down here for the celebration."

"Yeah, sure I guess," I say, noticing I can no longer see him or my wife.

I stand and open the door to enter, barely managing to move in time as Mac, Liv, and Zoe run full tilt out the door and onto the beach squealing.

"Don't worry, I'll keep an eye on them," Riva says chasing after them.

I look back a Dell, feeling wary about letting Riva look after Liv, alone.

"Just go, have some fun!" Dell winks, "I'll keep an eye on all of them."

I smile in appreciation and take one last look at Liv chasing Mac in circles hollering 'bad puppy' as Zoe teases him with a stick. Riva stands watching them intently and then looks back at me giving me a thumbs up before I head inside feeling somewhat reassured.

I scan the crowded bar but don't see Vix anywhere, so I head to the counter.

"What can I get you, birthday boy?" Jack asks.

"The location of my wife would be pretty neat!"

"Not this again," he gripes, "please tell me you're not going to freak out and shut the place down again."

"No," I laugh. "She's here somewhere with Gabe, have you seen them?"

"They went to the back," Jimmy says, gesturing behind him. "I think it was too loud out here for them."

Too loud for what? I swear if she's giving him a hate-blow I'll kill the son of a bitch.

I nod and step past the counter into the back, checking the stock room and then the washroom. No luck. Then I exit through the back door surprised to see them arguing before they notice me and fall silent.

"Well, I'm glad to see your pants are still on," I tell Gabe. "Now I just need to know what the hell is going on out here."

Vixen puts her hands on my shoulders, her eyes dancing with confliction as my heart starts to pick up speed.

"I think we should head home and have a talk. Jimmy agreed to take Liv for the night, and I'd like Dell to join us as well."

My first thought is that we've been busted for the plot to kill Helen, but then I look over at Gabe and the pained look on his face tells me I'm off base.

"A talk? Why? Are we in trouble or something?"

"No, Liam," Vixen sighs. "Now can you please just trust me and not ask questions until we get home?"

I bite my lip, hating that she won't just tell me, but if I've learned anything about my wife, it's that she has a good reason.

"Fine, lead the way then."

I open the door for Vixen and then gesture at Gabe to follow her, but he shakes his head.

"You go first, I'm a gentleman," he says smiling goofily.

"Bullshit you are," I laugh, "you're still a schmuck and we both know it."

* * *

Five days later...

There are no words to describe the crushing feeling when you are told someone you love has died.

There are no words to take away the pain when the world is spinning and all you want to do is make it stop.

There is no way to stop the questions that take over when you wonder if somehow it's your fault. If somehow, you could have stopped it from happening.

I have never been to a funeral besides Robert's. I'd never told Vixen that being there, surrounded by sad faces and emotionless people reminded me of my time in the basement. It was a gathering of hurt, pain, and suffering that was familiar to me. I hated being there, but now, somehow, I have to find the will to attend another one.

I wipe the tears from my eyes and take a staggering breath through the pain as I button my suit shirt. *I wish I had told her how much I loved her.*

But Verna is gone. The first person who taught me what love is, and what a supermarket and zoo were. The same person who always thought she'd find a fairy-tale at the end of the nightmare.

It hurts like hell knowing now that she will never get to meet Liv, or know my name, and all because the past has come back to haunt us all. Call it fate or shit luck, it doesn't matter, but it's what drove Verna over the edge. She hadn't given up searching for her parents and some cop finally listened to her story. He'd taken her seriously and without her knowledge, he'd set up a team of undercover cops to investigate the imposters. What they found was an abandoned house in a field somewhere, with a dark basement that held two abducted kids. They'd also found old evidence that supported everything Verna had told them about our lives eleven years ago. When the cop brought the news to Verna, he still hadn't located her parents, but instead, he asked her and Ken to testify at the new trial. They have been officially charged with child abduction, child abuse, and child exploitation just for starters. Verna refused, said it would kill her to have to relive it all, and instead she gave them the name Kirsten King and told them to look for me. During their search, they learned that Verna had taken her life on a morning last week while they sat at a table with Helen King and her partner Claire. Having a lot to say, Claire told them everything she knew about me and the things I'd told her. From there, Helen and Claire then called Gabe and told him I was in need of a lawyer, a friend, and someone to tell me about Verna's death before the cops could.

It was not the birthday I had hoped for and not the death my sister deserved.

The sound of Vixen's heels approaching tell me I need to dress faster as she enters the room.

"I've got Liv buckled in the van with Jack and Jimmy. We're ready to go as soon as you're done dressing."

I look back at her comforting face in the reflection of the mirror as I adjust the collar of my suit jacket and I smile.

"Do you really think Ken can win in court with the new evidence that was found?"

"I don't know," she shrugs. "But if he wants to try as a way to bring justice to Verna, then we are going to support him. Now come, Liam, we can't be late for the funeral."

"I need another minute and then I'll be ready."

She kisses my cheek and then leaves the room as I pull out a folded paper from my pocket. On one side is the eulogy I've written to represent Verna's life and on the other is question number ten.

If I looked back upon my life at all of the good, bad, and indifferent moments, what would I change?

Written below that is my answer.

I, Liam Whiskey King, cannot change the past, only the future. And if I ever get the chance, I swear on everything I am, that I will make them pay.

BOOK III
TAINTED LOVE
The Complete Trilogy

CHAPTER 29
Monsters
LIAM KING

It's been six months since my sister Verna's funeral. Six very long months full of police interviews that have felt more like interrogations at times, and still, *I'd rather be doing that than sitting here.* Vixen and I are over two thousand miles from home in a place called Billings, Montana. The official place the new trial against the Paulson's is set to be held in just one year's time.

I hate this place, *everything about it*, especially the news crazed reporters that stand outside the front door waiting to attack. For some reason they think my life is the biggest news ever, or that I have more to say than I've already told the cops. It's a nightmare if you ask me, one I can't seem to wake up from, but I'm really trying.

I stand quietly, feeling overdressed in the suit Vixen made me wear, and in an unfamiliar sitting room taking in the family photo of the Whitmores'. It hangs on the wall above their marble-encased fireplace mantle, and it's hand painted.

The portrait consists of Verna's parents, Susan and Lyle Whitmore, and her two younger sisters, Margaret and Valerie. I could easily have mistaken both of them for Verna when she was their age; the resemblance is uncanny. But there is no Verna in the picture. Instead, her photo sits directly below the portrait because her sisters hadn't been born until many years after she was taken.

"Can I offer you something to drink?" Susan offers.

"No thanks," I say, unable to pry my eyes from the photos.

Her family seems nice, I'd only met them once, briefly at the funeral when Ken buried her in Clancy. I'd heard rumors that her parents weren't thrilled about it. They wanted to bring her body 'home.' But both Dell and Gabe were kind enough to reach out to them on behalf of myself and Ken, and they made it clear that it was in their professional opinions, it would be in the Whitmores' best interests to support 'the victims' and our wishes. I didn't like being referred to as a 'victim' but for Ken's sake I let it slide. Verna was his whole life once we'd made it out, and I wasn't about to let anyone tell him how to handle her death.

"Liam, they have questions. Do you want to come sit?" Vixen asks.

I want to say fuck no, but I take her offered hand and follow her to the sofa. Across from us are Verna's parents, her mother isn't so hard to look at with her blonde hair tied to the side and her warm smile. But her father, he's not so easy to look at. He's clearly the genetics master; it's like looking at Verna if she was just a few inches shorter, wore a suit, and was still alive.

I look away from him not wanting to see the struggled look on his face. It's as if I manage to both disgust and intrigue him at the same time. I've been in their house for the last half hour and he hasn't said one word to me. I can tell he resents me.

Susan clears her throat and pushes a plate of cookies toward me.

"Please, help yourself, they are fresh baked. Our oldest, Margaret, made them."

"But she's not your oldest," I remind her, feeling a sense of anger. "Alive or dead, that title should go to Verna."

Her expression turns guilty as her husband looks down at the floor.

"I'd love a cookie," Vixen says.

She leans forward to get one and then grabs my hand before she sits back and looks me in the eyes.

"I'm sure that's not what Susan meant, Liam. This isn't a contest, and we aren't here to judge each other."

"Could have fooled me," I say, focused in on Lyle. "I'm always being judged, if not by these two, it'll be by the reporter assholes outside on the lawn. We shouldn't have come here."

I stand to leave, but Lyle stands as well.

"Please don't blame Susan, it's me who shouldn't be at this meeting," he assures.

His eyes are the spitting image of Verna's, so dark they are unreadable.

"Why don't you show me around Lyle?" Vixen asks. "I'd love a tour and a quiet place to call my mother to check up on Liv anyway."

I can tell what she really wants is to leave me alone with Verna's mother and judging by Susan's face, she agrees.

"Sure, I'd be more than happy to show you around," Lyle offers, leading Vixen out of the room.

I glance between the front door that I know is crawling with the press and then back at Susan before I hesitantly take my seat again.

"So..." Susan smiles awkwardly, "I assume Liv is your daughter."

"She is."

"How old?"

"Almost three."

"Three... wow! I miss that age. Margret just turned thirteen and Valerie will be twelve in May. Is your daughter an only child?"

I nod, thinking about how old Verna would be, annoyed that Susan can't seem to say her name.

"We adopted Olivia and we are currently in the process of adopting a son."

"Right, I forgot you weren't able to have children because of what they did to you—" Susan covers her mouth. "Oh God, I'm sorry, I don't know why I just said that."

Her embarrassment is kind of humorous, the way her face is instantly seven hues redder like Verna's used to get.

"It's fine, really. You aren't the first person to be curious about what we went through. But can I ask you something personal?"

She fiddles with her pearl necklace as if it's somehow helping her regain her composure.

"Of course, please, ask me anything."

"Why did you have more kids after Verna?"

"Well, to be honest, my husband thought it was time. Eight years had gone by, a long eight years of searching and praying Verna would be found. It was such a long, dark time. Seeing her face plastered over windows and lamp posts, never sleeping, never eating, it was like time had just stopped the day they took her. Eventually, it all took a toll on Lyle, he wanted to feel whole again. And for as much as I felt responsible for taking my eyes off her that day, I felt I owed him. It was never about replacing Verna; I hope that's not how you see it."

I smile thinking back to when Verna said she bet they were searching for her.

"I try not to judge, and I know it might be pointless to know this now, but Verna knew you guys wouldn't give up. I just wish she could have seen you once more before she—"

Unable to say it out loud, I bite my lip to the thought of her pulling the trigger.

Susan's eyes light up, flashing a glimmer of relief.

"She talked about us while she was with you in that horrible place?"

"All of the time. She never stopped talking. She said her house was a mansion, and that she had a cat she hated. She told me her parents were the best. She searched for you guys for years once we got out, but we all had our ages wrong and couldn't remember enough... well, you know the rest."

A tear falls from her eye and she sighs.

"I'm just thankful she had you and the other two there with her. I know that is a terrible thing for me to say, and maybe that makes me a horrible person," she breathes out, "but I'm so relieved she wasn't stuck suffering alone for all of those years."

I open my mouth to speak just as I hear Vixen gasp and turn to take in her expression of repulsion.

"Holy fuck, lady! Are you insane? Did you just say you're happy my husband was molested and abused? You bet your ass your goddamn right to admit you're a heartless fucking monster!"

I stand instantly, trying to block the view between Susan and Vixen, forcing my wife to look at me. Her face is angrier than I've ever seen it, and I think Susan may end up getting strangled.

"Vixen," I say calmly, "I don't think she meant—"

"I don't fucking care what she meant, Liam!" she scolds, trying to look around me. "Who the hell says that kind of shit to someone who's survived the things you have?"

Her face is full of fury and each time she moves to the right or left of me in an attempt to yell some more, I block her.

"Vixen, calm down please," I beg.

"I will not calm down, Liam, that bitch just said some unforgivable shit! Get your jacket, we are leaving."

"If I could just say something—" Susan pleads.

"Oh no, lady, you may not say fuck the fuck all!" Vixen

growls. "Sit the hell down and do not try to talk to my husband again."

Vixen hands me my jacket as I shrug at Susan and then follow Vixen down the hall, passing Lyle who looks just as distraught as I feel.

"Thanks for the tour," Vixen says, "and you might want to beat that shitty wife of yours into finding her goddamned manners in every single room of this place."

He says nothing in response as Vixen rams the door open and drags me into their backyard.

"You were right," she says looking around for the gate. "We should not have come here."

"Why? Because of Susan's desire to find comfort in her daughter's time of need?"

"At your fucking expense, Liam. Did you miss that part?"

"No," I say pointing out the latch on the fence. "I just don't think she meant it the way that you're taking it."

She growls and kicks the gate open, starting to speed walk down the street.

Not wanting to make her angrier, I try to keep up and glance behind us at the reporters who were smart enough to keep tabs on the back entrance.

"Fuck," I mutter, now walking faster than Vixen. "Do not look behind you, and when we hit the next house with a yard, follow me."

"Oh God, they're onto us?"

"Yep!"

Both of us now sprinting, I grab her arm and pull her into the next yard, stopping to boost her over the fence before I climb my way over.

We land hard on the other side, interrupting what appears to be a child's birthday party.

"Hello," I say to one shocked elderly lady. "My name's Liam, and this is my wife, Kirsten. We just need you to point us in the direction of the exit, please."

I smile my best *we aren't crazy* smile as she points to her left, speechless and gobsmacked.

"Thanks, and happy birthday, Josie!" I say reading the banner across the trampoline.

"That says Jose, the J is silent," Vixen points out.

"Right, I knew that... happy birthday to whichever one of you is Jose," I correct, dragging my wife quickly passed the bouncy tent to the exit.

I look both ways and then we jog to a nearby park and take a breather in some bushes.

Vixen reaches out to inspect the tear in my suit jacket as I scan over the matching rip in her blouse.

She shrugs and laughs.

"At least we made it away from the frenzied reporters, even if we are lost in some crappy city miles from home."

"We shouldn't be laughing," I say pulling her up against me. "You weren't very nice to Verna's parents."

"What's your point? Neither of them was very nice to you."

"I think Susan was trying until you snapped on her, Vixen. It's Lyle who seems to loathe me."

"He doesn't loathe you," she says, peeking around the bushes. "He just has a hard time looking at you and imagining the things you all went through. I don't see the reporters; I think it's safe to call a cab."

"Well, why is he trying to imagine it when I'm always trying to forget it?" I growl.

"I don't know, it's just the way people are built. Curiosity I guess, some people probably wonder if they could have survived something so brutal if it were them."

Searching around for a landmark, Vixen dials a cab and gives them the name of the park.

I stand and help her up from the ground, unsatisfied with her answer.

"So, then that would mean Susan wasn't completely wrong to say what she said... I mean if she was only trying to envision how Verna made it through."

Vixen shakes her head and scowls.

"I'm not going to debate this with you. She was dead wrong to wish that life upon you and that is the end of it."

I decide to drop it, *for now*, and follow her to the bench, keeping my eye out for the cab. I'm thankful we are only staying two more days and heading back home after we meet with Gabe tomorrow. He's been handling the case and working with both Ken's lawyer and the city prosecutor, making sure every charge they want to enforce will stick. Between mine and Ken's statements, plus the two kids that were abducted after the imposters' original release, we think there is enough evidence for the DA to seek the death penalty if they are found guilty. The statute in the state of Montana upholds special provisions for sexual crimes committed against minors that were twelve or under. Vixen says we are getting front row seats on that day if it comes, and I'll be holding an empty chair for Verna.

The cab finally arrives, and we climb in the back. Vixen tells the driver the name of our hotel as I mess around with the window button.

"Quit that," Vixen grumbles, "you always give Liv trouble for doing that exact same thing."

"That's because I didn't realize how fun it is."

I press it up and down a few more times and then she smacks me.

"Play with your phone if you want to press buttons," she scolds. "And what's with you anyway? You haven't said one word about the meeting tomorrow."

"Why would I be thinking about that?"

"Because it's a huge part of why we're here. I want you to be prepared for whatever Gabe might have to say. Come May, the trial will be in full swing and it's going to come faster than you think."

It can't come fast enough, I think to myself. This isn't just about justice for me, Ken, Cliff and those other two kids whose names haven't been released due to their ages. It's really about the retribution the imposters deserve for Verna's suicide. For her family who will never get to see her again, and for Ken, who has to somehow move on without her. The news and Vixen seem to view this as some kind of fight for justice, but if you ask me, there is no such thing. Nothing can give any of us back those years, and sure as shit can't bring Verna back. What festers in me now isn't strength, it's hate. Dark, charcoal-colored hate worse than anything I've ever felt. Sometimes I feel like I'm going to explode from the rage that burns in me when I think about having to face the imposters again. I haven't told anyone, but I know it's going to be like trying to contain a nuclear weapon the day I do.

"Shit!" Vixen mumbles.

I look over at the hotel entrance that is swarming with reporters and we duck.

"Pull around the back please," Vixen instructs the driver. "Jeez, don't those vultures ever fuck off?"

"Nope they are the predators searching for their prey, except sadly they can't go to jail for the way they behave."

"We are here, ma'am," the driver says. "It looks clear."

Vixen peeks her head up and nods at me, before she pays the man and we exit the car.

"If they are inside, just put your jacket over our heads and we'll head straight for the elevator," she tells me.

"Maybe I should just talk to them for once. Seems much simpler then running from them all of the time."

"Gabe told us not too, Liam, and besides they only want to

bring up Verna. We both know how hard it is for you to stay composed when her name gets mentioned."

I agree, knowing she's right as usual, and slip past her through the back door. Taking a quick look around and seeing no press, I wave her in, feeling more like the Pink Panther than a hotel guest. We sneak our way to the elevators, and I hit the button just as Vixen grabs my shoulders and turns me toward her. She does not look happy as she squints her eyes and leans left to look around me.

"Liam King! Please, just one comment," a man calls out.

"Do not turn around," Vixen orders.

"Did Verna Whitmore kill herself because of what they did to her or what you did to her? The public wants to know your take on it sir."

I watch Vixen's face turn furious as my fists tighten.

"This fucking elevator better open right now or I'm going to step out and kill that son of a bitch," Vixen roars.

"You and me both."

"Come on, Liam," the reporter taunts. "It's not like she was really your sister. The world deserves to know if you even apologized to her, or did you just continue to abuse her until she took her own life?"

I squeeze my eyes closed listening to the sounds of camera flashes as I grab Vixen's hand, trying to place myself anywhere but here. Half of the world sees me as a victim, and the other half a monster, both sides are wrong, and I'm not even allowed to speak freely or defend myself. How fucked is that?

"It's okay Liam, you're doing good, just block that fucking pig out of your mind," Vixen hisses, her hand gripping mine as if she too wants to tear his throat out.

The ding of the elevator reaching our floor sounds but does nothing to ease the tension in my gut. I pull Vixen inside to the corner and hit every button on the panel, silently begging for the door to close.

The sound of the man's unrelenting voice finally disappears as I stand speechless but tormented by my thought's.

I have no clue how any of it is going to look to a judge, let alone a jury who might paint me just as awful as that reporter did. And then there's the defence lawyer, *David Schneider*, a real fucking schmuck if I ever laid eyes on one. His job is to cause probable doubt regardless of the crimes the Paulsons committed. Gabe warned me that the focus wouldn't just remain on our time in that basement, that my character would be judged. Same for Ken, Cliff, and Verna, God rest her soul. He said that rumors would fly, and gossip would spread, and he was right.

"What are you thinking about?" Vixen asks as the elevator doors open.

I follow her to the room and step inside, wondering if this nightmare will ever end.

"I hate it here, Vix."

"I know, but this isn't going to be forever," she comforts. "You cannot let those reporters get in your head."

"Easier said than done," I sigh.

I remove my jacket and take a seat on the bed, feeling lost somewhere between anger, confusion, and hopelessness watching as Vixen begins to undress.

"You know they're wrong, don't you?"

Her voice is soft, and her eyes give off a sense of pity, which angers me further. *If I don't want the world to view me as such, I don't need Vixen doing it either.*

"Are they really so wrong?" I ask harshly. "Maybe it's you who is wrong about me."

"Why would you say that?" She asks irritably.

"I'm not exactly the ideal man," I point out. "I mean look at me. I'm a walking fucking art exhibit, one who plotted to kill your mother, not to mention the way I use your body on the regular to escape my own flaws. I think they're pretty accurate with their assumptions, and maybe it's more likely I'm the monster they say I am."

"Are you losing your God damned mind?" she scoffs. "This exhibit you speak of, is beautiful for one thing. It's a part of you with its own mind-bending story. Secondly," she says ripping my suit shirt down the middle, "we both plotted to kill Helen, and no one will ever know that, so stop feeling guilty about it. And third," she says removing my shirt and pushing me back onto the bed, "the way we fuck is nobody's business. What you are calling a flaw, I see as an orgasm. And if the way you need to release your anger is through hate-fucking than I guess I'm just as *flawed* as you are."

I look at her unchanging dark expression and it gets my dick twitching.

"Why do I get the feeling you want to argue?"

"Not argue, fuck," she corrects. "And because it's exactly what we both need right now."

"I won't argue with that then," I say, unbuckling my pants and removing them. "But just tell me if I'm too rough, because I'm still pretty mad."

"I'm not afraid of you, Liam," she says boldly, stripping down to nothing. "One day you will understand that."

I breathe in deep as she takes my dick into her hand and begins to stroke it, my eyes locked onto hers. The sensation is nice, a little too slow for my liking, but I get this is her idea of taunting me. She likes to test my limits and see if she can't stir up all of my anger into one giant ball. I get the feeling she thinks I'm capable of letting it all go during sex, for it never to return.

I watch as she kneels down, wanting to take me into her mouth and for as much as I would love it, I stop her and shake my head.

"What now?" she asks crossly.

"I love that you are so angry right now, but I am not going to hate-fuck your mouth."

"Why not? We haven't done it in a while, this could be good for you," she states.

"No. It won't be good for either of us," I warn. "Now get up here and get on my dick."

Ignoring me, I feel the warmth of her mouth enclose around my dick and I'm instantly lost in the divine feeling.

"Fuck, Vixen," I growl.

I close my eyes, taking deep breaths as she begins to move up and down my length in a steady rhythm, my dick becoming harder with each pass.

I swallow, attempting to control my heart rate and my growing urge to fuck her mouth much faster and harder than she's moving.

Do not be the monster, do not be the monster.

Talking to myself is not helping at all.

I open my eyes and realize my hands are tangled through her hair, now completely controlling her head forcefully but she isn't stopping me. It feels incredible, between the power of her pull and how she doesn't react at all to how hard I'm driving myself in and out of her mouth.

Shit, maybe I've always been the monster.

I stop her abruptly and pull her to her feet.

"Seriously?" she hisses. "I'm pretty sure you were enjoying that."

She wipes her lips and stares at me unhappily.

"I don't want to be this *monster* anymore," I mumble.

"What did you just say?"

She takes a seat beside me and forces me to look at her.

"Tell me what the hell you just said about yourself," she demands.

I look away, but she redirects my face back to hers waiting for my answer.

"Of all the things I am... the man who can't read good, write good, and did horrible things to his family as a kid, I can't do this. I can't be the monster who doesn't see you while we're fucking. It will make them right about me."

"That's a load of fucking bullshit if I've ever heard it. God, Liam, you are NOT a monster. And if you are... then what the hell does that make me for letting you feel like you are?"

I shrug, upset by the pain in her eyes, pissed that I've clearly not expressed myself properly. I never know how to say what I'm feeling or thinking. *I hate words*, they are not my strength.

"I think we should just take a minute and reflect."

"You sound like Dell," she opines, shaking her head. "Fine, reflect all you want, I'm going to call my mother again to check on Liv."

I slip my underwear on as she grabs a robe and makes her way out to the sitting room. Nothing in this world could make me love that woman less than I already do, but I'm terrified it won't be the same for her by the end of this. The things she will hear, the way their lawyer will scrutinize every shred of self-worth I've managed to scrounge in this life. I don't think it will be enough. My wife will one day see what I see when I look in the mirror, and then my life as I know it will be over.

CHAPTER 30
Ruthless Creatures
VIXEN KING

How do I make it clear to him? The big fucking dummy in the next room might be infuriating at times, but he is no damn monster.

Fuck the press, and fuck anyone who says otherwise.

I hate that they hold so much power over him, yet they don't even know him. They can't possibly understand who he is, let alone what wounds they are opening in him, but I do. I see the way he struggles with his thoughts, questions his worth, and tries so hard to find himself underneath all of it. This place sure as fuck isn't doing him any good, but I wasn't about to let him hide from the world while Verna's death ate away at him from the inside. There were no good options when the news broke. It was as if the entire world knew their names in the blink of an eye. For the last six months they have been dubbed as 'The Forgotten Four' which is bullshit. No one ever forgot them, they just didn't open their eyes wide enough to see them. Not until it was too late... for Verna at least.

The week after her funeral, Ken and Cliff got news about their father, Richard Dodd. It was their story that broke first and made national headlines. It detailed the story about a father whose two sons had gone missing twenty years earlier from a carnival just two towns over from where Verna was taken the same year. It wasn't long before the rest of the story broke, detailing Verna's abduction from the supermarket and then going full circle back to the boy who'd been kidnapped two years before all of them from an orphanage. That orphanage was just six hundred miles from the supermarket, and where the Paulsons had lured one four-year-old, Liam Kristopher O'Connell into their van.

My Liam.

If you were to look at a map and put a pinpoint marker in between all three locations between Helena, Billings, and Great Falls you would find an area called Livingston and the abandoned shithole they were held captive in. It sat just half a mile from the highway or one thousand two hundred and thirty-three strides as Liam would recall. The place was entirely secluded by wheat fields and because there was never electricity or city water being billed there, it was completely off the grid. One of the hardest parts for me to wrap my head around is how Verna never knew that where she and Ken ended up living in Clancy was just a three-hour drive from where her parents always were. I don't understand why the world is so cruel, it's something that will bother me forever.

It also irritates me to no end that people only know what details the paper has printed and the news has reported, but they don't know the entire story the way I do. Not the way Liam, Ken, and Cliff do. They have no idea what it's like to watch the world both rip apart the names of the people you love, while others offer their support and undying hate for the Paulsons. No one gets what it's like to have watched Ken bury his wife and then learn that his father was dead too. And no one sure as fuck gets what it's like to know their husband feels like a monster. Because if they did, they would be sitting right where I am, smack dab in the center of hell.

It's a good thing I'm Kirsten King and was born in the seventh circle, I can and I will take the heat.

"Dial Helen," I say into my phone.

I take a sip of whiskey as it rings twice and then my mother answers.

"Hello, Kirsten, hold on one second."

I listen as my mother asks Claire to take Liv to another room so we can talk privately. It's been hard trying to keep Liv protected from the negativity and out of the news.

"Sorry, about that," my mother says. "So, how did it go with the Whitmores' this morning?"

"Shitty, Mom, it was a fucking disaster. But I only called for an update on Liv."

"Liv's doing great, she keeps talking about My Chew," she laughs.

"Matthew," I correct with a smile. "Maybe we should teach her to call him Matty, it might be easier for her to say."

"I'll give it a try when I show her his picture again. He's an adorable little thing. Are things still looking good for the end of the month?"

I bring up his picture on my phone and smile, our son is almost a year old. We are adopting him from the same orphanage we found Liv at, and in the midst of all of this ugliness, his beautiful face makes it all melt away.

"Yes, Mom, Matthew is set to finally be ours in eleven days. Let's just hope none of this frenzy causes a problem because God is he perfect."

"Well, they can't just turn away a perfectly loving home because of some malicious clowns, can they?"

I hate the worry in her tone because it's the same worry in my heart.

"I would hope not, but if they do, Gabe will have to fix that too."

"Speaking of Gabe, have you seen him yet?"

"Not until tomorrow, but I have to go, Mom. Please give Livy kisses from me and Liam and tell Claire I say hi."

"I will do that darling, and hey," she warns, "you had better try and relax, I can tell you're letting this stuff get to you. Have a strong drink in my honor, and know that everything is going to be fine, sweetheart."

"Thanks, I appreciate the support."

I laugh as I hang up, thinking about how far she's come from the booze hound she once was. I never thought in a million years I'd have my mother's support, let alone trust her to watch our little extension of a daughter. It's one of the hardest things about all of this, being away from Olivia.

"How's Helen?" Liam asks.

He takes the glass of whiskey from my hand and slams it as he takes a seat beside me.

"She's good, still trying to get Liv to call her brother Matthew instead of My Chew."

"Why? I like the way Liv talks, besides as long as she doesn't pull on his ears like she does to Mac, I think My Chew is going to have the world's best sister."

I laugh and kiss his cheek knowing he's the only person who loves the dog as much as his kids.

"And the world's most heartfelt father," I add. "So, are you done demonizing yourself, or should I go and pour us both another drink?"

"I wasn't demonizing myself," he growls. "I was trying to tell you that I want to learn to be different."

"Different how?"

I stand and take the glass with me to the counter.

"Different as in I want to practice non-hate-fucking."

"Oh," I say pouring two glasses and handing him one. "We're back to this are we?"

I take a seat on the sofa beside him and sip my drink.

"Yes, we're back to this. I don't feel like you're listening to me, Vix."

"I am listening, Liam, trust me. I just think you put too much pressure on yourself trying to get out of your own skin instead of accepting that you are who you are."

He looks at me and shrugs.

"Well you'd feel differently if you were me. You'd want the world to see you as more than just a monster."

I'm instantly aggravated and it makes me want to slap him so damn hard.

"I hate it when you use that word, stop it!"

"Mon...ster. Monster, monster, monster, monster, monster," he repeats.

"Fuck you. Fuck you, fuck you, fuck you, fuck you, and fuck you," I say back. "I'm going for a walk so you can sit here and be a stupid fucking monster by yourself."

"You're only wearing a robe," he points out.

"Like that's going to stop me."

I slip on the hotel slippers by the door, grab the key card from the table and leave.

Sometimes it feels like we are going in circles and I can't take it. Can't take him, because he's so childish and petty when he wants to make a point. Sadly, that's also why I love him so much. The way he's able to push me and show me that I've at least taught him something, even if it is how to stand up for himself.

I press the lobby button in the elevator hoping the press has fucked off by now. Maybe a walk around the place will do me good if I can manage to feel like I'm on vacation for a few minutes. The doors open and I scan the area before I step off, pleased the place is pretty much empty besides the lady at the desk. She's a slim, dirty blonde with nails that look way too long and painted a hideous shade of brown. She eyes me over and smiles, presumably wondering why I'm wandering around in a robe.

"Can I help you with something?" she offers.

"No, I was just trying to take a walk, clear my head," I say trying not to slip. The flooring is overly polished and hard to walk on in slippers.

"We have a gym, a pool, and a spa, all complimentary if any of them sound appealing."

I lean against the desk taking in her curious expression, the one that tells me she recognizes me from the news.

"Thanks, but the only thing I'd find appealing right about now would be my own home, bed, and kid. That or a motorcycle ride."

"I can understand that," she says tapping her nails nervously on the desk. "I'd like to apologize to you for earlier and the way that reporter treated you and your husband. It's not the way we want our guests to be treated. We've instructed the security not to let the press inside if that's of any consolation."

I lean in closer and shake my head.

"Between you and me, the only thing that would console what that man said to my husband would be if I got to stuff his condescending head in between the frame and the wall of the rotating door over there. That would be an excellent start."

She looks at me feigning shock and then laughs before she holds out her hand.

"Melanie," she introduces, as if I hadn't read her name tag.

"Vixen," I say shaking it. "I'm sorry if I'm overly cynical, but God I hate those pricks."

"From what I've seen on TV, I don't blame you," she says. "The Forgotten Four, it's so sad, I don't get how people can be so heartless."

"They aren't forgotten," I say sternly but as calmly as I can. "And it isn't them the world should be focused on. The Paulsons are. They are the sick fucks that destroyed the lives of how many kids and families? Even now, while they get to hide in some prison with cable TV and food better than what they forced those kids to eat, they get to enjoy life while the world depicts my husband and his family as monsters. It's disgusting and unfair. It's a fucking crime in itself."

I take a deep breath realizing I'm ranting to this poor woman and her face is now bewildered.

"I never thought about it that way, wow, you've just opened my eyes to the other side of it," she admits. "I'm truly sorry and wish there was something I could do to help."

I put my hand over hers and smile.

"You already did. You listened."

She nods and I walk back toward the elevators knowing nothing else needs to be said. I feel better and I'm hopeful that the next time she watches the news or hears someone bad mouthing any of the amazing people this has affected, maybe she will become one more person in our corner. Another person to set the record straight in whatever way she can. And if not, at least she knows where the blame should lie.

The elevator doors open and I step on, pressing seven on the panel. Paying no mind to the man in the suit, I adjust my robe and stand in the corner.

"Mrs. King," he says.

I turn to look at his face and my stomach tightens into a knot.

"Mr. Schneider," I nod.

He smiles and extends his hand.

"Just David is fine. I didn't realize we were staying in the same hotel."

I look at his hand and then at his smug face. The Paulsons' lawyer is as shady as it gets with his greased back blonde hair, and beady little brown eyes indicative of what I would call pure evil.

I hit the stop button on the elevator without thinking, and

imagine myself gutting the man with my bare hands before I clear my throat.

"Why are you here, Mr. Schneider?"

He reaches for the panel on the wall but I place myself in front of it and cross my arms.

"You really are a feisty thing, aren't you?" he asks, looking amused.

"Not nearly as feisty as my husband, but I'd like an answer. Why. Are. You. Here?"

My heart is pounding in my chest and I will not let this piece of shit anywhere near Liam.

"I'm meeting with the DA tomorrow if you must know. Now do you mind?" he asks, eyeing the panel.

"What's the matter, David? You afraid to have a conversation with a woman in a robe?"

"Afraid, no," he laughs, "but your husband should be. Because when I get through revealing every dark, dirty, and immoral thing him and those two 'brothers' of his did to that poor girl who killed herself, no one will give two shits about the Paulsons."

I swallow, digging my nails into my hands as I clench my fists willing myself to stay calm.

In a composed whisper and very slowly I say, "Then you don't know fuck all about the law David, and when Gabe is done with those ruthless creatures, they're gonna fry while you watch, and my husband and I will be in the front row watching them squirm and squeal like the filthy pigs they are."

Angered, I slam the stop button so hard my fist goes numb as I pry my eyes from his.

"Are you really so naïve?" he asks tauntingly. "You can't seek the death penalty unless the accused has been charged with a prior crime of the same nature."

I look over at him and he smiles, shaking his head, which makes me grind my teeth.

"Is that right?" I ask sarcastically. "Then you're even more of a fucking idiot than I took you for," I say, smiling as the doors open. "It won't be Ken and Cliff Dodds' case, nor Verna Whitmore's, or even my husbands that will put the nail in their coffin, David. It will be those two nameless kids that the Paulsons will be on trial for after theirs that will, and Gabe will be leading that case too. And guess who will be front row championing that death sentence? Me, motherfucker, Vixen King."

I spit at his feet and let the doors close feeling queasy as I brace myself against the wall. My head is spinning with emotion and I need to catch my breath before I enter the room.

If my husband thinks he's a monster, he clearly hasn't met David Schneider.

I wipe my hands down my robe and then enter the suite, needing a drink like nobody's business. I can hear the shower running, which is perfect, gives me more time to figure out how to tell Liam about David's presence. I slam a shot of whiskey and pour another as I take a seat and stare at my phone. My nerves are shaky as I send Gabe a message and find my way to the bed. I take a seat preparing myself as the sound of the shower stops and I drink back my second glass of liquid courage.

Liam smiles as he enters the room wrapped in only a towel, and I love what I see. He is the vision of tainted beauty, the one thing that can restart my cold dead heart in an instant.

"Did you manage to clear that head of yours?" he asks, lying beside me.

I run my hand through his damp hair and take in the perfection of his art ridden body.

"Clear... no, more like cluster-fuck," I confess. "But there is a pool, spa, and gym here as Melanie pointed out."

"Melanie?" he asks raising a brow.

"The front desk clerk, and don't worry, she's a fan."

He removes my hand from his hair and kisses it.

"I don't need fans, Vixen, I just need my wife to listen to me," he states. "Remember when it used to be you who wondered if I was ever coming back?"

I nod, wondering what he's getting at.

"I now know what that feels like. And I wouldn't blame you if you took off and wanted for all of this to end."

I entwine my fingers with his and sigh.

"You, Liam, *are all of this*. You are all of *me*. And since when have you ever known me to backdown from a fight?"

He grins happily and rests his head on my stomach.

"That would be never," he states. "So, tell me more about this Melanie and the amenities we haven't explored yet."

"I can't, because we won't be exploring them. David Schneider is in the hotel with us."

Liam rolls onto his stomach and props his head up with his hands.

"What the fuck is he doing here?"

"He's meeting with the DA tomorrow. I've already texted Gabe and told him to come here first so he can handle the press and keep David at a safe distance from you."

His face turns confused.

"From me? I'm pretty sure you'd be just as likely to kill the fucker too," he points out.

"I thought about it, but managed to curb my desire although I did spit on his shoes."

"Wait... what? You spoke to him?"

I nod.

"More like threatened him, but not illegally, while I imagined de-gutting him. I wonder if that makes me a psycho or not?"

"It totally does, but I like your kind of *psycho*," he says convincingly. "Do you know what room he's in?"

"No," I say smacking his arm. "Don't get any bright ideas. We have Liv and My Chew to think about."

"And Mac," he adds.

Him too, I laugh in my head, taking in his way to innocent smile.

We lay silently for a long while I continue to brush through his hair with my fingers, trying to imagine his head when it was much smaller. Pretending that someone has always loved him the way I do. Loved him enough to do something so simple, and touch him with a loving hand. I don't even know if it really soothes him, or if it just makes me feel better to pretend. It's moments like these that really make we wonder if I'm even normal trying to consciously place myself in that basement with him. Fantasizing I somehow could have shown him the love he deserved. I hate myself for even thinking it, but I do. I imagine it all of the time, I think about the things I would have done to show him love and protect him, to guard all of them if I were there. Then it always comes back to me that it's exactly what the four of them already had, flawed or not. They loved each other unconditionally. And because of it, Liam and Ken were always trying to simplify the darkest parts by offering themselves up in place of Cliff and Verna. Because the truth remains that both of them are the heroes of this nightmare just like Verna once told me, and in a way, Verna must have been Liam's hero too.

"What if it were Liv?" Liam asks cutting the silence of my thought's.

"What if *what* were Liv?"

"In the basement," he says. "I'm just asking for the sake of the Whitmores... for Susan. Put yourself in her shoes, Vix."

My heart stops and I try, but I can't do it. I cannot imagine placing Olivia anywhere near that dark pit in my mind.

"I'd never let it happen, Liam."

"I'm sure Susan thought the same thing when it came to Verna," he states. "She didn't just let it happen, Vixen, the Paulsons stole her kid."

I try again to imagine standing in an aisle with Liv as an eight-year-old and looking up to find her gone. My heart breaks for Susan and the fear she must have felt. The agony of the blame she must have placed on herself has got to be excruciating.

Liam runs his hand down the side of my face and I know he can see how uncomfortable I am.

"Now," he whispers, "just try to think rationally. If it were Olivia, our sweet, perfect, curious, entirely innocent little girl that we would lay down our lives for in an instant, would you want her to be down there all alone?"

I feel the tears well in my eyes and take a deep breath, fully understanding what he is saying. The answer is no. I would want her to have someone with her who made it less scary. Someone who could give her hope, or at least comfort in knowing she wasn't alone.

I wipe the stray tears that escape my eyes, now fully understanding what Susan meant by her comment.

"You're a fucking asshole for making me think about Liv in that place, Liam. But you've clearly made your point," I say flicking him on the arm.

"That's what I love about you," he laughs, "you can see things from all sides. And even when you're on the verge of tears you're just like me."

"Like you?" I ask, baffled. "You don't cry," I point out.

"I'm talking about how you turn it into anger and either become really mouthy, or totally violent and then slap me or flick me as payback."

"Are you calling me abusive?"

"No, I'm saying you make me feel normal."

I roll onto my side and smile into the beauty of his kind blue eyes that always seem to captivate me.

"Neither of us are *normal*, we are beyond fucked up. Nothing about *us* will ever be defined as normal. So stop trying so hard to be something that doesn't exist for people like us."

"Fine," he mutters, "I'll agree to try to stop caring about what people think of me, if, and only if, *you* agree to apologize to Mrs. Whitmore tomorrow before we leave."

I cringe and contemplate my options.

A self-loathing Liam, or an embarrassing apology.

"Fuck, fine," I cave. "I'll apologize to Susan but I want to get hate-fucked first or it's no deal."

He growls that growl. The one that sends my heart into a fleeting fury of hellfire and sin.

What this man does to me, he may never know, but I'd go to hell and back to make sure he never sees it as a flaw.

Because Liam King might be a tainted man, but he is also the master of my fucking heart.

CHAPTER 31
Gone but Not Forgotten
LIAM

If I ever found a shred of respect for Gabriel Morris and his schmuck-driven lawyer tactics it would be now. I never used to like him, he pissed me off with his fancy car, impeccable hair, and douche-bag attitude. Not to mention the time the prick let my wife give him a hate-blow. But that's all in the past, and I see now the man definitely has balls of steel when it comes to handling the press. That and he looks pretty great on TV from what I've seen. He's always got a strong sense of conviction in his voice when he talks and because he is hell-bent on keeping the world focused on the Paulsons, his face is now branded. Gabe Morris is now known as the high-profile attorney for the 'Forgotten Four.'

I'd never noticed how green his eyes were until I seen him get mad this morning, the man used to seem harmless, but I think this case is starting to wear on him.

That or my wife's unedited outbursts are.

We've been sitting in a small room at the courthouse waiting for Gabe to finish up with his meeting with the DA and the Paulsons lawyer, David Schneider. Gabe made it clear that he doesn't want me or Vixen talking to the press, but he said it was important for them to see my face. I don't understand what my face has to do with anything, I'd rather just show them the inside of my heart, it would simplify things. But this morning as we left the hotel to get in Gabe's car, some reporter made some off-handed comments that got under Vix's skin, mine too, if I'm honest. We'd managed to sluff it off and once we'd arrived here, the press was stationed outside the doors like sharks waiting for blood to spill. They became loud and pushy; they all raised their voices at once and sometimes it's hard to drown them out. This morning was just that, they were like rabid animals, trying to come at us as we pushed our way toward the doors. Everything was fine until Gabe was holding the door open for us and then came the loud, echoing question.

"Liam, how do you plan to explain to your daughter about the things you've done? Is she even safe having a father like you? Liam, the world wants to know how you managed to adopt. Or did you kidnap her and think it was normal, acceptable even?"

I just kept walking, not realizing I'd lost Vixen's hand in the process. But when I'd turned around, it was too late. She'd already stopped and turned around to face the woman who asked the questions. Between her reaction and Gabe going straight into the crowd at her defence, it was fucking insane. I'd never seen anything like it.

Now we are sitting here waiting to find out how badly it's impacted the case. I can tell Vixen feels foolish, and she hasn't said a word to me yet. She's got her head buried in her arms on the desk and I know she's embarrassed by her reaction, which will be all over the news channels by lunch. But do I blame her? Abso-fucking-lutely not.

I run my hand over her back in circles, knowing there is nothing I can tell her that she isn't already thinking. This whole thing is a giant mess of gossip and politics.

Vixen sits up and finally looks at me, her face drained of emotion.

"How do they even know about Liv?" she breathes out hard.

I shrug, knowing they have their *'sources.'*

"If it wasn't Liv they would have found something else to entertain the public with. I think that's why Gabe keeps calling them a circus," I point out.

"Yeah, well, I hate how they are trying to tear our lives apart. I wanted so badly to rip that woman limb from limb," she seethes. "And how do you always manage to stay so calm?"

She looks at me as if I'm hiding some secret ability from her.

"It's hard to explain," I tell her. "I've just always kept my anger to myself, let it brew in my chest like a storm for a while. It's not easy, but I learned it was better to react with no emotion than to get punished for letting it out."

She sighs and grabs my hand, her eyes penetrating mine as if she understands.

"They were so fucking awful to you and the further we go into the fucked-up world of seeking justice, the more I realize how devastating this must be for you. And then there's Liv. How are we going to protect her?"

We look up as the door opens and Gabe enters.

"I just got off the phone with Helen. The press is already on the Hill standing on her lawn," Gabe notifies. "But don't worry, I've instructed a few associates from my firm to go over there and move Helen, Claire, and Olivia to a hotel."

"What about Mac?" I ask.

Vixen pops me one upside the head.

"I'm sure the dog will be fine."

Gabe laughs, "I'll make sure they find a hotel with a kennel."

"A kennel?" I growl. "But Mac didn't do anything wrong," I state. "Can't you find one that allows pets in the suite?"

"Oh, my Jesus," Vix hisses. "Enough about the damn dog,

Liam. Thank you, Gabe, for looking out for them, now what happened in the meeting?"

He proceeds to tell us that the DA is going to try all four cases at once. Mine, Ken, Cliff's and Verna's. The bulk of the charges are in place, but they are looking at adding more as the evidence continues to get sifted through. Mr. Schneider had been in there to try to sway the prosecutor from considering new charges but so far, he has failed which is good for us. The bad news, however, is that without Verna's testimony, her case will be harder to prove and normally 'hearsay' is inadmissible in court, meaning that my, Ken's, and Cliff's accounts of what happened cannot be used as evidence in Verna's case. Her case alone will have to rely on the evidence collected which Gabe now has access to.

"Are you going to ask Ken, Cliff, and Liam to examine the evidence?" Vixen asks nervously.

Gabe nods.

"They will need to be prepared and get their accounts of what happened straight. Every detail needs to be told to the jury. But we have plenty of time to work on it, and back home where you'll be more comfortable."

"What about Ken and Cliff?" I ask. "Maybe they should come and stay with us for a while."

Vixen nods and sighs.

"I'll go call Ken and see if he's up for it. If he is, I'll ask him and Cliff to meet us at the airport at four and they can fly back with us. There is no way we are staying in this fucked up place another night."

I half-smile, unsure that Ken will agree, but I'll be glad as shit to get out of here. I haven't seen either of my brothers since the funeral and things started to get crazy. Ken Dodd is a hard guy to talk too, and even harder to look at with all of the pain in his eyes. At the funeral it was like looking into a mirror, in his eyes I could see myself, a man broken into small fragments and held only together with a burning hate that keeps forcing you to exist.

"Okay, bud," Gabe says squeezing my shoulder. "I have to go and file some paperwork for disclosure, so we'll have copies of the evidence. I'll keep you guys posted on a time we can meet next week to discuss and possibly go through some of it. You two gonna be alright to make it back to the hotel without me?"

"Yeah, go do what you have to do, we'll head out the back once we call a cab. And thanks," I say shaking his hand.

"For what?"

"For standing up for Vixen earlier. I never knew you could be so hostile."

He crosses his arms and his face turns serious.

"Then you haven't seen me in court."

I watch him walk away, and I'm enveloped in a renewed sense of faith. No wonder Vixen insisted on him, he is one stubborn bastard.

The schmuckier the better, I guess.

By the time Vixen and I make it back to the hotel to grab our things and then over to the Whitmores', it's close to noon. We managed to avoid the press, but as precaution, she asks the driver to take us around the block a few times so we can make sure we weren't followed. Once Vixen is satisfied, she pays the guy three crisp hundreds and tells him to keep the meter running and to wait at the back of the house for us. It wasn't easy, but Vixen also managed to talk Ken into coming to stay with us. *Nothing can twist a man's arm faster than the mention of free all you can drink alcohol on the beach.* He's decided to make the drive up with Cliff and should be at our place by sometime mid next week.

"How do I look?" Vixen asks inhaling sharply.

"Incredible," I say.

We stand at the back door as I scan her over and adjust her fallen wisps of hair, tucking them back behind her ears. She pulls off the 'professional teacher' look well, dressed in a blush pink blouse, black pencil skirt and leather heels that make her almost as tall as me.

"And how do I look?" I ask brushing off the front of my suit jacket.

She smiles and tousles my hair.

"Like a freaking dork. But the handsomest one I've ever laid eyes on."

I growl under my breath and then pinch her ass as she knocks before smacking my hand away.

Quick to answer, I meet eyes with Mr. Whitmore.

"Have you come back to berate my wife some more?" he asks, looking directly at Vixen.

"No, sir," she says guiltily. "I came to apologize. May I speak with Susan?"

He gestures for her to step inside and then he eyes me over hesitantly but lets me in too.

"Susan," he calls out, "The Kings are back, and Kirsten would like to have a word with you."

I stand at Vixen's side, eyeing the jar of jellybeans on the countertop that looks old with its brass lid and some sort of engraving on it. Then I see Susan enter the kitchen looking surprised but yet oddly welcoming.

"Hello, Kirsten, Liam," she smiles warmly. "What can I help you with?"

Clearing her throat, Vixen says; "I feel I owe you an apology for my behavior yesterday. I shouldn't have yelled at you the way I did and I am truly sorry."

Susan begins to laugh and takes Vixen's hands into her own.

"Seems you like to say what's on your mind, dear. You gave that bitch on the TV even more of an earful than I got."

Vixen's face turns awkward and she bites her lip.

"Shit! You saw that?"

"I did," Susan continues, no longer laughing. "None of this is easy for any of us, and I imagine it has stirred up more inexplicable emotions and answerless questions for each of us than we want to endure. But," she says, her voice cracking, "I am an advocate for my daughter... I am Verna's only voice in this mess, just as you are very quickly becoming Liam's. We need to stick together, and to be patient and understanding toward what we are all feeling. This is a fight we won't win otherwise."

Her words hit home and my heart races thinking about everything Verna's lost in this mess.

"I'll be her voice too, and so will Vixen, maybe even Ken. I promise you, Verna will not ever be forgotten," I pledge.

Susan smiles and her eyes fill with tears. I think they are a mixture of happy and sad ones.

"And to think they are dubbing you as a monster," she says heatedly.

She steps closer to me and brushes her hand across the side of my face, the way a loving mother would.

"Boy are they wrong," she continues. "You are an incredible man. No matter what anyone says, you are a warrior, and that daughter of yours is lucky to have a father as strong as you are."

The belief in her tone is just as convincing as Verna's once was and it feels good to have her support. It feels incredible, actually.

I look over at Lyle who nods but says nothing, and then at Vixen who winks as if to tell me Susan is right.

"I'm only as strong as the woman who stands beside me," I say pulling Vixen closer. "And this woman, she's like a pit bull, mess with her and she will come back at you with a bite you won't ever forget."

"No kidding," Lyle weighs in. "I haven't seen the news yet," he says nodding in Vixen's direction, "but after her assertive and dramatic exit yesterday, I can only imagine what must have gone on."

Vixen's face flushes, and I almost feel bad for her.

"I apologize for that as well, Mr. Whitmore. I honestly have no excuse for saying what I did."

"Consider it even," he says deadpanning with me. "Seems we've all needed to stop and take a step back to think about who the real predators are in this situation."

I freeze, caught in the man's softened expression as he holds out his hand.

"I'm sorry, Liam," he continues. "I was just as guilty of judging a book by its cover, and I realize after listening to what Susan had to say, that none of what happened is your fault. Can you forgive me for being so terribly mistaken?"

I've never looked another man in the eyes and watched him work so hard to hold in his suffering. I can feel what he's feeling just by the anguished look on his face, and I shake his hand, working just as hard to hide my own.

"I loved your daughter, sir," I push out.

He doesn't let go of my hand, his eyes seemingly begging for me to tell him more, so I continue. "Verna was like a light at the end of a very long, dark tunnel. She was the best sister I could have asked for, and she was as tough as nails. Everything she did was always with grit and spunk. She taught me so many things, and she believed so strongly in family. Regardless of the things you *will* hear during the trial, I want you to know that's what we were down there. A family, and she will always be remembered by me as my sister."

The man doesn't hold back any longer as the tears fall from his dark, Verna-like eyes and he pulls me into a strong embrace. It's a weird sensation, but I give in and hug him back almost feeling like I'm hugging her.

When he finally lets go, he steps back and begins to wipe his face.

"You have my word on the life of my beautiful daughter, that

Susan and I will be in that court room with our unwavering support, no matter what those bastard's say."

And out comes the other side of Verna right before my eyes.

I smile and nod in appreciation as Vixen hugs Susan and then Lyle.

Vixen tells them we will keep in touch and meet up with them when we come back next, mentioning we have a plane to catch and a cab waiting for us. I feel like it went much better than I'd anticipated as we say goodbye and I follow Vixen to the door. I stop and turn around, realizing I can't go without saying just one more thing.

"Is that candy for eating or is it just to look nice?" I ask.

"You have got to be shitting me!" Vixen laughs. "I should have warned you guys, this husband of mine cannot look at candy without needing to eat it."

Susan picks up the jar and hands it to me.

"Take it, the jar was Verna's, and she would have wanted you to have it. See?" she says running her thumb over the inscription.

'Verna *Margaret Valerie* Whitmore'

"Gone but never forgotten," Susan smiles proudly.

I nod, not knowing what to say, so instead I lean in and kiss her on the cheek and then I whisper.

"Gone, but never forgotten."

* * *

The airport is packed when we arrive. I don't think I've ever seen Vixen as quiet as she was for the hour-long ride it took to get here. I suppose we were just taking in the good parts of the day, that and daydreaming of getting Liv and heading home. I grab our bags and follow her to our gate letting her go deal with the tickets. We'd packed lightly knowing this wasn't a vacation, which as far as I can tell makes this flying stuff so much simpler. I take a seat and glance around at the flight screens praying ours will be on time. The one coming out here was delayed by two hours, and if I've learned anything about airports, it's that they are *Boring with a capital B*.

"Oh shit, no," Vixen gasps.

I look over at her horrified expression and then up at all of the TV screens that are playing the daily news.

I force her to sit beside me as she hides her face in my chest while I look around at all of the people watching the screens. The volume isn't as loud as it could be, but I can hear the whole thing plain as day.

"Liam, how do you plan to explain to your daughter about the things you've done? Is she even safe having a father like you? Liam, the world wants to know how you managed to adopt. Or did you kidnap her and think it was normal, acceptable even?"

On the video you can see Vixen lunge at the woman, missing her attempt to hit her but managing to swipe the mic from her hand.

"Our daughter is none of your *beeped* business and how dare you," Vixen roars. Her face looks like she's a raving lunatic, and it even gets my heart racing. She goes on to say, "I'll tell you something you filthy *beeped*! The only thing Liam King will be telling our daughter is how *beeped* incredible he is, and that will be *after* he wins in court and when he does," she pauses, her voice becoming so low it's scary, "I hope the horrible, evil, head-*beeped* people like you end up suffering in some filth ridden basement while someone tortures, starves and molests—"

It's at that point Gabe gets a hold of Vixen and takes the microphone from her.

"Oh my God, is it over yet?" she asks into my chest.

"Almost," I whisper, trying not to look at all of the people now staring at us.

I look back up at the screen as the camera zooms in on Gabe's fierce but composed expression.

"I have asked you people nicely several times to stop harassing my client. You guys are like bugs, pushing and pestering them until you get what you want. Now you might think this is entertaining, that it's your job to report fake news and gossip about the private lives of the Kings, but I can assure you this is not news. What you are doing to these people is unwarranted, and let me tell you, if this doesn't stop, the next place I go is straight into the judge's chambers to get a press ban on the case before it goes to trial. So, unless you all want to be banned from knowing what goes on in that court room less than a year from now, I would advise you to back off of Liam and Kirsten King and direct your focus to the real news. No. More. Comments."

Holy shit do I enjoy the wicked green hue in that man's eyes when he smiles cool as all hell before he hands the lady her microphone back. The clip then ends quickly once the cameras record Gabe turning to enter the courthouse.

I lean down and whisper into Vixen's ear, hoping to cheer her up.

"Remember that one time you sucked our lawyer schmuck's dick?"

"Oh gross, Liam, why the hell are you bringing that up?"

"Because," I say trying not to laugh. "You never told me that son of a bitch was so damn manly underneath the suit, yet he got my hard nosed wife to suck his dick. Un-fucking-real."

She peeks her head up at me and rolls her eyes. It makes me smile inside because now I know it means she's no longer mortified. She's annoyed instead.

"You're *un-fucking-real*," she hisses. "I hate that you won't just let that go!"

"What husband would?" I ask, knowing full well she's angry.

"Clearly not mine. Christ, Liam, the hate-blow happened years ago and the last thing I want to be picturing is that humiliating oversight, especially when the guys defending us."

"And he fucked your mom," I remind.

"Are you seriously trying to make me lose it on you right now?"

I raise my brows up and down before I give her the warning growl.

"Hate-fuck city in the bathroom could be interesting," I whisper.

Vixen stands and drags me behind her to the washroom, body checking the door open before she pulls me into a stall and locks it.

"Drop your pants, you asshole."

"Lift your skirt and drop the panties, you vixen."

We both do as we were told and I'm hard as hell, while she's wet and needy, rubbing herself against my leg.

"I should hate-blow you right now," she threatens, kissing me forcefully.

"I should let you," I growl, "but I think what you really need right now is to get on this dick."

I rub my fingers over her damp folds, and she moans deep from the pit of her stomach.

"Fine but only because we don't have time for both, because of the flight," she reminds, "but don't think I won't drop to my knees and do it the second we get home."

Knowing it's the one thing I refuse to let her do lately, with every dark emotion I've been feeling, I smile and lie.

"Sure, I'll let you hate-blow me when we get home. Now turn the fuck around so I can hate-fuck that tense and needy little pussy."

The stall is compact, so I help her spin her back to me and hike up her skirt around her waist before I drive myself into her hard.

"Fuck yes," she groans.

I cover her mouth, knowing other people are probably listening to us as I fuck my wife with slow, calculated thrusts.

"You like this dick, don't you?" I taunt. "I'm going to fuck you in this airport until I make you cum, and then if we have time I'll do it again."

"Holy hell, Liam," she says muffled and drooling into my hand.

With my other hand I work her clit over firm and fast, the way I know she needs it. I love the way her nub hardens between my fingers; this gorgeous creature is so easy to please, and her moans drive me wild. I don't miss a beat, drinking as much of her in as I can while I continue into her, harder and harder, feeling the blood pressure in my dick mounting. I no longer hear the sound of the walls rattling and the world is starting to dissipate around me as I try to stay focused on the needs of her body. Where my mind wants to go is back into that basement, but I fight the thoughts as Vixen backs herself up closer to me.

"Harder, Liam," she gasps. "Hate-fuck me harder, I'm about to explode."

I do just that, now gripping the top of the stall with one hand and continuing to tease her clit with the other. Slamming in and out of her, I feel her body begin to tremble as she releases, tightening all around my dick as I work to keep her orgasm going.

"Holy, fucking shit," she pants giving in to her orgasm.

My hand is wet, and her moans are louder than sin, but I don't give a fuck because in this moment I feel awake. I feel needed. I feel like I'm about to spill every bad thing from inside me into her.

"Holy fuck is right," I growl, pushing myself as deep inside her as I can get. I cum hard, feeling my hate empty into her as I try to catch my breath, both of us now standing still and gasping quietly.

We stay silent for a few seconds before I remove myself and crouch down to lift her panties.

"How long do you think that took?" she asks, still breathless, and adjusting her hair.

"About as long as it needed to, but round two is out of the question, I think we are being called to board."

I smile at her sexy, completely devious smirk and then kiss her as I zip my pants. I know that what we just did has erased any negative thoughts from Vixen's mind. *For now, anyway.*

CHAPTER 32

Not What I See

VIXEN

2 months later...

This has got to be some sort of world record. Likely for *the world's strangest looking family to ever walk the planet.*

"Daddy, Daddy!" Liv squeals, "Mac broke it again! He broke My Chew's diaper off!"

I look to the left at Matthew running naked down the beach past Helen and Claire while Liam tries to get the dog to let go of the diaper. Our little boy seems to fit right in here and has had zero problems adjusting to the King clan over the last seven weeks. I love the way his golden hair shimmers when he runs, and how he'll stop on a dime to check something out that catches his eye.

"Matthew! No, stop that!" Helen laugh shouts, swatting at him lightly with her Bible. "You do not bite Bama's leg!"

"He thinks that mole is candy," Liam laughs. "Come here My Chew, leave grandma's dirty old leg alone."

349

I laugh and take a sip of my iced tea, as I enjoy taking in the view.

Our family has tripled in size and thank God for Jimmy and Jack offering up a room at their place because this, *as fun as it is*, it's nuts.

Staying with us, we now have Ken the 'skull man' as Liv calls him because of his tattoos, and Cliff 'the shhh man' since he never talks. And trust me, Liv has tried everything to make him talk, I swear she'll crack him one of these days. Then there's Helen the Bible-spewing mother of mine and her soon to be wife, Claire who are now staying three doors down with the Marron brothers, and at least twice a week Gabe stops by to talk about the case. On top of that, we now have adorable one-year old Matthew who is inseparable from Liv, Mac *the dog-son* whom Liam insists is a person and not an animal, and then we have Dell, our well-needed therapist. Thankfully, Dell, has not asked to bunk with us. You add all of that up and you get what I'm witnessing at the moment. But I'm not complaining. I love it. I also love that the press has managed to tone it down and doesn't seem to bother us much out here. Not since Gabe's well-executed ultimatum. And having Mom and Claire around has been nice; Mom helps a ton with the kids and Claire, well, she helps a ton by keeping Liam busy with cooking.

I lower my sunglasses down my nose, watching as Olivia climbs her way onto Cliffs lap.

"What do a cat say?" Liv asks. Her eyes are wide and curious as she twirls his hair between her fingers waiting for him to answer, but he says nada.

Then Liv squishes her fingers against his belly as if to tickle him, but still nothing.

"He say mow!" she tells him. "And my bad puppy, he say woof!"

Matthew gets right in there too, mounting Cliff's leg and barking as if he is Liv's bad puppy.

In the chair next to Cliff, is Ken, who is clearly pretending to be asleep. I watch as he peeks his eyes open like Frankenstein and then he leans over really close to Liv and Matthew's face's as their expressions turn scared but excited. "Boogedy, boogedy, boo! The skull man has awoken!" Ken snarls in his mock monster voice.

Liv stumbles back, yanking Matthew by the arm and they take off hollering and squealing as Ken chases them down the beach.

It's one of the sweetest things I've ever seen considering the wreck he was when he first got here. It's taken him more time to warm up to the adults than it did the kids, and he's the kind of man who needs to keep busy. If he's not repairing something or messing with the bikes, he's down at the bar working. I guess it helps that he used to be a bartender because it's really the only place he seems to be comfortable enough to talk about Verna. And as a bonus, it's kind of a bonding place between him and Dr. Dell who is now quite the regular at The Olive King. Dell likes to go in there and pretend he's 'learning how to make drinks,' but I know he's really there as shrink support.

I'm positive Ken knows it too, but I think he appreciates the non-tainted company and most of Dell's advice.

Then there's Cliffy, now he's a completely different story, and even though I know about some of his past, I really don't know *him* at all. I wonder if anybody really does, besides Ken. Maybe Verna did, it's hard to say, but when I look at Cliff I see nothing but desolate sadness. The kind that stays forever treading behind his dark eyes that I wish I could get just the smallest glimpse of his thought's from. I've seen him smile here and there, but rarely, and when he does its usually to be polite or tell you that he's listening. Other than that he's pretty much like living with a ghost. If it weren't for Ken bribing him all of the time with a telescope and an hour under the stars, I swear that man would never leave the house, let alone man the bar with Ken.

I look over as Liam takes a seat beside me with Matthew on his lap.

"Ken and Cliffy are headed to the bar to open and your mother and Claire are heading back to Jack's place to start dinner," he says excitedly. "Would it be okay if I take My Chew, Liv, and Mac over to help cook?"

I study his less than trustworthy smile questioning him with a smile of my own.

"Do you mean help them? Or *harass them* with thousands of cooking questions and another lesson on how to spell jalapeño?" I ask pressing my nose to Matty's.

He smells like baby formula as he giggles, slobbers all over me, and then pulls my hair.

"Help of course," Liam boasts. "I'm an amazing cook, Claire said so. And I already know how to spell jalapeño."

I raise a brow and look at him doubtingly.

"Okay, then you can go if you can spell it," I challenge. Truthfully I'm positive he only wants to go there so he can play video games with Liv and the boys, but it keeps his mind off of the trial and that is a very good thing.

"Okay, I'll spell it," he says believably. "But I also want something else when I do."

"Wow, is it just me, or is Ken's bribing tactics wearing off on you?"

"Never," he grins. "I'm not seven anymore, I don't need lessons from Ken. I get all of the lessons I need from you."

My heart shatters at his words. I've noticed how much Ken's presence here seems to make him talk a lot more about their childhoods. I don't even think Liam realizes he's doing it when he does, so I always try hard not to point out how much it stings me.

I look into Matty's big pale-blue eyes and then into Liam's pleading blue-grey ones that are begging for the go-ahead.

"Okay, fine, what are you after this time?" I ask reluctantly.

The man is damn near impossible to say no to. He's even worse than the kids with his pouty face and boy can he melt my heart like salt on ice. He takes a deep breath and lets it out slowly, his eyes seemingly searching mine for permission.

"I want to go with Ken and Cliffy back to the basement," he mumbles quickly. So quickly I'm caught off guard and fighting to process the words.

"Ken said we should—"

"Stop talking, Liam."

It's all I can muster out as my breath halts and my fists clench to the thought of the basement. I've seen the pictures that was enough to tell me every nightmare I'd ever had never even touched what that place is like.

"But Ken—"

"No, Liam," I snap, trying not to look at the disappointment in his eyes. "The answer is no, and that's final."

I stand to walk away needing a minute, but he grabs my hand and tugs me back toward him.

"Would you just listen to me for a second?"

Now he's whisper growling, and it's making Matthew fussy. I jerk my wrist from Liam's grip and hold my arms out.

"Give Matty to me and take Liv to your cooking lesson. We are not discussing this topic in front of the kids."

He hands Matthew over and I don't know what to make of the fact he doesn't just look sad anymore, he looks downright angry, as if he wants to scare me into listening. Not winning the cold-hearted staring contest, he backs down and glances at Liv all wide-eyed and watching us.

"Olivia," he says taking her hand, "lets go see the grandmas, since Mommy wants to be a bossy b-i-t-c-h like those evil sister princesses again."

"Don't teach her that, and I'm not being bossy, you're being an absolute, thoughtless, mind screwed i-d-i-o-t right now. And there is no reason for it," I add, stepping past him and into the house.

I take Matty upstairs to get him changed and fed. The only thing running through my head is images of a damp, cold, dark basement and I don't understand why in the hell Liam would want to go back there. I don't even want to ask, because if this is what having Ken here is doing to him, I'll be the first to throw Kenneth Dodd out the fucking door and onto his ass, *brother or not*.

"There you go, Matty, all snuggled in a clean diaper and a nice warm blanket."

He snuggles into me with his bottle and for a moment, I imagine he's exactly what Liam looked like at this age, but with messier hair and a slightly bigger head. I take a seat with him in the rocking chair that sits in the middle of the room he and Liv now share. The little guy is tired and so am I. I'm emotionally drained and seriously wondering what the hell my husband is thinking wanting to go back. What could he possibly gain from going there? And Ken of all people, the leader of The Forgotten Four, *fuck*, who does he think he is suggesting something so deranged. Why would he ever want to bring Cliffy back to that place? All of these questions are driving me insane, and if I want an answer, I should probably go to the source.

Out like a light, I place Matty in his crib, kiss him, and cover him with the blanket before I head back downstairs.

I grab the bottle of Jack I've had hidden since we returned from Billings and take a seat on the sofa. I feel deeply guilty that I even have it, but with everything that's gone on these past few months, I really need it sometimes. Just the scent of it is enough to ease my tension somehow, maybe because it reminds me of less dark days with Liam, the way things were before Verna died, or maybe I just need an excuse to rationalize the fact I'm hiding it. It's not even like Liam would be mad or unsupportive, I just know he's always been weary of me winding up like my mother. Hell, I used to dread the possibility of turning into what she used to be for most of my life. But she proved people can change, so in my opinion, that would mean I have nothing left to fear in that department. I put the bottle to my lips and savour the burn as I swallow back several mouthfuls and shut my eyes.

Fuck you shitty basement, you aren't taking him back.

I laugh to myself thinking about how insane I must be to be holding a conversation in my head with that evil place. But it's how I feel. No matter which way I think about it, I can't see it being a wise decision for any of them to revisit that hell hole.

Startled by a loud knock at the door, I half-choke and half-swallow the booze in my mouth and jam the bottle in between the sofa cushions.

"Come on in, it's open," I say coughing. I'm assuming it's Dell or maybe Cliffy, but am surprised when I see Gabe enter the house. I like the guy and all, but seeing his face isn't particularly amusing when he reminds me of the purgatory of news he tends to bring with him.

"Kirsten," he says smiling and looking as sharp as always. The guy is practically the cover model for Armani formal wear, which used to annoy me, but now it *suits* him with the 'high profile' lawyer gig and all. *No pun intended.*

"How's the Addams family doing tonight?" he teases.

"Ha! Ha! You're so funny," I laugh understatedly. "All of them are either over at Jack and Jimmy's, The Olive King, upstairs in his crib, or right here pining over their stupid husband's un-bright ideas."

"Whoa," he says eyeing me over. "You alright? What's the matter? Liam say something to upset you?"

He takes a seat beside me as I debate telling him anything further. I know he's trustworthy, and he doesn't tend to take sides which is odd because that's kind of the point of his job and all. Gabe's always been easy to talk to, and besides, if anyone other than Dell might understand how completely ridiculous Liam's suggestion was, it's Gabe. I sit up, trying to gain my balance and realizing I'm definitely feeling the effects of the whiskey, and then I blurt it out.

"My twenty-eight going on twelve-year-old husband says he wants to take a memory lap around that fucking pit the Paulsons used to abuse him in."

Gabe's face pales and his eyes narrow.

"He said what?"

"That was exactly my reaction," I tell him.

"Why the hell would he want to do that?"

"Don't know," I shrug. "It was Kenneth damn Dodd's stupid idea."

"Really? But Ken has barely even written a proper statement about what happened there, never mind talked about it. The man also outright stated that he thinks the house should be burned to the ground. So, I'm not sure why he would suggest going there, nor am I convinced it was his idea."

I scoff and dig around in the cushions until I find the bottle.

"Well it sure as shit didn't get implanted in Liam's head by Cliffy," I say taking a swig, "so I don't know which one of them came up with the stupid plan, but the point is, it's crazy. Tell me I'm right."

Gabe shakes his head at me and swipes the bottle from my hand sliding it onto the table. I always forget the two years he spent with my mother makes him think I'm prone to the same disease. I can tell by his face he's irritated and likely thinking about the entire situation from every angle. The man tends to say what he means and mean what he says for the most part.

His dutiful lawyer senses are kicking in.

I drum my fingers on my leg watching him, he's attractive, not gonna lie, even though I'm positive it's the alcohol highlighting those powerful eyes of his.

"First off," he says bluntly, "you shouldn't be using liquor to deal with this stuff. Second, I'm thinking maybe Liam came up with the idea. And third," he says pinning my eyes with his, "I really think you need to stop trying to look out for everybody else and take care of yourself, Kirsten."

I roll my eyes to his unhelpful answer and sigh.

"You don't know me very well do you?" I ask, annoyed. "Your opinion on how I want to deal with the very few moments of silence I get lately is not helpful, and for the record, this is how I'm trying to take care of myself," I say pointedly. "And when it comes to the whole basement scenario, there is no way in hell Liam thought of it on his own."

His face doesn't budge from the stone wall look of *I'm not done talking* splashed across it. Adjusting his suit jacket he leans forward and clears his throat.

"I worked for the infamous Robert King for five years when he was alive, Kirsten," he reminds. "Your father was no pushover when things got hard. Then I dated your spitfire of a mother, the notorious Helen King, and guess what I got?" he says in a heated whisper. "I was invited to witness a first-hand view of what kind of hell you must have survived as a kid. So don't sit here and think for half a fucking minute that just because you and I had one indecent moment of an attraction I knew damn well I should have walked away from, that those things mean I don't understand which King I'm talking to. Because I do, Vixen."

Holy hell he's hot when he gets all attitudish.

I swallow and dismiss my slight attraction to him and fuck am I mad with his condescending tone.

"Nice speech, Gabe," I clap mockingly. "Is that the same one you're gonna use to make sure the Paulsons pay for what they did to Liam with their lives? Because I don't give two shits what you *think* you know about me or what I am, Gabe, I. Am not. Your client. Liam King is. Now find a way to talk him out of going back there, that's what the fuck I pay you for."

I reach out and grab the bottle from the table daring him to take it from me again, but he raises his hands and watches me take a swig.

"You can't even see it can you?" he mutters.

"See what?"

"That you are just as scared of failing him as your mother was to fail you."

He sits there just staring at me with what I can almost describe as a tsunami in his eyes. My pulse is racing, pounding in my chest and I have never felt so blindsided by a single sentence in my life. Half of me feels enraged that he sees me as scared and the other half is shattered because I wonder if he's right.

"Fuck you, Gabe."

It takes everything in me not to let the alcohol intensified feelings in my chest come flooding down my face.

"That's all you've got to come back with?" he pushes. "You're not even going to yell at me? Get mad and break something like she used to?"

I can feel my blood beginning to boil as he continues to press me and stare at me with that stupid pitiful look on his face.

"Come on, Kirsten," he goads. "If you're gonna act like her with a bottle might as well play the part properly. Maybe wait for your sweet kid to walk in the door so you can—"

The bottle leaves my hand and smashes into the wall behind him before he finishes the sentence.

"And there it is," he says, wrapping his arms around me. The tears that are coming from me are silent but unstoppable and I'm caught in a web of confusion between feeling helpless and wanting to burn everything around me to the ground.

His hand caresses my head as I focus on trying to stop the tears and the voice in my head that tells me he's right. *I'm an alcoholic just like my mother.*

"Lif? Momma?" I hear Matty call out.

"Sit," Gabe says as I try to stand. "I'll go and hang out with him until you've sobered up. He shouldn't see you like this."

I nod, knowing he's right about that too and hate him for it. When did that man become so much smarter than me?

I wipe my face with the front of my sweater and grab a glass of water before I check out the broken bottle and the mess I made.

Hearing the front door open, I look up from the floor as Liam enters.

"Is that Gabe's car out front?" he asks.

"Yes, he's upstairs hanging out with Matthew," I say trying not to let him see my face.

"Cool. Maybe he brought the papers I asked for."

Having no clue what he's talking about, I finish getting the broken glass swept up and he notices.

"What happened? Gabe piss you off again?"

"You could say that."

I toss the shards into the garbage and take a seat at the counter beside Liam. It takes him all of two seconds to realize I've been crying before he jerks my chair closer and lifts my chin so our eyes meet.

"Did he say something bad about the case?"

I shake my head thinking that would have been my first question too.

"Then what?" he asks. "Is this about me wanting to go back there?"

"No, but I hate that you are even considering it," I confess.

"I'm not considering it, Vix, I am going with or without your permission."

"Then why did you bother to ask me in the first place?"

He lifts a shoulder.

"We can talk about it later. First tell me why you were upset so I can go punch the schmuck in the face."

"You're not punching your lawyer in the face, Liam, and technically he did me a favor even if it made me break the golden rule."

He looks at me and growls, his eyes narrowed and his head tilted.

"So what did the weasel do? Spit it out before I go up there and ask him myself what the shit he did."

I lean in and press my tongue into his mouth, forcing him to taste the whiskey that lines my lips.

"He simply pointed out to me that I am my mother's daughter."

"Because you had a drink?" he asks, confused.

"No, because I only seem to drink when I'm stressed, or when I'm afraid. And he's right, Liam, I'm terrified of not being strong enough to make it through this."

"Me too," he whispers.

"Sorry to interrupt," Gabe butts in. We look over to see him holding a wide-awake, cheery faced Matthew in his arms. "He keeps asking for his sister... mind if I take him next door for a bit? I think you two could use some time alone."

I nod, feeling like an ass.

"Yes, by all means."

Lord knows I wouldn't want to be trapped in this house with us either right now.

I stand and give Matty a kiss and then look Gabe in the eyes.

"Please don't tell my mother about tonight."

He smiles and looks between Liam and me.

"Client confidentiality," he reminds. "Isn't that what you pay me for?"

Ouch, guess I deserve that.

I hand him the diaper bag and Matty's bottle as I walk him to the door.

"Thank you, Gabe, for being so good to us. To me," I add, ashamed.

"Don't thank me yet, Kirsten," he says, now looking behind me at Liam. "The papers you asked for are in my car in an envelope with your name on it," he continues, "but I suggest you talk to your wife about them before you make any decisions. You know where I'll be if you have any questions."

With that he leaves as I try to decipher what the cautionary tone in his voice is about.

"What papers is he talking about, Liam?"

I turn to take in his uncompromising expression. The one he uses when he's telling me his mind is made up about something.

"They're permittance papers for the abandoned property. It's taped off as a crime scene now, so I asked Gabe to get permission for me to enter the house."

"Oh, wow," I say, offended. "So this was your idea, which means you lied to me and you went behind my back to do it."

"I had too," he states, "you never listen to me, Vixen. I tried to tell you but you said no before I even had a chance to explain."

I cross my arms, frustrated.

"Don't you dare try to make it out like I'm unreasonable. You went to Gabe before you even asked me what I thought, and you blamed Ken for this stupid idea. That's messed up."

"It's not stupid," he shouts, slamming his fist against the countertop. "And I wouldn't have to lie to you if you would just fucking listen to me once in a while. Let me make my own decisions. But you never do, you always have to be the fucking hero, talk louder than me, tell me where to go, what to do, what to say, how to spell it. Fuck, Kirsten! Can't you see I don't need you to protect me anymore? Let me learn to be a man for fuck's sake!"

My heart is pounding and I don't even know who I'm talking to right now.

"Fuck all of what you just said. It's bullshit. I've listened to every fucking crushing word you have ever spoken and then I've done what I thought was best. Not for us, you asshole, and certainly not for myself... for *you*! Do you know what that feels like? Listening to you talk about things so dark, muddy, and fucked-up it hurts to breathe. Watching you hate yourself and tell me you don't want to be who you are anymore because of it. What the fuck did you expect me to do? Stand by and watch you degrade yourself and fall apart on me? Fuck you. Seriously. Fuck you for not giving a shit about what I've tried to do. Fuck you for not seeing how much I've tried to help you. And fuck you, Liam, fuck you the biggest for chasing that stupid red ball."

In an instant, I feel his hand on my chest as my head smacks against the wall.

His face is so violent and close to mine I can see the flecks of gold around his pupils as my heart pounds and he stares at me like I'm his enemy. My chest hurts and I can't move, *I dare not move*, deadpanning with the man holding me against the wall.

"You are still not listening," he growls. "What is it going to take? This?" he asks tightening his grip. "Do I have to be forceful with you outside the bedroom to be heard?"

I say nothing and look away from his eyes, not wanting to see the agony that burns in them.

"Fucking look at me when I'm talking to you," he hisses.

I feel his hand ease up and look into his eyes, unafraid of him, knowing he would never hurt me.

"I've tried so hard not to be this fucking person, this horrible monster that lives in me. I've tried to tell you, but you never fucking listen and now look at me," he breathes, "I'm everything I never wanted to be. Not to you," he finishes, finally removing his hand and stepping back.

I take a sharp breath, but I don't move because I'm spellbound, completely riveted by the tears that are streaming from his sapphire eyes. I have never seen him cry and it's heartbreaking.

A very long minute of silence goes by as we stand just breathing and staring at one another. This beautiful man that I would die for is utterly broken to the core. Begging me to see him as a monster, yet I do not.

What I see is courage and strength. Survival and pain. Want and need. And the man I finally see after five years of hell, standing so close I can taste him, is Liam Kristopher O'Connell. A tainted man who never needed my protection, he just needs me to love him enough to let him be who he is.

CHAPTER 33

Guilt & Ghosts

LIAM

"I swear if you apologize to me one more time for last night, I'm going to drop Mac off at the animal shelter before we head next door for breakfast," Vixen warns.

I pull the blanket to my side of the bed wondering why she's threatening to give the dog away instead of me.

"Here you go again not listening," I tell her.

I hate making the bed, but she insists its important, so I fluff the pillows and place them neatly against the headboard.

"I am listening." she says sternly. "I'm still thinking about what you're asking, but I need you to stop beating yourself up over last night. It wasn't a big deal."

"Yes, it was," I say feeling the guilt in my soul. "I put my hands on you and I shouldn't have. Fuck, I really am so sorry."

"So what, Liam! You had a meltdown, it happens. It's no different than me yelling at the cunt-faced reporter a few weeks ago. Or the fact I launched a bottle of Jack at the wall last night. People have breaking points, it just so happens that Gabe found mine, and I found yours."

I catch the other side of the blanket she likes to leave folded across the foot of the bed and help her straighten it out.

"Yeah well, neither of the things you did hurt someone else," I point out.

"You didn't hurt me," she laughs. "I'm Vixen King remember?" she asks pointing to her head. "I can take abuse with the best of them, and last night was no comparison, nor do I classify it as abuse. All you did was make a point, and I get it, so can we please move on?"

I want to say yes, but I can't get the images of her face from last night out of my head. The way she couldn't even look at me until I yelled at her and how she didn't even try to fight back. It bothers me, and sure didn't help me feel like less of a monster.

"Is that a yes?" she asks, tossing a pillow at me.

"I'll say yes when you do."

"Wow," she scoffs. "You're such a pushy bastard lately."

"I know, but I really want you to say yes. Agree to go with Ken, Cliff, and me. I really need this."

She looks at me and sighs before she flops down onto the bed, covering her face with her arms.

"You are such a brat, Liam, I'm really trying to understand why you have the need to go back there so badly, but I don't get it."

"Because," I say now lying beside her, "it's about getting closure. It's important."

"Closure?" she asks suspiciously. "Why does it sound like you've been taking advice from Dell?"

I lift her arm and take her hand into mine.

"He says this will be good for me, Ken too. He's not sure about Cliffy but Ken wants to drag him along anyway. Dell finally said something that made sense to me for the first time in almost three years."

"Oh yeah?" she asks rolling onto her side. "Tell me what he said."

I smile loving how she always looks so interested in what I have to say when it comes to Dell. It's the only time I really feel like she's listening and not just stuck teaching me something I should already know.

"When I was at his office last week, we were talking about how I tend to hold in my feelings. I told him how sometimes all I can think about is are the things that make me feel like I'm suffocating, like I'm still trapped in that place looking for a way out. Then he mumbled something that made sense to me, *sometimes you can take the man out of the dark, but you can't take the dark out of the man.*"

She looks at me and takes a profound breath, her eyes flickering with terror.

"And you think this trip back into that dark basement they tortured you in is going to cure you?"

I don't blame her for being hesitant, it scares me too, but I'd rather try anything than sit around feeling like I'm drowning.

"Yes, Vixen, I think it's worth a try. Besides, maybe a road trip on the bikes with just the four of us will be refreshing."

She groans, almost as if she's both irritated and orgasming at once.

"You had to throw that last part in there, didn't you?" she asks, annoyed. "The bikes sound fun but it's the whole dirty ass, haunted basement setting that has me at odds. But since I know you are going no matter what I say, fine, I'll go with you. Lord knows you guys are going to need a babysitter."

"Yesss!!!" I shout and then kiss her face. "You're the best, Vix, and I swear this trip is going to be good for us."

I know she must think that sounds crazy, but a part of me feels like maybe I'll be able to leave the blackened pieces of me there where I found the damn things in the first place.

"So, which one of us is telling Liv that we're leaving again?" Vixen asks.

"Sham you for it?"

"You know you always lose at rock, paper, scissors," she prompts. "But sure, put your dukes up, best of three."

As usual, she wins using two rocks against my scissors and one piece of paper to cover my rock. I growl and then kiss her forehead thinking maybe we should flip a coin next time.

"You guys decent in there?" I hear Ken ask through the door.

"Are we ever really decent?" Vix asks naughtily.

"Not that I've ever witnessed," he laughs. He opens the door and hands me a blank check.

"What's this for?"

"I need a bike for me and Cliffy, and I don't know nothin' about ridin' them things, only fixin' them," he says. Then he looks Vixen over adding, "Gonna need some helmets and gear or whatever too, and are you coming with us tomorrow, Vix? 'Cause if you are, I'm going to spend today puttin' in work on your bike, it's a long, hot drive down to hell."

Vixen nods and half-smiles.

"Honestly, I think this plan is fucked, but I'm no wuss when it comes to Lucifer's playground so I'm in. But are you really sure this is a good idea for Cliff?"

Ken begins to roll up his sleeves exposing the skulls that line his arms and extend over onto his hands.

"Cliffy might come off as delicate to you, lost even, but I can assure that boy don't want to miss this trip. He goes where I go, same as y'all," he says looking between us.

Vixen and I nod in acceptance as Ken walks back to the door but then stops in the doorway.

"And don't you go and buy me some fucked-up girly lookin' thing either, get me something badass, something big and mean lookin' we're gonna be ridin' back to hell for Verna after all."

Vixen and I look at each other and smile, knowing that's the first time he's mentioned her name outside of being half-cut.

"You got it," Vixen says.

When we make it over to Jack and Jimmy's place, the kids are already up and stuffing their faces with Claire's breakfast special, pancakes and bananas. I take a seat at the table with Liv and Matthew, leaning towards Liv's plate with my mouth open.

"No! You get, Daddy!" she growls. "Not haffing Liv's bannan-cakes."

I give her the pouty face and she giggles as I make my way over to Matthew hoping to have better luck.

"Liam King," Claire scolds, "do not steal the kids' breakfast. I will make you your own."

I look up at her, unhappily as Matthew smothers the side of my face in syrup and laughs.

"What did you just do you little Chew-bacca?" I say, tickling him. He giggles even louder and claps, his face filled with mischief.

Vixen hands me a wet wipe as I wander over to Helen and Claire, kissing them on the cheeks and managing to steal a sliced chunk of banana in the process.

"I saw that," Vixen says, "and that too," she continues, appalled that I fed the banana to Mac.

I smile and blow her a kiss as she rolls her eyes.

"What got you two up so early and where are the other two heathens?" Helen asks.

"Don't call Ken and Cliff heathens, Mom," Vixen says, annoyed. "They are working on the bikes in the garage."

"I didn't mean it in a bad way, I meant hungry men," she clarifies.

"It's fine," I tell her. "Ken and Cliff don't take offence to much, but where are the Marrons this morning is the better question?" I ask, looking around for Jack and Jimmy.

Claire places a plate of pancakes stacked high as heaven in front of me and takes a seat.

"I think they found some female companions that aren't Helen and me to stay with," she cringes. "I can't say I blame them, we have kind of taken over their 'pad.'"

"So have our kids," Vixen adds, stealing a bite of Liv's pancake.

Liv's eyes widen and she scrunches up her face.

"You not eat Liv's bannan-cakes! Only for the shhh man! Where he is?"

Vixen pinches her cheek and kisses her forehead.

"The shhh man is busy, but Mommy will tell him you saved him some pancakes."

"But he no talk, Momma," she says, now covering her plate. "Why he is broken?"

Her questions always make me think of me when I wasn't too much older than her.

"Cliff isn't broken," I explain, "he's mute."

"Moot?" she asks. "Cow say moot!"

"No, Livy, cows say moo," Vixen corrects. "I don't think you can explain it to her just yet, Liam."

"Me either," I say, now watching Matthew throw banana slices at Mac.

"Don't just sit there watching him feed the dog," Vixen gripes. "And you better tell my mom and Claire about tomorrow."

I take Matthew's plate away from him before I hear the sound of a male yawn, followed by, "You guys are leaving tomorrow?"

I look behind me startled to see Gabe and, in a robe, no less.

"Jesus fu—" Vixen says, stopping herself from finishing the sentence.

I look at her bewildered expression and then at Helen's and Claire's faces that are smiling awkwardly.

"I am not even going to bother asking," Vixen states.

"What?" Helen says casually. "It's not like he's mine or

Claire's lawyer, and I did date the man once."

"Oh, gross, Mom... seriously? Liam is eating and our kids slept here!"

"Don't worry about it," Claire weighs in, "we made sure the dream machine was playing lullabies once they were asleep, these two little monkeys didn't hear, see, and will speak no evil."

Vixen shakes her head, disgusted.

"And what do you have to say for yourself, Mr. Go Getter?" she asks, eyeing Gabe up and down.

"I plead the fifth," he says smiling like a nerd.

"That's probably smart," I say, unable to look at him. "Schmuck doesn't quite cover how I want to describe you anymore," I add, pleading subliminally with Vixen to tell him to get some damn clothing on.

"I think Liam wants you to take that housecoat off and put on a show," Vixen says.

"What? Hell no I do not! Couldn't you tell I was thinking the exact opposite?"

Vixen winks at me as the four of them start laughing and the kids jump in clapping with excitement.

"Very funny," I say not laughing at all.

"I beg to differ," Vix says, "you should have seen your face, it was priceless."

"Well you've already seen his d-i-c-k," I remind. "So naturally it wouldn't be a shock to you would it?"

"Okay, you two, cut it out," Helen says, "we don't need to be discussing this any further in front of the tiny ears."

Vixen smiles at me tauntingly.

"Sure Mom, we'll drop it, since Liam has something else he needs to say."

I look around at everyone's expressions, it's as if they're waiting for a bomb to explode.

"It's okay, Liam, just say it," Vixen nudges.

I take in Liv's face. Her eyes are huge and filled with question.

"Daddy buy Liv nother My Chew baby?" she asks.

We all start laughing and I shake my head.

"No, Liv, one My Chew, a Mac, and a Liv are plenty," I tell her. "Daddy and Mommy are taking a trip."

Her face turns sad and she pushes her plate toward me.

"I give you bannan-cakes, you not go, Daddy? Okay?"

"See?" Vix says. "Even Liv's picking up on Ken's bribery tactics and he isn't even here."

"You never mind," I tell her, returning my attention to Liv. "Daddy and Mommy have to go, but we won't be long. Do you think you can be a big girl and help the grandmas take care of Matty and Mac for a few days?"

She nods her head up and down and then her eyes light up.

"You bring Liv and My Chew a present when come back?"

Impossible to say no to the precious smile on her face, I nod.

"I promise I will."

"So, where you guys headed?" Helen asks, clearing the table.

I look over at Vixen and she shakes her head at me.

"You said you wanted to be heard and allowed to make decisions, so don't look at me. Tell them the plan, just nobody freak out please, because it's definitely going to come across as insane at first."

"It's not *insane*," I say defensively.

Everyone stares at me, including Gabe, who is at least dressed in his regular attire now.

"I'm taking Ken, Cliffy, and Vixen back to the property in Jefferson City. I'm determined to find closure," I say confidently.

I watch both Helen and Claire's jaws drop.

"You mean the place where the Paulsons—"

"Yes, that place," Vixen says cutting Helen off.

"Well why on God's green earth would you think that can bring you closure? Isn't that what the trial is for?"

I don't like the judging look on Helen's face as Claire stands to excuse herself.

"I think I should take Liv and Matty to get washed up and dressed," she offers.

"I'll come and help you with them," Gabe says, plucking Matthew from his highchair.

"To answer your questions, Helen, I can't be sure which is supposed to do what. Even if we win, what are we really winning? And even if the Paulsons are sentenced to death, who's really gaining anything? It won't change the past, it won't make the nightmares, or the pain lessen. It sure as hell won't bring Verna back."

I pause to take a breath and calm my emotions that I used to be good at controlling, but lately seem to sneak up on me.

"Look, I don't really know what I'm doing, but I have to do something. I feel like I have to prove some things to myself, because no matter what anybody sees me as, the thing that sucks the most is how I see myself. I don't expect you to understand it, but I need to go back there for me."

"Well then I wish you luck, Liam, and I will continue to pray for you."

Just those words coming from Helen's mouth are enough to ease the tension in my chest. I look over at Vixen, holding her mother's hand and I realize the two of them are the world's most fearless women I've ever met. When things were at their worst for Helen, with the drinking, the loss of her husband, and the days when she used to lash out on Vixen, she still never gave up. She never gave in to her suffering or her failures, she just kept moving forward. And when she was faced with the hardest part of all, asking Vixen for forgiveness, she didn't cower and she's kept her word to this day, trying to be a better mother.

Then there's my wife, who has never been anything but a solid presence of strength and grit in my corner. She was right when she said I have no clue what that must be like for her. I'd never really thought about it. I've always known she's tough, smart, beautiful, and verbally dominant. It never occurred to me that underneath all of that she's probably more like me, used to holding all of the anger in, and drowning it out with hate-fuck sessions and liquor. Vixen has never been frightened to speak her mind since the minute I met her. She tells everything like she sees it, and regardless of how we handle our demons, I know one thing above all else about Kirsten King. She's not afraid of me or whatever the hell I am, because if she was, she'd have made it crystal clear and she would not be standing here beside me today.

That's not to say I haven't learned my lesson about knowing that what I did last night was wrong. *I know it like I know every rotting crack on the walls that are in that basement.*

"Are you done eating yet?" Vixen asks. "Everyone is clearing out of here which means we're left on clean up duty."

"Bye-bye, Daddy," Liv says, kissing my hand and then running to catch up with everyone who's heading out the door. "And don't dare be a bad princess! You not forget Liv and My Chew's present right?" she stops to ask. Her face is stern as if she's warning me.

"I would never," I say convincingly before she smiles and rams her way out the door. "Where the heck is everyone going?" I ask realizing the house is empty.

"Gabe has court stuff to deal with and Mom and Claire are taking the kids, and *cheese head*, to the farmers market," Vixen answers.

"His name is Mac, not cheese head," I say, helping clear the rest of the dishes. "So, I guess this means we have a free morning to shop online for Ken's new beast then. Woo hoo!"

"Start rinsing the dishes, please. You are way too excited about this trip."

"No, I'm excited about finally getting to press all of the buttons on Jimmy's computer, that thing is state of the art."

"Right," she's says, not believing me. "In that case, I think we should get Ken a hot pink bike with a matching glitter helmet. Think you can press enough buttons to find one of those?" she asks, sideways glaring at me.

"Well, aren't you a badass vixen this morning. If that's a dare, then, hell yes, I know I can find one, but I'm pretty sure he'll just end up swapping you bikes if we do that."

"That's fine, I'll just swap it with yours after that happens."

I look at her unchanging *bring it on* expression and continue to stack the rinsed plates on the dish rack.

"I'm cool with driving a pink bike for four thousand miles, but I'm skipping the helmet, or making Cliffy wear it, because I know at least he won't bitch."

We both start laughing, which is fucking terrible, *I know*.

Handing me the last glass, I watch as Vixen glances quickly at the computer screen mounted to the wall in the living room.

We both bolt over to it, but as always, I'm faster and snag the chair before she can get to it.

"You cheat," she says standing beside me with her arms crossed.

"Do not. I'm just faster than you, I've had practice, one thousand two hundred and thirty-three strides were once gained with these feet, multiplied by two," I say, wondering why I still don't know the exact math on the numbers. "And with no shoes on," I add, "so don't be so hard on yourself about being slow, Vix, I am the master of speed."

I lift the keyboard and inspect all sides of it, before I search the entire monitor, but I can't seem to find a power button.

Leaning over me, Vixen presses a weird looking symbol on the glass screen and the thing magically turns on.

"You might be Usain Bolt when your shoeless, but you are no Bill Gates," she says winking at me. "Need some lessons on how all of the buttons work now?"

I smack her hand lightly as she tries to take over the keyboard.

"What ever happened to 'I can't learn if I don't try?'" I ask mockingly.

"That was before we were tasked with finding a motorcycle for a closed off man and his mute brother so we can all go on one seriously screwed up trip to the netherworld. Nothing at this point seems valid in this situation, let alone makes much sense to me, but there is nowhere on this God forsaken planet I won't follow you."

"I feel the same way about you," I tell her, pulling her onto my lap. "Go ahead, press the buttons, I don't know how to spell Kawasaki anyway."

She laughs and kisses my cheek.

"Nice try, you might be able to sway me into taking a trip, but you are not getting out of homework or learning to spell. Sound it out and start there. I'm heading back home to start packing for the road trip or 'The hell ride for Verna' as Ken named it."

"It's not just for Verna, although I like that Ken's found a strong inspiration," I say, stopping to breathe in the scent of her skin. I rub my hand over her breastbone where I was less than gentle with her last night, and I look into her eyes, silently apologizing. "This trip," I continue, "to the fires of hell, is for all of us, the kids included, Vix. I swear on every hate-fucked inch of you that I am going to come back a changed man. One way or another, I will be better."

"Alright, Liam," she sighs supportively. "Just as long as you come back still being *my man*, it's all that really matters."

She leans down and kisses my lips with a sultry hint of passion that hitches my breath. It tells me Vixen is willing to do whatever it takes. This woman doesn't do things half-assed and I know she expects me not to either. When she stops, I stay lost in her charm as I watch her leave out the door, and in the instant, I know exactly how the trip has to end.

CHAPTER 34
Two of A Kind
VIXEN

It's quiet, too quiet in the house today. The silence that occupies the space around me is no good when all I can think of is how badly I want to say no. No to Liam and this trip, no to the fear that sits burning in the pit of my stomach urging me to take a fucking drink, and no to the possibility that this whole thing could turn out to be a complete nightmare.

Not that most of it isn't already.

But I can't say no because the rational side of me understands him. What I saw in his eyes last night told me everything I need to know. My husband is finding his voice and telling me what he needs. Who am I to hold him back? I'm no hypocrite, and since I've always tried to push him forward, I see no sense in stopping now.

For better or for worse, right?

Besides, if I know Liam, I'm sure he's still badgering himself over yelling at me which is pointless. It never used to work when my mother did it, so I'm not sure why he thought it would have any affect on me. Especially when I let the man hate-fuck me, I mean did he *really* think him being rough with me would scare me? I was turned on for the most part up until he cried, and that in and of itself is a breakthrough as Dell would call it. Last night was a turning point for a man smothered in darkness, that's how I see it, and truthfully, I can't stand that Liam would think wanting to be heard is a crime. For years, he's been so used to doing what he was told that this is a huge step for him. It's monumental, actually.

I grab the duffels I packed and haul them downstairs, tossing them by the front door.

I'm trying to be practical, but knowing what to pack for this situation isn't exactly simple. I can't decide whether we might need candles and flashlights for the creepy basement or gasoline. Should I be bringing my mother's Bible and praying to a God that didn't exist in that place for strength and forgiveness or a sledgehammer to beat down the cursed fucking walls with? And what about the memories it might bring back for the three of them? It's not like I have a mind erasing contraption for shit's sake. I mean fuck, this whole thing seems impossible to prepare for. The more I think about it, the more I wish I could have a damn drink.

I look up as Liam enters the house, damn near tripping over the duffels. He kicks them to the side and waves a piece of paper around excitedly.

"Damn you're fast at packing," he says, "but guess where I'm heading?"

"To hell?" I ask, sarcastically.

He smirks and squints at me.

"Not just yet, we need Ken's bike first," he reminds. "I found one. It's a mint condition 83 Harley-D, 1340 Wide Glide. It's perfect for two riders and the guy says he's willing to throw in his gear too. Want to come and check it out?"

His face is stupid cute and full of a happiness I haven't seen in a while.

"No, you go on ahead and take the guys with you so they can

inspect it for themselves. They should probably take it on a test run and learn how to drive it too, I can't believe Ken can fix them but not ride them."

"That's because he can read, Vix, so he self-taught himself how to repair them, but never had the desire to drive one, until now. Are you sure you don't want to come check it out?"

"Can't, I need to finish up packing and making sure the kids are all set before we leave."

"I won't be long," he says leaning in to kiss me, "and can I just say I'm really sorry about last—"

I cover his lips with my fingers and shake my head.

"Go, Liam, before I make good on my promise to give Mac and his nasty diaper stealing habit away."

"Love you," he says licking my hand.

"Love-hate you more."

I wipe his slobber down the front of his shirt and then nudge him toward the door and watch him exit.

That man is able to drive me wild in ways I don't think he grasps most of the time. Between his need to repent for things that aren't even on my radar, and how hard it is to feel even slightly okay about this thirty-two-hour one-way trip, I'm in desperate need of a hate-fuck fest. *That or a drink.*

* * *

It's cooling off and the sun is beginning to set on the I-90 as I notice the signal light on Liam's Hog come on and his arm swing out to the right. We haven't even reached the halfway mark of this trip even though we've been riding for close to nine hours and only stopped to refuel and rest once. My ass is literally numb and so are the insides of my thighs, but I've missed the hum of the bike between my legs regardless. I put my signal on and glance back at Ken in the mirror before I throw my right arm out making sure he knows we are pulling over. I watch his signal come on and ease right, parking beside Liam and switching my four ways on as I hop off my bike at the rest stop. I remove my helmet and stretch as Ken pulls in and cuts his engine, him and Cliff both removing their helmets and getting off to stretch as well.

I rummage through my bag and toss them each a bottle of water before I grab my own and take a seat next to Liam on the grass. He's got the map out and he's studying it as if to make sure we are making good time.

"What does this say?" Liam asks. "I think we are getting close to halfway."

"Not quite half yet," I yawn, "sound it out."

"Gimme that fuckin' thing," Ken says grabbing the map. "If you can't damn well read, you can't be the navigator."

"He's trying to learn, Ken, give him the map back," I instruct.

Ignoring me, Ken pulls out a lighter and holds it to the map for light.

"Massac County, Illinois. That's where we are, now what's the hold up?"

"The hold up, Ken," I say, snagging the map back, "is that my crotch hurts and we need a damn break. I'd also like it if you'd cut Liam some slack and help him read it instead of discouraging him."

Ken scans me over, seemingly irritated as he swishes a pile of chew around inside his mouth. He spits on the grass and then reluctantly takes a seat beside Liam.

"Ain't nothin' hard about readin', it's livin' that don't make no sense," he states.

I look over at Cliffy laying in the grass, staring up at the sky as the final hint of the sun goes down. I take up a patch of grass beside him wondering what he's thinking, because whether Ken knows it or not, life doesn't make sense to most people, mute company included I'm sure.

"My phone shows there's a motel a few miles ahead," Liam says. "You guys want to check in or keep going?"

"Why you askin' me?" Ken says, now standing. "Ask your wife and that crotch of hers that keeps bitchin' about everything."

I flip Ken the bird as Liam stands and shoves him back a few steps.

"Do not disrespect my wife. She's been nothing but good to you."

Ken spits and then shoves him back as I stand and shake my head, hoping this won't turn into a pissing match.

"What the fuck, Pax? It ain't my fault the woman's got you turned into some kind of pussy now, is it?" he laughs. "You sure are stupid if you think having kids, some stupid bar, and a wife changes what we are. You are sorely mistaken, brother. You isn't hiding nothin' from me, I know what you are and so does she, even if she won't admit it."

"Fuck you, Ken. My name isn't Pax, it's Liam, and I don't know what your problem is but you need to take that shit back."

"Or what?"

"I'll show you or what," Liam growls. Grabbing Ken by his jacket Liam jerks him closer so they are eye to eye.

Pissing contest it is.

"Jesus Christ, you two," I hiss, managing to stuff myself in between them. "What the hell are you guys even arguing about? You're supposed to be friends, brothers, so cut this shit out."

I feel oddly small in between the two of them but I am not afraid to knee a man in the balls if I have to.

"Not until he takes that load of shit back," Liam warns.

"I ain't takin' it back, fuck that," Ken spits. "Come on, Pax, just admit it. Say it out loud just one time that this whole fuckin' shit show is a joke. Stop pretendin' you belong with this girl when you damn well know you're just as ugly inside as me and Cliffy."

I can feel Liam's fists tightening his grip on Ken's collar.

"Really, Ken? What are you trying to prove right now?" I ask as calmly as possible.

I look over and see Cliff standing beside his brother, his eyes looking straight down at his feet.

"I want Pax to admit the truth, that's it," Ken states.

"Why? So you can feel better about Verna's death? Is that what this is about? If you can't be happy, Liam shouldn't? Is that it?"

"Just get out of the way, Vixen," Liam growls, "I don't need you trying to defend me."

"Yeah, now there's a real bright idea," Ken smiles maliciously. "You do realize you're in between two of the world's most dangerous men," he whispers, "and it ain't no good place for you to be unless you know what kind of kinky, fucked-up shit me and Pax is really into."

I inhale sharply, taking in Ken's cold eyes. My mind is spinning, wondering where this darker version of him came from when I realize my throbbing knee has already reacted. I cover my mouth and watch as he grabs his balls and drops to his knees groaning, my heart pounding in my chest.

"Shit!" I say stunned. "I don't know whether to apologize or kick you again you sick son of a bitch."

"Just leave him be," Liam growls, pulling me back.

I catch eyes with Cliff, and he smiles. If I didn't know better I could swear he's laughing to himself.

"I'm not going to kick the fucker while he's down," I say, winking at Cliff and then turning my focus to Liam.

"You shouldn't have kicked him at all. He's always been like this, Vixen."

I take in his disappointed expression as he helps Ken to his feet.

"You're actually going to side with him after what he just said to me?"

"I'm not siding with him," he says, pushing Ken toward his bike. "Get the fuck on it with Cliff and we'll meet you at the next motel you see."

"Whatever," Ken groans. "You shouldn't have brought her if she can't handle the shit this is going to bring out in us."

"In *you*," Liam corrects.

I watch the way my husband looks at Ken, as if he's both hurt and terrified at the same time.

It takes a few minutes for Ken to start the bike, bitching like a wounded dog, but Cliff waves as they finally pull away. I take my coat off and lay in the grass, not wanting to ask why Liam is upset with my reaction. I don't even care at this point. I'm satisfied in knowing that whatever Ken's twisted statement was referring to, it's been put to rest by my knee.

I don't bother moving as Liam sprawls out beside me with his hands underneath his head.

"I apologize," Liam mutters.

"What for?"

"Not preparing you for what Ken can be like sometimes."

I roll my eyes feeling an excuse coming on.

"You're still defending him."

"He's fucked up, Vix. He's still grieving and lost. You confuse him."

"I confuse him?" I ask infuriated.

"You confuse everybody," he laughs. "Don't act so surprised."

"Well it's news to me. How the hell am I confusing?"

He rolls on top of me, straddling either side of my legs holding his hands up until I link my fingers through his.

"It's weird for him, seeing me fit in somewhere and comfortable. Having a real family and witnessing how far I've come. I think he's jealous, and it's hard for him to understand why and how you're able to love me knowing the truth."

I shake my head, not understanding.

"He had Verna, and she knew the truth."

"That's completely different."

"In what way?" I ask, not buying it.

"She was an insider, one of us," he clarifies. "She was just as messed up as we were. It made it easy for Ken to relate to her."

"Well, have you ever bothered to tell Ken the pig that I'm not as untarnished as he thinks?"

He laughs and kisses my fingertips one by one before he responds.

"You're a tough cracker, Vix, I get it, but it's not the same thing, surviving what you did versus living with what we did."

"You mean cookie," I point out, "not cracker. And I don't give seven hate-fucks about what the asshole went through. He threatened me Liam, and I won't tolerate that shit for a second."

His eyes pin mine as he shakes his head.

"You mean you were scared," he states. "Just admit it."

"Fuck that, I don't get scared. Ever."

"Is that right?" he asks doubtingly. "You reacted the same when that reporter said Liv's name. Then again when Gabe brought up your drinking. You only ever fight back when you're afraid, Vixen."

My breath halts as I take in his words, the deep-seated meaning of them coursing through my veins like adrenaline. He's right. How is it that he noticed this and I didn't?

He leans down and kisses me, telling me it's okay to be afraid because he is too.

I sit up and push him off of me.

"It still doesn't excuse his disgusting behaviour, Liam, and when this trip is done, so is he."

"What does that mean?" he asks, confused.

"It means he can fuck off and stay the hell away from me and the kids."

His face turns conflicted, but he nods.

"If that's what you need then fine. But I swear, Vixen, he's not as bad as he makes himself out to be."

"Stop defending him, I've heard enough, and I'm tired. We need to get to the motel."

I can tell by his face he's upset with me but he says nothing and helps me with my jacket. The roads are now black as the streetlights flash past us down the highway. I can't seem to get Ken's dark stare out of my mind as I tail Liam. I feel like I'm on the literal Highway to Hell questioning if I want to go any further down this path with a man as disconnected as Ken seems to be. It makes me question if I'm even safe around him. Maybe he hates me even more than he did before I kicked him in the nuts.

Oh, thank fuck, I think as I watch Liam's arm go out and his signal turn on. We pull into the parking lot of a seriously scummy looking motel attached to a liquor store. The motel itself looks eerily like The Bate's Motel from that fucked up movie which rattles my nerves even further.

Fuck do I need a drink.

I wait for Liam to grab his duffel and then mine as we head inside and get the key to a room. My mind is all over the place, but we pass Ken's bike on the way to room 110 just underneath the staircase, so I know him and Cliff are here.

I take a look around the room as we enter, locking the door behind us.

"Why do you look like you're prepared to kick someone's ass?" Liam asks, flopping onto the bed.

The place is even uglier on the inside then it was on the outside.

Tossing my jacket onto the chair, I say, "Because you brought me all the way out here, away from our really clean, comfortable home, to this shithole straight out of a horror movie. And not only that, the man we're traveling with is a loose fucking cannon, not at all the same person we've been sharing our home with."

Looking offended, Liam sits up and pats the bed.

"Come over here and sit down, please, your pacing is killing me."

I take a seat, feeling his eyes sear into me.

"I'm sitting."

"Stop worrying about Ken," he sighs. "The guy would never do anything to hurt you. He's harmless."

"Were you not looking at the same psychotic looking man I was an hour ago? I am not overreacting and I don't trust him."

"And you actually think I would let him mess with you? Come on, Vixen, give me some credit here. I've known Ken my entire life, he isn't a threat."

"Why are you defending him?"

"He would defend me too if the situation was reversed."

"Oh, so the two of you have some sort of twisted pact, great," I say, disgusted. "I'll remember that while he's looking at me funny and creeping me the fuck out."

I look around the room, displeased there is no mini bar and wanting a drink so badly it hurts.

"Why don't we just get some sleep and I'll have a talk with him in the morning?"

Giving in, I agree, but only because the conversation seems to be getting me nowhere except drowning in my own saliva, salivating for a drink, and craving a night of drunken freedom.

I lay down watching the shadows sway across the walls as the vehicles pass on the highway. I am anything but tired and my nerves are a mess. I can't shake the look in Ken's eyes, or the way he talked to Liam as if his life with me is a fraud and he doesn't belong.

Maybe it really is just like Dell said. *Sometimes you can take the man out of the dark, but you can't take the dark out of the man.*

It makes my heart race thinking about it. What if Dell is right?

What if no matter how much I try to support any of this mess, it's pointless?

Unable to sleep, I peek over at Liam, happy he's sleeping.

If I want to have any hope of settling my overactive brain, I know I need a drink. *That or a seriously good hate-fuck, but my anger buddy is already snoring.*

I tiptoe my away around the room, grabbing my jacket, shoes and the room key, then shut the door behind me.

Slipping my shoes on, I scan the dark parking lot feeling uneasy as I walk toward the flickering sign in the liquor store window. It's the only light around this place and I can't be sure if my anxieties are a result of the spine-chilling surroundings, or if it's because I know I shouldn't be doing this.

"Good evenin'," Ken says, startling me.

"Jesus fuck, Ken."

My heart is beating rapidly as I back away from the staircase and he shakes his head as if I'm entertaining or something.

"Ain't no need to be all jumpy," he says spitting his chew. "You want a drink? You look like you could use one."

I look at the bottle of Jack in his hand and grab it quickly, stepping no closer to him than I have to. His eyes are even darker than I've ever seen them, terrifyingly twisted, so I take a swig hoping it will ease the adrenaline in my body.

"Where's Cliff?" I ask.

"Sleepin'... and good ol' Mr. King, where's he at?"

"Same."

He glares at me, expressionless, as I take another drink and place the bottle on the bottom step.

Leaning down, he takes the bottle.

"I meant what I said, Kirsten."

The sound of my name rolling off his tongue makes my heart race as I watch him take a drink and then he continues.

"Pax and me, we ain't cut from the same cloth you is cut from.

Don't matter if you teach him to spell, dress him up like he's a Catholic, he's infected. Same as I am. Ain't no amount of money, no woman, and no court's ever gonna change what we are."

I steady my breathing and swallow down the obscure tone in his voice.

"Liam says you're jealous," I mutter, trying to stay calm. "Isn't that what the real problem is?"

He smiles wickedly and looks at me as if he can see right through me.

"Darlin', if you knew what my real problem was, you wouldn't be standin' here talkin' to me. Now I think you'd be wise to be a good girl and listen when I tell you to go on inside, and climb into bed with your husband."

I take his maddened face and flat tone as a solid warning and nod. Still rattled by the man, I turn maintaining my composure, and head to the room, refusing to let him see that he scares me.

I climb into bed, getting as close to Liam as I can, feeling only pity for Ken. I didn't see it before, but that man is exactly what my husband once was. Tormented by the things that haunt him and I can see it now. I'm just not sure that I'll know how to fix it.

CHAPTER 35
Hate-Fuck City Revised
LIAM

She's breathtakingly beautiful, my wife. Watching her sleep is one of life's most fascinating gifts. The way her foot hangs off the side of the bed just like Liv's does, and how her golden hair is in disarray across her face, yet she sleeps peacefully. I could sit in this chair and stare at her forever, lost and in awe.

I don't want to wake her just yet, I think as I hit send on my phone. It's probably poorly spelled, but I want to check-in with Helen and the kids, and also Dell who has been incredibly supportive of my mission. I know how hard he's been trying to work with Ken the last few weeks, but the progress has been slow. I figure the things that have taken me three years to achieve will likely take Ken closer to ten. I see so much of me in him and him in me, it's distracting at times. It's like looking into a broken mirror, there is no difference between the fight that wears hard on our faces. It's always there, the hurt, the hate, and the feeling of being unworthy. I never wanted him to feel like I was his responsibility when we were kids, but he did. And for as far back as I can remember, I know I am guilty for a large part of who he is. I owe

Ken irreplaceable moments of time that I won't ever be able to give back. Specifically, when it comes down to the fractions of time he sacrificed for me and for all of us when we were in the basement. He's the kind of man who would call it even, but I remember who the leader was, and I knew what having a brother meant. Even now, he's the only person who understands me completely, the same man who is struggling to breathe just as much as I am at times.

The sad truth to Ken is that I'm positive if it weren't for Cliffy, he'd have followed Verna straight to the other side, and not a soul would have blamed him. Now, he's just a broken man marked by the Devil himself and trying to figure out where he belongs. I want that place to be with Vixen and me, I want him to know that there are people who can love us. People who still want us just as we are. Most of all I don't want Vixen to give up on him, because him and Cliff deserve every beautiful gift I've been given just as much as I do, maybe even more.

I brush Vixen's hair from her face, and she groans.

"No, please don't tell me it's time to get up already."

"Sorry, but it is," I whisper. "We still have a lot of road to cover and I need to go have a talk with Ken."

"Don't bother. I already talked to him last night."

I lean in close and pry her eye open with my fingers so she can see the grin on my face.

"And did he apologize?" I ask, praying they made up.

"No, he did not," she groans.

She slaps my hand off her face and sits up. "He basically gave me a warning growl and sent me to my room like he was my dad. Now can I please have ten more minutes of quiet?"

"Wait, he did what?"

My mind is racing in every direction. Was Ken seriously hitting on my wife?

She rubs her eyes and yawns.

"You heard me, Liam, and stop looking at me like that."

"Well then tell me what he said, Vixen."

I can tell by her face she's just as confused about whatever happened as I am. Ken has never been with any woman other than Verna; I don't think the guy would know where to start if he tried.

"Come on, I need to know what he told you," I plead.

"Shit, Liam, I don't know, I can't really explain it. He kind of reminded me of you when we first met. All trying his darnedest to villainize himself and angry I guess."

"And then what?"

"And then nothing, I came back to bed," she says, looking insulted.

"But you said he growled."

"So? He was mad, people growl when they're mad."

"Not the way we do," I tell her.

I watch her face turn awkward.

"Oh gross, Liam, you're kidding me, right?"

I shake my head and shrug, knowing she's catching on to the underlying situation.

"It's been over eight months since he lost Verna, the guy has needs," I state.

"I'll bet," she says sarcastically. "But that's what hookers are for."

I shake my head and remove my shirt.

"You've seen what we look like; women are terrified of us, Vix. No hooker wants to be with a man with his kind of issues."

"Twenty bucks is twenty bucks," she says running her hands over my chest. "I don't think hookers are too picky about what a man's kinks are, only what his wallet holds."

I grab her wrist, stopping her from messing with my mind.

"You're missing the point," I growl, frustrated. "Listen. To what. I'm trying. To say. There is no hooker in the state of Indiana who isn't gonna go to the cops after Ken's hate-fucked her."

"We are in *Illinois*," she corrects, "and what. The fuck. Is your point?"

Compelled by the irritated tone in her voice, the words come barrelling out of my mouth.

"You need to hate-fuck Ken."

Her mouth falls open and she covers it, beginning to laugh hysterically.

I cross my arms waiting for her to let up, but she doesn't stop. She continues to laugh to the point of tears and just when I think she is done; she starts all over again.

"What the fuck? Will you stop laughing, please?"

She shakes her head and continues which is really starting to aggravate me. *Is she laughing at me? Is she laughing at Ken? Why the fuck is she even laughing? I'm being serious.*

I throw my shirt back on and begin to tie my shoes and she finally stops.

"Where are you going?" she asks, trying to control herself.

"To get Ken."

I look over at her poker straight face happy she's no longer laughing.

"You're fucking with me, right?"

"Uh-uh, why? What's the problem?"

She crosses her arms and gives me the look of death.

"Jesus, Liam, I am not a child's toy for shit's sake, you can't just pass me from hand to hand. And exactly what part of me hate-fucking Ken do you think I'll be okay with? You are out of your damn mind."

"I won't deny that, Vixen, so is it a yes?" I smile.

"No, it's a straight up fuck no, and fuck you, Liam. I'm going to shower and then eat breakfast before I hop on that bike and pretend you never said any of this shit to me."

Well, fuck, guess that means she's not attracted to him the same as me.

Assuming I can work on it for Ken's sake anyway, I head out the door and make my way to the diner inside the lobby. Upon entering, I scan the tables and see Ken and Cliff stuffing their faces and I make my way over.

"What happened to your feisty little guard dog?" Ken asks, motioning for me to sit.

"You can save the prick-based attacks on my wife; I know why she pisses you off."

I exchange nods with Cliffy as I spin the chair around and take a seat.

"Is that so?" he asks.

I don't take my eyes off of his as he tries to stare me down.

"I'm not intimidated by you, Ken, and I don't think Vixen is anymore either. You hit on my wife last night, didn't you?"

"Is that what she told you?"

I lean in close and smile.

"She didn't have to tell me, but we both recognize exactly what you were doing. I just haven't convinced her to accept your offer yet."

"I don't know what the hell you're talkin' about, I didn't offer your wife shit," he snaps. "And you are fuckin' crazy if you're sayin' what I think you is."

"You're talking to me, Ken, and it's no crazier than the shit you did for me as a kid, I owe you. So, if I can get Vixen to agree, are you in or not?"

I watch him stir his coffee and then in the blink of an eye he's got me pulled across the table and so close to his face I can smell his aftershave.

"Now you listen here, and you listen good," he hisses, "I know I ain't no sinless man, but I also ain't no home wrecker either. What in the fuck is wrong with you? Offerin' your wife up like this? You need to grow the hell up and stop tryin' to fix shit that don't need no fixin'."

He lets go of me, shoving me back in the seat and all I can do is take in the madness in his blackened eyes.

"I was only trying to—"

Slamming his fist on the table, the spoon lands on the ground as I look quickly at Cliff shaking his head before he gets up and walks away.

"You ain't listenin' to me," Ken whisper-shouts. "That wife of yours is a fucking godsend. She's more than you know you'll ever deserve you stupid prick. She's come all the way out here on this fucked-up trip, for you, and this is how you treat her? You're a bloody fool. So, don't you sit here and think in that mashed in head of yours that you're doin' me a favor. You is even more of a shit head than I thought if you're too stupid to see you'd be puttin' her right where Verna was for all them years? Don't you fucking get it? She is dead because of this shit, and yet you sit here lookin' at me like I'm the crazy fucker at this table. Get a goddamn grip on yourself and go apologize to your lovely little wife before I knock them shiny teeth down your throat."

I watch his fist tighten and know he isn't kidding so I nod and get up to leave, feeling like an idiot.

"And one more thing," Ken says, as I stand with my back to him. "Stop bein' a fuckin' follower and learn to lead, brother. I can't always be the one in charge and neither can your wife."

I stand waiting to make sure he's done taking in his words for the value they hold. He's right and I know it, Verna would be mad as hell with me for putting Vixen in this position. I walk back to the room feeling ashamed and unworthy not knowing how to face Vixen. I get it now, why Ken was always the leader when we were kids. I hate that even as the man I'm trying to be, he can see through my faults and stop me from doing something unforgivable. And now I owe him yet again.

I enter the room smelling the strong aroma of strawberry shampoo and hearing Vixen's music cranked and coming from the washroom. It's her 'angry playlist' as she calls it, which means she's just as unhappy with me as Ken is. I take a seat at the table trying to come up with the right words as Vixen comes out of the washroom, in her panties. Her damp hair is dripping from the ends as she pulls her t-shirt down over her stomach and turns down the music. The look on her face is that of uncertainty, disappointment even, as she takes a seat beside me and combs her hair.

"Did you find Ken?" she asks.

"Yes, he's in the diner, probably bitching to Cliffy about what a moron I am."

"Why? What happened?"

"Ken's wisdom happened. He pointed out what an asshole I was being. I'm sorry that I asked you to do something so cruelly unfair."

She lets out a sigh and hugs herself.

"It's not that it was cruel, it was kind of thoughtful in a weird Liam-like way," she states. "But sometimes I feel like you think I'm built to withstand and ease the pain of others."

"I don't think it, Vix, I know it. You do it for me all the time," I point out.

"Only because I love you enough to do it," she says with conviction. "Because I know what you can't see when you hit that broken, blackness, the empty place in your mind when we fuck. I know you don't see me when you're there, Liam, that you can't, and I get it. You have to block everything out because it's too much. But what I don't understand is why you would think I would ever let someone else use me like that."

The hurt in her eyes is enough to tell me she's just as disgusted with me as Ken is.

"I wasn't looking at it like that, I swear it Vix. I guess I never realized it bothered you."

"It doesn't," she says sternly, "not when it's with you. Never. When it's with you, Liam."

"Okay," I say knowing she means it. "Ken was just as appalled as you are if that helps any."

Her face turns inquisitive.

"Really? So, are you saying he rejected the idea?"

"Something like that, among an earful."

"Wow," she says placing the comb on the table. "I kept telling myself that you couldn't be serious, but then I realized it's *you* I've been talking to. You are always serious when it comes to your strange ideas. So, what did he say?"

I clear my throat and lean forward, hating myself, but knowing Vixen needs to know how decent Ken really is underneath his criminal facade.

"He said things I should have already known, but I was an idiot. He knew that I was putting you in a horrible position, the same fucking spot Verna died trying to get out of. Then he said what hurt the most, and he was right, which is that I'm like a child and I need to grow up. And lastly, he said the one thing I've always known to be true about you Vix. The simple reason for my very existence."

She smiles as if to say go on, her face as supportive and beautiful as ever. He's completely right; *she's more than I'll ever deserve.*

"He pointed out that you are a godsend. *My* godsend. Even Ken knows how incredible you are, fuck, I can't believe how stupid I was."

She laughs sceptically and pulls her chair closer.

"Ken *'the skull man'* Dodd said all of that?"

I nod.

"I told you, he was only trying to scare you yesterday with his thoughtless bullshit, Vixen. He just doesn't think you should be on this trip. And after the stupid shit I just asked of you, I'm starting to think that maybe he's right."

"Fuck that," she scoffs. "You just asked me to hate-fuck the man, so I'd say that disqualifies you from having any right to tell me where I do or don't belong."

Taking in her *you know I'm right* smirk I cross my arms.

"Well, do you accept my apology or not?"

"Of course I do," she smiles genuinely.

"Good," I say, leaning closer to her, "because I won't be apologizing again after I tell you I want you to head back home."

She looks at me as if I have no say.

"Well, sorry to tell you, sweetie, but I'm already here and that's not going to happen. I don't take orders from you. Not to hate-fuck your brother or when to call it quits."

"Vixen," I warn, irritated and lowering my voice. "I need to be a good leader, and this is not up for debate. I am not asking; I'm damn well telling you. I'm in charge now, and you don't belong out here with us. So just go home, hug and kiss the kids for me, and I'll meet you there when it's over."

She looks at me daringly, as if I'm playing with her, trying to get her angry. Then she stands and lifts her shirt over her head and drops it onto the floor, exposing her perfect tits.

"And I'd like to know in what world you plan to make that happen, Liam?" she pushes, now straddling my lap.

I watch her nostrils flare and I know she's becoming angrier with me by the second, which is turning her on. The sight of her naked makes my dick harden as she presses her tits against my chest and whispers in my ear.

"Hate-fuck me for Ken for all I care, but I am not leaving you no matter what you do to me."

"Fuck," I growl, "I'm serious, Vixen, I'm not trying to get laid, I'm trying to do the right thing."

"Could have fooled me," she says rubbing my dick. "Growl again, God, I love that shit," she taunts.

She begins to rub herself against my now full-fledged erection as I grab her hips and ass, trying to stop her. But in the moment, I can't concentrate on anything else other than the way she feels on top of me. This woman makes me want to fuck the sarcasm right out of her mouth until she obeys me.

Pressing her lips to mine, she kisses me and jerks my hand to her pussy. I can feel her heat and dampness through her panties as she continues to fuck me with her eyes and her mind, the way only Vixen can.

"Fine, I'll hate-fuck you," I hiss, "but you're still going home when I'm done."

"Then I'll just have to make sure you never finish," she says, cupping my balls. "Either that or I'll let you fuck me until you change your mind."

Is she kidding me?

Now I'm mad as hell as I grab her ass and stand up with her wrapped around my waist while I walk her to the bed. Dropping her on it, she gasps excitedly as I tear her panties off and then hastily remove my pants.

"There's no rush," she says, smiling, "I can handle whatever wrath comes out of you and then some."

I ignore her attempt to aggravate me further as I run my fingers over her wet pussy and spread her legs roughly. I grip her wrists in one hand and yank them above her head as she wriggles beneath me, her eyes penetrating mine as if she's permitting me to take what I want. What I need. To unleash whatever festers within me into her until I can't any longer.

This woman that knows me even better than I know myself, gives herself to me fully and without hesitation.

"Godsend indeed," I growl, filling her slowly.

She moans out, her eyes still hellbent on holding steady with mine as I press into her inch by inch, allowing my mind to take in every bit of pleasure she offers. I continue my slow and unhurried assault on her as she wriggles beneath me trying to quicken the pace.

"Stop moving," I warn, "you wanted it to last, well, I'm going to take my time. I plan to keep fucking you just like this for three days if that's what it takes to prove my point."

"Fuck," she moans from deep in her throat. "I'll be holding out for five if you want to play this game."

I smirk down at her, willing myself to stay focused on her eyes. The feeling of her around my dick is intense and hard to control when everything in me wants to let go and slam into her with brute force. Holding back I continue in and out of her, my dick throbbing in her warmth as she arches her back needing to feel my friction.

"Tell me what you want, Vixen. What you need," I urge.

"Ah," she groans. "I need only what you're giving me, slow and gentle," she moans again. "I kind of like it."

I press myself into her hard and groan as she swells around me.

"No, you don't," I grind out, grazing my thumb lightly over her clit, causing her to shudder. "You like it rough, and fast, hard as hell but you want to test me."

Her body shakes to the pleasure I'm inflicting, but still she holds back, admitting nothing.

It hasn't been ten minutes never mind three days and I don't think I'm going to win this argument.

"Come on, Liam, we both know how this is going to end, so just give in and hate-fuck me already. I promise I will never look at you any differently."

"That is the fucking problem," I growl. "I want to be the leader."

"Then lead us both to an orgasm," she mocks, rocking herself over me.

She bites her lip and it drives me wild that she never gives in.

"Damn it! Fine," I groan.

She winks at me as I grip her hips, taking control of her and I start to drive myself into her, hard. She claws at my arms, spreading her legs further apart, trying to take in every part of me she can get.

"Oh, God, fuck yes," she mumbles.

"I. Hate. That. You. Feel. So. Fucking. Good," I say with each thrust, not letting up and feeling her climax build.

"And I love the way you hate me," she pants. "Don't stop, Liam."

I couldn't if I wanted to, I tell myself, now losing my focus. My mind is wandering into the darkest places of my memories as I stagger on the edge working to hold this image of Vixen over everything else. *I want to see her, be here with her, only her.*

"Jesus fuck, Liam," she gasps. I feel her body surrendering as I continue to impale her rapidly, shutting my eyes and wanting everything I hate to disappear.

No longer paying attention, I'm moving on instinct as I feel Vixen's body convulse through her orgasm, and her pussy tightening around me.

"Open your eyes and look at me," she demands.

I do, taking in her stunningly beautiful gaze as I continue to fuck her. She's like an angel, her face flushed and her expression perfectly at peace, even though I am now the monster underneath the man.

"Now stay focused on my face, Liam, stay with me, I am right here," she breathes. "God, I love you, seeing this side of you. You are so beautiful, so worthy of love. You are not bad, Liam; you are not a monster. Now fuck me harder and let it all go."

Her words impale my heart like an electric shock, and I unburden into her like a storm as she grips my face and holds me steady.

"Holy fuck," I mutter, astounded, "I can still see your face, Vix."

"Yeah? For real? You stayed with me?" She laughs as her eyes fill with tears.

"Yeah," I nod, loving how warm her fingers are on my face. "I opened my eyes and it was still you, and fuck are you beautiful."

"So are you," she says, wiping the tears from my eyes. "But am I still grounded or are you going to admit that I belong on this trip now?"

I help her sit up and toss a t-shirt at her thinking about it as we dress.

For the first time, it feels like I can breathe, like I accomplished the impossible. I kind of want to go outside and shout it to the world. *I, Liam King, just hate-fucked my wife and wasn't the monster today!*

"You're ungrounded," I tell her, watching as she throws her jacket on and packs the rest of her belongings.

She smiles and holds up my bike keys, swinging them back and forth.

"Good answer, because if you would have said anything else, I'd have made sure you weren't going either."

"I don't doubt it, you little badass," I say, swiping the keys from her hand. "But I'm still the leader okay?"

She gestures for me to lead the way as we head down to the bikes. The truth is I never would have sent her home, there's nowhere else she belongs other than by my side, and I know it. I get our duffels secured to our bikes as I pull out the map and lean against my seat.

"You make good on your apology?" Ken asks. I look over, watching as he straps his bag to his bike and I nod.

"I did and you were right," I admit, handing him the map.

"I know I was," he says proudly. "Why you givin' me this fuckin' thing?"

"Because even though I want to be a good leader, I still can't read good. So, I figured you're the better man to lead us there, and I'll be the one to lead us home."

"Sounds like you're skippin' out on your homework to me," he says shaking his head.

"Me too," Vixen says. "But I agree with Liam, you were one hell of a brother to him as far as I know, so he's right, you should lead the way."

I watch Ken eye her over and half-smile.

"I still don't think you belong on this trip, but not because you ain't one of us, I was wrong about that part. Anyone who can love a man as tainted as we is, has got to be equally as fucked in the head."

Arching a brow, Vix stands there, smiling.

"Mmm... well is that supposed to be a compliment, an apology, or an insult?" she asks, now laughing.

"I'll let you know when I figure it out for myself," Ken states crabbily. "Now we better get moving, it's another twenty-one-hour ride to the inferno."

Vixen and I shrug at each other as we hop on our bikes and get our helmets on. The only thing I know as we rev our engines and hit the I-90 as the sun comes up is this: there is nothing in the world that can stop us now. We are all riding this highway for something. For Ken, I know it's Verna he's riding for. Cliffy, I'd like to think it's for his freedom, and Vixen, well, I know that badass is riding for me, and what I ride for is simple; to rid myself of everything unholy and to become the man I need to be.

CHAPTER 36
Sins of The Sinner
VIXEN

If seeing is believing, then I *believe* my husband and his crew of brotherly bandits have lost their minds. We drove a total of fifteen hours yesterday but only gained eleven thanks to their insistence to detour, stopping to reminisce in the strangest of places.

No wonder they didn't want me on the trip.

Seems the years they'd spent drifting together from place to place are still engrained tightly in their memories, although it was Ken who knew where most of the events took place. Every time they'd stop to piss, a new memory of something they'd done with Verna came up and they'd wager on which one of them could find the place it happened first. They'd lived off the land mostly and only ever took odd jobs for cash when they could, ones that didn't ask for proof of education or residence because money was scarce. If things were really bad, they'd sometimes wait for restaurants to throw out their expired food and eat it, and other times they'd have to beg. But apparently Verna wasn't one for begging, she didn't mind stealing but she said she could never look a person in the eyes and feel pitied. That's when Liam mentioned the time she once went on a rant about wanting to eat a real meal. It was in the summer one year, close to when she and Liam thought it was time to celebrate their twentieth birthdays, which we now know would have really been their eighteenth. She had it in her head that they deserved only the best dinner that night and went into some restaurant. After she'd ordered enough food to feed a football team, literally, she had them pack it to go and then ran out the door with it without paying. That was the memory that had these boys laughing in tears outside at a random diner rest stop in Kentucky. They'd said Verna ran for an entire mile with those bags, as they followed close behind her, but that she was right. It was a fake birthday they never forgot.

Then there was a field trip over in Missouri where Ken made a campfire in her memory at the very spot they said they'd resided for weeks one year. It must have been a good year for all of them emotionally speaking, because even Cliffy smiled a few times as they told stories. Watching him was like watching Liam in the goody aisle of a supermarket. The only thing I'd wished as I drank in their happiness was that I'd brought a real camera, not just a cell phone. By the time we crossed over into Iowa, I'd learned more about Verna than I had the chance to find out when she was still alive. I know that she was a badass, but in a good way, and that she had no problem beating the shit out of anyone who messed with her brothers or Ken. I heard she even got into a fight at a biker bar once somewhere on the edge of South Dakota. Seems they'd been crossing state lines in circles for years, stopping into cop shops to search for their families, but they always came up short. It was on one of those particular days when the tensions were high, and their hopes were dwindling that she'd dragged them all into some bar and decided to conjure up some free drinks using her God given charm. *Now, I've met Verna, so by charm, I'd swear they were talking about her unrivalled beauty.*

Anyway, as the story goes, apparently Verna decided to drink back a few too many and ended up getting a little touchy feely with a few of the bikers who were covering her tab. Ken being Ken and in love with her at that point, didn't like it so he'd gone over to pull her out of the mess she'd started. The bikers didn't take to kindly to it and tried to rough him up, but that's when Verna hauled off and busted one of their noses, but not before she cranked another one over the head with a beer bottle. While this was happening, Cliff sat there eating peanuts like it was a live action movie, up until Liam stepped in to drag both of them out of the bar, Cliff not far behind. I've never seen Liam laugh so freely as I did when he talked about the real reason Verna was getting so touchy/feely with the men in the bar. That girl had pickpocketed three of them and ended up with close to twelve hundred dollars and a liver full of free drinks that night.

Like I said, badass.

When our bikes crossed over into South Dakota, *where we are now*, we'd made one last stop in Verna's memory. The zoo.

"There you are," Liam says, handing me a glass of water. He takes a seat beside me out on the balcony of the motel we are staying at. It's a beautiful night and although I should be exhausted I don't want to close my eyes to this day just yet.

I look over at Liam and smile and then down at the glass of water I wish was a stiff glass of whiskey.

"I had a drink last night," I mutter. "I shouldn't have, but I did."

"Was it after Ken growled at you?" he asks, as calm as always.

"No, it was *while* he was growling at me. I wasn't even out there to talk to him, I was actually heading to the liquor store."

Liam sighs and then lays his head in my lap.

"Was it because of something I did that made you want a drink?"

I shake my head no, listening to the crickets chirping as I run my hands through his silky hair.

"It was because of what Dell said," I admit nervously.

"What, the thing about taking the man out of the dark, but not the dark out of the man?"

"Yeah, that's the one. I'm just scared he might be right. What if this trip does nothing at all to help the way you feel about yourself?"

He smiles up at me, tracing his fingers up and down the side of my face.

"That's not possible, Vix, I already feel differently than I did."

"Because of yesterday's hate-fuck/love-fuck?" I ask curiously.

"That is the biggest reason," he laughs, "but also because of today at the zoo."

I laugh at his face that looks like he's a sugar happy kid in a candy store.

"Yeah, I could see how much being there and thinking of Verna made you happy. You looked like Liv the day we brought Matthew home. All dumbstruck and full of excitement at the same time."

"It's the same way I've always looked at you."

I smack his arm and shake my head.

"Don't get all sappy on me or we might have to venture back into love-fuck land."

"Are you threatening me with an incredible time?" he asks, groping my breast.

"Nope, not tonight, we need to get to bed because I'm guessing tomorrow is going to be another enchanting adventure."

Liam growls in fake disappointment as he helps me up and I follow him inside.

I lay my face on his chest when we hit the bed, instantly melting in his embrace as my eyes close to the wonder of what tomorrow holds.

* * *

"Do you smell that?' Ken asks with his arms out as he stretches, spinning in a circle. "That there is the smell of hell itself and it's as if the Devil is whisperin' to us, *welcome home minions*."

We crossed into Montana a little over two hours ago and are now stopping to refuel and rest after another long and eventful day. It's getting dark out, cooling down too, half past nine, and the only thing I personally happen to smell out here is donuts.

"You want anything while I run inside to pay?" Liam asks.

"The donuts smell mighty good," I say, mocking Ken's accent.

He laughs and gives me a thumbs up as I watch the three of them enter the store, knowing by Ken's unimpressed glare he must hate that I find his voice amusing. He's starting to grow on me, although I still have no clue why the kids were so quick to like him. I'm still trying to wrap my head around his always pissed off demeanor, but I think it's just who he is.

I glance around, feeling uneasy about being back here, and not for good reason as far as I'm concerned. I keep praying that no one will recognize any of us because the last thing we need is for the press to get wind of us being here, let alone the reason for us being here. They would have a field day turning it into a headline that would most likely only make the world view this as another reason to berate them. I will never understand the way the world perceives them and I've never been able to get over the fact everything that happened to them was done in this very state, the same one all of them were born in. Yet their strength and determination is always overlooked. The fact they'd spent years travelling together, the wrong way mind you, and ending up in Georgia. But after everything I've heard them say about the woman Verna was, at least I can smile knowing they had each other. I just wish they'd found the answers they deserved, but now all they can hope to find is justice and closure.

"Your donuts, my evil Vixen princess," Liam says, dangling the bag in front of my face.

"Don't call me that, please," I say taking the bag and cramming a half donut in my face. "And speaking of princesses, my mom just texted about Liv and Matty. She said they are good but missing us and 'the shhh man' like crazy."

"Fantastic," he says stealing the other bite of my donut. "And how's Mac?"

I watch his eyes light up like they always do when he talks about the dog and I shake my head.

"I didn't ask about Cheese Head, Liam, he's still a dog, not our kid."

"Evil princess," he mutters, "just like I said."

I hold the bag of donuts out in offering toward Cliff as I curiously stare at Ken strapping down a large box of fireworks to his bike.

"So where to now?" I ask, wondering what it is he plans to celebrate.

"Don't look at me with them judgin' eyes," he says. "I got a plan, but first we're headin' back to my trailer to get some gear."

Liam and I look at each other, confused.

"But Clancy is close to three hours past where we are supposed to be going," I point out.

"I know that, woman, but I'm the leader, so what I says, goes," Ken snarls. "And I say we is goin' to my place first. We can spend the night there and head back out tomorrow mornin'. If you don't like it, you can always turn around."

"Don't be a dick, Ken. Vix goes where I go," Liam states.

"Yeah, Ken," I say sticking my tongue out.

"You two is just as juvenile as Cliffy and them kids of yours. I'm startin' to see why y'all get along so damn good."

I look over at Cliffy and my heart evaporates into a puddle as I witness the man smile proudly. Even without talking, his dark eyes represent a playful side of him that Ken might hate, but I've grown to love.

"It's okay, Ken," I say optimistically, "we love you too, even though you're too grumpy to admit that deep down you love our delightful companionship."

Ken snarls and tightens the strap forcefully before he looks me in the eyes.

"Just stuff another donut in that pie hole, *companion*, and get on that bike."

I do as I'm told and shove an entire donut into my mouth, chewing extra loud and with my mouth open. Liam laughs but Ken ignores me.

I guess only Verna could bust down the man's impenetrable walls.

* * *

By the time we make it to Ken's trailer in Clancy, it's midnight. His place is on a large piece of land in a remote area but it's nice with wide open landscaping surrounded by fully matured trees. You would never know this place even existed unless you were looking for it. Then there's his trailer, I can tell Verna picked it by the fact it's a dusty rose pink with white trims around the entire thing and matching wrought iron security bars on every window. I stare up at the three signs nailed to the walls around the door and realize that this wasn't just their home, it was more like their hidden barricade.

The first says, 'Get the fuck off my lawn, ALL TRES-PASSER'S WILL BE SHOT ON SIGHT!'.

The second one says, 'I bet my gun is bigger than yours!'.

And third, 'Can't fix stupid, but you can always kill em' instead.'

I look over at Ken and watch as he stands in the doorway unshackling a bunch of chains and padlocks to his own front door. In a way, I want to laugh, but I realize this is how he tried to protect what was his.

"Nice place," Liam says, also eyeing the signs. "So, do you really have a stockpile of guns inside?"

Ken tosses the pile of chain onto the deck and laughs as he pushes the door open.

"Fuck no, but the signs did their jobs and got you thinkin', didn't they? Verna wasn't takin' no chances when it came to respectin' what we loved."

Liam nods and steps inside and all I can think about is asking where Verna got the gun from that she killed herself with. Instead, I follow them inside and take a look around.

The place is small, but so different than what I imagined they lived like. I'd only ever been able to picture living how they did when I'd met them in Fairmount in that dirt-infested shack they'd once called home. But this, this is nice. It's clean and organized with a spacious kitchen to the left and sitting room to the right. If I had to guess just by looking around at all of the photos and romance novels that line the mantle above the fireplace, I'd say nothing that was Verna's has ever been touched.

"Drinks are in the fridge but the booze is out back by the fire pit where Verna spent most of her time. Help yourselves, I'm goin' to shower," Ken states.

I look over at Liam whose eyes seem to be questioning if I caught the part about the liquor as I place one of Ken and Verna's photos back on the shelf.

"I'm good, stop staring," I tell him.

He puts his hands up and sighs.

"I'm only trying to be supportive. We could always call Claire for advice if you need it."

"It's after midnight, and I wasn't exactly planning to tell my mother or Claire about my issue, I can deal with it on my own, thanks."

I turn on my heel, almost bumping into Cliff and knocking the drinks from his hands.

"Shit! Sorry Cliff, sometimes I forget you are even around," I say, taking a glass. I sniff the contents of what appears to be orange juice as he looks at me funny and shakes his head.

"Oh right, your ears still work just fine," I smile. "Promise not to say a word to Ken?"

He flips me the finger and smiles making my heart feel overloaded with joy again.

At least one of the Dodds seems to find me amusing.

Giving me the *hold on one minute* signal, I watch Cliff head down the hall that I assume leads to the bedrooms and washroom as Liam and I take a seat on the sofa. The exhaustion starting to set in is brutal, but I can't help but let my eyes wander around the room that holds so many memories of the Verna I wish I'd known better.

"Heads up," Liam says as a pillow nails me in the side of the head. I turn to Cliffy and laugh as he lofts a blanket at me and gestures for me to stand.

He removes all of the sofa cushions which reveals a hidden bed inside and Liam's eyes practically bug out of his head.

"Holy shit! There's an entire bed inside of your sofa!" he gasps. "Why don't we have one of these, Vix?"

I laugh at the thrill on his face, loving how even the smallest of things still excites him.

"Because the kids could get hurt, or worse, they could get trapped in one of these," I state. "And don't give me the pouty face, it's not happening."

He lets out a muffled growl and helps Cliff make the bed as Ken enters the room.

"Washroom's free if any of y'all want to shower. Cliffy will put some towels out for you guys. Make yourselves at home, I'm headin' to bed. Oh, and don't fuck around with Verna's miniature statue collection or I'll bust you up."

"Got it... and goodnight to you too, Ken," I say scanning the room for the so-called collection.

Cliffy points to the mantle above the fireplace where a small collection of gnomes doing highly inappropriate gestures with their fat little hands is displayed. I can't help but laugh at their roguish expressions and then to my surprise I turn to see Cliff holding his arms out.

I move closer to him wondering if I'm reading the situation wrong as he jerks me into an embrace.

Son of a bitch, Cliffy Dodd is actually hugging me.

The guy smells like one of those car fresheners in the shape of a tree and his grip on me is solid. Not the kind of hug I would have suspected a man of his serenity would possess.

"Don't get any ideas," Liam states, undressing into his boxers, "Vixen is a one-man woman, which sucks for you because she'd probably hate-fuck you so good she'd unmute you since she's the very cure for all things hate-fuck related."

Cliffy lets go of me and his face is flushed as he shakes his head rapidly trying to reassure Liam he was thinking of no such thing.

"Don't listen to him," I tell Cliff while rolling my eyes at Liam. "Feel free to hug me anytime you want, I know you were just being friendly. And despite what Liam thinks, I am not actually the cure to anything, but if I was, for you, I'd do it in a heartbeat."

With that, Cliff gives Liam a proud but playful smirk before he heads to his room.

Liam cocks a brow, looking surprised by my answer.

"You'd seriously hate-fuck Cliffy but not Ken?" he asks, perplexed.

I shrug and undress into my panties and a clean t-shirt, too tired to shower.

"You are such an ass sometimes," I say climbing underneath

the bedding. "And no I wouldn't, I only told him that because he hugged me which means he likes me, *unlike* Ken. I thought after yesterday's breakthrough we were going to refer to our intimate moments as love-fucking now."

Wrapping his arms around me, Liam pulls me close against him so my face is pressed into his chest.

"It's complicated to me sometimes," he says, his breath ragged and warm in my hair.

"What is?"

"Trying to title what we have. This love, hate, sex stuff. Maybe we should just call it something different altogether."

"Like what?" I ask breathing him in. The man smells divine, intoxicating, just like home as I close my eyes to the feel of his heartbeat against my face.

"How about something unique to us," he says stroking my hair, "like outlawed lovers, or distorted lovers?"

"Or tainted lovers," I add, realizing nothing really covers whatever it is we are.

"I don't know, Vix, Tainted Love-Fuck City doesn't have quite the same ring to it," he reasons.

"Okay... well I wasn't aware we were renaming the entire city of our love," I laugh, "but let's just sleep on it until we come up with something we both like. Goodnight, Liam, I love you."

"Night, Vixen, love-hate you more."

★ ★ ★

I awake in the morning hanging halfway off the bed to the obnoxious sound of the blender and Ken's eyes clearly plastered to my ass and checking me out.

Either that or he could be plotting to leave me here judging by the intense look on his face.

"Good morning," I shout over all of the noise. I slip my jeans on and notice Liam must be up already.

"Mornin'," Ken says in between stopping and restarting the awful racket with his eyes glued to the television. "If you want coffee, you're goin' to have to make it yourself, I ain't got no clue how to work that machine."

I have to piss, bad, so I motion at the hallway and find my way to the washroom. I can hear the shower running and the door is a crack open, about to knock I see Cliff come out of his room and beeline toward the washroom.

"You gotta go bad too huh?" I ask, moving out of his way.

He nods but juts his head toward the washroom and then points to himself and then the back door.

"Oh, you're gonna take a leak outside?" I ask cringing.

He nods again and shrugs as if this is a normal occurrence so I smile and then lock myself in the washroom with Liam.

After living with the three of them in the same household the last few weeks, I get that they have no issues with privacy around each other, but I am not like them. *Ain't no one looking at my junk except Liam's feral stalking eyes.*

After going to the bathroom, I drop my clothing on the floor and climb into the shower, finding those exact eyes as he turns to look at me, his smile wicked as all sin.

"Don't even think about it," I say stopping his nomadic hand from exploring me. "We are not screwing in Ken's shower."

"Well why not?" he asks trying his luck again. I slap his hand and pass him a bar of soap before I spin around so he can wash my back.

"For lots of reasons," I say gathering my hair over my shoulder.

"Like what?"

"What do you mean *like what*? For one, we are guests here, and for two, we will probably break something and then Ken will want to kick our asses for sure because you still don't exactly know how to 'play nice' when it comes down to it."

"Oh, I can play very nice now," he tells me in a low rasping growl. "Let me prove it."

I turn to meet his pleading eyes with mine and shake my head, also stealing the bar of soap back as I tell him to turn around.

"I will wash your back and then we are finishing up in here, without hate-fucking... I mean love-fucking or whatever we're calling it now. Understood?"

He nods and mutters something under his breath as he turns the other way.

"What was that?" I ask, contemplating smacking his solid, beautiful ass.

"I said, maybe I should just take it from you."

The words pierce my chest like daggers sending feelings of shock, confusion, and rage throughout my body. Unable to process it, I toss the soap into the stream of water and say nothing as I grab a towel and dry off.

If he's smart, he'll keep his mouth shut and think about what the fuck he just said.

I don't know if it's this stupid trip in general, or the way he's learning to find his voice, or if it's simply the pressure he's facing with heading into the tempest of that basement today that's bringing this aggression out in him, but I do know one thing for sure.

It'll be a frosty day in the fires of hell before I ever let him think he can threaten me.

CHAPTER 37
Closure
LIAM

I shouldn't have said it. Fucking hell, I'm an idiot and I hate myself for it. For saying it out loud and seeing the stained disappointment in her eyes. Vixen should feel protected by me, but instead, I'm exactly the evil villain I've been trying to defeat this entire fucking time. It feels like the harder I try to expel the darkness that festers in my soul, the deeper it attaches itself to me. I wonder how she ever loved me at all, and I don't know if she will forgive me, not that I've asked, nor am I deserving of it.

I take a glimpse back at her tailing me, wishing I could see her face through her tinted visor and wondering why she still wants to be a part of this. She hasn't spoken a single word to me since we packed up and left Ken's place more than three hours ago, which means we can't be more than thirty minutes from our destination, and if I'm honest, I'm starting to feel tense. I don't want to admit it, but maybe this was a bad idea, and since Ken seems so gung-ho to get there, I don't think there is much point in me saying anything now. I found he seemed, I dunno, off this morning, not his usual fury fired-up self. He was worse, the guy was more miserable than I've ever seen him, as if being back at the trailer brought back his loathe for life ten-fold. I would have asked Vix if she'd noticed it too, but I figured she would have told me to screw off or to ask him what his problem was myself. It's at times like this I wish Cliffy could talk, I don't do so good when I feel alienated.

I follow Ken as he pulls into the rundown looking service station on a remote backroad and we hop off the bikes.

"Just gonna top up the tank before we ride straight down that road and into purgatory," he says, pointing behind me.

I turn and lock eyes with Vixen, noting the bitter look of *fucking asshole* on her face before my eyes wander out to the fields of wheat across the road. It takes a minute to kick in, but I recognize exactly where we are as I walk back to the edge of the road and scan the street as far as I can in either direction.

Motherfucker, there it is.

My mind floods with the images of the pitch-black night I'd made it to the very payphone that stands just one-hundred yards from me. It's weathered and probably not in service, but it still holds up as the marker for all 1233 strides I ran through the storm that night, and the most fucked up part is that it still feels like yesterday. I can feel the pain of it in my feet, smell the rain coming down, and the fear that was driving me the entire time.

"Where are you going?" Vixen asks, catching up and grabbing my arm.

I point to the payphone and keep walking.

"That's it," I whisper, "the very phone I used to report what evil things lay hidden way down there, on the other side of those fields," I tell her.

"Shit, Liam, are you okay?" she asks concerned. "Do you want to stop and talk about this for a minute?"

I shake my head as we get closer, remembering how all I could think was that my family would be dead by the time I found my way back. That it would be my fault if they were, and it's what kept me going regardless of the rocks and thistles that were ground into my feet or the fact I was soaked and freezing.

"What the fuck are you two up to?" Ken hollers from behind us.

"He's showing me the very spot he saved all your lives, Ken."

"Well, fuck me," Ken hisses. "I'll be down there in a sec, just gotta grab somethin' first."

I don't bother to wait for him as I reach out and pick up the receiver. It's broken, which seems fitting considering that's how I feel most of the time.

"Is there anything I can do to help whatever it is you're going through?" Vixen asks.

I look over at her and force a smile.

"You're already doing it. Just being here is all I need."

She smiles back and sighs.

"Yeah, well I wouldn't have missed this fucked-up trip for the world, even if you are displaying signs of PTSD."

I can't tell if she's referring to my behavior now, or back when we were in the shower and the stupid shit I said.

"I'm sorry, Vixen," I say pulling her close. "I know this can't be easy for you either and I didn't mean what I said. I would never—"

Shoving me out of the way, Vixen gasps as Ken comes running full tilt at us with a sledgehammer in his hands. In his eyes I swear I can see the Devil himself as he hauls back and then swings the hammer with so much force it sends parts of the payphone casing flying in every direction.

"Jesus fuck, Ken!" Vixen yells. "What the hell are you doing?"

"Gettin' closure. Ain't that why we're here? Now get the fuck outta my way, this bitch is goin' down."

I pull Vixen further onto the grass as we watch Ken stand

there destroying the thing, piece by piece and blow by blow. I have to say it does look pretty fun as Cliffy makes his way over and gestures at Ken for a turn.

"Be my guest, little bro," Ken says, handing the hammer over. "Ain't gonna be nothin' left of this fuckin' thing when we is done here. Now this my friends, is what Kenneth James Dodd says is closure."

Vixen mock laughs, both of us wondering if he's lost his mind, although part of me wants to have a go at it too. We watch Cliffy for a few minutes as he smashes it with a blaze in his eyes, one I've never seen sweet and silent Cliffy possess.

"Come on, you two, batter up," Ken states, taking the hammer from Cliff.

He holds it out in our direction, his face determined to tell us we aren't leaving here unless we pay our dues. Vix and me look at each other, and she shrugs, reaching for the hammer.

"So, if I do this," she says pinning eyes with Ken, "does it mean I'm officially part of the crew?"

He laughs and nods.

"I ain't never taken you for stupid, Vixen, but I guess you need people to be real clear with you. You always was one of the crew, it just took me a while to realize it. Now fuck that thing up before I do somethin' dumb like hug you."

The beautiful smile that takes over Vixen's face is one that leaves me breathless. Not only does she look proud like I've never seen, she looks bad-fucking-ass, and that payphone has no clue what's coming.

I watch in anticipation as she lines it up, gets a strong stance like she's about to hit a home run, and then she nails that thing so hard it tilt's sideways as chunks of plastic start to fly. The sounds of sheer madness that escape her lips are loud as hell as she strikes it repeatedly until she runs out of steam.

"Your turn, Liam," she says handing me the hammer. "Knock it out of the fucking park for Verna, and for everything that haunts you."

I stand and take the hammer from her, filled with a sense of both honour and hatred. The privilege of knowing Verna would have loved everything about this moment, and the hate that runs through my veins when I think of the Paulsons. Every swing I take connects, each one harder than the last as the handle vibrates through my palms with each blow. With each swing I take, a vibrant vision of Verna's face enters my mind and then it becomes replaced with one of the Paulsons. Over and over I smash it and by the time I finish, breathless and blistered, I realize I've demolished the thing completely down to its wiring.

"Christ! You are one twisted son of a bitch," Ken laughs swiping the hammer back.

"No, he isn't," Vixen states. "It had to have felt good, didn't it Liam?"

I high five her and smile.

"It was alright, but I'd feel a lot better if I knew you forgave me for this morning."

Vixen wipes the bead of sweat from my brow and then kisses me.

"Like I said, I'm chalking your little slip of the tongue up too PTSD, but if you ever threaten me again, let me assure you, your face is gonna look worse than that payphone."

The dead serious glimmer in her eyes tells me she isn't kidding.

"I give you my word, Vix, I won't ever say it again."

"Good, because I really happen to love your face exactly how it is. I just need a couple of minutes to call and check on the kids, I'll meet you guys over at the bikes," she finishes, pecking me on the cheek.

I jog back toward the fuel station and watch as Ken struggles to get his hammer back inside his duffel. I have no clue why he felt the need to bring a sledgehammer with him but decide not to ask since it practically led to the outcome of Vixen no longer being pissed with me. I also haven't figured out why the man bought a box of fireworks either, but Ken has always been a hard man to figure out.

"I got a question," Ken says, eyeing me from the side. "How long did that Dell fellow figure we'd been locked down in that basement for again?"

I'm positive he already knows the answer but tell him anyway.

"Eleven years."

"That's what I thought," he says walking toward me. "It's a long fuckin' time to get to know your cellmates' nasty habits ain't it?"

I nod unsure what he's getting at.

"Yeah, I guess... what's your point?"

"Your face, brother, that's my point," he laughs. "I can tell you're holdin' back askin' me some stupid question like usual, so just go on and damn well ask already."

"Okay, fine, I will," I say crossing my arms. "I want to know what your plan is with the fireworks, and what was the deal with your extra cranky attitude this morning?"

His expression turns almost demonic as his spectral eyes drill firmly into mine.

"You ain't never lost the woman you love," he whispers. "In fact," he says poking me in the chest, "you ain't never lost nothin' at all, have you, Mr. King?"

I grab his hand and shove him.

"What the fuck are you talking about? Verna was my sister, you ignorant prick."

He laughs and shakes his head as Cliff steps closer to me and crosses his arms, seeming just as confused about Ken's remarks as I am.

"Your sister, huh?" he says laughing like a lunatic. "You need to quit sayin' that shit out loud, ain't you been watchin' the news? The entire world thinks you was fuckin' the same woman you be callin' your sister. Do you know how that makes us look?"

I can tell by the wrath in his eyes it's a rhetorical question and hold my tongue. I've never seen Ken look so volatile and I don't want Vixen or Cliff to see what I'm about to do to him if he doesn't calm the fuck down.

Pulling a flask from his inside pocket, I watch as he takes a few swigs, realizing the asshole is not only off his fucking rocker, he's hammered.

"I'll tell you how it makes us look if you ain't gonna admit it," he slurs. "Like fucking animals, Liam. The world hates us, they don't like people like you and me, nor do they give a shit about what went down in that sinister pit of a basement," he spits and then takes another drink.

Every muscle in my body is tense to the tone of his voice and the hate in his eyes, but I understand every repulsive thing he's feeling.

I also now know this is exactly why Vixen has a no TV rule at our place, unless it's on the kids' channel, no news coverage allowed.

I notice Vix stop to my right, covering her mouth with a shattered look in her eyes, so I gesture at her to stay where she is. I can't guarantee whatever this darkness is that's starting to spill out of Ken won't turn even uglier.

"What?" he starts in again. "Ain't none of you got fuck all to say about it? Or am I the only one of us whose got the balls to admit how vile we is? All of us is fuckin' worthless and our story sure a shit ain't gonna win the hearts of nobody in that courtroom a few months from now."

"That isn't true, Ken," Vixen says gently. "Verna's parents will be there, and they said they'd support you guys every step of the way."

"Are you stupid?" he asks moving toward her. I step in the way and put my arm out.

"You better get that fuckin' arm outta my way if you know what's good for you."

I shake my head.

"I don't think so, Ken. Whatever you need to say can get said from right here," I state firmly. It takes everything in me not to growl at the man and give him a fair warning on what will happen if he fuck's with my wife.

"Both of you is stupid, ain't ya? I don't need this shit," he whispers. "Least of all from the two of you and your perfect fucking lives. Well I got news for you, it ain't gonna be so perfect no more once that lawyer tears you to shreds for bein' a sister fucker, a goddamn rapist piece of shit, no better than the imposters, and guess what?" he asks, slamming yet another drink and wobbling back toward his bike. "I ain't gonna be there to help you no more. I'm done, Liam, Pax, whoever the fuck you are. I'm done, and I ain't never gonna let *nobody* call me no *brother* fucker, let alone tarnish Verna's name for the sake of some dumb fuckin' crusade. Some bullshit battle for justice that don't exist anymore than we do in the world's eyes."

The pain on his face looks rabid.

I bite my tongue as he gets on his bike and starts it, and I grab Cliff's arm, stopping him as he tries to follow.

"Just let him cool down. He needs a minute and the roads out here are empty. We'll follow him to the house in a few minutes."

Cliff nods and I pull Vixen closer as Ken hauls ass out of the parking lot, howling in the air and speeding like an asshole.

"Jesus, that was an earful. Are you okay?" Vixen asks. Somehow, she can still look at me after hearing all of that, but the look on her face is the same as it always is. Non-judgmental and completely in love with me, yet I have no clue how.

"Yeah," I swallow, "perfectly fine, besides the fact my so-called brother just drove off drunk and told me how he really felt for once."

"Well it's not true, Liam, he's wrong. You did what you had to, just like Ken did. He knows it, I know it, and Verna knew it too."

I appreciate the love in her tone, but it doesn't do anything to alleviate the hurt in my chest, or the fear of wondering if he's right. What if the world never sees the truth? What if the Paulsons' lawyer is even more of a smug schmuck bastard than Gabe could ever be? Maybe I should stop referring to Verna as my sister, even though the thought of that alone kills me inside.

I sigh and pull Cliffy into a hug that he fights against for a few seconds and then embraces.

"I'm sorry Ken is losing his shit, bud. I'll try to fix it when we get to the house. You wanna ride on the back of the Hog or Vix's Ninja?"

He points to Vixen's bike which doesn't surprise me at all. *Who wouldn't want to press their dick up against the back of the world's hottest wife?*

Vixen's face flushes as she catches the dirty smile across my face, and she laughs.

"You're so gross sometimes, Liam. Come on, Cliffy, get your helmet buckled and hop on."

"It's not my fault you have such a great ass," I point out. "But now you'll just have to stare at mine until we get there, past all 1233 strides through those fields."

"Are you sure you're ready to go back there?" she asks.

I want to say no, but Ken's already headed there so I nod, thinking I don't have much choice.

"And what about you?" she asks Cliff.

He shrugs, looking terrified, but I can't tell if it's going to the place itself making him nervous or the fact his brother left here in a drunken rage.

"You have a choice you know," Vixen tells him. "You don't have to go in there just because Ken dragged you all the way down here. You know that, don't you?"

Cliff takes a deep breath and shakes his head, pointing to himself before he circles his heart and then indicating toward the direction Ken took off in.

"Brotherly love prevails, huh?" I ask.

He shakes his head up and down and smiles a toothy grin, seems the guy has smiled more in the last two months than he did his whole life. Well, the whole stretch that I've known him for anyway.

"Alright, follow me," I say, starting my engine. "And do not punch it down those roads, Vixen, they are narrow and nothing but straight gravel."

She flips her visor down and gives me the thumbs up as I pull out.

I know I am not ready in the slightest for what we are about to face. My mouth is dry just thinking of it, the old abandoned house of horrors that holds nothing but broken pieces of my soul and the memories I am hell-bent on confronting. I can only hope Ken has had enough time to confront some of his own, because it hurts like hell to know he feels as shameful as I do. I never really thought about it from his perspective, but the anger he carries makes sense to me now. He hates himself for having been forced to do things to his own brother, and even I can't imagine the scars that must have left him with. Maybe we should have been more open to talking about it when we first escaped, or perhaps I should have done more than plug my ears and shut my eyes because I was too damn weak and hungry to fight anymore. I wish I had done so many things differently, but most of all I wish I could show Ken a way out of the pain I know so well.

"Jesus Christ!" I shout, turning the throttle and pinning it. The entire field ahead of us is burning out of control as thick black smoke fills the air.

I glance back making sure Vix is still right behind me and I motion at her to pull over just as we approach the hundred-yard mark from the house. My heart is pounding as I hop off the bike and remove my helmet trying to see any sign of Ken's bike.

"What the hell is he doing?" Vixen asks, her voice startled.

It's hard to see through the smoke but we can hear his engine in the distance as Cliff starts to run ahead of us. I barley manage to grab the back of his jacket and haul him back just as the house explodes before our eyes. The sound is like thunder rolling through my ears and into my veins as I watch in horror, reaching for Vixen's hand.

The entire world is silent, and, in the blink of an eye, Ken is gone. There is not a single word I can use to describe the agony as tears fill my eyes and I look over trying to decipher what the strange sound I hear is.

In twenty-nine years, I have never heard Cliffy Dodd make a sound until this very second. A sound so tormenting I can feel his anguish in the depths of my soul. I'm frozen with fear and unable to breathe.

"No, Cliff, don't go in there!" Vixen yells.

I try to stop him but miss as he bolts toward the house, pieces of old siding and paint chips are still falling from the sky as me and Vixen start to chase after him.

"Fuck, Cliff, stop!" I shout. He doesn't listen as I look at Vixen, panicked. "Fuck, fuck, shit, I have to go in there and get him. You need to stay out here."

"Oh, no I don't," she says still keeping pace with me. "If you're going in there, so the hell am I."

"Jesus fuck, fine!" I growl, having no time to argue with her. "We will go in, grab Cliff, and then we get the hell out! Cover your face with this," I say removing my shirt.

"Cover your own face with it," she says removing hers too and tying it around her face.

If ever there was a time I realized my wife is a complete freak of nature, just like me, it would be now.

Never has my heartbeat faster as the smoke and flames billow all around us and it's damn near impossible to see Cliff. Listening to only the faint sounds of his wailing, I grab Vixen's hand and pull her behind me trying to get to him until the piercing sounds of—*motherfucker, this is insane*—firecrackers going off within feet of us. I can't see where the hell they are igniting from, but the flashes light up through the smoke just enough that I catch a glimpse of Cliff tossing debris around. My eyes are watering and it's hard to breathe as I reach out and grab Cliff by the collar and jerk him back.

"Fourteen steps, Vix, I counted. Turn around," I choke out, "and walk back fourteen steps. We will be right behind you."

"You fucking better be," she wheezes.

Trying to fight me, I hear Cliff make all kinds of noises I've never heard. The panic of it all is setting in and I don't know whether anything else in the place is about to detonate so I grab his lanky ass and toss him over my shoulder.

He's not too compliant about it but I walk the hottest, most unbearable steps I've ever taken and grab Vix's hand just outside where the porch used to be. We get a few feet away from the place and I drop Cliff to his feet as we all struggle for air, congested and listening to the sounds of sirens in the distance as the fields continue to burn. I look over at my soot-covered wife and nod that I'm okay as I feel the tears form in my eyes at the sight of the ones already streaming down her face, and then we hear a clicking sound and look over at Cliffy.

The forsaken look in his eyes tells me there isn't a fucking thing I can do to stop what's going to happen next, so I grab Vixen, clutch her head into my chest and hug her for dear life. Then I nod my final goodbye into the eyes of my brother, tell them both that I love them, and inhale hard as I stand, waiting for him to pull the trigger.

CHAPTER 38
Where Are You Mr. King?
VIXEN

Six months later...

And then there was one.

A worn down, broken shell, the living ghost of the man I married. What's left of him is only darkness, a vengeful anger he can't seem to control most days because he blames himself. It's been painstaking watching him pull away from the kids, especially Liv who doesn't understand where 'the shhh man' went. As a mother, I can't put into words how devastating it is to see your three-year-old daughter dressed so pretty all in black and then have to watch her drop flowers onto the coffins of the men she never understood laid dead inside. Her world is broken, my world is malfunctioning, and Liam's world is shattered. And still I am standing here, trying to hold it all together, knowing the upcoming trial looms in the air over Liam like an obscure cloud.

Thank God for my mother's once imbalanced golden rule; King's don't cry.

It's what's been keeping me going, although it's sad to admit. But in a way, it's my saving grace at the moment. If I wasn't so used to suppressing the pain, the shit that's gone on in the last six months would have drowned me alive in my own tears and I know it. Losing Ken and Cliff has destroyed Liam. The culpability that he feels because it was his idea to go back there has burdened him with a guilt I can't imagine living with, even though it isn't his fault.

Then there is the horrific experience he endured having watched Cliff blow his brains out while he sheltered me from having to see it. But I understand my husband, why he thinks it's his fault, and although it's fucked-up to say, something good actually came of his brothers' deaths. After the police interrogated Liam on what happened the day the Dodds took their lives, they did an investigation. That investigation eventually led to a news broadcast in which Dr. Dell informed the world of the reasons he'd felt they took their lives according to what I'd told him. The way Ken had become so fed up with the news tearing Verna's name down, ripping his life apart, and labeling them all as monsters. Dell spoke of how all of it had damaged him in ways that were irreparable. He went on to say that in the short time he'd known Ken, he would have guessed he was contemplating death, although he never could get Ken to talk about much at all.

As for Cliffy, it ended up coming out that the gun he'd used to follow Ken to the other side was the same one Verna had used to take her life with as well. It was registered to Verna and given to Cliff as a gift knowing he was always striving to feel protected. *The hindrance of not having a voice, I guess.* Whatever the deal was doesn't matter, but the guilt of Verna's death had been riding on Cliff's conscience from the second she died. It was in Dr. Dells opinion that Cliff also suffered from a deep depression much like Ken's, but that he'd always held on out of respect for Ken and everything he'd done for Cliff when they were kids. The bond they had was unbreakable, but eventually the memories of their childhood had infected them both to the point of no return. Dell was very clear in his final statement, pointing out that all of them were victims of the press's shameful decision to attack the Forgotten Four rather than support them. He asked them how many lives had to be lost at the hands of the real monstrosities before they would be happy.

It took a couple of weeks after the statement aired for it to sink in with the public, that the crucifixion of the lives forced upon each of them as children was not their fault.

And of course, *now*, after everyone Liam loved is fucking dead and buried, the world decides they love him. *Go figure.* There have been rallies of support for him across the country and the reporters haven't gotten off our front lawn in three months. They want to know Liam's side of the story, which according to Gabe, has to stay under wraps until after the trial. But even if Liam was allowed to talk, I know he wouldn't. He hates the press almost as much as he hates himself because they too are the reason he lost everything.

Everything except me, and I ain't goin' the fuck nowhere, as Ken would have said in that accent of his that I miss so much.

* * *

"Momma, Momma?" Liv asks, tugging at my leg.

"Yes, sweetie, what's up?"

I dish out the macaroni I made as she points at Matthew.

"My Chew is being so bad! He color on the table again!" she tattles.

"It's fine, Liv, I will wash it off in a bit. Now scoot your butt up to the table for lunch, please."

She climbs onto the chair next to Matty's as I set their lunch down and check the time. Liam's been in the garage messing with the bikes the entire morning because he can't leave the house. It's impossible to get past the shit storm of press stationed outside our place. Thankfully, my mother has no qualms about driving out here with Claire to grab the kids every second weekend. We haven't even been able to work at the bar, let alone get a minute to ourselves without the kids. It's not easy being locked in the house 24/7 with two toddlers and whichever version of Liam appears each day.

"Is the Bama's coming to get Olif and My Chew, Momma?" Liv asks, smacking Matthew's hand. "I said you not go color on the table, that's bad and Mac will eat you crayon if you do it again," she threatens.

I laugh, knowing I shouldn't condone her hitting her brother, but the fact she still thinks the dog is *the punisher* kills me.

"Yes, Liv, the grandmas' should be here right away, so hurry and finish up your lunch so you can get ready, okay?"

She nods as Matthew takes a handful of macaroni and launches it at the dog.

"Matthew, do not feed the dog, please."

I take a seat beside him as I hear the back door open and Jimmy comes barrelling inside.

"Hey Vix, your mom's parked out front of my place chatting with Riva and waiting for the kids. She asked me to come and grab them for her because she can't get onto your driveway."

"Oh for Pete's sake," I say rolling my eyes. "Yeah, just let me get the kids' shoes on, their backpacks are over by the door." I'd forgotten Jimmy and Riva recently started seeing each other; it's kind of sweet if I think about it. Jimmy's great with kids and Riva's daughter, Zoe, would love him I'm sure.

"So, how's Liam?" he asks, grabbing the bags. "He still going all Jekyll and Hyde on your ass these days?"

"Why don't you ask him yourself? He's been in the garage all morning and I haven't seen him to be able to answer you," I inform.

He looks at me as if he's concerned and starts to get Matty's shoes on as I tie Liv's.

"I'm worried about him and wish he would go back to seeing Dell once a week. I'm worried about you too, Vixen. Is there anything I can do?"

"Not besides stop worrying, Jimmy. I'm fine, and I wish he'd go with me to see Dell too, but he refuses," I say, kissing Liv on the cheek. "There you go sweet girl, now you're all set for a wild weekend with your crazy Bama's!"

I give her a hug, breathing in her sweet little scent and then give Matty some love too.

"Will you tell Liam I said hey? Maybe try to bribe him with my computer and send him over if he can sneak out after dark," Jimmy offers.

"Yeah, right," I laugh. "I'll tell him you said hello, but we both know Liam won't leave the house for nothing. He's like a freaking zombie and it'll take something far more inspiring than your computer to get him to snap out of the funk he's in."

"I guess you're probably right, but what about you? Why don't you come and hang out with us then, Riva will be there and I promise we won't do any drinking. We can just hang out like old times."

I lean in and kiss his cheek. He's too sweet with his 'distract the damsel' ploy.

"Alcohol, my friend, is no longer an issue for me, but thanks for the offer. And if this were like old times, you and I both know that would mean partying until the sun comes up, so I'll have to pass. I don't want to cramp yours and Jack's style by turning you into lame anti-social freaks like me and Liam. But please say hello to Riva for me."

"Alright," he sighs, "but if you change your mind you know where I live," he says taking the kids by the hands. "Oh, and if things get out of hand or you need *anything*, Vixen, call me," he says sternly. "You don't have to try to help him on your own, got it?"

I nod and half-smile knowing he means well, but have no intention of involving him in my personal affairs.

"Bye, you two, have a great time with the grandmas," I say, kissing them both one last time.

"Bye-bye, Momma," Matty says.

"I love you, Momma, and say it to Daddy too okay?" Liv asks.

"You know I will, Princess, and Daddy loves you guys so, so, so much too."

"But he love the shhh man bigger than Olif, right, Momma?" she asks, twirling my hair around her finger.

The sadness in her eyes breaks my heart and I swallow.

"No sweetheart, he doesn't. Daddy's just misplaced... kind of like Cinderella's slipper. I promise you I will find him soon and then he's gonna tickle you all over until you pee your pants!"

Liv giggles and waves goodbye as Jimmy winks at me and mouths the words *call me*.

I exhale and shut the door, wiping the tears that I'm sucking in knowing Olivia thinks Liam doesn't love her the same anymore. It destroys me inside, literally pummels my soul knowing I'm not sure if I can fix it for any of us.

I take a seat on the sofa in the silence as Mac jumps up and lays in my lap. I know he too feels neglected as I sit petting him, wishing I knew what to do. Wishing even harder that I didn't have the urge to drink because battling the remnants of what's left of my husband is insufferable at times. Instead, I shove the thought way down and turn on the TV.

Oh, look, it's my front yard, wonderful!

Fuck, don't those people ever leave? I mean it's nice that they are actually standing out there in support, but seriously, I want some privacy for once. I hate how dark it is in here with all the curtains closed. It makes everything feel suffocating.

I flip through a few channels until I land on one displaying images of missing kids. Instantly irritated, I chuck the remote onto the floor as Liam enters from the garage, looking just as annoyed.

"Hey," he says, walking past me toward the kitchen.

"Hey," I say back.

I watch Mac follow him, whining for food, but Liam ignores him.

"He's hungry you know, poor guy only got a handful of Matty's macaroni earlier, so I think you should feed him," I notify.

I roll my eyes as Liam tosses a day-old hamburger patty into his bowl and continues rummaging through the fridge.

"Liv asked me to tell you that she loves you before she and Matty left just a bit ago," I say trying to strike up a *real* conversation. I swear it's been weeks since he said anything more than *hey* or a grunt/growl, unless we were arguing or fucking. *Which by the way was more like Hate-Fuck Hell,* because Liam is hell-bent on punishing himself, which also means punishing me, not that I can't handle it.

"Thanks for the message," he says, stealing back half of the patty from the dogs bowl and eating it.

"That's disgusting, Liam, why don't you sit and let me heat up the rest of the macaroni I made the kids for lunch?"

"If I wanted that crap, I'd heat it up myself," he mutters.

I sigh and walk over to him.

"We need to talk Liam," I pause, trying to find the words. "I know it's untrue, but Liv thinks you don't love her so much anymore. I need you to reassure her that she's wrong."

Slamming the fridge closed, he turns and locks eyes with me.

"And how would you like me to do that?" he asks in a growl.

"I don't know, talk to her, hug her once in a while, answer some of her questions when she asks. She misses you."

"No she doesn't," he hisses, "she misses *them*. They're all she ever talks about, Vixen, and fuck, aren't kids supposed to have like some sort of short-term memory or something? What she needs is to do is just forget them for fuck's sake."

"Just like you're doing?" I ask sarcastically. "She's three for the love of God, she doesn't understand *where* they went, Liam, and it's not her fault. And just maybe if you would *stop* storming off every time she asks about them, she wouldn't think you love Cliff more than you love her."

His expression turns guilty and he rubs his face as I swallow down the ache in my chest.

"Did she really say that?"

I nod, feeling like an ass for admitting it but this is destroying us. I want my husband back already.

"Look, I get that you are still grieving, I really do. But you've been so distant from us for so long, and I feel like I'm not reaching you anymore. Not even when we're together in bed which hardly ever happens at all anymore," I add, regretting it instantly.

His eyes turn cold again and he growls. *Not the good kind of growl either, no*, this is more like the sound a wounded animal makes while trying to fend off a predator circling its prey.

"We've been through this already," he says bluntly, "I'm not touching you after what happened last time, so just fucking drop the topic."

"I'm not dropping it. Either we verbally hash it out or hate-fuck it out, but one way or another we are dealing with this because I'm tired of watching you suffer."

"That's the part you aren't getting, Vix, are the bruises even fucking healed yet? Because seeing the way I marked you last time makes me suffer more than you could ever know."

I rip my shirt over my head, toss it behind me, and drop my pants to the floor.

"See for yourself. I. Am. Fine. It's been a month Liam, the bruises are gone, and I told you they didn't even hurt."

His eyes scan over my hips, my arms, and then my collarbone before he lets out a sigh of relief.

"I don't know what to do with all of this anger," he says almost inaudibly. "This is worse than anything I've ever felt. I wish I could just shut my eyes and plug my ears to make it go away, but I can't, that just makes the images worse."

"Then fucking use me, use my body to get rid of some of it," I breathe. "I'm giving you permission and I am not afraid of a few marks if that's what it takes to help you let go of some of it."

I can see the torment fluttering in his eyes, the way he questions himself, afraid to stop feeling guilty for even a second. He's been holding his breath for weeks because everything is different now. He no longer sees my face when we fuck and he carries the guilt of that too, but what's worse is that he admitted his mind now mostly displays images of Cliff's suicide instead. *PTSD at is finest*. I hate that he relates sex with negative things, but I get why, it's all he knows. And all I want at this point, is to feel his warmth on my skin, his breath on my neck, his fist in my hair, and ease some of the burden he carries. I'll let him use me, my body, in whatever way necessary and until I have nothing left to give, as long as it brings him back from the deep end.

"Fuck, Vixen, put your clothes back on. Please."

"Nope, not happening," I say, unclasping my bra and slipping my panties to the floor. "Don't make me beg, you know it's not my style, but I will if you don't say the words."

I stand exposed, my body covering in bumps from the cool air, my breathing ragged to the untamed look in his eyes. It's both scary and irrationally sexy at the same time because I know what dark beast lays dormant in him.

His movements are quick, predatory as I end up against the wall, at his mercy, my heart racing while he runs his hand down and in between my legs and then he whispers.

"Is this what you want?"

I nod, unable to speak as the sense of his breath on my skin has me fighting for air. His fingers are rough as are his movements, he's premeditated, taunting me.

I try to close my legs to feel all of it, but he forces them open with his knee and holds me steady, looking down at me with a carnal expression.

"You might think you're helping me," he says ominously, "but all you are really doing is feeding my obsession by offering yourself up to me," he continues, now using my dampness to heighten my awareness of his fingers. "And I have to warn you, I'm not sure I can stop until I've used every part of your body to my advantage. So, you'd better tell me now if you've changed your mind."

I inhale sharply, closing my eyes to the feeling of his hand, wanting desperately to feel him inside me, to fulfill and experience the depth of his craving.

"I'm waiting," I breathe out. "You should know me by now, Liam, I never back down from a challenge."

The growl that leaves his lips is unlike anything I've heard before as he spins me forcibly away from him and presses me into the wall. I decide to be smart this time and use my forearms to rest my face against. *The phrase no pain no gain, is bullshit.*

I listen to the clink of his belt being removed and stand panting in the darkness of our kitchen anticipating the arrival of his animosity. My heart hammering in my chest as I swallow, trying to contain my nerves.

Is the way we connect completely insane? Maybe. Do I care? No. Am I afraid? *Fuck yes*, but I'm the only one who can tame the wild part of him long enough to keep him alive.

At least that's what I tell myself because I've never been more afraid of losing him than I am now.

I close my eyes tighter as the madness takes over him, in turn taking over me as I imagine all of the darkest moments in my life. Collecting the anger from them and allowing it to flood my body that is now completely in his possession. The angrier I become the more I can handle as his hands grip my skin and his thrusts become more aggressive. What he gives, I accept with mercy and together we are colliding into the gravity of our newfound hate-fuck hell.

My moans and his grunts fill the space around us as I turn my focus to the perfect vibration of his fingers. Growing ever closer to my impending release, thinking only about making sure he gets to his.

My stomach tenses as I moan into my arm, teetering on the edge. With one of his hands tugging my hair and the other gripping my hip, he continues into me with everything he has.

"Jesus, yes! Holy fucking hell," I mutter, muffled by my arm.

He growls, saying nothing at all, just continues as if he's on the warpath for vengeance against my pussy as my orgasm rips through me.

"Fuck, Jesus, fuck," I chant, breathless.

Every part of me is on fire—including my muscles—and my body feels like it's being annihilated, but for him I hold steady.

This is the essence of my affection, what I can offer the man I love whose mind only works in jagged moments of pain. Agony so foul I don't want to imagine it, only expel it.

His vigor is ruthless and with each dig of his nails against my skin, I grit my teeth knowing the home stretch has arrived, he's about to become whole again.

"Fuck, I'm close," he growls, "Do. Not. Move."

"I couldn't if I wanted to," I groan, "I think I have lock-body at the moment. So take your time, I'm not going anywhere."

One of his hands unfastens from my hip and finds its way between my breasts and locks around my throat. It's odd to me, but I stay completely still, waiting for the final crash of thunder to end his storm, and with his last thrust I feel his release begin. In a low growl, he surrenders the hate that consumes him, filling me as his hand tightens around my neck, so I hold my breath. I count twenty-five seconds before he lets go, and if I'm honest, I enjoyed it. I exhale and then inhale hard a few times as we both catch our breath, my body sluggish to recover from the unreserved violation, but as I turn to face him, I see it.

He's come back to me from the edge of the cliff with a semi-smile, *it's better than nothing*, and fuck is he beautiful. Like a thousand tiny diamonds gleaming in the sunlight.

Grabbing a blanket from the back of the sofa, he studies my body where his hands have been and then he wraps me in it.

"Don't look so distraught, I'm fine," I smile authentically. "It's nice to see you again, I've missed you, Mr. King. Now get your fucking clothes on so we can finish our conversation, please."

That's right, the man can boss my body all he wants, but I get to boss him when he's done.

CHAPTER 39
The Beginning of The End

LIAM

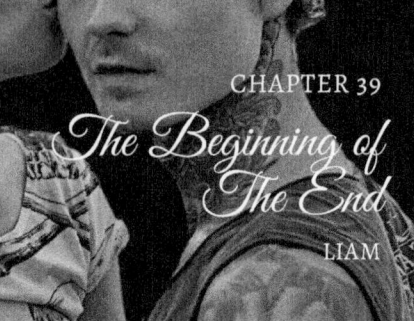

Fuck am I angry.
Furious as hell.
It feels like a storm raging inside my chest with every breath I take and all I want to do is make it stop.

I drive myself harder into my wife, searching for the release from this darkness. I don't know why she offers herself to me this way, thinking it'll help me, but it won't. Not while I'm rage fucking her with this agony bearing down on my chest and in my head.

It's the same agony that made me want to end my life while I was in that basement. When I was at my weakest ready to give in, but then there was always Ken standing in my way. The person who pulled me out of the squall and forced me to continue on. Told me to be a man, to grow up, and to snap out of my self-pitying thoughts of wanting to end it.

He told me never to let *them* win.

I continue on fucking my wife, gripping her savagely and trying to focus, but all I can think of is my hate for Ken at the moment. The way he stopped me from ending my suffering, it was a selfish thing for him to do.

Maybe he only did it for the sake of protecting Cliff and Verna like he'd wanted me to, but I hate that he used me. Forced me to exist in that hell and for what?

So he could in turn do the very thing I'd wanted to do my entire childhood?

The more I think about how much I miss him, the more I hate him. The more I hate him, the harder I fuck my wife into the wall. My anger is building with each breath, as is my release, but not my sympathy for Ken.

I hate him for so many reasons.

I hate him for cheating me out of my chance to avoid this vile fate, and then taking the easy way out like a fucking coward.

For being a goddamn hypocrite.

And most of all, for leaving me here to face the predators all on my own and then taking Cliff with him. The stupid motherfucker is responsible for Cliff's death, after all, Cliffy was just following his leader, *our leader*. And for as much as the images of Cliff's brains blowing out of his head have messed up my ability to sleep, I will never hold Cliff responsible. Out of the four of us, I could have expected it from *him*, but not from *Ken*.

I feel Vixen's pussy tighten around my dick as she releases, moaning wildly into her arm. I continue on doing what I do best, what the world has hated me for, fucking her like the untamed animal I am, as my palms jacket in sweat and I impale my wife with the morbid lessons of my childhood.

I grit my teeth, listening to her grunts, knowing I'm overly aggressive, but she doesn't give in. She's like a brick fucking wall, taking every unharnessed thrust I feed her, and yet she refuses to crumble. She believes *this* can cure me, and I *think* she's crazy. There is *no* cure for what this life has stained me with. There is no forgiveness in my soul.

The press will never earn my absolution for the hell they've caused anymore then the Paulsons will ever care about what they've taken from me.

I feel my muscles tense and I'm ready to spill as I run my hand up between Vixen's tits and around her throat. I want her to feel my wrath as I pour into her this darkness. I want her to experience this pain, this hate, this hurt.

This anger that's consuming me alive. The fucked-up demon in me she foolishly loves so much.

With each thrust I get closer to my limit, focusing on the only thing I now know.

I'm on the warpath.

They wanted to push me, to see what the fuck I am, wanted me to be a monster, well I'm going to show them a fucking hellhound. This shithole world forsook me long ago and I'm done being its bitch.

With my final thrust, I feel all of the hate empty from me, my dick releasing inside her. It feels fucking incredible, and for just a flash of time I can breathe again because I've completed my mission. Done exactly what was expected of me and earned the right to praise myself for it.

I let go of Vixen and back away as she turns toward me.

Our breathing is erratic, as are my thoughts.

I force a half-smile as I study the red marks I've left upon her skin and then drape a blanket around her, feeling both ashamed and relieved.

A fucked-up combination, I know.

She smiles a wickedly beautiful smile, as if she's just conquered the impossible, and I realize it's this tarnished side of me that she lives for, and I created her addiction by providing it for her.

"Don't look so distraught, I'm fine," she insists. "It's nice to see you again, I've missed you, Mr. King. Now get your fucking clothes on so we can finish our conversation, please."

I swear nothing fazes her.

"What conversation?" I ask, slipping into my pants.

"The one where you call our daughter and fix her broken little heart."

"Oh, that one," I say feeling like a piece of shit. "I'll video chat with her after I shower and figure out what to say to her."

"There's nothing to figure out, just tell her that you love her, that she's still your princess, and then maybe read her a story tonight before bed."

She makes it sound so simple, like our daughter can't see what a fraud for a father I am.

"Sure, I guess I can manage that."

"Don't guess, just do it or you'll hate yourself even more in the end," she warns.

"I don't think that's possible."

I walk away before she can continue with her pep talk. I don't want to hear it. She's under the impression this is fixable, well it's not. No matter what I say to our daughter it won't change anything. *Nothing can save me now.*

* * *

I jolt up alarmed and gasping for air as I clutch my chest, trying to shake off the images in my head. The clock says 3:36 am and my shirt is damp at the neckline. I'm cold from the sweat that lines my collar, hating that I haven't had a decent night's sleep in months.

Vixen groans sleepily as she rolls toward me and rests her chin on my chest.

"Another nightmare?" she whispers. "I can get you a sleep aid if you want."

I move her off of me and sit up, frustrated, trying to peel my soaked shirt from my skin.

"Why would I want that? What I need is to never sleep again."

Vixen yawns and stretches as I stand and throw my sweatpants on.

"Well then let me go and put some coffee on and we can talk about it," she says rubbing her eyes.

"You're tired, Vix, it's fine. I can deal with it on my own just go back to sleep."

"I don't want to sleep, what I want is to help you," she states.

"And *I* just said I don't need your fucking help. I need some air. I'm going for a walk."

I change my shirt and throw a sweatshirt overtop, ignoring her spiel about the press keeping tabs on the house. Grabbing a ball cap from the closet, I throw it on and head downstairs continuing to ignore her as she follows me.

"Are you even listening to me?" she hisses. "You can't go out there."

I continue to lace up my runners, trying to disregard her incessant nagging, but she just keeps talking.

"Seriously, would you please just listen to me for a second?"

Now blocking the door with her body, she crosses her arms and challenges me with her riled expression. If she thinks I won't pick her tiny ass up, she's got another thing coming.

"Move, Vixen," I say calmly. "I'm not sitting in this fucking house trapped for another God forsaken minute with you."

She cocks a brow and smirks.

"With me? Really? Are you saying I'm the problem right now?"

"Yeah, that's exactly what I'm saying," I admit, grinding my teeth.

All I want is to get the fuck out of here and clear my head because what I see is haunting.

"Fine, fucking go," she says, stepping aside.

I hesitate for a fraction of a second caught in the fear dancing in her eyes and then I open the door and leave. When she closes it behind me, I hear the sound of her body slide against the other side to the floor and I know she's hurting.

Maybe she thinks I'm not coming back and *maybe I'm not*, I don't know. I have no clue *what* I'm doing anymore. I take a deep breath, inhaling the moist salted air and all I do know is that it feels good to breathe freely, no longer trapped in dreams of terror.

I take in the dark, empty streets trying to check for hidden reporters, whichever fuckers might have the gusto to sit outside the house all night like stalkers waiting to attack. Not seeing any sign of the scavengers, I start to walk through the breeze, having no real clue where I'm going, but it's peaceful. Once a drifter always one, I suppose.

My mind has been nothing but a filthy mess for months and half of the time I don't even recognize myself. Nothing makes sense to me anymore, not even Vixen. I know she means well but it's hard to rid myself of this all-consuming ball of fire that swelters within me and all I can ever seem to imagine when my head hits the pillow is revenge. Then I fall asleep.

That's when it all turns insufferable, the dreams start to eat at me from the inside out. Spreading through me like a disease are the images of my childhood, the indescribable moments of the monstrous things I somehow have to prepare to talk about in court. Things that I'm now alone to explain in a place where nobody knows who I am or how I feel. Up until a few months ago the world didn't even care, but now that my family is gone, they want to pity me. I don't want fucking pity; I want my existence back.

I want my soul returned.

I want to close my eyes and not be afraid.

And I want to know if I'm even human anymore. Having all these fucked-up thoughts of slaughtering an army of reporters and then walking into a court room to blow the heads off of two child molesters, what does that even make me?

The sensor light above the bar door comes on and blinds me as I realize where I am.

Seems my demons have minds of their own and want to drink.

I flip the lights on as I enter and take a seat behind the counter. Lining it with shot glasses, I pour myself a row of whiskey, one shot for each of my siblings and two more for the bullets I want to put in the Paulsons' heads.

"For Verna," I say aloud downing the first one. "Cliff, your next buddy."

I feel the welcomed burn as the alcohol enters my chest, sending fire through my core. I tilt my head back, inhaling the serene comfort of Cliff and Verna's eight-year-old faces flooding my mind. Their goofy looks make me smile, remembering how Verna used to fuck with Cliff, trying to make him talk the same way Liv used to. It always pissed Ken off, made him extra lispy with his missing teeth when he'd yell at Verna to cut it out. One time he got so mad when I joined in just to be an asshole. Me and Verna were teasing Cliff relentlessly about how he was afraid of spiders, even captured a few and put them in his hair when he was sleeping. He'd ended up pissing on the mat he was sleeping on with Ken because of it, which wasn't our intention. If we'd only known that being voiceless made him super sensitive to fear, we wouldn't have done it. Anyway, Ken being a good brother, and not so happy to wake up soaked in Cliffy's piss, got his payback. The son of a bitch waited until we were sleeping the next night and me and Verna woke up damp and freezing, thinking he'd pissed on us. It wasn't until a few years after we were free that he told Verna it was just well water he'd dumped beside our mats to give the illusion of urine.

"Here's to you, fucking asshole," I say slamming another shot. "And don't think for one hellish second this means I forgive you for blowing yourself up either. You hear me down there?"

"Who are you talking to?"

I look up at Vixen from the floor after imagining Ken condemned to hell underneath it and with Verna, *probably pick pocketing the Devil at this very moment.*

"Nobody special," I say gathering the glasses closer to myself. "You shouldn't have followed me here, I'm in no shape to babysit an alcoholic along with myself right now."

"Too bad I own this place, so I don't have to listen to you," she says grabbing the bottle.

I stand, jerk it from her hand, and slam it down on the counter.

"I'm not in the mood for this shit," I growl.

"Mmm, right then," she smiles amiably. "Well at least I know you still love me somewhere underneath all of that hate."

"That's a fucked-up thing to say. Being angry doesn't delete love, it just overrides the ability to show it sometimes."

"Six months of sometimes," she points out.

I shrug, swallowing down the flecks of hurt and neglect in her eyes, wondering why she puts up with me. Questioning why I can't seem to do anything right anymore except hate life in general.

"What do you want me to do? Lie to you and say I'm okay? Put a fake smile on? Would that make you happy? Or do you want me to keep using your body as an escape while I leave marks on you like a fucking savage? It's bad enough I'm caught in this abyss of torment wanting to kill everyone who wronged me, but now I'm abusing you to drown it out. Tell me what the fuck it is you want me to do, Kirsten, because I'm failing here at being your husband and living in general."

Taking a seat beside me, she runs her fingertip around the rim of one of the glasses in thought.

"If I had the answers, I'd tell you, believe me," she mutters.

"I'm about as lost at this point as you are, but I'm holding on as tight as I can. Forcing myself to hold it all together while holding my breath, waiting for you. And not only for the kids or for you, Liam, I'm holding on for me. Because I'll suffocate without you and it feels like all of those times you used to leave for days on end. When I'd worry that you weren't coming back. But this is worse," she says as tears roll down her face. "It's cruel and it hurts because I'm terrified, you're not going to come back from this, and if I lose you," she says wiping her face, "then there is no me. Without you, there never was."

I watch the tears stream from her eyes, turning them greener than the ocean, as my own fall down my face. I can feel the soul I thought I'd lost to the darkness, shattering into thousands of tiny pieces, and I realize Vixen isn't just part of my soul, she's the whole God forsaken thing. She's like the reinforced Goddess of war, she's never backed down, and never will, so neither the fuck should I.

"Okay, Vix," I whisper, and then clear my throat. "I'm coming back," I breathe, "you know why?"

She shakes her head, unable to stop her tears that I think she's been gathering together her entire life for this moment.

"I'll tell you why," I say, jerking her chair closer to mine. "Because you should know me by now. I always come back."

Her face instantly lights up and she throws herself onto my lap, wrapping every part of herself around me.

"Holy fuck, Jesus, thank you," she says into my neck. "Thank you for not giving up on me. Fuck do I love you. *Love-love* you. Still really love-hate you too, but really fucking love the hellfire and sin out of you."

"I fucking *love-love*, love-hate, and whatever the fuck else you just said times two, whatever that equals," I say breathing in her scent as deep as I can.

She laughs, sniffling in the tears that are still coming, and I wonder if they'll ever stop.

"Can we go for the jugular now?"

"Pardon?" I ask, lifting her face from my neck.

"The Paulsons," she growls. "I want her bloody beating heart and his balls, dick and all, on a fucking platter. Then I want to take that proverbial platter and douse it with gasoline and light it up so we can watch it burn at the same time those heinous fucks get their death injections. Sound fun?"

I cock a brow and laugh at her lethal expression; *my wife is out for flesh just as much as I am.*

"Yeah, not gonna lie, that sounds pretty interesting, you are one hell bent badass," I say loving how sick in her head she is, *just like me.* "But I have a question."

"Shoot."

"What the fuck does proverbial mean?"

* * *

"Just remember, Liam, deep breaths," Gabe says, messing with my suit collar.

"I got it, schmuck," I say, slapping his hand away. "And would you stop messing with my suit already. I'm not four anymore, or weak, I have Vixen now. And worst-case scenario, if Carl tries to look at me, I'll simply look at my gorgeous wife."

"Yeah, Gabe," Vixen echoes, "just do your thing in there and we'll do ours."

"That's not entirely reassuring to me," Gabe admits, showing us into the empty courtroom. "You two have a *thing* that's off the charts insane and nobody wants to witness it."

Vixen scowls at him, knowing Jimmy and his big mouth told Gabe about how Vix got all of the bruises from our six-month stay in hate-fuck hell.

"Yeah, well that info is attorney-client privileged and isn't that what the shit I pay you for, smart-ass?" she asks, smirking.

Gabe points to his watch and then gestures at the benches behind the prosecution's table. Today is the day I'll finally get to see Gabe *the schmuck* Morris in action while he presents the opening statement in my case. In fifteen minutes, the gates to my personal hell will open and my story will start to unfold for the entire world to judge.

Fuck me, this is painfully unnerving.

Vixen and I take a seat. I'm anxious; my chest feels like it's on fire as I watch Gabe take a seat at the table and mess around with his briefcase sorting out some papers.

"How are you doing?" Vix whispers.

"Okay so far, but how the fuck does Gabe look so calm?"

"That's his job, he's gonna crucify that son of a bitch, nail him to the cross, and turn it the fuck upside down, where that monster belongs. He's got this," she says compellingly.

Hearing what sounds like hordes of footsteps, I glance behind me at the hailstorm of people and press flooding through the doors.

"Jesus, it's like they've come to witness the launch of a new Apple device," I mutter nervously.

"No, Liam, they've come to witness the slaying of the fucking Devil," she says viciously.

She grips my hand and juts her head toward a side door where two armed officers and David Schneider walk in with one Carl Dean Paulson as my heart begins to beat feverishly. He looks much older than I remember with his cold dark eyes and he's clean shaven, something I'd never seen in all the years I was his captive. He lowers his head never looking my way as they walk him to the table across from Gabe's. They take a seat as yet more people crowd into the court room, but I ignore the commotion and stay focused on the back of the two evils in the room. Carl's grey suit seems far too nice and I bet his dirtball of a lawyer bought it for him, trying to make him look respectable, I guess. *That predator is anything but.*

The side door over by their table opens again and I watch as the jurors enter the room, there are twelve. Seven women and five men. Nothing about any of them stands out to me, but I try to study their faces wondering if they've already made up their minds about me. A dark-haired woman who looks to be in her forties meets eyes with me and she smiles awkwardly and quickly looks away.

I think I have my answer, fuck.

"Liam," Vix whispers, "look behind you."

I turn and smile instantly as Verna's mother waves at me and her father nods. I feel a sense of relief knowing the Whitmores' didn't go back on their word.

"See?" Vix says, kissing my cheek. "I told you they'd be here. Just. Like. I. Said."

"Don't be cocky about it," I warn teasingly. "There is a washroom stall somewhere in this place I could easily take you to if you want to start an argument."

She smiles naughtily and leans in closer, so her breath is hot on my neck.

"Don't threaten me with a good time, Mr. King. This suit turns me on in ways you don't even know."

"As does this dress," I whisper back, running my hand in between her thighs. "And I thought you said dresses were for weddings and funerals," I add as she stops my hand from going any further.

"This is the beginning of one very long funeral, don't forget it."

"Ahhh, right," I growl.

Is it odd that imagining watching the Paulsons die by lethal injection is kind of a turn on? Could be, but I'd be lying if I said I give a shit.

"All rise. The honorable Judge Marilyn Montgomery is now presiding."

Vix and I stand as the judge seats herself at the head of the courtroom at her bench. She's an older woman with silver hair and glasses. She looks mean and tough as hell as I study her face while she scans over some papers on her desk and we all take our seats, except for the jury. I watch as the bailiff begins to swear them in, each of them looking serious in their expressions, especially the dark-haired lady.

I squeeze Vixen's hand and don't take my eyes off of the back of Gabe as the judge asks him to stand and present his opening statement. My palms are sweaty, my heart is racing, and I know that whatever Gabe says needs to be solid enough to stain the jurors' minds, infect them with the pain of the truth. It needs to be hard hitting and hellbent on pinning them with the evil injustices of my life, for my family, for Verna, Ken and Cliff, and for myself. This speech needs to carry so much weight it will destroy the character of the sinister bitch at the other table, and above all it absolutely must pull the jury into my corner. Should it accomplish those things, I'll know Gabe was the right choice.

"Good morning, your honor, jurors, members of the gallery, my name is Gabriel Morris and I have a story to tell you."

He pauses for a minute and grabs a stack of paper from his desk.

Vixen's grip on my hand is so firm I feel like she might break it as she leans over and whispers in my ear.

"This is it, the beginning of the end. The end of every horrible thing that happened to you. Just breathe and know with each breath how much I love you."

I grip her hand a little harder.

"I know, Vix, and I'm terrified. Falling apart inside, but I'm working it out," I say, focused on Gabe. "I don't know what he's handing out to the jury members but if he manages to nail this, I swear on everything holy your gonna owe him another hate-blow."

She flicks me in the thigh, hard, and growls under her breath.

"You are such a dork. Pay attention."

I wink at her and smile naughtily as the dead silent room erupts into gasps, every single one coming from the mouths of the jurors, and my heart stops.

CHAPTER 40
Let the Games Begin
VIXEN

Well if I didn't know it before, I certainly know it now. Gabe is a fucking genius.

His opening argument did not fail us, nor did the photo he handed every member of the jury. He had each one professionally printed and he designed them himself. On one side of the top half of the photo was a reproduced image of the missing child flyer that was handed out the year Liam was abducted. Beside it was a picture of the living conditions in the basement and the mats they'd slept on that weren't even big enough for a dog. No pillows, no blankets, and no toilet, just a bucket. The bottom half is a picture of Liam now and down the side there was something written.

This is what a kidnapped child who endured unspeakable acts of torment looks like twenty-four years later, after spending eleven of them in this basement. This is what he looks like now, after getting every single one of those tattoos pierced into his flesh at thirteen years old. His name is Liam Kristopher O'Connell, and he's twenty-nine years old this year. Two things he never knew up until eight months ago, in which he's spent all of that time also learning how to read and write. None of these things you see come even close to touching what this man has survived. Look at his face and I will tell you his story.

The pictures alone caused reactions that made me shiver. Almost every juror had tears in their eyes before Gabe ever spoke a word. Then he started in on his opening statement, which blew my fucking doors off. It also managed to cause a riot of slurs and hostile remarks from every person in the gallery to the point the judge had to strike her gavel just to shut them up.

I'm not one for expecting a victory before the final round is through, but shit did Gabe nail it. The things he said left nothing to the imagination nor unsaid, not one person had to guess what Liam was subjected to. It was so fucking gritty and raw, David Schneider was throwing up objections left and right, but the judge is a beast of a bitch, *my kind of woman*, and she shut that fool down every time he opened his mouth.

Thankfully, we made sure the asshole is not in the same hotel as us this time, but Gabe is. He thinks we'll be here for at least four weeks depending on what cards Schneider has up his sleeves, so in the meantime, Liam and I are basically trapped inside the suite like hermits. It's been rough on Liam, his emotions have been all over the charts. I know he's terrified inside, and I'm trying my best to keep him grounded. He always acts as if the trial doesn't bother him, but I know it does, although he puts on a decent show. I've recently caught on to his act though and I can tell when he's lost in his own world, it's like watching an asthmatic struggle to breathe. I can see it in his eyes, the way his mind torments him, especially when the nightmares start, and then he spends the rest of the night cramming sugar down his throat, trying to stay awake. My sweet as sin husband is battling both his demons and depression, but he refuses to take the pills Dell prescribed. Instead, he'd rather just pretend we can cure it by ignoring it.

"Look who I have on video chat," Liam taunts, handing me his phone.

I rip it from his hand smiling at Liv and Matty making a giant mess on my mother's countertop with cookie dough and flour.

"What the heck are you guys doing to Bama's kitchen?" I feign shock.

"We making cookies, Momma! And My Chew keeps giving it to Mac, he's so bad right?" Liv shouts excitedly.

I laugh at her flustered face as she swats at Matty with a wood spoon.

"Not hit me, Olif!" Matty yells back at her.

It's a total war in there as my mother takes over the phone from Claire's hand and laughs into the camera.

"Hi, dear, how are things going out there?" she asks.

"It's going okay," I sigh, "Gabe's holding his own as I'm sure you've seen on the news."

"And Liam? How is he feeling?"

I look over at him sitting next to me, watching him stuff his face with handfuls of mini marshmallows and washing them down with chocolate bars.

"I'm pretty sure he's about to be sick if you want my honest answer," I say, turning the camera toward him.

"Hi, Mom," he gargles.

I shake my head at him.

"You need to cut it out with sending room service over to aisle four to fulfill your nasty little candy fetish," I tell him.

"Oh leave him be," my mother insists. "At least he's dealing with his stress with sugar and not alcohol," she points out.

"Gee, I dunno, Mom, I think I'd rather him smell like whiskey then end up becoming diabetic. Besides, it's only me and you that are disastrous alcoholics," I remind.

"Oh, sweetheart, sometimes you're so cynical, you need to learn to let it go. In the Bible, God says—"

"Love you, Mom, kisses to Liv and Matty," I say quickly and then hang up on her.

God's a douche and He's fake, and if He's not, then I dare Him to stop Liam from hoarding sugar this instant.

"That wasn't very nice," Liam says with his mouth still full. "Helen is only trying to bond with you over her faith."

Point proven, the almighty is a fucking fraud.

"Faith, smaith," I mock. "I hate her ridiculous Bible babble, and I sure hope she isn't filling the kids' heads with that crap."

I steal a marshmallow and lay my head on Liam's torso.

"Why would that be bad?" he asks.

"Why would *what* be bad?"

I'd rather play dumb than tell him the million reasons why God doesn't exist.

"Teaching our kids to have faith. I think it might be good for them," he states.

I roll onto my stomach and look up at him, trying not to laugh at his sugar high smile.

"How does that even make sense to you? After everything you've been through, you have to know God is fake," I lecture him.

"Maybe He or She is real, I did end up meeting you," he says kissing my forehead.

"Gross, Liam, your lips are sticky. Lick them or something," I complain. "And if you want to get technical, then I'd say it's more likely the devil brought you to me than God."

"Why is that?" he asks, wiping his face on his shirt.

I roll my eyes at his childish behavior and groan.

"What do you mean why? Because look at us, we aren't even normal people. We come from a history of violence for shit's sake, we hate-fuck, we beat down pay phones, and then watched your brothers kill themselves, and we even plotted to kill my mother once too. Take your pick, but we are definitely *not* in God's good grace's if the fucker does exist, and if He does, *who cares*? It's not like we'd forgive Him for bailing on us when shit was so bad we wanted to die. What kind of parents would teach their kids to believe in an asshole like that?" I ask, staring into his still curious eyes.

He shrugs and smiles ear to ear and then his eyes light up bright as hell like he's having an epiphany.

"I just realized something. Remember that time you shoved money underneath my pillow to give me the tooth princess experience?"

"Tooth fairy," I correct. "And yes, why?"

"Because she was fake and so is the fat Santa guy we've been celebrating with the kids, and also the creepy leprechaun you told me about."

"I know that," I say, laughing. "What are you getting at?"

I can't believe he's still mesmerised by the traditions I taught him.

"What I'm saying is that you let me and the kids celebrate those very strange events because it's fun, so why can't God be one of the fun occasions too?"

I cringe and cock a brow, cornered.

"You cannot be serious, Liam. Lying to the kids about Santa Claus is not the same as lying to them about going to some fake magical Heaven when they die."

"It's not about lying to them," he argues. "I just think it would be good for them to have hope. I wish I'd known about a God, *fake or not* when I was a kid. Maybe if I did, I wouldn't have felt so lonely the whole time until I'd met Ken, Cliff, and Verna."

Fuck my sceptical Godless heart, he's too adorably honest to say no to.

"Damn you, fine. Helen can tell them a couple children's tales, but I have limits."

"No way! You have limits? How did I not know this?" he asks, pinching my ass.

"Don't be a dick," I hiss. "Do you want your way or not?"

"Yes. Very much," he says straight-faced and nodding. "I want my way with you," he then finishes smartly.

I roll my eyes and push myself off of him, annoyed as I move to the other side of the sofa.

"Okay, I take it back," he laughs. "Tell me your demands on the God zone and I'll listen, I promise."

I chuck a marshmallow at him in retaliation and he's like a lizard, catching it in his mouth and swallowing it whole. I shake off my urge to laugh because I'm trying to be serious with the world's least serious person at the moment.

"My terms are this," I say firmly. "One, there will be no going to an actual church, she can only recite crap from the Bible with them in her own home. I don't want to hear it. Two, Liv and Matty are not getting baptized unless they are old enough to agree to it themselves. And three, even if our kids start singing hallelujah, and fall in love with the false entity, I want us to still be us, fair?"

"Sure, I guess, but what does baptized mean?" he asks.

"It's just a thing Catholics practice on kids by dunking their faces in holy water or tossing them headfirst into a lake so they can be blessed by God or some crap."

"Oh, sounds kind of awesome, maybe I should do that," he says excitedly.

"No, it's not happening. I already said *no* churches."

"Come on, Vixen, please? It'll be a one-time thing, and besides, you're still wearing the cross I gave you so technically you're already blessed and I want a turn too."

He gives me his best begging face, the sweet one he uses unfairly to his advantage.

"Seriously, Liam? A necklace and a ride on your anaconda

doesn't exactly amount to being doused in some sham concoction of holy water. But fine, if it makes you *so* happy then go ahead and get your God fix."

"Really? It was that easy?" he asks, crawling on top of me.

"Yeah, why? Were you expecting an argument?"

"Uh-huh."

He rubs himself against me, his excitement expanding in his pants as his eyes penetrate mine with a fierceness.

"Mmm, someone wants to come out and play," I say, massaging his dick through his sweats.

"Fuck yes he does, Benjamin Button has a rather devious mind when it comes to you. But you know the drill," he says, planting kisses down my neck.

My body reacts in waves of heat as his breath lingers on my skin.

"What drill is that?"

"Don't play dumb with me," he growls, jerking my lips to his. "I'm a machine, not a man, remember?"

"How could I forget?" I taunt. "I also remember thoroughly enjoying our little trip to hate-fuck hell, which means I can, and will love whatever you want to do to me, Terminator."

"Termi-what?"

"Terminator, it's a movie about a machine that looks like a man and it's badass."

"Cool, well does this robot man have a metal dick to by chance?"

I shake my head, "Nope, his junk is non-existent I'm pretty sure."

"Well what kind of half man is that then? Who builds a machine man without a dick?"

I laugh at his puzzled expression and realize he's missed out on far too many great films and I can't take it.

I lean over, grab the remote from the table and hand it to him.

"I think it's time we got you caught up on your movie knowledge."

"Right now?" he whines unhappily. "But what about Benjamin?"

"I'll take really good care of him later, but first we are going to watch some movies from the ever-growing list I've been making. Search up *The Terminator* and I'll see if I can get us some popcorn."

I throw on my sweater, then my shades, and tuck my hair underneath Liam's ball cap while I listen to him sound out the word terminator.

"It has a y in it right?" he asks, pressing way too many buttons.

"Nope, keep trying, I won't be gone long," I say, kissing him on top of his head.

"Be careful out there," he calls out, "and see if they have gummy bears down there too, please."

"Will do," I lie.

Screw that, he's already so hopped up on sugar he *thinks* he's getting baptized.

I slip out of the elevator into the lobby and keep my head down. It's nice to be out of the suite even if it is only to go on the hunt for snacks in the lobby gift shop.

At least Liam didn't beg to come with so he could stand here and stare into the abyss of Candy-land.

Trying to ignore the whispers from the women to my left, *who clearly my disguise is not fooling,* I grab a package of gummy bears and saunter over to the next aisle. I can hear them getting louder as I scan over the selection of chips. They look and sound like nineteen-year-old Barbies for fuck's sake, I'm ashamed to be blonde at the moment.

"It's definitely her," one of them says, both of them now following me.

"I think so too, maybe she'll give us an autograph if we ask."

"A picture with her would be better. I wonder where her other half is though," the other ditz says, now scanning the store.

I glance at them and offer a half-smile, irritated that they see us as celebrities, and even more annoyed by their fake eyelashes and too much lipstick.

Finally deciding on cheese puffs, I grab the bag, ignoring them, and take it to the counter to pay.

The clerk rings it through and looks me over peculiarly.

"That will be $7.75," she says, pausing in thought for a second. "Hey, aren't you the wife of that bizarre looking guy with all of the tattoos who was—"

I fucking dare you to finish the sentence, lady, I think to myself, ready to pounce.

"She is," Gabe interrupts. "And she has no comment, so here, keep the change," he says slamming a ten down, paying for the snacks. "Come on, Vixen, let's go."

He grabs the cheese puffs and leads me by the arm back out to the lobby and toward the elevators. I feel like a reprimanded kid, but I'm also relieved.

"Thanks for the save," I say, pressing the button. "Two more degrading words out of that lady's mouth about Liam's appearance or his childhood, and I probably would have smacked her upside her ugly mug."

"The audacity," Gabe responds, sarcastically. "I told you not to leave the suite and to call me if you needed anything. But here you are busy not listening to my direction as usual."

"That's what vixens do," I point out. "We don't make rules, we break them. Besides, I'm not going to send you on errands every five seconds just because my husband can't get his sugar fix from room service alone."

"Then find a different way to fulfill his needs if you have to," he states. "I cannot afford to have you stirring up trouble. Everything the two of you do and say is being scrutinized."

I scoff and cross my arms.

"Then it's your job to fix it! Why should we have to be trapped, away from our kids and hiding when we haven't done anything wrong?"

"Excuse me, you forgot this," one of the Barbies says, handing me the package of gummy bears.

Gabe sideways glances them over, seemingly impressed with the size of their chests.

"Thank you," I say, taking the package.

"No problem, but would you mind if I got a picture with the two of you? You guys are the hottest shit on TV right now."

She hands her phone to her friend who looks gobsmacked and dumber than a sack of hammers.

"Actually, we would mind," Gabe says with a cocky, self-confident smile. "But here's my card, call me when the trials over and I'll gladly get a picture with you. That is, if you're still in town by then."

I roll my eyes, disgusted by his attempt to flirt right in front of me knowing the douche has slept with my mother and Claire. Gross! Then again, Gabe is a nice looking man and should be screwing someone a little closer to his age, *but still, these two, ew.*

She giggles annoyingly, slips his card into her bra and winks.

"Oh, I will definitely still be here," she says, pulling out a card of her own. "But in the meantime, why don't you call me if you get lonely?"

Slipping it into Gabe's pocket, she then yanks her still-speechless friend by the arm, waves cutely and walks away.

"Well, that was both nauseating and fascinating," I say enthusiastically.

"Shut up and get on," he laughs as the elevator doors swing open.

"Yes, counselor, sir, whatever you say," I tease, mocking Barbie girl.

I hit seven on the panel since Gabe's room is just four doors down from ours.

"She didn't sound that obnoxious," he declares. "And she was cute. I like being the object of her affection."

"I could tell... but I'm pretty sure she isn't quite up to your intellectual standards. She could be very hard to hold an intelligent conversation with."

"Who says we'd be doing any talking?"

"Good point, although if you plan on wooing her with your dick, that might be tough too, I know what it looks like, remember?"

I wink at him as his face turns unimpressed. *I think he's butt hurt.*

"Don't you dare be spreading rumours about my dick, Vixen, I happen to know a few stories of my own involving a lawn tractor and not only that," he says, stopping to hold the elevator door open as we arrive on seven.

Continuing as we walk, he says, "I also know about the trips to hate-fuck hell as Jimmy so oddly worded it."

"You think that bothers me?" I ask rhetorically, smiling at his heated expression. "Oh, sweetie, you don't know me very well do you? I'd let the man in that room hate-fuck me to Mars if he wanted to, and I am not ashamed of how we operate, especially when it comes to sex. So, go ahead, spread all the rumors you want, just make sure they help you win the case because I'd *hate* to have to expose my other skillset and end up needing *you* to defend *me* next."

He stops in front of his door and grabs my arm, preventing me from passing him.

"I will win this case, Vixen."

His tone is cold, dark even, sending a shiver down my spine, and so does the wicked green tinge in his eyes that spear mine.

"Carl Paulson will pay," he continues, "but if you're thinking of doing something unethical I'd advise you to put it to rest."

I step closer, wanting him to see the wrath in my eyes, that I'm not afraid, as I take a sombre breath and speak calmly in a hush.

"I won't be able to rest until that fucking monster pays with his life. Same goes for that twisted bitch wife of his. They destroyed my husband, they've devastated my daughter, and they've taken the last lives they are ever going to get the day Ken and Cliff died. So don't talk to me about ethics, not when the man I'd die for is still fighting to find reasons to live."

Gabe nods and grabs my hand.

"I said I'd win it, and I will. In the meantime, stay out of trouble and in your damn room," he says with a smug smile of his own.

"Sure thing, schmuck," I tease, wanting to level off as I walk away. "Oh, and have fun with Rockstar Barbie," I call out as I swipe my card and enter the room.

I hear him yell something back, but stop dead in my tracks as I look over at Liam, his eyes fixed on the TV as he kneels directly in front of it.

I move closer, unable to see the screen from this angle as I tiptoe concealing my presence. Then I watch from the side as his mouth drops open and his eyes grow wide in anticipation because whatever he's watching has him either fascinated or frightened, I can't tell. He looks like a kid experiencing their first firework display and it's taking everything in me not to laugh as I sneak around behind him.

Oh dear, he's in deep, watching a horror flick. This should be interesting.

I stand directly behind him watching over his shoulder as the actor enters the notorious shower scene with a knife, and then just as the eerie music starts to play even louder, I make my move.

"Boo!" I shout.

"Motherfucker!" he hollers, jolting forward in a panic.

The crunch of his fist connecting with the TV is unreal as I cover my mouth and back up to assess the damage.

"Oh. My. God, Liam. You just busted the TV! What the hell?"

I'm laughing inside, but I'm also relieved it was the TV he hit.

He looks at the screen and cringes before he turns his attention to me, seemingly out of sorts as he shakes off the sting in his knuckles.

"Shit, Vixen! It's not my fault, you shouldn't have snuck up on me while the creepy guy was about to kill the lady in the shower! Fuck me! I almost had a damn heart attack," he sputters.

"A *heart attack* or a *hard-on*?" I tease, wondering about the lady in the shower.

His fright turns to a wickedly naughty grin.

"You know this dick only works for you," he reminds me with a low growl. "But I did really want to see what happened next and since you made me break the TV, I think you should remove all of your clothes and show me what was about to take place."

I laugh at his deviously sweet flirting skills.

"Uh-uh, there was no sex about to happen in that movie," I assure him. "And what movie was it anyway?"

"I dunno, I couldn't spell Terminator and some random list came up so I picked the cover that looked coolest," he says proudly.

"Yeah? Well I don't think you should be watching horror flicks considering you hardly sleep as it is. I think I'll have to put a parental code on the TV we're going to have to replace that one with thanks to *your* beast mode reaction."

He grabs me by the waist and jerks me closer smiling cunningly, it's a total turn on because I know what improper thoughts flicker in his eyes.

"This whole thing could have been easily avoided had you serviced my so-called beast in the first place," he says pointedly.

"Now we have a broken TV, and nothing to do until court starts again tomorrow, except wait in this room. Tsk, tsk, Vixen, now what are we gonna do?"

"We could always get Gabe in here to help us prepare some more. Maybe we should go over what's going to happen tomorrow again," I offer.

His face turns serious and I know court is the *last* thing he wants to think about.

"I don't think so, Vix, nothing can prepare me for that. We both know you are the only thing that's gonna keep me properly sated through this godforsaken battle. I hate tomorrow, please don't make me think about it."

My heart sinks to his broken tone, and the fear in his eyes, knowing he's petrified and trying so hard to hide it from me.

If I'm honest, I'm scared too, there's nothing worse than imagining him up on the stand being forced to relive what he's wanted so badly to forget. And I want it for him too, at least for tonight.

"Hate-fuck-Mars it is then," I say, removing my shirt.

"What? We're venturing to Mars this time?" he asks, his eyes igniting with fire.

"Yep, screw hell, let's aim for somewhere closer to the Heavens instead."

His beautifully innocent face breathes life again, as his eyes scan me over, outwardly hungered.

"You know what, Vix?" he says taking my hands into his. "You are the one person I wouldn't hesitate to do it all over again for," he whispers. "Because having you by my side is worth a million broken memories. Ones I can overcome because you love me and stand with me. You make me feel like I'm armed with a powerful angel, but more like a mouthy and sinful one from hell."

I cock a brow, slightly confused by his rambling.

"Okay, you are so grounded from sugar."

He covers my lips with his hand.

"Shhh, I wasn't done. My point, Vixen, is that you never give up on me even when I want to give up on myself."

I lick all of his fingers until he laughs and then wipes them down the side of my face.

"Well, I'm going to take that little spiel as a compliment, I'm proud you've finally realized I'm no saint! Definitely more of an angel from hell," I agree, completely unashamed. "But you're right, I won't ever give up on you, wanna know why?"

I draw his anticipating and curious face closer to mine as he nods.

Kissing his lips, I then part them with my tongue as I whisper my affection into his mouth.

"Because, Liam Whiskey King, without you, there can be no me. And come hate-fuck-hell or hate-fuck-heaven, I'll always be in love with you."

CHAPTER 41
Once a Schmuck
LIAM

There is no shame on her face. Not in her eyes, her body language, or her love while she sits there looking at me from the bench behind Gabe's table.

My wife is a pillar of strength, and justice when she looks at me. A beautiful mess of everything I fell in love with and the freedom from all that makes me want to hide my head in this court room.

I keep my eyes focused solely on hers as I sit up here feeling like I'm being crucified by David Schneider. It's hard not to tune him out because concentrating on her means I can still breathe no matter how quickly the walls feel like they're closing in around me.

In Vixen's eyes I see a storm of potent might, a shadow of mercy, and an arsenal of power. The same kind of dominance it took me to get through the most harrowing years of my life. Not just when I was a kid, but when I carried the caskets of the only people I'd ever related too in this life to their graves.

Now I'm up here on the stand, alone, and bearing my soul to strangers. People who think they know me, or the things I've outlived, but respectfully, they know nothing at all. I'm trying to keep my breathing steady and my nerves controlled because everything I hate is sitting at the table to my right. I can feel Carl's eyes bore into me, but I refuse to look at him. Instead, I stay focused on Vix's face trying to answer Mr. Schneider's harsh and condescending questions feeling like his prisoner now. He clears his throat and steps closer to me, but I stay deadpanned with Vixen.

"I asked you a question Mr. King."

Still focused in the depth of Vixen's wild eyes, I grit my teeth and heave in a hard breath.

"Ask it again."

I don't pry my eyes from hers as he continues, my heart racing in my chest.

"You are under oath, Mr. King, and we cannot proceed with this trial if you don't comply," he reminds, "now, can you please point to the man you claim abducted you?"

I wipe my palms down the front of my thighs, searching my mind for the strength to lift my arm in his direction, but it feels heavy. Anger is boiling underneath my skin to his demanding tone, and if I were to raise my arm, I feel like I might hit the son of a bitch. I'm also sleep-deprived and feel like I might conjure up the image of a gun in my hand if I were to point to Carl, and then I'd pull the fake trigger. But everything I do, and everything I say is imperative to the case as Gabe has so often reminded me.

With her fist gripping the cross pendant I gave her, Vixen nods her head, her eyes pleading with mine to point him out.

You can do this, Liam, I'm right here, is what I hear her saying in my head.

I lift my arm and as I do my eyes travel with it in what feels like slow motion as I meet eyes with fear incarnate himself, my chest swirling with adrenaline.

"That demon right there, Carl the whack job Paulson, is the

man who abducted me, then fucked me, and also destroyed eleven years of my existence from within hells basement."

The words come crashing out of me in the silence of the room as gasps emit from several people. But not David Schneider, no, he holds steady in his plight to tear me down to nothing.

"You will watch your tongue in my courtroom please, Mr. King," Judge Montgomery states.

I don't bother to acknowledge her as Vixen smirks and mocks her, contorting her face up like a child. I hold in my laughter and then look at Gabe who also looks rather impressed. It gives me a sense of pride as I wait for Schneider's next assault, preparing for battle.

"Alright, Mr. King," David says smugly. "Can you tell me about the day you claim my client abducted you?"

I think back to the homework I'd done for Dell; about the orphanage and the red ball I'd wanted so badly. It fills me with a sense of fear, so I look up at Vixen trying to find my voice.

"I remember his shoes," I push out. "They were shiny, nicer than yours even," I say, inspecting David's leather loafers. "I was reaching for the ball when it stopped against his shoes and then his wife offered me something much nicer than a rubber ball, a bear, so I reached for that instead."

"And then what happened?" he continues as if he doesn't know.

"What the fuck do you think happened next?" I growl.

"Language, please, Mr. King," the judge requests, again.

I bite my tongue, again, ignoring her because she has no clue how infuriating it is for me. Having to sit here and go over things that have already been stated how many fucking times?

"I will ask you again," David says sternly.

My fists clench to the sound of his patronizing tone.

"What happened after you say Carl Paulson's wife offered you the bear?"

"I told you, I reached up to take it," I say, feeling the panic set in. "And then before I knew what was happening, I ended up in the back of a dark vehicle. Are you fucking happy now?"

I can't help but look the smug prick in the eyes as my body betrays me, starting to tremble in reaction to the memory.

"Mr. King, I will hold you in contempt of this court if you do not settle down and mind your tongue," the judge states yet again.

I look over at Gabe, now standing.

"I think my client needs a break, your honor, would you be so kind?" he asks politely.

Jesus, fuck yes, I do.

Vixen winks at me and then her eyes land hard on the judge as if she's willing the virgin-eared woman to agree with Gabe.

"Alright, counsellor, I will allow a thirty-minute recess. This court will reconvene after that time."

Asked to rise, we all do, but my legs feel like jelly as we wait for the judge to leave the room. I then wait until Gabe waves me over, confirming I can leave my post. I make my way over to Vixen, doing everything I can to make sure I don't look at Carl as the room starts to clear out.

"You did great!" Vixen says, cupping my face and smiling. "Fuck that grouchy old bitch, she doesn't get that it's in our DNA to curse."

"Yeah, well you'd better find a way to cut it out," Gabe interjects. "You cannot let David get under your skin, Liam."

"I'm trying, I really am," I assure, "but he's such a self-righteous prick when he talks."

"I hear you, bud, but you're gonna need to tone it down, just until we win and then you can stick it to him with every curse word you can think of, okay?"

I nod, trying to think of ways to get through this without resorting to profanity as Gabe leads us out of the courtroom. Being that we are somewhat celebrities around here, we've been instructed to wait until the room has officially emptied and to use the exit that avoids the press. The same exit, I might add, that Carl uses, and it terrifies me that I may run into him at some point.

Gabe leads us to a small room and shuts the door behind him as Vix and I take a seat. It still sounds like a circus out there since the walls aren't as insulated as I wish they were. On the table there are two bottles of water and a tray of crackers which look brittle as hell, but I take one anyway as Gabe starts in on me again.

"When we go back in there, I need you to be calm and collected, no more of the F-bombs please. Also, Liam, the questions are going to get harder so you need to be prepared to hold your tongue and just answer them as truthfully as you can."

"That's what I've already been doing," I groan, whistling out cracker pieces across the table.

I gesture at him to hold on a second and wash it down before I continue.

"I feel like a child up there getting forced to repeat shit that fucker already damn well knows the answers to. It's embarrassing."

Before he can respond there's a tap on the door and the court stenographer opens it and pokes her head in.

"Sorry to interrupt," she says out of breath. "Judge Montgomery would like a word with you in her chambers promptly please, Mr. Morris."

"Hold that thought," Gabe says, "I'll be right back and hopefully I can mention Dell's PTSD diagnosis and maybe get her to cut you some slack on the stand."

"Works for me," I say appreciatively, also wanting to ask him to come back armed with something much sugarier then these stale crackers.

"Shit," Vix mutters. "What do you think that was all about?"

"Don't know," I shrug, "but I wish all of this could just be over. I don't know if I can do this."

"You can," she says squeezing my hand. "You've already been through the worst of it and survived, so just look at this as the end game, okay?"

Easier said than done, I think just as she pulls a package of gummy bears from her pocket and dangles it in front of my face.

"You didn't," I say reaching for them.

"Uh-uh, gimme your word first," she entices.

"You have it, I'll treat this like it's the Nintendo game."

"End game," she revises. "Tell me how you're going to do it."

"Really, Vixen? Just give me the damn bears, please," I groan, knowing I'm extra moody today.

Her attention turns to the door as Gabe enters the room, so I rip the package from her hand.

"Wow, Liam, you really are something else," she hisses.

I smile, still not knowing what that means, but happy I am in control of the candy.

"I have news," Gabe says, sounding at odds. "The judge has decided to postpone the trial for a week in light of something that's just occurred."

Vixen and I look at each other curiously as he continues, and I munch down on the delicious candy.

"I'm not sure how you two will take this, but I'm just going to say it straight up," he pauses seemingly trying to choose his words. "Dana Paulson was found dead this morning in the women's prison."

Motherfuck, holy shit! Is this for real?

"Wow, shit, that's awesome! What happened?" Vixen asks, pointedly. "I want details, the gorier the better," she then adds, not even attempting to hide her delight at the news.

"Well, it's pretty graphic from what I was told. Maybe we should wait for the official report."

"Fuck that," Vixen laughs, "spill it Gabe."

He looks to me, ignoring Vixen's demand.

"How do you feel about it, Liam? Do you want to hear the details?"

"The fuck?" I say with my mouth crammed full. "Don't be a schmuck. Tell my wife what she wants to hear."

"Yeah, *Gabe*," she goads, her face sexy and sinful, craving the dark details as the naughty little vixen she is.

He begins to tell us how there was an error in her paperwork, and she'd been moved and placed into general population which is not where accused child predators are supposed to be incarcerated. Apparently, there is some code and they are usually placed in their own confined group due to the other prisoners having certain morals and becoming violent towards felons accused of such crimes. In a way I guess I can sort of understand it. Had Vix and I ended up in there for the murder of the satanic-like Helen back in the day, we too may have opted to get our hands on such predators in the name of vengeance. Still enlightening us, Gabe goes on to say that not only was the woman beaten to death in the shower, she was first humiliated and tortured in ways I can confirm are not something I'd like to repeat.

"Right the fuck on!" Vixen gloats pretty much cheering. "So, what does this mean for our trial?"

"Like I said, the judge agreed to postpone for a week in order to give Carl time to grieve his loss, so, in the meantime—"

"Wait, what?" Vix cuts him off. "That grizzly old bitch who hates swear words is giving that perverse child predator time to grieve for fuck's sake? Is she insane? A few cans shy of a six pack or what? I don't get it, that piece of scum should be forced to deal with it after the things he's done."

"Calm down," Gabe instructs. "The law says innocent until proven guilty, Carl has rights and if we don't do things by the books, it will leave room for David to have it declared as a mistrial in the end. Patience," he says firmly. "All bad things come to those who deserve it. Besides, maybe another week of preparation will be good for Liam."

"More like a week of celebrating the violently awesome death of that cunt will be what's actually good for him."

"That too," Gabe mutters, trying not to laugh at Vixen's unashamed victory grin.

The acknowledgment of her death spikes my heart rate and I have to question what it means.

"So now it's just me versus him?" I ask feeling both relieved and nervous at the same time.

Gabe nods.

"It won't be easy, but one less trial is good for us. Once this one ends, it'll come down to the testimony of the other two captives that were found. Between the sentence I'll be asking for and the outcome of the other trial, there is a strong chance he will receive the death penalty if convicted in both trials. We just have to make it through this prosecution first, alright?"

"Sure, thing schmuck."

I stand and stretch, feeling anxious yet excited at the same time. There would be no greater feeling in the world than to know the two of them were wiped off the face of the planet entirely.

"Is there anything else I can answer for either of you or should we book our flights home for the week?"

Vixen's mouth hits the ground and I look at him and grin ear to ear.

"We can go home?" we both ask simultaneously.

"Who's not so much of a schmuck now?" Gabe asks arrogantly. "And yes, I cleared it with the judge. Straight home and no talking to anyone about the trial. Sound good?"

"Fuck yes," Vix hollers as I say, "You're still a schmuck."

"One for two ain't bad," Gabe laughs.

* * *

We make it off the Hill just after dark with the kids and Mac in tow having sung them (but not Mac) to sleep, during the car ride home from Helen's.

It's been a long day, one that started with me not wanting to be alive, but that ended with me praising Vixen for not letting me give up. Being back home with the kids is just what I needed, and I plan to make it the most spectacular week for all of us. I made a deal with Vix on the flight home that there would be no discussions of the trial between us (unless it was with Gabe) in return for my promise to get things back on track with Liv. I'm her father and I've sucked at it the last several months, but this is my chance to redeem myself and show her that she can count on me no matter what.

Once she's not sleeping of course.

I place Liv carefully in her bed remembering not to cover her feet because she hates it. Then I tuck her fuzzy blanket underneath her chin and kiss her forehead as Vixen does the same for Matthew. We tiptoe to the door and stand silently for a bit admiring the warmth of being home with the world's greatest kids. I'm positive all parents think it, but I'm fairly certain that we are the only ones that are actually right.

"Okay, come on," Vix whispers, nudging me to follow her.

I leave their door open just a crack and slide my way down the hardwood hallway and into our room feeling like a superhero.

"I am Metal Man," I announce in my best Robert De Niro Junior voice.

"You mean *Iron* Man," Vixen laughs.

I can't help but watch her as she slips into a baggy t-shirt. It's such a turn on because it always happens to be one of mine.

"Now get over here and lay with me," she says, patting the bed, "but keep your iron dick in your pants, tonight we are going to practice the art of decompressing sexlessly."

I look her over suspiciously as I undress quickly down to my boxer shorts and climb in beside her.

"What are these big words you are using, and are you just trying to fuck with me?"

"Not in the slightest, I just want to try something a little different tonight because I'm exhausted."

"Me too," I admit, although I'm still very unnerved by the idea of going to sleep.

Vixen rolls toward me and pulls my hand to her chest, holding it there as she stares at me. I could lay here awake forever memorizing every feature on her perfect face. The way her eyes glisten and change colour according to her mood and also the way she always seems to be planning something devious by the manner in which her eyebrow twitches. I can tell she's studying my face the exact same way by how she bites her lip in thought. And the more I stare at her thinking dirty thoughts of visiting the city of hate-fuck, the more serious and aggressive I feel my face become, which for some reason she usually finds irresistibly attractive.

"Okay, quit it," she hisses, "I know what you're doing."

"I'm not doing anything, just looking at your incredible face is all," I lie.

"Oh, because that's *not* precisely the particular look you *always* give me when you want to fuck?"

"No?" I say back in more of a questioning tone than an answer.

Seeing right through me, she laughs and continues to hold my hand, caressing it gently.

"You're afraid to go to sleep, aren't you?"

"Afraid, no. Trying not miss out on what's right in front of me, yes."

"You lie."

"Never," I say, kissing her smooth forehead. "Go to sleep and decompose, I'll see you in the morning."

"Decompress," she whispers, barely holding her eyes open. "Goodnight, Liam, I love you."

"Night, Vix, love-hate you more."

Watching her drift off into a place of comfort, I lay taking in the view, wondering what she will dream of. Perhaps it will be of something fun like hitting the highway on the bikes or taking the kids down to the beach. Then again, it's more likely she's dreaming of the same thing I'd been thinking all the way home. Envisioning all of the gruesome things that happened to Dana during her final breaths. Imagining that her last thoughts were of my face and those of my siblings. Hoping, her last feelings were that of pain and regret for all of the horrible things she took part in. Craving that her screams were filled with worse anguish and suffering than she'd ever gotten out of any of us. And wishing that for just a moment of time I could have been in that room with her and gotten to join in on her demise. *Twisted, I know*, but forgiveness for the agony she's caused me is beneath me. Now all that's left to do is to pray that Carl is faced with the same fate. It's just too bad it won't be nearly as rewarding as watching him suffer would. Maybe that's what my lovely wife and her spank-able, lacy, pink panty covered ass are dreaming about. The death of Carl and getting to watch the life drain from his septic eyes. If I had my way and got to choose how he died, I'd opt for burning him alive while he was stark naked and hanging from a pole in the ashes of the basement he'd kept us in. Not only that, I'd want every parent who'd ever lost a kid to a pedophile to be offered a front row seat, along with any person who'd been lucky, or unlucky enough, *depending on how you view it*, to have survived what I did. Sick or not, that's what he deserves, and I'd be the one to light the flame as he looked into my eyes and begged for mercy. I would have none, not an ounce, and I know I'd be smiling as I listened to him cry out and then finally watched him take his last breath. My smile would be the last thing he ever saw. Now that would be righteous.

I wonder if the fact that entire thought has me completely turned on right now is normal. I'm gonna guess not, but what is normal anyway? Certainly not my wife's current sexually eliciting moans while she presses that tight little ass of hers against my groin, and yet she remains fast asleep. *So much for wondering what she's dreaming about.*

* * *

Wanting to start off the morning right, I make sure to begin by throwing together the kids' favorites. Bananas in milk for Liv, porridge for My Chew, and *leftover whatever the fuck this is that Helen sent home with us for Mac*, I think to myself, dumping it into his bowl.

"Yay! Thank you, Daddy," Liv cheers, clapping her hands as Matthew copies.

"You're welcome, my little monkeys, and you too," I say, looking down at Mac.

"What the heck did you slop into his bowl?" Vix asks, sounding unhappy.

"It's just porridge."

"Not Matty's bowl, you big dummy, Mac's bowl," she clarifies.

"I dunno," I shrug, "whatever it was Helen sent in the container home last night."

"Oh. My. God, Liam. You didn't," she says swiping the bowl away from Mac. "It's cookie dough and dogs can't have chocolate!"

"Well, shoot, I didn't know... it just looked like a mushy mess of goo that no one would have wanted to eat," I say in my defence.

"Whoa! You so bad, Daddy!" Liv squeals. "Momma you need to smack he ass!"

"Smack ass!" Matthew then repeats.

Vixen and I turn our backs to the kids holding in our urge to laugh, surely both of us now wondering where they picked up the word ass from.

"Okay, Liam," Vixen finally musters out. "You need to keep a watchful eye on Mac, and he might need to get looked at if he gets sick."

I nod in compliance, still refusing to look at either one of the two tiny troublemakers behind me. It's more likely this is all their fault considering it was actually their unwholesome looking leftovers that tricked me.

"Right, Vix, if he gets sick, I'll take him straight over to see Dell."

Arching a brow and looking crossed between sneezing or choking, Vixen ends up laughing and farting, in turn making me too, bust out in laughter yet I have no clue what we are laughing at.

When it finally subsides, long after the kids join into the infectious moment with their giggles to the sound of Vixen's toot, we compose ourselves and then she kisses my forehead.

"Okay, Liam, first off let me just say excusez-moi, that was not super ladylike of me," she says turning a rosy red. "Second, we really need to go over what Dell's qualifications are because he cannot treat sick dogs, only people. Nor can he attend to physically injured children *including* ours. Where would you have taken the kids if they got sick or hurt?"

I can tell by her face I am supposed to know the answer, but I'm still baffled to know that Dell isn't qualified to help Mac, yet the man is a doctor, so I decide to go with the safest answer I can think of.

"To your mother's house of course."

I give her the *I bet you thought you had me face* as she punches me in the arm and shakes her head. *Fuck me, really? I suck at this.*

"Wrong answer, tough guy. I think it's about time we take a

family trip down to the hospital for a sight-seeing adventure, then we'll head over to the veterinary clinic, because boy are you something else."

I smile excited by the sound of this so-called adventure and loving that she thinks I'm something else, although someday I plan to ask exactly what it is. But for now, I think I should stick with the one question I've been dying to ask since last night.

"What does decompress mean?"

CHAPTER 42

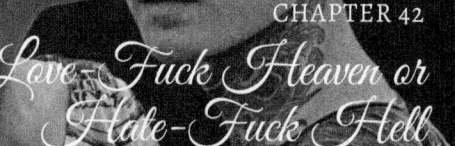

Love-Fuck Heaven or
Hate-Fuck Hell

VIXEN

You know what they say about time... it flies by when you're having fun. Not at all like how I used to feel when it felt more like time was dragging on in a slow torture back when Liam would disappear. Or like so many of the days when I'd spend an entire afternoon gluing my head shut and removing glass from it after one of my mother's drunken rage fits. Nope, now I enjoy every second I get even though it never seems to last long enough. The week of being home with the kids was exactly what Liam and I needed, I'm just sad it's over and that we are now back in Montana, fighting the good fight as they say.

I can't complain though, because Liam did accomplish what he said he was going to; he repaired his bond with Liv, *and in the strangest way if I might say.* I'm not sure if it's their shared experience of having lived in an orphanage, or if it's just because of their shared love for sugar in general, but they stood giggling together over an hours long session trying to read, name, and identify all of the colors of every treat in aisle four at the grocery store.

If only I'd recorded it, my God they were sweet, no pun intended.

To my surprise, it wasn't the hugs or kisses Liam drowned the poor girl with repeatedly. It wasn't the shoulder rides down the beach while chasing Mac, nor was it the many I love you's he told her the day they watched *Cinderella* three times in a row while he let Liv put makeup all over his face. *Nope*, all it ended up taking was their once forbidden, now undeniable, undying love for *candy* to rekindle their father/daughter bond. *Go figure*.

Nonetheless, it was a much-needed surrender from the press hype and pressure of what now only happens in Montana, thanks to Gabe. He was kind enough to ensure the judge issued a press ban so that we could spend our time at home in peace. The ban was only in effect during the last week and kept them from hounding us during our private time with the kids, but now that we are back here, it's no holds barred.

Liam and I stand staring at the airport exit plastered with a mass of gathered reporters just waiting for us to step outside. *Fuck me, this is the shit I did not miss, time to get my game face on.*

I dig something out from my purse and then hand my bag to Liam.

"Hold this for a second. I have a plan."

Throwing my purse over his shoulder, I point to the taxi waiting behind all the reporters as I tell him what we are about to do to make it there.

"Wait," he says looking confused. "Why do we have to give them anything at all?"

"Just follow my lead, this will work," I assure him. "Follow me out there and as soon as I have their attention, get in the cab, I'll be right behind you. Got it?"

"Yeah, sure, I guess," he says, still puzzled.

I grab his arm and push through the doors just as they all start hollering out into their microphones asking questions. Keeping Liam to my left, I hold my right arm in the air and wave it around.

"Look what I have," I shout as loudly as I can. Several of them look at my hand as I nudge Liam toward the cab and then toss what's in my hand into the air. "This should be enough to tide you savages over," I say, watching as the pile of pictures from the last week flutter through the air to the ground. "Report all you want about us, but when it comes to the trial, Liam King and I have no comment."

With that, I back away quickly as some of them pick up the pictures, but others continue to spew out questions. In the moment all I really want to say as my heart beats wildly, is a big old *suck it, assholes*, but instead I climb in the back of the cab with Liam.

"Nicely done," he credits.

I smile at him as we sit watching most of them continue to fight over the last of the photos on the ground and then I tell the driver the name of our hotel as we pull away.

"It was the only thing I could think of that those freaks would want more than money," I tell Liam. "Plus, it will be good for them to see first-hand what an amazing father you are."

Without warning, he grabs my face and kisses me as if there is no tomorrow. His lips are warm and full of passion, he's rough and demanding with his hand tangled in my hair, leaving me breathless and slightly damp down below.

"Jesus," I pant as we stop. "If this is what a week of sexless decompressing brings out in you, we may just have to do it more often."

"That's not what has me wound up," he growls *that* growl.

"What is it then?"

"You, Vix, it's the way you somehow think of everything and then boss handle the fuck out of everyone. But I am a little upset that you gave away our pictures too."

I reach across his lap and grab my purse before digging out the second set I'd printed. I was going to give them to Mom and Claire but forgot during the heart-wrenching goodbyes with the kids when we dropped them off. I hand the envelope to Liam and smile my *I'm fucking awesome* smile.

"Have I ever told you how badass you are?" he asks, tracing his fingers up and down my thigh.

I wink knowing I've just tipped the man into the potential route to love-fuck territory. *I've brought him there once; I can do it again.*

* * *

It's not yet nine in the morning when we enter the empty courtroom and take our seats. Liam at the table beside Gabe, and me on the bench directly behind them as they mutter dumb shit to each other like usual. Equally as annoying, is Gabe's persistence to make sure we are first in and last out of this wooden box of lemon polish, but I get why. He want's Liam to have some time to take in his surroundings, process the feel of the room as if it's going to alleviate some of his tension, but I say nothing, knowing that isn't at all how my husband's mind works.

I've always been able to read Liam's face like a book, it's both a curse and a gift if I'm honest. I'm able to see his anxiety in his hand gestures, when he looks at them or picks at his fingers anxiously. Sometimes his stress is less subtle, and he'll shift in his seat or scratch his head when he's becoming frustrated and it tells me he needs me to help him breathe. I use small, basic signals whether it's something that makes him laugh, like making a face at him or the judge, *God forbid she ever sees me.* Other times it's as simple as a wink or a hidden bag of candy I'll even purposely eat from that will keep him going. Then there's the harder emotions that want to take over him. The one's that make me wonder if he's going to blow out of his stark black suit and become a giant

TAINTED LOVE

ball of rage like the Hulk. Anger induced by fear is the one emotion I can see most prominently when I look in his eyes. They turn dark and venomous; his brows drop and pinch at the center and I know it's at that point when he thinks he has to hold it in yet all he wants to do is detonate. Being in the courtroom means I can't relieve him of it with a simple hate-fuck, so instead I find myself holding my breath right along with him as I talk him through it in my mind.

I remember I used to do it a lot as a kid, trying to bite my tongue around my unpredictable mother. I'd learned the flip side of holding in all of the anger was that I was taking a risk. If I let too much out at once, or said the wrong thing, chances were, I'd get nailed with a foreign object. From everything I've learned about dealing with said anger, it's taught me one thing that brought me to the here and now.

Fuck Darwin's theory, it's not survival of the fittest, it's survival of the angriest and whoever can withstand the most pain.

For Liam and me, it's where we connect the deepest. The anger and resentment inside us fill our lungs until we can take no more, but the pain of our reality when we exhale is what keeps us alive.

Hence, what I'm positive spurred on my morbid addiction to the violence of hate-fucking.

As for Liam, I don't think he comprehends a whole lot past his need for sugar which leaves me in the one place I value the most. By his side and ready to take on whatever I need to that will get him through this.

The court room starts to fill as I look over at Gabe, looking calm and prepared as usual as he spins in his chair and whispers something in Liam's ear.

Nodding, Liam then turns to me and grabs my hand. "Gabe says he has this morning's paper in his car and that Liv, and My Chew are plastered all over the front. He says he'd bet his career on it that jurors have seen it and he wants you to watch for their reactions when they enter."

Hearing the excitement in his tone and seeing his face glow proudly impales me with a sensation I don't know how to describe.

"I will, I'll watch," I whisper just as the jurors are led through the door.

I let go of his hand and focus on them as they enter. Sure, as shit the first one through, an elderly man in a plaid button-down glances over at Liam and smiles. Next through the door, a woman with long dark hair also smiling and blushing if I'm not mistaken, looks our way and I can tell she's quite smitten with Liam. Either him or Gabe, it's hard to say, the guy is technically eye-candy. I keep watching as the jurors enter one by one, each of them looking like they are all dying to laugh about something. It makes me want to jog out to Gabe's car to see what the hell was on the front page.

Turning in his seat, Gabe smiles smugly at me.

"Don't think I'm not still a tad perturbed with your little stunt," he undertones.

I stick out my tongue and twirl my finger in the air motioning for him to turn back around and do his damn job.

As if I care what he thinks. Those press fucks took the bait and I'd do it again if it meant keeping them off Liam's ass.

The whole room that is chatting quietly amongst each other goes dead silent as Carl gets led in by the bailiffs and his lawyer. All eyes are on them, including mine until Liam turns toward me, his nerves teetering on edge once again as I watch him swallow.

"Just breathe, it'll be okay," I whisper, "I'll tell you when he's seated."

Liam nods and shuts his eyes. If ever there was a time, I wish I'd listened to every bizarre thing I'd heard him ask me, I now wish

I'd taken him to get baptized. He needs God now more than ever, fake or not.

I sideways peek over at the two worthless scumbags and then squeeze Liam's hand.

"You're good, they are seated and talking away about something to one another."

"Thanks, Vix," he says opening his eyes. "And just in case I fuck up today, I just want to say—"

"You are going to be fine," I state, not letting him finish as I lean in and press my lips to his. In the heat of the moment I do it without thinking because of the fear in his eyes. My only intention as I savor in the heat of his tongue, is to bring his focus back to feeling in control, at least for the moment.

"Cut that shit out," Gabe says kicking Liam's chair. "The judge will be in here any second."

I remove my lips from his and smirk at Gabe.

"I highly doubt that just because the old bag has virgin ears also means she has a virgin pussy too," I tease.

Gabe's face flushes and Liam laughs.

"Yeah, schmuck, the judge probably gets more action than you do."

About to respond, we are cut off by, "All rise... Judge Marilyn Montgomery is now presiding."

Once she takes a seat, we are all once again instructed to do the same.

I watch David Schneider stand and ask to approach the bench to which the judge agrees and then Gabe quickly makes his way over. Then I glance over at Carl and my heart stops as I turn and look at Liam.

Jesus, fuck.

The two of them are in a stalemate, their eyes locked on one another's as my heart races to the animalistic manifestation engraved on Liam's face.

I stand and grab his hand fearing he will do something insane just as Gabe steps in front of us looking shocked.

"What?" I sputter out. I'm panicking inside and my mind spinning in every direction.

"You're about to find out."

I don't dare move as David Schneider returns to his table beside Carl and begins to address the court.

"Over the last week, my client, Mr. Paulson, has been grieving the loss of his wife as we know," he pauses.

I feel Liam's hand sweating as it tightens around mine and I'm terrified of what's about to come next as once again David discusses something with Carl before he nods. The echo of my heartbeat is ringing through my ears and it's hard to slow my breathing.

Clearing his throat, David finally continues.

"As I was saying, my client has had some time to reflect and against my advice he wishes to change his plea. Let it show on the record that Mr. Carl Paulson now wishes to enter a plea of guilty on all counts."

"Jesus fuck!" falls loudly from my mouth as I stand vibrating with adrenaline. "Did we seriously just win?"

The judge looks at me, her expression entirely unimpressed.

"Language please," she states. "And the answer young lady, would be yes," she finishes, turning her focus to Carl and David.

I freeze, feeling stunned as Liam grapples and hugs me harder than I think I've even been fucked or pegged in the head with anything, *ever*.

"Holy shit," Liam sighs, spinning me around. "Can you even believe it?"

"Put her down and pay attention, guys, please," Gabe says, almost laughing.

The judge continues to address David, Carl, and the jurors I'm pretty sure, but I can't focus on anything other than the fact we just won. The realization that the hardest part is over, and I can only guess this is what a full body orgasm feels like. It isn't coming from anywhere near my pussy; not even close. I feel the rush throughout every nerve in my body.

All I can feel is Liam's grip and I can imagine he too, feels a wild array of emotion at this moment as we continue to stay locked in an embrace. I take in the happy whispers and cheers around us as the judge finishes up instructing the jurors or whatever she's still rambling on about.

"You did it, Liam King. You held on with both hands, and you did it," I praise.

He says nothing, just smiles a beautiful, proud smile that leaves me no choice but to kiss him some more. *Fuck is he pretty.*

When the full-blown chatter of the room finally starts to die down as people begin to shuffle out, Liam drops me to my feet that have officially fallen asleep. We take a seat waiting for Gabe's instruction as Verna's parents come over and join us, the triumph of it all still sinking in. Both Susan and Lyle have tears of what appears to be joy and pain in their eyes as they congratulate us, and it feels surreal. Like I'm not even in my own body anymore.

"Wow, this outcome was completely unexpected," Susan says, wiping her eyes. "Do you think he feels remorseful?"

"Who?" I cringe, wondering if I heard her correctly.

It sends fleeting pulses of hate through every nerve ending in my body instantly ending my happy high as his name falls from her lips.

"Carl Paulson."

If I wasn't in such a state of astonishment, I wouldn't even consider holding back the fact I really want to haul off and punch her straight right now.

"No, Susan," I say bluntly, "there is no way in hell I believe he's remorseful. Not after what he did to your daughter, Ken and Cliff Dodd, or my husband for eleven years in that basement. All I can think is that the sick fuck just has finally recognized that there is no one left in the world he can relate to, so he's giving up."

Susan shrugs and takes a deep breath.

"I suppose you are probably right," she says unconvincingly.

I sit waiting for a but, expecting one, yet she says nada.

Smart woman.

She stands with her arms out, wanting to hug us as we say goodbye, all of us agreeing to keep in touch as we await his sentence. In the meantime, at least Liam and I can collect ourselves and celebrate the huge step toward victory.

"So, what's next, Gabe?" I ask, still held hostage by the robust smile that graces Liam's gorgeous face.

"If you were listening instead of making out while the judge was speaking, you would know what's next," Gabe says brazenly.

"Don't be a douche... just tell me that when Liam and I leave those doors we have permission to mingle with the reporters."

"As a matter of fact, you do, but I'd advise you to mind your tongue."

"Have you learned nothing about Vixen?" Liam asks. "The only person who can control that sweetly foul little tongue of hers is me while it's in my mouth. Other than that she says what she wants."

Gabe lifts a brow and laughs.

"Well then I suppose I'll leave you guys to it then and I'll see you back here in the morning for sentencing. I need to go and catch up with the Whitmores' to see if they have an impact statement they'd like to read. You might want to prepare one as well, bud," he finishes, shaking hands with Liam.

"Consider it done, and hey," Liam says, pulling Gabe into a hug. "Thank you, you're a good friend and lawyer, but don't let it go to your head, you're still a schmuck too."

"Thanks, and you're still an undereducated meathead, but I'm glad I could help."

"You two are so ridiculous," I say rolling my eyes. "Now beat it, Gabe, Liam and I have some serious celebrating to do."

We watch as Gabe adjusts his suit and then his hair before he winks and exits into the noisy surroundings of the flashing cameras and reporters shouting out questions.

I pull out my phone and we skim through the pile of messages from everyone who's been following along with the news. There are messages of congratulations and love from Mom, Claire, Jack, Jimmy and even Dr. Dell.

"I still can't believe this," I tell him. "Maybe we'll get super lucky and he'll plead guilty in the next case too."

"Yeah, and then hold is arm out and beg for the injection," Liam adds.

"Hell yes, and then while that's happening we should be allowed to chuck rocks at him. I'd aim for his balls mostly and laugh the entire time."

"Fuck that, we should be allowed to set his ass on fire, I've actually dreamt about it. I'd want to see him burn alive."

"Mmm, yes, that'd be disgustingly fabulous. Man, is it weird that talking about this is kind of turning me on right now?" I ask, wanting desperately to climb on top of him.

He shakes his head and laughs wickedly as his eyes glide up and down my body in thought.

"You ever been hate-fucked in a court room?" he whispers.

"You know I haven't and although it sounds interesting, I don't feel like getting arrested. Besides, I'd rather take this back to the hotel and see if we can't find our way back to the city of love-fuck."

"Hmm, I guess it's a reasonable request, but I have to warn you this dick of mine has been unreasonably deprived since you began forcing me to decompose sexlessly."

I laugh at the serious expression he's trying so hard to pin me with.

"It's still decompress not decompose, Liam. Decompose means that Benjamin down there is rotting, which we both know that is so not the case."

"Well how would you know that? You haven't even seen my dick in over a week," he points out.

With my arms crossed I squint at him.

"Are you deliberately trying to cause an argument with me right now?"

"Of course not," he says, feigning innocent. "The city of love-fuck does not require total anger on your part. Now move that nice ass and go tell off some schmuck reporters so we can get on with the best part of today."

"Oh, you know I will," I say, dragging him through the doors.

We stop and for a brief second, take in all of the blinding camera flashes and overlapping questions and then I clear my throat before I take a deep breath.

"Alright, listen up fuckers, and don't look at me all funny like you're all shocked and stupid. I know you vultures have bleepers to fuzz over my profanity. So I'm only gonna say this once... and believe me when I say that my husband and I mean it from the bottom of our hearts. Get fucked."

With that I take my husband's hand as he laughs and they all start to follow us with their thousand questions and loud, obnoxious voices, until Liam stops and turns toward them.

"Did you assholes not hear my wife?" he asks as they all stop abruptly, practically up each other's asses. "She said get fucked. That means go now and get some, you shameless bastards. Oh, and all of that is on the record."

I laugh as we exit the courthouse, no longer paying attention to the horde behind us. They are still tailing us which I expected, but I love the way my husband now holds his head up high, no longer feeling like an outcast or a villain, I'd imagine. He finally seems unafraid to speak up, as he should. All he needed was vindication, to know that the world saw Carl as the guilty monster he is, and Liam as the hero he's always been. He is a survivor and he's learned how to become a man with a voice and a beautiful one at that. I'll have to help him harness it come tomorrow though, because come hate-fuck hell or love-fuck heaven, he's going to need it for his impact statement come the morning.

CHAPTER 43
Ashes to Ashes
LIAM

Fucking homework, again. Why? I'm beginning to hate this shit.

Mostly because we are in a damn hotel room and we should be celebrating, not sitting here sounding out the vowels in the word su-i-cide, which is spelled dumbly in my opinion. If I had a silver coin for every time Vix looked at me with her *I know you can do this* face I'd be a zillionaire. But still, I sit here staring at the eighteenth page I've tried to write and refuse to crumple it like the rest. Why? Because my awesomely hot wife refuses to take me to love-fuck city until I finish my impact statement.

Thanks a lot, Gabe. Fucking schmuck.

I should have said fuck that to the dirtball, because not only do I not want to *write* this, I don't want to *read* it either. It's Stupid with a capital S and I'm positive I'm just going to embarrass myself with how slow I am at reading. Of course, I know Vixen won't see it that way, *noooo*, she'll tell me how cute I am or bribe me with some freakishly delicious gummy bears, which will work. Because she is pure and total vixen, that wife of mine. She can be so unfairly persuasive sometimes, *I swear it*, even worse than the evil, vixen sister princesses from *Cinderella*, and I think she damn well knows it too.

"Are you ever going to get more than two sentences finished or do I have to make Benjamin go another night without any special attention?" Vixen entices.

"I'm trying here, it's not my fault all of the words I want to use are big and confusing to spell."

"Then sound them out, Liam."

"I don't want to."

"Why not?"

"Because even if I write this stupid thing, I'm not going to read it anyway."

"Yes, you are."

"No, I'm not."

"Want to make a bet?"

"Depends what kind of bet," I say, pointing to my dick and then crossing my arms.

"You really think I'm going to reward you *twice* for completing *one* task? Boy are you something the fuck else," she scoffs.

I smile at her, thinking my tactics are spot on, but then she removes her shirt and sprawls out on the sofa. Her beautiful body barren and on display as my eyes trail over her and *wow, she's sexy as hell*, wearing nothing but her black lacy panties.

I stay focused, watching her hand travel over her perfect tits, her nipples hard and begging for my attention, but her hand doesn't stop there. It continues on downward over the piercing in her navel and then, *fuck me*, she slips it into her panties.

Is she really going to get herself off just to spite me?

My dick is fully awake and constricted hard against my pants as I continue to watch her tease herself.

"That's it," I growl, "I can play dirty too, and you're going to watch me."

"Go for it, you know I'm down to watch you manhandle my buddy Benjamin," she says in a moan.

I say nothing and rip my dress shirt open straight down the middle as all of the tiny buttons pop off and fly in every direction. Now fully having her attention, I smile as I watch her eyes light up and wander over my colorful nakedness, loving how she can never resist studying me.

"I know you Vix," I say moving closer to her. "You'd rather *I* manhandled you than my dick," I say, removing my pants. "But if you want to be a bad girl, I have no problem making you watch."

"You don't have the willpower," she retorts, moaning even louder and then licking her fingers.

"Don't be such a tease, Vixen," I growl, wanting to lick them too.

Mother shit she's good at this game.

Wanting to up my own game, I decide my smartest move is to get even closer and make her watch me enjoy myself even more than she seems to be.

"Check this out," I say stroking my dick as close to her face as I can get.

"Move that shit or I'll bite it."

"You wouldn't."

"Try me. I will."

"Well fuck, go for it then."

I instantly regret saying it as she lunges forward and takes me into her mouth. But fuck does it feel good and hot and wet.

My mind is in overdrive as she continues to lick and taunt the length of my dick and it makes me want to drive myself further down her throat. She's fast and aggressive in her pace. The vibrations of her throaty moans are bringing me close to release as I shut my eyes to relish in the sensation, but then she stops.

"Wait... what? Don't stop," I breathe out.

She licks her lips and smiles before returning her hand inside her panties.

"I was just giving you a taste of what you could have if you agree to read and write the statement. Otherwise, have fun finishing yourself off," she states.

I want her so badly, watching as she continues to play with herself, one hand teasing her pussy and the other palming her breast. The harder she squeezes her legs together tells me she has every intention to orgasm right in front of me if I don't stop her.

I know I can't take anymore of watching her, as the agitation mounts in my chest. I need to be inside the wicked woman filling and fucking her.

"Fine," I hiss, "I'll write it and then read it."

"Mmm, smart choice," she moans and then spreads her legs.

I stand, thinking and lost in her seduction, knowing what I want to do, but not entirely confident in how to do it.

Knowing that if today were yesterday, I'd have already torn her panties off and fucked her over the arm of the sofa like an animal, but it's not yesterday. I'm not the same inside as I was yesterday because today, I was freed. Unchained from the pressure of having to remember why I am the way I am. Correction, why I *was* the way I *was*. Today I no longer feel like the ruthless creature from the basement and I want to show her I can be gentle.

"What are you doing?" she asks, jerking me closer. "I just gave you permission—"

"Shhh, Vix, just let me see you."

Her eyes turn a deep tint of green and her breath halts, her skin covering in bumps as I take my time studying all of her with my fingertips. From her flawless face I trace them down along her neck as her chest rises and falls, embracing the sensation. She's the most enchanting being I have ever seen, and her staggered moans tell me she knows it.

"Fuck,' I whisper into her skin, "you are utter perfection."

She lets out a gasp as I begin to follow my fingers with my lips, placing light kisses down her silken stomach as her breathing deepens further. My own need to occupy her is intensifying quickly, but I continue to hold back as my hand reaches the top of her panties, her body trembling to my touch.

"Are you going to tease me all damn night?" she asks, vexed.

"This is not teasing, it's called instigating."

"Exactly what I just said."

"No, it's not, now shhh."

She laughs and squirms her way out from underneath me before forcing me to sit as she takes my hands into hers.

Fuck, what did I say wrong this time?

"Don't look so disappointed, you know I'm only trying to better your vocabulary. Now repeat what you just said."

I growl under my breath and cover us with a blanket. *Here we go with another lesson, way to wreck the moment, Liam.*

"I said I was instigating your body, and I thought I was doing a good job of it," I inform.

"Oh, you were definitely doing an incredible job. I was horny without a doubt and my body was absolutely *activating* from your touch, which is another word for *instigating*, but I don't think that's what you meant to say, is it?"

I shake my head and realize instantly what I meant to say.

"Investigating," I say, yanking the blanket off of her. "That's what I meant to say... I was investigating every part of you with my lips and my fingertips."

"That you were," she says jerking the blanket back. "Now spell it."

"What? Now?"

"Yes."

"Uh-uh."

"Come on, please?"

"No, Vix, I want to investigate you some more."

"Then spell the word."

"What the fuck? This is getting out of hand," I tell her, throwing my arms in the air.

I'm really starting to feel frustrated, but as always, she crosses her arms waiting for me to give in and spell the stupid word.

"Challenging or not, I love you, Liam, and this is an important part of me showing you just how much," she says sincerely.

"I appreciate it, Vix, but this is ruining my day, and fuck is it really starting to mess with our extra-circular activities."

"Curricular," she corrects with a smirk. "Now stop stalling and spell the damn word."

"Which fucking one?"

I'm now even more confused, completely irritated with myself and she's laughing to make matters worse.

"Oh my God, Liam, you should see your face right now," she says, still laughing.

"It's not even funny and it makes me so mad that you think it is."

"I know."

I look at her face, trying to determine why she's got tears from laughing so hard until she finally stops, still saying nothing.

"What?" I growl. "Why do you keep laughing at me?"

I feel like I'm about to flip the woman over and fuck her until she's remorseful just to teach her a special lesson of my own.

I wonder who would be laughing then.

Now quiet, but still smiling as she wipes her eyes at my expense, she finally says something.

"Just how angry are you, Mr. King?"

My mouth falls open as I stare at her, stunned.

You have got to be kidding me, un-fucking real. She just tipped me into hate-fuck territory.

* * *

My wife is really something else. I'm exhausted from being up all night in the city of love-fuck, but I finally understand what the *'something else'* phrase means. *All thanks to her entirely shady ploy to trick me last night.* It was solely her intent to use my own methods against me in an attempt to get me riled. Having a taste of my own medicine is what she called it, not that I fully get what that means. I refuse to complain though, because the best part about last night wasn't that I learned how to spell and define two big words, uh-uh, or the fact I've written and am prepared to read my impact statement. *Nope,* the most amazing part was the fact that even as angry as I was, we made love. *Well, a red-hot version of it anyway.*

I saw Vixen, all of her, and it was nothing short of mind-blowing. From kissing her flawless lips, all the way down her beautiful silk-like, decadent body, and into every part of her sinfully sweet soul. I saw my wife with my eyes wide open.

It was like nothing I've ever seen, nor experienced before, and with each moan I extracted from her, I also saw myself. The hidden parts of me I never knew existed, the new ability to be calmer and gentler, at ease with myself, not feeling pressured to hurry through it or punish her for my hate, because there was none. I felt only love and freedom aside from Vixen's eventual hellfire, demanding nature to persuade me to fuck her harder, but that was to be expected.

It was a night I will never forget.

"I've got an early morning surprise for you," Vixen calls out from the bedroom.

"I'll be right there," I holler from the washroom. "And it had better not be you wanting a repeat of last night because we have to be at the courthouse in—" *Shit, I hate this watch.*

"One hour," she finishes for me. "The small hand tells the hour; big hand tells the minute."

I finish buttoning the last button and grab my tie from the countertop as I exit the washroom.

"Well why can't I have a watch like Jack's? It just tells him the *real* time and it glows red."

"That Rolex, which was my dad's also tells you the *real* time, you just have to learn to read it," she informs, as she hands me the phone.

I take it, expecting to see Liv's sweet face, or My Chew's troublemaking grin, but instead I see a very bald smiling Dr. Dell on video chat.

"Looking sharp this morning," he says chipperly. "I just wanted to call and tell you that I'm proud of you, Liam, and I wish you luck today."

"Thanks," I say, feeling proud. "I'll try my best."

"I'm sure you will, and I know Kirsten has your back should you need a little nudge. Just remember, Liam, I'm always here if you need to talk."

"Yes, sir, I know, and hey, don't let your other patients eat all of the candy before I get back. I think with Vix's permission, I might want to sit and tell you another story about a little place we visit here and there, I could really use your doctorly insight on how to make sure I continue the practice of surviving abuse and trauma. Especially when it comes to Vixen, I think we had a breakthrough," I update.

His sly smile turns into an all-knowing grin as he nods.

"Now what would make you think that the V in vixen would make your wife stay silent?" he laughs. "I already know about hate-fuck Hell and love-fuck Heaven, and even hate-fuck city, territory, and Mars, Liam. But I am more than happy to help you out with whatever's on your mind. In the meantime, *son*, go and tear that imposter a new one for me and get back here safely."

He winks and then hangs up as I wrestle with the idea of Vix telling him things she clearly hasn't told me. I realize that in all of the months I skipped the sessions and let her go alone, she must have been battling things I didn't bother to support her through. More so, battling *me* and what *I* put her through. I was selfish and too caught up in my own misery to see how she must have been suffering. I feel like an asshole knowing it must've been such a burden on her that she felt she had to tell Dell about the monster in me. *Fuck, how do I apologize?*

"We should get going, Gabe texted and says he'll be waiting downstairs for us. Oh, and I booked our flights home this evening, so Mom and Claire said they'll be waiting at our place with the kids. Sound good?"

I nod, biting my lip and trying to separate my guilt from my happiness and my nerves.

Vixen's brows furrow and she looks at me peculiarly.

"Liam, what are you thinking about right now?"

"You," I mutter, ashamed. "What did you tell Dell about us? And why?"

Her face pales and her eyes meet mine with a guilt of her own.

"I told him the truth," she says, her voice cracking. "I needed someone who would understand us and not judge you, Liam. I wasn't trying to go behind your back or keep things from you. I just needed to get it off my chest."

"Get what off your chest?"

She steps closer, her eyes studying me as if she's worried, I might be pissed.

I stay waiting wondering whether or not I should be as she swallows and then answers.

"I told him I felt like I was stuck. That I was afraid for you and for myself and whether I'd be able to get through to you. That's it, I was looking for his reassurance, that's his job."

"And? What did he say?" I ask growing more frustrated by the second. "Because he just told me he knows about shit I certainly *didn't* tell him, Vixen. Things I would have asked *you* permission for first. Private things," I add, wanting her to admit it.

"So what? Yes," she shouts heatedly. "I told our shrink about the fucking marks and the way I was letting you use me. I wasn't sure if I was doing the right thing and I felt like I was losing you, terrified you would end up killing yourself too. Yet, on the other hand, I felt like I was crazy for somehow liking it, and even *crazier* for not knowing whether I'd end up dead on the flip side of things," she pauses, trying to compose herself as a single tear runs down her face. "I was scared, Liam, and I know you understand the feeling, so I asked Dell for his opinion. That's it."

"Is it?" I ask, feeling worthless. "And what was his opinion then? Did he tell you to go home and let me treat you like dirt? Because I remember very clearly telling you to put your fucking clothes back on after the first time," I remind.

She rolls her eyes as more tears slide down her guilt-ridden face.

"Yeah, I remember too, and no, he didn't give me his blessing. He told me to admit you to the hospital for a psych eval, but you know what I did? I told him to go fuck himself because it would be over my dead body that anyone ever locked you up anywhere for a second time. And then do you want to know what else I did?"

"What's that?" I ask, beginning to realize how wrong I am to be questioning her.

"I'll tell you," she says passionately, "I went the fuck back home and called Gabe to make sure he would save our asses if Dell decided to report you."

"Shit!" I mumble, wordless otherwise.

She wipes the tears from her face looking upset, somewhere between anger and guilt.

"Can we just get going please? Gabe is waiting."

I nod and follow her out to the elevators, holding my tongue but admiring how incredible she looks. Her pant suit, a black and white pinstriped fabric, fitted entirely to her frame, was designed by none other than the notorious Rebecka Davenport, the CEO of Davenport's Formals. From what I've heard, if there is anyone else in the world that is as vicious at grabbing life by the balls as Vixen is, it's Rebecka. I remember Vix reading a write up in a magazine once and bragging about how the woman faced some pretty fucked up family issues.

I get why my wife became an instant fan and went to her directly to have this specific suit made only to be worn if we won. The suit is perfect, as is my wife's ass along with the stark white embroidery across the back of her suit jacket. They are the wise, spoken words of Rebecka Davenport herself:

Kings were meant to be castled; you just have to know when to make your move.

"Come on, Liam, stop staring at my ass and get in here," Vixen says, holding the elevator doors open.

I step onto the elevator and without thinking I back her into the corner and kiss her until neither of us can breathe.

"Is that your attempt at an apology?" she asks smirking as the doors open to the lobby.

"Nope, this is."

I head straight for the gang of reporters just outside the front entrance and stop when I get there, waiting for Vix to catch up. I watch her face flush, probably unnerved and wondering what my plan is as I grab her hand and pull her to my side, now facing the reporters who are staring at us in wonder.

"I know you've all met my gorgeous wife, Vixen... or rather Kirsten King I should say, *my Vixen*," I say proudly before I continue. "Take a long look at her, she's not only what you see, or what she shows you. She isn't just sexy as fuck, or to put it simply, a no-shit taking bitch in which I respect her wholly for. Nope, she's a warrior and as such, I have to apologize to her publicly so that I can tell the entire world something she'll probably kick my ass for later—"

Stopping me there, Vixen tries to pull me away, but instead I cup her face that expresses her uncertainty and I kiss her up against the hotel doors and then whisper in her ear.

"Just let me do this, they need to know how I feel, and so do you."

Breathless, she nods but pulls me into another compulsive kiss igniting everything unholy in me before she lets me continue.

I clear my throat.

"As I was saying... my wife has given me the confidence to be the man I am today. She's supported me through things that would make most men feel weak, or lesser, or like a monster. I know this because I felt those things, but Vix, she made me realize something along the way. She made me understand that it doesn't matter what other people think of me, it only matters what *she* thinks of me," I pause, gripping her hand and she smiles up at me as if I'm the only person who exists. "This woman," I say, turning to look her in the eyes, "is the lightning to my storm, and I just want to tell you that I'm not ashamed of what we are. I love you, Vixen, and I'll hate-fuck, love-fuck, fuck-fuck you upside-down, backwards, and into the netherworld for the rest of my life, simply because it makes you smile. But I want you to know that I'm sorry for not always giving you the recognition you deserve."

She wipes the pooling tears from her eyes and smiles.

"Are you done now?" she asks.

"Yep, I said what I wanted to."

"Good, because I forgave you inside the elevator, and now these fucks are looking at us like we are insane. But you know what I think?"

I take in the wicked gleam in her eyes and smile because I know exactly what she thinks, but I ask anyway.

"What do you think?"

"These fools still need to go get fucked."

I laugh as she grabs my hand and we walk toward Gabe, who's been watching from behind us the entire time.

"Wow," he says, shaking his head. "You two are really something else."

"I know," we both say at the same time, happily.

"Well, if you're done performing for the circus, let's make our way down to the courthouse, shall we?"

Obliging him, Vixen and I get in the back of the cab, letting Gabe take the front seat. The drive isn't too far from our hotel as we sit holding hands while I stare out the window, pressing the button up and down for fun.

"So, Liam, are you prepared?" Gabe asks.

"Yeah, Liam, are you?" Vix then adds, slapping my hand.

"Ouch, yes! Just leave me be and talk amongst yourselves," I suggest, wanting to play some more with the button.

"Verna's father plans to read a statement on behalf of his family," Gabe says. "It should go a long way in swaying the judge toward my recommendation of a life sentence. I'm hoping the deliberations will be quick given the evidence and Carl's plea."

"How quick?" I ask.

Gabe lifts a shoulder and turns in his seat.

"Your guess is as good as mine, a couple of hours maybe, it all depends on the judge and whatever she finds to be a reasonable sentence."

I look at Vixen and cringe.

"Try not to worry, Liam," she says supportively. "No matter what she comes back with just remember *you've* already won."

I smile and grip her hand harder, feeling both confident yet nervous. I know there is a lot riding on what I've written, and I know I will never truly feel like I've won unless he's dead.

I take a deep breath as we pull up outside the courthouse and I take in the crowds of people that line the sidewalk. Some of them have signs that are rooting for the injection even though that isn't on the table at this point, but it makes me feel supported. Others have signs that say, 'get fucked' and 'Vixen King rules' printed underneath, I can't help but laugh.

"Jesus, you two," Gabe mutters. "I can't believe the shit you can stir up."

"Sorry, not sorry, Gabe," Vix says, smiling her most devious smile. "I only told them what I know we were all dying to tell them for the last year, and for that I will not apologize."

"Yeah, Gabe, Vixen's right," I add. "Those schmucks deserved it and look... we have more fans than ever. I'd say Vix is fucking brilliant."

"You and me both, bud," Gabe says lifting his brows up and down.

For a second, I wonder if he's referring to her badass tactics to stonewall the press, or if he's thinking about the time she gave him a hate-blow. I guess either way it doesn't really matter, because regardless, he's the best lawyer I could have asked for and I should probably forgive him at some point.

"Alright, Liam," Vix says confidently. "Lets go in there and give that sick fuck a statement he won't ever forget."

We exit the cab and I adjust my suit feeling like a King, not the kind in a palace, but more so the kind that's married to an enchanting vixen. Because of her, I'm ready to put my past to rest, to tell the man who stole so much from me what the cost was. I'm prepared to face all of the hurt, the torment, and the anguish in the name of justice.

Ken, Cliffy, and Verna, this is for you.

CHAPTER 44

Get Fucked

VIXEN

It's finally here. The day I've dreamt about for so many endless nights, since the first time Liam told me about what he'd survived as a child. There are no words to describe the emotion flooding through my body as I take a seat beside him. He is the one person who gave me hope once upon a time, and a reason to exist. It's funny he calls me tough and thinks of me as some kind of miracle, or vixen-like entity that's helped him find himself. *Ha*, boy was he wrong. It was the other way around; he's always been the real champion in my eyes. I'd always been fairly certain that being born the daughter of Helen King meant I was automatically hell-bound, and maybe I still am, but one thing is evident: running into Liam that night in the park changed everything. It wasn't until my father answered the door while Liam held me upright that I saw the look in my father's eyes. It sobered me up instantly. The look on his face that said *you have got to be shitting me,* as Liam's eyes turned a glorious shade of confusion and it all just hit me. That's when I put the pieces together... the tent in the park that no one *ever* tented in because we all had motorhomes or vacationed away from the Hill, and the indescribable look of defeat meshed with failure written across Dad's face. A look that told me not only could he guess that the job he'd hired Liam to do, (killing Mom) wasn't going to get done, but he'd also predicted the start of what was sure to become a bond between us that no one could break. Do I believe I am partially responsible for my father's death three years later? I do.

In many ways I know I'd seen the signs of a broken man but figured it was a natural reaction for a husband who'd felt trapped in a loveless marriage. I also thought he would have been wise enough to hire someone else to do the job. But it's different now, and I'm not sure that was the right solution either, now that I see how good Mom is with the kids and how much she's changed. I've thought about what I would do if given the chance to do it over again and as sad as it is to say, I wouldn't change any of it even though I miss my dad. Then again, *at least I had one.*

"Hey," I say, rubbing Liam's leg to get his attention.

The courtroom is starting to fill as he turns to me looking slightly unsettled.

"I don't think I can read this in front of all these people," he says anxiously.

"Sure, you can, just breathe deep and read slowly. You'll be great," I assure.

"Okay, Vix," he says, visibly struggling to find his brave face.

We watch as Carl and his lawyer are led in and then we all rise as Judge Montgomery enters. She looks extra bitchy this morning, and her tone is firm as she reminds the room to stay silent while the statements are being read. Gabe has recommended a sentence of life and David is seeking a sentence of ten years minus time served. If the judge comes back agreeing to ten years that would mean Carl will be eligible for parole before his seventy-third birthday.

It also means I'll be waiting for him should he manage to survive.

"Alright, at this stage, I'd like for those who have prepared impact statements to stand and address the court. You may do so from your place in the gallery, but please speak loud and clear," Judge Montgomery instructs.

We watch as Gabe turns and gestures at Mr. Whitmore to stand, telling him to begin when he's ready. I grip Liam's hand, feeling the stress of both Liam and Lyle linger in the air as we watch him unfold a piece of paper, his hands shaking as he does. The room is entirely silent, there is nothing to be heard except the sound of Gabe's endearing and subtle remark to let Lyle know he can take his time.

"My name is Lyle Whitmore, Verna, my daughter, was abducted from a supermarket when she was just eight years old," he pauses, working to compose the shake in his voice. I watch as Liam stares at him intently his palms becoming coated in sweat as Lyle continues.

"I spent many sleepless years searching for her and then many more blaming my wife for not paying more attention that day. I kept telling her if she'd only not turned her back, or if she'd held Verna's hand instead of letting her wander down the aisle, then maybe—"

He pauses again as his eyes fill with tears and he wipes them away before he crumples the page in his hand and continues.

"I came down here wanting to talk about the grief and undefinable pain Carl caused my family the day he took her. But no matter how hard I try to word it; our little girl is never coming home. And the hardest part about knowing that it isn't just the fact Carl Paulson destroyed her beautiful, innocent little heart the day he took her. Nor is it the fact he then devastated her a second time so much so, that years after she'd made it out, she still ended up taking her life just to avoid having to face him here today." Stopping to recover, Lyle takes another sharp breath and continues as tears line his cheeks.

"The part that guts me the most is knowing that the monster not only took our daughter from us twice, he also managed to turn me into a man full of hatred. A husband tortured by the guilt of blaming my wife for something that was beyond her control. Now, I am a man also haunted by my guilt for listening to the press. They said that my daughter's hero, Liam King, was rabid. They said that the same man you see here, who was just a boy back then, was no hero at all. Christ, he was just a child no older than my youngest daughter who turned fifteen this year, yet, barefoot and scared as I've been told, he ran the half-mile back through those fields without a second thought. The truth is, Liam could have saved himself and just left them behind, no one would have blamed him. I mean, Hell, anyone who's ever watched a horror movie knows that when you escape you never go back. But then again, none of them understood anything more than what it was like to have each other. My daughter was loved, she was like a sister to him and he went back to save her, yet the press called the courageous child an animal. How sick has this world become when they could depict an abducted child as a monster far worse than Carl was ever dubbed?"

Lyle's hands clench into fists as he closes his eyes, seemingly trying to swallow the anger in his tone, before he begins again.

"I am ashamed to say, I fell for it, I believed Liam was a vile person because of what he looks like, I judged him and I felt that maybe he was part of the reason Verna's now dead, and I hate myself for it. So, tell me... as a man, how do I apologize to him for hating him for the things he too, like my daughter, my wife, and Ken and Clifford Dodd had no control over? For not realizing sooner that he too has suffered as all of them did, and for each other despite the cost. And for not grasping until now, that all of this, every single ounce of pain this has rippled throughout so many lives, is solely on the hands of the only monster in this courtroom. My apology can only begin with this: Carl Paulson deserves to spend the rest of his life in a dark, damp, cold hole, with no power, no bed, and nothing on his wall but the faces of the people's lives he shattered. It's the only thing besides his death that will be of any justice for his crimes. That's all I have to say, thank you."

Quiet murmurs amongst several people float around the room as the judge addresses Lyle.

"Thank you for sharing your statement, Mr. Whitmore. You may be seated. Are there any other people who wish to make a statement?"

"Yes, your Honor," Gabe says respectfully. "My client, Liam King, wishes to address the court."

"Very well, he may do so now."

Gabe turns to Liam and nods as Liam turns to me looking terrified.

"It's fine, I'm right here and I will be right beside you the whole time," I say, standing.

I offer him my hand and he plants himself directly in front of me as we face each other, so it's my eyes he can see.

"Excuse me," the judge interrupts.

I turn toward her slowly as Gabe shrugs and gives me the 'behave yourself' look.

"Me?" I ask, pointing at myself.

She nods. "Yes, Mrs. King, you," she says firmly. "I just wanted to double check that your standing beside Mr. King will not end up disrupting these proceedings."

I half-smile debating my answer carefully, knowing she's likely mad about the whole 'get fucked' news ordeal.

"No, your Honor, I'm just standing as moral support and possibly phonics support."

"Very well then," she permits.

I turn back toward Liam and give him a quick contortion of my face, mimicking the old bitch, as I watch him work hard to hold back his laughter.

"Whenever you're ready," I whisper, "but don't take too long. She might end up dying of sex deprivation and need you to hellfuck her old ass back to life."

"Quit it," he hisses under his breath, partially smiling and barely composing himself. "I'm trying to concentrate here."

I nod and wait as he unfolds his wad of paper and I stay focused on his face. He takes an audible breath and then begins.

"Uh... My name is Liam King and I'm a little... what's this word?" he asks.

"Sound it out," I whisper.

"Just tell me for once, please Vix," he whispers back through gritted teeth.

I can tell he's uncomfortable so I decide he can cheat this one time.

"It says anxious."

"Right, okay," he mutters, clearing his throat.

"I'm a little anxious, because this is not an easy stat... statement to write. So, please beer with..."

"Bear," I whisper, rubbing his back.

"Please, bear with me, while I read it to you."

He looks down at me, his face flushed and his eyes starting to do the thing that tells me he's nervous.

"You're doing great, keep going."

He takes a hesitant breath and continues.

"I know I am supper, no, shit, I mean I know I am *supposed* to talk about how I was imported, wait... that's not what I meant... um, what does this one say?" he asks pointing to a word.

"It says impacted."

I smile at him and wink, seeing how hard he's trying, knowing I couldn't be prouder.

"Let me go again," he says clearing his throat. "I am supposed to talk about how I was impacted by the abduction, fuck yes! I nailed that word!" he cheers.

A few laughs erupt as I glance back at the judge, who is looking rather impatient, but I tell Liam to continue.

"For one thing, I have to learn to read and write and it's hard if Vixen isn't helping me. Also, I get easily forested, wait, why does this say forested?" he asks, puzzled.

"That says frustrated, Liam."

"Well no fucking shit this is frustrating!" he hisses.

I hold my breath as yet more laughter erupts throughout the room.

Liam scratches his head as the judge interrupts once again.

"Mr. King... would you perhaps like to have your wife read the statement on your behalf?"

"Fuck yes I would!" he answers honestly.

Again comes more amusement from all directions as I shake my head at Liam.

"Don't listen to her, you're doing fucking awesome," I say under my breath.

His face falls into a mixture of frustration and anger, so I do the only thing I can think of and hand him a gummy bear.

Squinting at me, he takes it, eats it and then continues, although I can see he's still not in good shape.

"Where was I?" he mutters, "Oh, right, so, as I was saying, when I look back at everything I've had to learn, it sucks. It's been hard to be me most days... mainly when I think about Ken and Cliffy. They were my brothers and my friends. There is no one left to speak for them, so I wanted to say a little about them. Ken was a straw, no... a strange, uh-uh, well yes he was *strange* actually," he mutters to himself, "but what I mean to say is that he was strong. And Cliff, well he was frag... frag—"

Before I can correct him, the judge opens her big yap, again.

"Mr. King, I am aware that you are struggling due to problems with literacy, but I'm going to have to ask you to hand the statement over to either your wife or your counsel, please. This court does not have the time to sit here all morning while you practice reading, am I understood?"

Is she fucking serious right now?

I look at the disappointment on Liam's face and instantly I'm filled with rage.

I turn my back to Liam and stand in front of him as Gabe makes his way toward me, his eyes pleading with me not to say anything, but it's too damn late.

"Are you trying to tell me that sick fuck sitting over there got to have *eleven* years of my husband's life while he did unspeakable acts of horror to him, day in and day out, but you refuse to grant my husband one measly fucking hour of *your* precious time to read his statement?"

Leaning forward in her chair, Judge Montgomery's face maddens.

"You will not use that language nor that tone in my courtroom," she says heatedly. "Now I'm sorry that your husband has a hard time reading, but it is unreasonable to expect this court to waste valuable time, so would you please be so kind as to read it or have Mr. Morris do so?"

My whole body feels like a pressurized ball of hellfire wanting to eject from the core, as Liam runs his hand down the small of my back and whispers in my ear.

"It's fine, Vix, just do your thing."

I smile at the smug old bitch and take a deep breath, knowing she didn't hear me very well.

"Alright," I say calmly, swallowing down my anger. "Before I read this out loud for my husband who spent much of his own *precious* time writing this out last night, I want it to be crystal clear that Carl Paulson is the reason my husband struggles with reading. He didn't just take away Liam's right to a family, to the possibility of a loving set of parents who could have adopted him and taught him to read. People who could have loved him, hugged him when he was sad, or kissed an injury when he was hurt. No, that's not nearly all Carl took from my husband. That monster silenced all of Liam's tears and crushed every single one of his dreams. A four-year-old boy's dreams. Carl Paulson is also responsible for eleven years of smothering that boy's right to breathe. He forced that same innocent child to adapt, survive, and live with years of perverse torture, that left him unable to bear children of his own. And after all of that was said and done, Carl still wasn't finished. What that man stole from Liam, was his dignity, his self-worth, and his right to a proper life that isn't full of pain so domineering he can't sleep at night. But you know what that, worthless, spineless, child stealing, piece of shit over there didn't get? I'll tell you. He didn't get to take my husband's dying breath. And do you know why? I'll tell you the answer to that too... because all it took was for one person to see him the way I do, past the ink, under the shell, and into the beautiful mind of a forsaken man. I'll leave it at that, and if you want to read his statement that is written by one hell of a champion, I'll leave it with Gabe. As for you, your Honor, I appreciate that you let me speak, but seriously... GET FUCKED."

* * *

Okay, so that probably wasn't the smartest decision I've ever made, but I have made worse, so whatever. At least after the uproar of laughter crossed with shouts of *'fry the son of a bitch'* and *'inject the sick bastard'* died down, I ended up being escorted out by the bailiff, because boy did I want to ring that old bitch's neck before I got hauled out. Now I'm stuck handcuffed in a little room waiting for Gabe to do damage control because she wants to hold me in contempt of court, but it was totally worth it. There was no way I was just going to let her toss Liam aside after he stood there scared and embarrassed, swallowing down his anxiety, as he tried so hard to read what took him all night to write. I glance at the clock. seeing its now 11:30, which means I've been trapped in here for close to an hour and yet I have no clue if the judge is deliberating, or if anything that I just said in there will mean anything at all. I wish Gabe would hurry the fuck up and tell me what's happening because I can still hear people chanting our names through the walls in protest. It seems they too wanted Liam to be permitted to finish his statement and they had no issues with what I belted out.

A tap on the door startles me before Gabe and the bailiff enter as I let out a sigh.

"Fuck, finally! Where is Liam?" I ask.

"Outside the door where he's been standing since the second you were brought in here," he laughs. "Where else would he be?"

I exhale in relief thinking I should have guessed as the bailiff removes my cuffs.

"So, I'm not going to jail?" I ask as Gabe takes a seat and the bailiff exits.

"Of course not... although the judge was pretty irritated with your final statement," he points out. "It took a lot of persuasion on my part to get her to understand what this has been like for you. But after a few compliments that were getting me nowhere, I may have used a few legal threats to get the woman to see it my way."

"Seriously? You shady fucker," I laugh, taking in his arrogant smile.

"Yeah, but she made it clear you are *not* allowed inside the courtroom during the sentencing which could be any time now, so we'd better get Liam in here."

I roll my eyes as Gabe tells him to enter. Liam's face is full of concern as he runs at me like the viking he is, grappling me in an off the ground hug.

"Shit, Vixen," he says squeezing me, "I was ready to bust you out of here and holy fuck was that speech brilliant."

"Thanks," I groan, "but can you please put me down?"

"Oh, sorry," he says placing me on my feet. "My phone was ringing off the hook, but don't worry, I told your Mom, Dell, and Jimmy that Gabe had everything under control."

We both look at Gabe smiling in appreciation as he stands there looking full of himself, rightfully so.

"You have a decision to make, Liam," Gabe says checking his watch. "Judge Montgomery has unfortunately banned Vixen from the courtroom, so I need to know if you want to be in there for the sentencing or out here with the tiny loudmouth when the jurors read the verdict?"

"Who are you calling tiny?" I tease, eyeing over the crotch of his pants.

He squints at me unhappily as Liam laughs.

"Yeah, Gabe, I didn't see you in there jumping to my defence," Liam adds.

"That's because I know better than to argue with a judge, being that I'm so well-endowed with a Harvard education… and not just a dick that inspires mediocre head," he taunts back.

"Wow," I say, pretending I'm offended. "Funny thing to hear coming from a douche who sleeps with cougars, *Gabe*, and I highly doubt you have any other experiences to compare that one-time, extremely ill-thought-out blowjob I regretfully gave you with."

Gabe's face flushes as I wink at him and he stays silent, unable to find a comeback.

"That's what I thought... so what's the plan?" I ask side-eyeing Liam.

"Same as it always is, Vix, I'll be wherever you are."

"Alright, then I'll go and wait in the courtroom and keep you two posted," Gabe says. "Just don't get into any more trouble, please."

"We'll try but I can't guarantee it," I say in all honesty as he exits.

* * *

"It took the judge how long?" Mother asks again, as she zips Liv's coat. "I'm sorry dear, I just love hearing the excitement in your voice when you tell the story," she explains.

"Two hours," I say grinning.

"Right, that's pretty fast as far as I know. I think your statement had a lot to do with it even if that contrite cunt of a judge disregarded your entire speech," she says openly.

I shrug and smile as Liam kisses Mom's cheek and carries the kids out to the car.

"I can't be sure, mom, but she came back with the sentence he deserved, life, so it doesn't matter to me what got her to reach the decision. I'm just happy Liam might be able to sleep through the night at some point."

"And what about you, sweetheart? How have you been sleeping?"

I see the concern in her eyes and shrug at that too.

"Don't worry about me, I'm good, relieved to finally be heading home. So, how were the kids while we were away?" I ask, trying to move on from talking about me.

"They were little devils as usual," she laughs. "But like their parents, they are unafraid to test limits and push boundaries. I wouldn't want them to be any other way."

"Thanks, Mom," I say hugging her. "Oh, and I meant to ask you how come the kids came home infatuated with the word ass last time?"

"It was a slip of the tongue as far as I remember," she recalls. "We had just finished watching a news clip and Claire accidentally called someone a Jackass in front of Liv. It spiralled out of control from there, I'm sorry."

"No worries, it happens," I say as I open the front door and stop in the doorway. "I love you, Mom, and thanks for taking the kids and also for staying sober."

She smiles a prominent grin.

"You're welcome, sweetheart, and I'm proud of you too in case I don't say it enough. I'm just sorry your father isn't here to witness how incredible you are... but I suppose, in a way, it's better he's gone and waiting for us in another place."

I cringe at her.

"Why would you make his death sound like a good thing?"

She laughs and places her hand on my shoulder.

"Well, I can only guess who would have ended up raising Olivia and Matthew if he were still here. Chances are you, your father, and Liam would likely be in jail by now if you'd done things his way," she says candidly.

My mouth falls open and I gasp.

"You know?" is all that seeps out from my lips as my heart pounds in my chest.

"Of course I know," she laughs, "I'm a King for Pete's sake. It's my business to know that my husband, daughter, and son-in-law plotted to kill me. But don't worry," she pauses, lifting my chin. "I've forgiven you guys, Lord knows I've tried to kill you more times than I can count. Let's just call it even, okay?"

I feel my eyes bulging out of my head as I half-smile.

"Sure thing, Mom, I'll call you once we make it home."

With that, I close the door behind me wondering how the hell she knows as I enter the car laughing to myself like a lunatic.

"You ready to hit the road, my little badass?" Liam asks.

I nod, deciding this is one thing he doesn't need to know. Not when everything we've fought for is in front of us, and the past belongs exactly where it is.

Far the fuck behind us.

CHAPTER 45

Ride or Die

LIAM

E IGHTEEN MONTHS LATER...

Images of the kids I once knew dance among the shadows on the ceiling as I lay thinking about my life to this point. I smile at the memory of my siblings, the four of us sitting by a campfire, talking about our hopes and our dreams as the gravity of our freedom started to sink in. A time when Vixen didn't exist yet, and the only thing I knew for sure was that I was lost. I remember Verna's biggest hope was to find her parents, Ken and Cliffy had the same notion, wanting to find their father as well, but me... I had nothing to return to. I remember thinking it didn't matter though because even if they didn't take me with them, I was free. But now that they are gone, and Carl is behind bars, I still sometimes wonder if it's me or my siblings that are truly free. It's a question I've asked Dell, but instead of answering it, he came back with another question.

"What do you think the meaning of freedom is? Whatever your interpretation of the word is will be your answer."

So naturally I've been laying here most nights, trying to define what interpretation means... along with what freedom means to me, yet I'm unable to find a solid answer. What I do know is that for as much as I miss Ken, Cliff, and Verna, I don't want to be dead, because the thought of missing out on Vix and the kids is more unbearable then my grief for my family.

I feel the bed shift as Vixen rolls toward me and slides her arm across my chest.

"You're still awake?" she grumbles.

"Yep... just trying to answer Dell's question still."

"Well, it's late and tomorrow is a big day, you should really try and get some sleep," she advises.

"I will soon. Don't worry about me and close your eyes."

I run my hand through her hair suddenly filled with anticipation at her mention of tomorrow's event. We've been following the news closely as the trial in the case of the other two kids who were abducted came to a close. It's been all over the TV for the past few weeks and the jurors have been in deliberations to reach a verdict since this morning. Carl complicated the trial and didn't plead guilty this time. His lawyer, *once again that David Schneider schmuck*, has managed to create a strong line of reasonable doubt (Gabe's words) by accusing his wife of being the enforcer. They are trying to make it appear as though Carl too was a victim under his late wife's control. *Sick sons of bitches.*

Gabe says it was smart because she's dead, which made her an easy target to pin it on as they fight to keep Carl from receiving the death sentence which is currently on the table. I feel for the two kids and I know what they are going through, although I'm glad their identities and testimony have been covered under a publication ban due to their ages. The only details we get are from reporters outside the courthouse and a few images of the kids that were blacked out as they gave their testimony via recording, so they didn't have to sit in the same room as Carl. I'm just happy it isn't Judge Montgomery presiding this time. At least those kids had the chance to say what they needed to, and tomorrow, should fate allow it, those kids will be able to breathe again.

* * *

"Daddy! Daddy! Help me," Liv pleads from out of my view.

I can hear her growling in the other room at something as I drop the spoon into the batter bowl and make my way over. Turning the corner, I see Olivia fighting against Mac and Matthew who are both tugging on her princess costume from either side.

"My Chew's dress, you gif it to me!" he demands.

"No! It's my dress, Mommy said so," she growls. "You get your own! Right, Daddy?"

I nod, "Yes, Liv—"

"I'm Sleeping Beauty," she corrects, taking turns kicking at both Matthew and Mac.

"I mean, yes, Sleeping Beauty, please let go of your sister, Matthew, and I'll help you find your own dress," I offer.

"But My Chew needs this one!" he hollers.

I pick Mac up, wrestling the little guy away from the dress as I glance around the room quickly until I spot a shiny purple dress on top of the laundry hamper.

"Look Matthew, this one is very nice," I emphasize, "and it has sparkly ribbons all over... why don't you come and try it on?"

He eyes it over hesitantly with a grumpy face, but finally lets go of Liv and I help him put it on. It's miles too long and rivers too wide but he smiles contentedly and turns his focus back to the princess movie as the two of them stand there singing along.

"Sing with us, Daddy," Liv says holding out her hand.

"Yeah, Daddy," I hear Vixen say from the kitchen. "I'll take over cooking whatever this crap is if you sing really loud for us."

"It's pancake mix with bananas and chocolate inside," I inform. "And challenge accepted, you are so on!"

Vixen half-laughs and half-cringes as she inspects the bowl of batter. Taking the kids' hands, we belt out the words to "Once Upon a Dream" and I'm thankful for the subtitles that pop up across the screen. Being the incredible singer I am, I focus on the high notes as I pick up the kids and spin them around making them giggle.

"Okay... so, I have to say that I'm slightly confused over here," Vixen interrupts.

"Why? Matthew wanted to wear a dress, so I let him, isn't he beautiful?" I ask proudly.

"Yes, he is, like a real princess if I've ever seen one, but that's not what has me baffled," she states.

I kiss the little princesses on top of their heads and place them back in front of the TV before I make my way into the kitchen.

"What's the problem?"

I watch intently, feeling on edge as I observe her digging through the batter bowl lumping portions of it onto a plate. Then she makes her way to the garbage can and shakes her head as I stand wondering if I'm in trouble.

"Liam..." she says, in a reserved tone, "why are there mini size candy bar wrappers in the garbage? Are these seriously miniature chocolate bars inside the batter?"

I smile my best *please don't be mad* smile and nod.

"We ran out of chocolate chips," I explain. "And the kids anted up their Halloween treats so I couldn't say no... not when they were begging with their sweet little faces."

"Okay... I'll admit they are hard to say no to, but, Liam, this is not the solution," she says, "if you want to substitute something in place of chocolate chips, your best bet is to use these."

I look at the box of M&Ms in her hand and growl, wondering why I never thought of that first.

"Damn Vix, you are bad-a-s-s," I spell out. "You never seem to be without an answer."

"Speaking of which," she says, eyeing the two dancing princesses, "you should probably turn the TV to the news channel while I run the kids over to Jack and Jimmy's. I promised to keep them posted on the trial results over text if they agreed to take the kids, so they aren't subjected to any possible emotions that might fly out of our faces depending on the outcome. I think those two have already seen and heard far too much over the past few weeks. And, just maybe, if we're lucky, the guys will have chocolate chips at their place," she adds with a glimmer of hope.

"Good call," I say as the kids cheer and I eject the princess movie from the disc player.

I put it in the case and pack it in Liv's backpack as Vix helps Matthew with his shoes. Liv doesn't need our help with hers anymore, apparently five-year olds want to tie their own shoes. *She is so much faster than I ever was.*

If I'm honest, she can already read and write better than me too, but it only makes me prouder of her. She's a beautiful version of Vixen and every bit the go-getter as well.

"I love you, Daddy," Liv says.

"Me too," Matthew copies.

"Love you guys more," I say hugging them and then kissing Vixen. "And I love-hate you the most," I add in a whisper.

"Ew, that's gross, Daddy!" Liv says.

"Yeah, so gusting," Matthew weighs in.

I stick out my tongue at them as Matthew fiddles with the remote and hands it to me.

"You save the boys, okay Daddy?" he says, his eyes wide and full of love.

I don't know where his sensitivity comes from; his kind heart and awareness have always intrigued me. I'm not sure why he thinks I can save them, or what leads him to believe they are both male, but I hug him close and gossip in his ear.

"Your aunty Verna already saved the kids, but I promise I'll keep cheering for them, sound good, bud?"

He nods and smiles a toothy grin before he turns, running to catch up with Vixen and Liv.

As I watch them exit, it finally occurs to me. *This is freedom.* Right here in the presence of the only things I've ever needed. To love and to be loved. My family is my freedom.

"Welcome to Fox News, early morning edition. We are currently broadcasting live, standing here outside of the Billings City Court house in Montana, as we continue to await the much-anticipated verdict of Mr. Carl Dean Paulson in his latest trial. As the jurors continue to deliberate the verdict, we stand here on edge acknowledging that the victims in this case are children. This is now the second trial he has faced in the last eighteen months as the accused in several charges of child abduction and predatory sexual crimes against children. It was just last year we stood at this very courthouse and brought you the breaking news on one of the worlds most watched cases in criminal history, the trial that shed light on the story of Liam King, one of Paulsons' victims more than two decades ago. Liam was abducted when he was just four years old not far from where we stand and from just a few feet outside of his orphanage at the time. Eleven years later, and after a lengthy battle to survive, Liam was able to escape his then accused captor's clutches. At the time he was fifteen years old, but that didn't stop him from seeking help and then returning to the very place he fled in order to rescue the three other victims he'd been held captive with.

"It was during the unprecedented trial that Liam King having been the only survivor still alive to testify, had captivated the hearts of millions around the world, and at the time, the then accused had a sudden change of heart and abruptly changed his plea to guilty. It is believed that the unexpected death of his wife and accused co-conspirator, Dana Paulson, is what sparked his decision, and as the trial moved forward, he was sentenced to life imprisonment."

"Again, we await with our hearts pounding and our minds reeling in the anticipation that could potentially see to Mr. Paulson's execution in the next decade should he be found guilty. As you can see, there is a rally of support that lines the streets, families marching for the victims and even chanting the names of Liam and his wife Kirsten King..

"It stands to reason that today's verdict may just very well be yet another victory for the King family, the unnamed victims of these heinous crimes, and the entire world as we await what could be the first time the state condemns a criminal to death since 1996. Please stay tuned as we continue to bring you the latest."

"Any word yet?" Vixen asks upon returning.

"Uh-uh, just a recap of last year's events, which by the way, kind of turn me on. You getting thrown out of the court was pretty sexy."

"Oh, yeah?"

"Yeah."

She gives me a naughty smile and begins to pick up some of the toys scattered across the sitting room.

"So, what's got you all hot and bothered? Was it my suit, or my speech?"

"Definitely the speech," I say, now helping her. "But the suit was a major plus, any idea how that Rebecka woman is doing these days?"

She lifts a shoulder, "Last I heard she has twin girls, same age as Matty I think, and she married their daddy. He was sick, some sort of rare leukaemia, but I think she managed to bitch slap his ass into fighting it. I should probably call her; I'd love to have coffee with her sometime."

"Sounds nice," I say, focusing more on her great ass than anything she just said.

"Oh shit, quick, turn it up. This could be it."

I turn the volume up as the same reporter starts to talk again.

"Hello, and welcome back to Fox News, where I'm standing directly outside of the courthouse, here in Billings, Montana. We have just received news that the jurors have reached a verdict in the case of Carl Dean Paulson. After twelve hours of deliberations, we have just learned that they have come back with a verdict of guilty on all six counts, which means we will now—"

The noisy cheers flooding the streets around her is so loud it's hard to hear her as Vixen jumps on my lap in excitement.

"Holy, fuck!" she shouts. "They did it, Liam, they fucking did it!"

I smile at her overjoyed face and hug her as a surge of empowerment crashes through me. I don't even know what to say, but it feels like nothing I've ever felt. It doesn't even touch close to the feeling I had at the first trial; this is a victory that could send the monster to his death. This is unreal.

"Say something, will you?"

"I don't know what to say," I admit, speechless.

"Then stand the fuck up and dance at least. Dance for those two kids who just put the nail in Carl's coffin, also for yourself, Liam, and then some more for Ken, Cliff, and Verna."

"Right, good idea," I say, standing and twirling her around.

In this moment I'm filled with an indescribable emotion as my entire life plays in my mind. It's a throbbing mix of sadness, pain, and love as I take a deep breath and set Vixen on her feet.

"Maybe you should shout and scream, or growl, Liam, we could even break some shit if that helps you react."

I laugh at the concern on her face and take a seat, trying to breathe through the feelings I'm not sure how to express.

"Maybe we should wait for his sentence," I say, pulling her onto my lap. "It only took the judge two hours last time; this time could be even quicker."

"Sure, but if it's not I know what we can do in the meantime," she says, removing her t-shirt.

"Are you trying to occupy my mind with a trip to love-fuck Heaven?"

"I most certainly am," she says, massaging my dick just as our phones start to go off.

"Well, fuck," I growl.

"Mmm, should we answer?"

"I'd like to say fuck no, but mine says Dell."

"Mine says Mom."

"Want to trade?" I ask.

"That would be a fuck yes," she says, swiping mine and handing hers over.

I wink at her loving that gleam in her eye that says she'll take over my dislikes if I takeover hers as I answer.

"Hi, Helen, how are you?"

"Ecstatic! Wow! A guilty verdict for the second time... praise Jesus, I am so happy for you, Liam, and for those poor kids. How do you feel?" she asks elatedly.

"A little horny at the moment if you want my honest answer," I admit.

She laughs as Vixen squints at me, somehow listening between my conversation and her own.

"A few years ago, I might have been able to help you with that, Lord knows you are one very nice-looking man...but now I'm afraid I'll have to repent for my impure thoughts. I just wanted to call and congratulate you."

"Thank you," I say making a nauseated face at Vix. "I'm

feeling a little on edge waiting for news of his sentence... but while I have you on the phone, maybe you can help me with something."

"Anything. What's on your mind, dear?"

I inhale a deep breath wondering if I should ask about what her God would think of me these days, but decide not to.

"Never mind, its nothing, it's fine I'm sure it was a dumb question anyway."

Still on the phone with Dell, Vixen kicks me and gives me an evil look as if she's mad I called my question dumb.

"Well, alright," Helen says, "if you change your mind just call me. Kisses to Kirsten and the kids, and hey, no matter what his sentence is, I want you to know that you are an amazing man."

Her compliment makes me blush. If I had a Mother, I could imagine she'd be almost as cool as Helen.

Thanking her, I then end the call as Vixen continues on talking with Dell, as I overhear something about homework, which gets me motivated. *Homework always means gummy bears for me.*

"Alright, Dell, I will tell him... thanks for calling and we'll see you next week," she says hanging up.

"Tell me what?"

"Dell says he wants you to write in your journal tonight. He expects a detailed statement of your experiences, thoughts, and feelings today."

"Oh, sweet, I can do that."

"Hold on... I wasn't finished, and I know you're only excited because he has candy," she says pointedly.

"Fuck yes I am," I smile, "so what's the rest of the lesson?"

"He wants you to read it in front of him out loud."

I cringe and shake my head.

"Uh-uh, no fucking way, Vix, and you can't make me."

"I'm pretty sure I could, but I want you to *want* to do it.

Come on, Liam, please? It'll be like a mini do-over except it will just be me and Dell listening, and I will even throw in a trip to aisle four," she nudges.

Why does she always bribe me so well?

"How much time would I have to practice if I said yes?"

"Until our appointment next week."

"Okay, fine, I'll do it and I'll just practice alone and in front of Mac until then, but only because I love aisle four, *not* reading."

"I know," she laughs. "The candy aisle always gets a yes out of you every. Single. Time."

"You are such a devious little tease," I tell her as the news lady starts reporting again.

"Shhh," Vixen says, grabbing my hand.

We both watch in anticipation as the woman says that the sentence has been determined.

"After just thirty-four minutes of deliberating, the judge has come back with a decision in the case against Carl Dean Paulson."

Every hair on my body raises as my heart pummels inside my chest and the faces of my siblings enter my mind. I shut my eyes, take a deep breath, and listen. "The judge has voted that given the nature of his crimes, the ages of the victims, and the impact his choices have left the survivors and families of the victims scarred by, Carl Dean Paulson is now condemned to death and will be placed on death row, until he is executed by lethal injection."

I expect to hear loud roars and praises as I let out the breath I was holding and open my eyes, but all I see is Vixen with her hand on the power button and tears forming at her momentary disbelief.

"You know that you're a good person, don't you?" she asks as tears stream down her cheeks.

I nod and smile through my own tear laced face that tickle as they continue to come.

"Just remind me of it again in a decade," I say, wiping her flawless face with my thumb.

"You fucking know I will... but I have just one question," she pauses, wiping my tears with her kind and gentle hand. "Just how happy are you, Mr. King?"

THE END.

Whiskey & Vixen

Thank you

THANK YOU FOR TAKING THE TIME TO READ MY BOOK, I HOPE YOU ENJOYED IT.
AS A NEW AUTHOR IT HELPS A GREAT DEAL TO RECEIVE HONEST FEEDBACK INCLUDING CONSTRUCTIVE CRITICISM. PLEASE TAKE THE TIME TO POST YOUR RATING, THOUGHTS, AND LIKES/DISLIKES ON AMAZON.
IT IS INCREDIBLY HELPFUL TO KNOW WHAT FLOWS THROUGH THE MINDS OF MY READERS.
AND IF YOU ENJOYED THIS STORY, PLEASE FEEL FREE TO CHECK OUT MY OTHER BOOKS THAT ARE ALSO AVAILABLE NOW ON AMAZON.
YOU CAN ALSO STAY CURRENT AND UP TO DATE ON MY PROGRESS BY FOLLOWING ME ON INSTAGRAM AND ON MY AMAZON AUTHORS PAGE.
IG: @RCCHRISTIANSENAUTHOR
HTTPS://AMAZON.COM/AUTHOR/RCCHRISTIANSEN
THANKS AGAIN. MY HUSBAND AND I BOTH WISH YOU WELL.
SINCERELY, R&C CHRISTIANSEN

Printed in Great Britain
by Amazon